The Mark of the King

JOCELYN GREEN

BETHANY HOUSE

a division of Baker Publishing Group
Minneapolis, Minnesota

Published by Bethany House Publishers
11400 Hampshire Avenue South
Bloomington, Minnesota 55438
www.bethanyhouse.com

Bethany House Publishers is a division of
Baker Publishing Group, Grand Rapids, Michigan

Printed in the United States of America

Library of Congress Cataloging-in-Publication Data
Names: Green, Jocelyn, author.
Title: The mark of the king / Jocelyn Green.
Description: Minneapolis, Minnesota : Bethany House, a division of Baker
    Publishing Group, [2017]
Identifiers: LCCN 2016034521| ISBN 9780764219061 (trade paper) | ISBN
    9780764230035 (cloth)
Subjects: | GSAFD: Historical fiction.
Classification: LCC PS3607.R4329255 M37 2017 | DDC 813/.6—dc23
LC record available at https://lccn.loc.gov/2016034521

Unless otherwise indicated, Scripture quotations are from the King James Version of the Bible.

Epigraph Scripture quotation and quotations labeled NASB are from the New American Standard Bible®, copyright © 1960, 1962, 1963, 1968, 1971, 1972, 1973, 1975, 1977, 1995 by The Lockman Foundation. Used by permission. (www.Lockman.org)

This is a work of historical reconstruction; the appearances of certain historical figures are therefore inevitable. All other characters, however, are products of the author's imagination, and any resemblance to actual persons, living or dead, is coincidental.

Cover design by Jennifer Parker
Cover photograph by Miguel Sobreira/Trevillion Images

Author is represented by Credo Communications, LLC

17   18   19   20   21   22   23   7   6   5   4   3   2   1

To all who feel marked by judgment.
May your life be marked by the grace of Jesus instead.

✜ ✜ ✜

"From now on let no one cause trouble for me,
for I bear on my body the brand-marks of Jesus."

—Galatians 6:17

PROLOGUE

"You shouldn't be here." With gentle authority, Julianne Chevalier ushered a man twice her age to the doorway of his young wife's lying-in chamber.

"You have what you need?" Toulouse Mercier looked over Julianne's head toward Marguerite. "My first wife died in childbirth. I cannot lose Marguerite too. Or the baby." He gripped Julianne's arm, pulling her close enough to smell the pomade on his wig and to see the powder dusting the shoulders of his black robe. "Marguerite lost the last baby. The last midwife did not bleed her, and so we lost the baby before it was fully formed. Please."

Gritting her teeth, Julianne peeled Toulouse's fingers from her arm and gave them a reassuring squeeze before releasing them. "*Oui*, monsieur, we have bled her monthly as required, and today of all days will be no different. Now, am I to attend any further questions, or shall I attend your wife instead?"

His watery blue eyes snapped. "If you require the surgeon, I'll fetch him posthaste."

7

"I'll notify you at once should such a measure become necessary." With a firm nod, she watched Toulouse bow out of the room and closed the door. As she unpinned her lace cap from the curls that crowned her head, she swept to Marguerite's bed, where Adelaide Le Brun already stood watch. Julianne had completed her three-year apprenticeship under Adelaide months ago, but Toulouse insisted on having the seasoned midwife present for the birth.

"You will help me?" Marguerite's voice quaked as she reached for Julianne's hand.

"With all that I am." She smiled as she unpacked her supplies and tied her birthing apron over her skirt, pinning the bib to her bodice.

"I'm so afraid." Marguerite's lips trembled. At sixteen years, she was nine years Julianne's junior and dangerously slight of frame.

"We have taken every precaution." Her fingernails trimmed short, round, and smooth, Julianne gently probed Marguerite's belly through the thin sheet covering her. "Today will be no different." Throughout the pregnancy, she had gathered this sparrow of a girl under her wing, providing linseed oils to help her skin's elasticity, wraps to support the weight of the child, and advice on what to expect.

Adelaide stood by Marguerite's head, speaking encouragement to her in low, practiced tones. With greased fingers, Julianne reached under the linen, and with her eyes still on Marguerite's face, skirted the neck of the womb. It was still small and unwilling.

"We have some time yet." Julianne wiped her hand on a rag. "Rest between the pains. Save your strength for the grand finale, oui?" She caught Adelaide's eye and cocked her head to ask if she wanted to examine Marguerite as well.

"It's you she wants, not me." Adelaide's eyebrows arched

innocently, but bitterness soured her tone. The mistress midwife had been practicing for three decades. But when clients began asking for Julianne, the apprentice, rather than Adelaide, something shifted between them. Julianne never intended to usurp her teacher, but her young practice had outpaced the older woman's.

Stifling a sigh, Julianne crossed to the window, opening it wide enough for healthful ventilation, and fragrances of orange and jasmine wafted in on the breeze from the *parfumerie* down the street. A hundred church bells chimed across the city. Rainwater gushed from the roof, cutting muddy channels into the road three stories below.

Marguerite stirred, and Julianne turned in time to see her belly harden into a compact ball. A grimace slashed the young woman's face. With her palms upturned in a helpless gesture, Adelaide retreated petulantly to a chair in the corner of the room.

"Breathe through it." Julianne seated herself on a stool and greased her fingers once more before reaching under the linen. During the next contraction, she pierced the membranes around Marguerite's waters with a large grain of salt. The familiar sour smell pinching her nose, she replaced the soaked rags beneath Marguerite's hips.

"Aren't you forgetting something?" Adelaide crowed.

Julianne had forgotten nothing. But rather than argue, she allowed Adelaide to bleed Marguerite from the arm to ease her breathing, lessen engorgement, and soften the cervix so it would stretch and open more easily.

"Forgive me for not asking sooner, Julianne, but do you have children?" Marguerite's eyelids drooped.

"Not yet," she replied.

"'Twould be a scandal if she did, given that she's not married," volunteered Adelaide. An unvarnished attempt to undermine

Julianne's credibility, as married midwives with children were preferred for their life experience.

Julianne could inform them both that her own mother had died giving birth to her little brother, Benjamin, and that ever since she had wanted to be a midwife, to help spare other families such sorrow. She could say that she had raised Benjamin while her father drowned his grief in wine until he joined his wife in heaven. Then Benjamin had enlisted in the army and sailed for Louisiana, and Julianne had felt his loss with a mother's heart.

But today was about Marguerite, so Julianne said none of this.

Shadows lengthened on the floor. The hands of the clock pointed accusingly at the hour, and still the baby's head did not crown. *Malpresentation.*

Breathing deeply, Julianne spoke. "Marguerite, I need to put my hand inside you. I need to know where the baby's head is. Do you understand? Just keep looking at my eyes."

Mercifully, Adelaide came and held both of Marguerite's hands. Julianne's gaze locked on the young mother's eyes as she slipped her hand into the womb and probed the baby's head for the V where the suture lines of the scalp met in ridges at the back. There it was. Slowly, she wrapped her fingers around the baby's skull.

"Your baby is face up. That's why we haven't been able to make the progress we were hoping for yet. I have to turn the baby." She stood up, gaining leverage, and decided not to explain that if she didn't turn him, his jaw would hook on Marguerite's pelvic bone. "It's going to hurt, but I'll be as quick as I can. Then things will be much easier for you, and for him."

Her right hand inside Marguerite, she felt through the abdominal wall for the baby's limbs with her left. A contraction hit, and when it relaxed, Julianne shoved with her left hand at the same time she turned the baby with her right until he rolled facedown.

Marguerite arched her back off the bed in silent agony, then fell back upon it, and still Julianne did not release the baby's skull. Through two more contractions, she held him to be sure he did not slip out of place.

At last convinced the baby was locked into the correct position, Julianne withdrew her hand and wiped it with a rag. The rest of the delivery proceeded normally, and the baby boy was born. He was nine pounds, she judged as she swiped her finger through his mouth and nose. Little wonder Marguerite had torn despite Julianne's best efforts at greasing and gently stretching the neck of the womb. She wiped him off and handed the mewling newborn wrapped in clean cloths to his mother.

Marguerite's arms shook as she accepted him. "My son," she whispered. "My son."

"You did well, *ma chère*," Julianne told the young woman. "He's perfect."

Briskly, she readied the room for Toulouse's arrival. She tied off and cut the navel string once the afterbirth slipped out. Because Marguerite was still bleeding, Julianne soaked cloths in a mix of water and vinegar, wrapped them around Marguerite's thighs, and placed one under her back.

Adelaide raised her painted eyebrow. "Shall we send for the surgeon?"

"Why? Is something wrong?" Marguerite's voice trembled.

Irritation swelled within Julianne. Marguerite was in no danger. "Nonsense. The bleeding will stop soon on its own." After all, she'd seen worse—and so had Adelaide, for that matter. "You'll be sore, but your body will heal."

Shrugging, Adelaide wiped the mother's face with a sponge and smoothed her hair back into place.

Julianne smiled at Marguerite as she washed her hands. "Ready for your husband?"

No sooner did Adelaide unlatch the door than Toulouse burst into the room and crossed to his wife in four long strides. Kneeling, he tentatively touched the baby's velvety crown with one finger before kissing Marguerite on the cheek.

With calm efficiency, Julianne dissolved a hazelnut's worth of Spanish wax into six spoonfuls of water and gave it to Marguerite to drink while Toulouse held the baby. "To help stop the bleeding," she whispered discreetly.

Peeking under the sheet, she noticed that the cloths were already dark crimson far too quickly. Alarm triggered somewhere deep inside her.

While Marguerite slowly sipped the concoction, Julianne pulled from her bag portions of wild chicory, orange blossoms, and a vial of syrup of diacode and capillaire. "Adelaide, could you brew this into a tea for Marguerite, please?" Her voice was steady. Her hands were not.

"I remember a time when it was you who brewed the tea for my patients. My, how times have changed." But Adelaide prepared the tea just the same. She gave the cup to Marguerite and coaxed her to drink every drop, though the girl drifted to sleep between shallow sips and needed to be gently wakened to finish. Clearly, she would need more time than most to convalesce.

A sickening thud. Julianne spun around to see that Marguerite's empty cup had slipped from her grip and tumbled to the floor at Toulouse's feet. Dread seized Julianne. Marguerite's pallor was not that of one asleep.

"Marguerite?" Toulouse rasped.

Julianne rushed to her patient's side. Lifted her hand, felt her wrist for a pulse, for a flutter, for some sign of life.

Felt nothing.

Toulouse yelled at Marguerite to wake up and the baby cried, but it sounded as far away as the muffled tumult of theatergoers spilling back into the street a few blocks away. Sweat prickling her scalp, Julianne grabbed her jar of smelling salts and waved it beneath the young mother's nose, her heart suddenly a rock in the pit of her stomach. But of course no scent or sound, not even that of a husband's heart breaking or of a baby wailing for his mother, could bring Marguerite back from the dead. Her soul had already taken flight.

The baby dipped in Toulouse's arms as he dropped to his knees beside the bed. He clutched his son tighter and skewered Julianne with his gaze. "What have you done? He needs his mother. *I* need his mother."

Words webbed in Julianne's chest. She could scarcely take in that Marguerite was gone at all, let alone form a defense of her actions.

"You did this!" he cried. "You put your hand inside her; I heard you say so! How dare you invade the body of my wife when you knew her to be so narrow!"

"No, that's a common practice. I needed to change the baby's position. . . ." She looked to Adelaide for help.

"You killed her!" Toulouse's voice trembled with grief-glutted rage.

Julianne reeled. "We took every precaution. The baby was so large . . . Madame Le Brun was here the entire time. If I had been close to making a misstep, she would have caught it."

Toulouse rounded on Adelaide. "What say you?"

One word from the mistress midwife could absolve Julianne from any suspicions. Just one word. The truth.

With a scathing glance at Julianne, Adelaide looked under the sheet to examine Marguerite's condition. "*Ma foi!* The girl has torn dreadfully! No tea could have repaired this damage."

Her breath suspended, Julianne sank to her knees beside the bed, watching Marguerite's complexion grow waxy while

Adelaide conferred with Toulouse in low tones. "A preventable tragedy. If only a surgeon had been called right away. Fatal negligence."

"What am I to do?" Toulouse moaned. "Oh, what am I to do?"

"I'll take care of assigning a nurse. As for Mademoiselle Chevalier, you know what to do. As a magistrate, you know this—an abuse of midwifery is a public crime."

The room swayed. Julianne clutched at the ache in her chest as her gaze dropped to the bowl of blood Adelaide had let from Marguerite's arm. Her reflection stared darkly back at her. *How could I have let this happen?*

PART ONE

The Deep

"We believe that We can do nothing better for the good of our State than to condemn [convicts] . . . to the punishment of being transported to our colonies . . . to serve as laborers."

—Royal Policy of France, January 8, 1719

Chapter One

✤ ✤ ✤

There it was again.

Suddenly wide awake, Julianne covered her ears. Straw crunched beneath her, needling her skin through the ticking as she inched away from the dank stone wall and closer to the warm body beside her. The bedding, like the damp air forever clinging to her skin, reeked of the waste dumped into the creek beside the prison. On the nights when it was not her turn to sleep by the wall, elbows and knees of bedfellows on either side jabbed her ribs and spine. But it was the screaming that bothered Julianne most.

"What is that? Julianne, what is that?" Whispering too loudly, Emilie propped herself up on her elbow, her hair a spiky halo around her head. Behind her, three more criminals shared the wooden platform that served as their bed.

"It is nothing, only the screaming." Julianne would have been lying if she told the newest inmate at Salpêtrière that she would get used to it in time.

"But why are they screaming like that?"

"They are mad," Julianne murmured. A tickle crawled across

17

her scalp, and she raked her fingernails through her shorn hair until she pinched the vermin off her head. Passing her fingertips over her linen, she searched in the dark for any other offenders, but all she felt were the sharp ridges of her ribs and the narrow valleys between them.

"They sound angry." The whites of Emilie's eyes gleamed in the moonlight.

"They are insane. And likely they are angry too, chained to the walls as they are. Maybe they know they will never get out."

Another shriek ricocheted against the walls tucking Salpêtrière away from the rest of Paris, and Julianne felt their despair reverberate in her soul. Shackled by a life sentence, she too would never leave Salpêtrière. The *maison de force* was her permanent home now.

In the northernmost section of her building, *le commun*, hundreds of prostitutes cycled through. In the adjacent *maison de correction*, libertine women and debauched teenagers were held in isolated cells by *lettres de cachet* at the requests of their husbands or fathers. And in thirty other dormitories in this massive complex, paupers lived in groups, four to a bed: the invalids, the orphans, nursing mothers, the diseased, the venereal, epileptics, the sick and convalescent, the deformed, able-bodied women and girls, destitute older married couples.

Of course, it was the dormitory holding pregnant women that interested Julianne the most. *"I can help them,"* she had suggested, then begged to be put to use. But though Sister Gertrude had known her before her incarceration, the nun pointed to Julianne's shoulder and shook her head. *Impossible.* A branded convict was not allowed near birthing mothers, even if those in labor were but prostitutes or mendicants.

Even if the convict was branded for a crime she didn't commit—for such was her suspicion now. Months of lying awake at night, replaying Marguerite's travail and death had revealed what shock and grief had kept hidden in the moment. The bowl that contained the blood Adelaide had drawn from Marguerite's arm was far, far too full. Whether by calculation or accident, Marguerite's fatal loss of blood had more to do with Adelaide's actions than with the birth itself.

Even so, if Julianne had paid closer attention to her client's weakening pulse, if she had humbly called the surgeon in time . . . but she hadn't. Whatever had driven Adelaide to go too far, was it pride that had held Julianne from going far enough in the care of her patient?

Poor Marguerite. There was no undoing any of it.

"We will never leave either, you know," Julianne whispered between the snores of the other women.

"Perhaps. There is talk on the outside."

Julianne frowned. "What kind of talk?"

"Talk of freedom, for the small price of exile."

Memories sparked. Of edicts read in the streets, of rumors swirling about a Scotsman named John Law and his plan to populate the Louisiana colony with his Company of the Indies. Of wagon convoys winding through Paris full of people and returning with naught but matted hay. Of her brother Benjamin, a smooth-cheeked boy of fourteen when she saw him last. He was a man of eighteen now, the only family she had, and still in Louisiana somewhere.

"They say Law is prowling for more colonists and taking another pass at the prisons to find them."

Julianne sat up and hugged her knees to her chest. "He wants convicts?"

Wrapped in shadows, Emilie shook her head, and Julianne could not help but notice the roundness of her cheeks. With only a bowl of soup and two pounds of black bread a day, the fullness would soon melt away. "Who can say what he's really after? They say this time he's looking for girls of good character, a great many of them. So many, in fact, that Mother Superior has failed to supply his demand."

Julianne quietly considered this. Scant moonlight squeezed through the small windows near the ceiling, skimming the outlines in the room. Her life, which had once been full-bodied and multifaceted, was reduced to the repeated shapes of rectangles. The blocks of stone in the walls that hemmed her in. The wooden beds lining the walls, each one holding four to six inmates. The worktables and benches in the middle of the room, where she ate and stitched and listened to catechism readings twice every day. The slices of black bread, served day after day. This was all. Unlike stained-glass windows, which only needed the sun to transform their panes into a riot of living color, this existence was relentlessly, despairingly grey. The only variations were the weather that snuck in through the windows, new convicts who arrived by force, and the inmates who escaped by dying.

"They say," Emilie continued, "that a large sum would be paid to Salpêtrière for the girls, but only if enough are given. But they must be very good girls this time, not like you and me, for they are meant to be mothers, to settle the land for France."

"Who says this?"

"I heard the guards talking. Surely they would know."

Julianne nodded while her thoughts spun. From some place unseen, another scream raked the night. If Salpêtrière was to be her home for the rest of her days, if she was never to see her brother again, or a newborn babe, or the beauty beyond these walls, she feared she would join the ranks of the insane long before her sentence expired. Adrift in meaningless monotony, her spirit was draining away with no lifeline in sight.

Until now. A smile cracked her lips as a plan hoisted itself up from her swirling thoughts, unfurling with a single word. *Louisiana*.

⚜ ⚜ ⚜

Mother Superior did not trouble herself to turn when Julianne, accompanied by Sister Gertrude, knocked on her doorframe and stood waiting for permission to enter. Against the window, the Superior's habit seemed all the darker for the light spilling around her figure and landing in pale gold latticework across this sacred space. The polished crucifix on the wall, the rich embroidery on the kneeler below it, the food and drink on the desk—all of it made the office an oasis within Salpêtrière. Clinging to the edge of it, Julianne felt like a smudge of tarnish on a silver chalice.

Sister Gertrude cleared her throat, and the Superior's head dipped in an unconvincing nod. Her pale hand emerged from the folds of her habit in a gesture so fleeting it could well have been missed.

At Sister Gertrude's touch on the small of Julianne's back, they entered. The smoky scent of cheese braided itself with the spicy steam lifting from the teacup on the desk and cinched a noose around Julianne's empty stomach. But she had not come for hospitality.

"I can help you." The words slipped out quietly and sincerely, but for speaking out of turn, Julianne bit her lip in penance. Sister Gertrude's eyes rounded in her softly lined face.

The Superior looked heavenward. "This, from a supplicant," she murmured, though whether to the saints above or simply to herself, Julianne could not guess. Slowly, the woman turned. "In what way do I need help, and how, pray, could you possibly be in a position to give it?"

"Forgive the intrusion, Mother," interjected Sister Gertrude,

21

her hands swallowed up by her habit, "but we have a proposal for you to consider, which I believe is worth your time."

"In regard to?"

"Your arrangement with John Law for a certain number of girls intended for Louisiana. I believe we have found a favorable solution." Sister Gertrude smiled, and her full cheeks flushed pink.

One eyebrow lifted on the Superior's paper-white face. But her thin lips remained pulled tight.

Julianne looked up, and the strings of her round bonnet tugged beneath her chin. "I volunteer. To be among them."

Now both eyebrows arched high on the Superior's forehead. "My instructions are quite clear. Girls of good moral character only, no exceptions. Taken from the dormitories of the poor. From the orphanages. But you—" Her hand flitted toward Julianne's shorn hair, a clear sign that she was from neither.

Sister Gertrude slipped Julianne a silencing look. Turning to the Superior, the nun smiled again and gave a slight bow of respect. "If I may speak on the inmate's behalf for but a moment. I have known Julianne Chevalier for more than three years, well before she was accused of the crime that brought her here. Before I began serving at Salpêtrière, I was attached to the church at Saint-Côme. As Saint-Côme is dedicated to the martyrs Côme and Damien, patron saints of surgery, the church has a special connection to medicine and to the poor. On the first Monday of every month, all sworn Parisian midwives attend holy services there, and afterwards, tend to the needs of poor pregnant or nursing women who have flocked there for that purpose. Surgeons also give lessons to midwives."

The Superior tilted her head. "I fail to see how this relates to the inmate." Languidly, she brought her teacup to her lips, and wisps of steam curled around her veil. She set the cup back on its saucer without making a sound.

Julianne rolled her lips between her teeth and prayed for favor.

"Mademoiselle Chevalier was there as a midwife's apprentice every month for three years. I watched her work with the poor. She is very good, rumored near the end to be better than the midwife she apprenticed with. I cannot believe she was guilty of the crime that has been assigned her."

Mother Superior looked at Julianne for a long moment, a ridge building between her eyebrows, her mouth gathering to one side. Tenting her fingers, her gaze landed on Julianne's left sleeve as though she could see the fleur-de-lys beneath her grey wool gown. "Nevertheless, the trial is over, and the mark of judgment is for life. You are not what Law had in mind for this shipment."

Julianne studied the lines framing the Superior's eyes and mouth but could not measure just how much condemnation or pity they held. "Surely my character is sufficient for that of a Louisiana colonist."

"Your mark says otherwise."

"Forgive me, but if they are so intent on this large number of girls, will we each be examined upon delivery?" Surely not, if the colonizers were desperate enough for settlers that they now turned to Salpêtrière. The idea that this very desperation, which she was counting on to work in her favor, could also suggest untold hardships ahead—this she blew from her thoughts like chaff. She was resolved to her plan. It was the only avenue to freedom. To Benjamin. "Mother Superior, you are sending girls to Louisiana so that they may find husbands and begin families, yes? My skills do no good in Salpêtrière. But send me with the mothers-to-be, and I can help settle the colony by caring for the well-being of mothers and their babies." Surely she did not need to point out that if the women died, so too would the colony.

"If I may be so bold, Mother, a midwife's skills are vital," Sister Gertrude said.

"Law was clear. He wanted only moral girls. And she is marked."

"He'll never see it. Besides, the Company isn't nearly as particular as they let on. We've given hundreds from our hospital, and they are combing the streets for more."

Mother Superior hesitated, and in that pause, Sister Gertrude grew bolder.

"It is one million *livres* for Salpêtrière. Think of it! What we could do for souls here with that sum . . . but only if we deliver all the girls we agreed to."

"I understood that we found enough already."

"We lost another one."

"Since Tuesday?" The Superior's tone lifted in surprise.

"Catherine Foucault has died. I've just come from Hôtel-Dieu. And Julianne's skills would be quite useful with this shipment in particular, even before they reach Louisiana. I warrant John Law has not thought of taking every precaution for the voyage."

Silence filled the room like water until Julianne felt as though she were drowning in it. She had to escape this place that swallowed up girls and kept madwomen in chains, that let them die and counted it normal. Louisiana was the only way out for Julianne, for the scores of Salpêtrière girls who had no hope of a future here in Paris. And the only way she would ever see her brother again. She dared to whisper, "I will go in Catherine's place. So that you may still fulfill your contract with the Scotsman."

"My child." The Superior's voice was low and tremulous. "You do not know what you are asking."

"Please. Let me help. Allow me to be useful once again."

At length, the Superior nodded. "You leave tomorrow." She crossed herself.

Air seeped back into Julianne's lungs, and with it, a quiet sense of victory. "May I ask—what is particular about this shipment that will require special precautions for the voy—"

But Sister Gertrude ushered Julianne from the chamber before she could finish her question.

Chapter Two

⚜ ⚜ ⚜

Sunrise spangled the River Seine as the caravan of horse-drawn carts trundled over the bridge, away from Salpêtrière. Guards in white breeches and blue velvet jackets escorted the train on foot. Julianne jostled between a dozen girls in the same wooden cart, enclosed on all sides, used to haul common prostitutes to Salpêtrière. But this morning, her hope could not be caged.

She peered from between the wooden slats of the cart, her senses quickening. While poor Catherine Foucault was being laid to rest, the city cried out with life. On both sides of the street, shutters and doors banged open as Parisians spilled outside. Above the muted tones of journeymen and apprentices working in their shops, street vendors competed for patrons.

"Brooms for sale!"

"Oysters in the shell. Oysters!"

"Knife sharpening here! Get your blades sharp!"

"Green walnuts!"

The aromas of coffee and pastries and baked apples and cheese entwined with the sharp smells of an industrious city: leather, bread, horse manure, shoe polish, lye, freshly tanned rabbit skins. A milkmaid balanced a huge jug atop her head with one hand. Chimney sweeps, shoe shiners, rat catchers, woodcutters, bucket and bellows menders, letter writers, and water carriers called out their specialties.

As the carts of girls from Salpêtrière rumbled by, few peddlers and pedestrians spared them a glance. Julianne thought she heard a passerby comment, laughingly, on "another likely shipment of hardy colonists for Louisiana."

Hardy, indeed. Every girl in her cart, and in all the others, was thin and yellowed from lack of sunshine, and many were ailing. Still, leaving Salpêtrière was the chance for a new life for all of them. Julianne could see the future no better than she could see the road ahead of the horses, but she rejoiced to leave.

As the caravan rolled farther from the flurry near the river, leaves trampled under hoof and wheel spotted the road with crimson, marigold, and bronze. Footmen and their carriages rolled by in a blur of powdered wigs and tricorn hats.

The carts slowed to a halt.

"Out, and be quick about it." Sunshine blinked on the guards' gold buttons as they unlocked the doors and hurried the girls out into the street.

Julianne shaded her eyes against the morning light as she gained her bearings. They had pulled up alongside a stone church only two stories high at its tallest point. "Where are we?"

"Priory of Saint-Martin-des-Champs," one of the men answered.

"For a blessing?" someone guessed.

"That's not all you'll be getting here." His gruff laughter sent alarm coursing through Julianne, though his meaning remained shrouded. "Enter in silence and do not break it."

With the guards at their heels like sheepdogs, the girls were soon herded into the nave of the church and found it already teeming with the dregs of the city. Grease-stained rags hung on bone-thin frames. Eyes too large for their faces were made even wider with curious confusion. With the number arriving from

Salpêtrière, Julianne estimated the sum at near three hundred people, maybe more. Men lined one side of the nave, women the other.

Once all the girls from Salpêtrière had taken their positions with the women, a man in a richly embroidered silk waistcoat stepped into the open middle aisle and clapped twice for attention.

"My name is Nicolas Picard, and I represent the Company of the Indies. It is our duty and pleasure to bring colonists to Louisiana under the authority of the illustrious John Law. You may have seen the broadsides and tracts advertising the colony—"

Across from Julianne, many of the men shook their heads. Little wonder. If they were poor plucked from the city's streets, as they looked to be, very likely they were also illiterate.

Monsieur Picard recovered himself. "Forgive me. I forget I'm addressing prisoners."

Julianne squinted at the men's tattered clothing. Were those prison uniforms? She'd never seen a male prisoner before, let alone scores of them. Her stomach rolled at the realization that she may share the same ship to Louisiana with them.

"Louisiana offers much to be desired," Picard was saying. "Gold and silver just waiting to be mined. The land abounds in game, and the soil is a miracle of fertility. Your new life there will agree with you, I assure you. As we speak, the carts outside are being loaded with new clothes and provisions for your voyage. Each couple will also receive a dowry of three hundred livres upon arrival."

Murmurs rippled through the nave. Strangers whispered to each other, "Does he mean for us to marry in Louisiana as soon as we land?"

"You will settle the land for France together. Be fruitful and multiply in the name of King Louis XV. The sooner, so much the better."

The nave buzzed. Gasps broke from young orphans who had never seen a man outside of the clergy. Some men grinned and laughed, winking brazenly across the nave at the scandalized and the willing alike. Pauper girls clutched the hands near theirs and muttered their defiance.

Picard raised his arms. "Silence! I will have order! You will not leave this church until we accomplish one sacred act." He lowered his arms to his sides and leveled his gaze at the women. "Girls, on my command, you will cross the room and choose for yourselves a husband. Do it silently; I must have order. You will all be wed within the hour."

Panic cycled up Julianne's spine and snatched her breath away, even as she uttered a silent prayer for help. Choosing a groom at a moment's notice, without passing a single word—how in heaven's name could it be done?

Picard crossed his arms as he looked out over the unmoving mass of prisoners and orphans. "What did you think? That we pay your passage for nothing? You were not rounded up for your brilliance in architecture, engineering, or botany, you know." His laughter grated. "You were purchased. You belong to the king. Thankfully, your chief end is so simple even the beasts of the field need no instruction to manage it. Populate Louisiana and help secure our hold on the land. Now find your mate."

Blood rushed in Julianne's ears so clamorously she barely noticed her *sabots* echoing from the floor to the vaulted ceiling. Following Picard's instructions, the men formed two lines, three paces apart, and faced each other. The women were to walk between them, considering their selection. If a woman reached the end of the rows without having made her choice, she would be matched with the last man in the line closest to her by default.

Heart banging against its cage, Julianne stepped forward for her turn. Bile rose, and she fought to keep it down. A rough hand reached out and grazed her sleeve as she passed. Step following step, she shuffled down the aisle as slowly as permissible while her mind whirred frantically.

Yes, these men had all been prisoners, but she'd been branded a criminal herself. Was it not possible, then, that among this ragged assortment there may be others unjustly detained? She searched not for comeliness but for clues of character in each man's form and posture. A jagged scar across a cheek—but was it from a drunken brawl or earned by protecting another from harm? A full set of teeth set in a roguish smile—was that the grooming of a gentleman imprisoned after a duel, or the charm of an adulterer, the deceit of a thief? Haunted, hollow eyes—but because he'd been hardened by a life of crime, or because he too could not stomach the fate handed to them here today?

Contradictions tangled together in Julianne's mind as quickly as she tried to unravel them. Head aching, she looked intently from one prisoner to another, willing herself to divine the heart of each man.

Impossible.

And then one of the men caught her gaze and held it, almost conspiratorially. His face was gently lined, either by age or by weather, and bronze enough that he could not have been in prison long. He smelled of salt and earth and woodsmoke. Beneath his shirt-sleeves, his muscles retained their masculine curves—another sign that he'd not spent much time stagnating behind bars yet. A sign, she hoped, that he also retained more of his humanity than those whose bodies had wasted away.

"Hurry up," called a guard. "Many are waiting!"

It was such a small gesture, to offer her hand to this blue-eyed prisoner with the frank gaze. As she did so, Julianne felt as though she were stepping off a plank, bound and gagged. But she'd made her choice, and he accepted. The touch of his skin as his hand swallowed hers sent a charge through her body. It was not attraction that shuddered through her, but finality.

Together they moved to the end of the line and waited for the rest of the matches to be made. She could barely hear above her galloping pulse. She looked at the man she had chosen and wondered what a life with him could offer. Could they navigate the colony as partners, though they were only together by force? Would he support her desire to practice midwifery? Would he turn to alcohol for solace like her father did?

His eyes met hers, and he gave her hand a light squeeze. Bending to her ear, he whispered, "Courage."

The first word between them. Julianne nodded and managed a shaky half smile. It occurred to her that one day they would tell their children this story—of the moment in which they met and married all at once. *Children!* She pressed her cold hands to her burning cheeks to cool them. The prisoner rested his hand on her shoulder, and she wondered whether his instinct ran toward protection or possession. Or both.

As soon as the last couple was paired, a priest appeared at the altar, made some remarks about holy matrimony, and instructed the grooms to repeat after him, inserting their own names into the space he would allow. As nearly two hundred grooms recited the vow at once, Julianne strained to hear the name of her new husband.

"Simon?" she mouthed to him as the priest gave instructions to the brides.

He nodded. Simon. She would have to learn his last name— and hers—later.

She straightened her bonnet on her shorn head, retied the strings beneath her chin. It was her turn to recite the vows, and Simon leaned in to hear her choke out, "Julianne." Silently, he formed her name on his cracked lips.

Tears blurred her vision. She was falling. Flailing. She felt stripped by his gaze already. Around them, prostitutes grinned and puckered their lips while pauper girls hung their heads, shoulders slumped in shame. A waif-like orphan stared unblinkingly through her blond hair. Overhead, a sparrow chirped madly as it fluttered among the beams in the vaulted dome, and Julianne gritted her teeth. She too knew what it was to feel free, only to realize she was trapped instead.

In a fleeting moment, the priest pronounced one hundred eighty-four husbands and wives joined together in holy covenant, though surely God himself would not call this forced mating holy. If any took the opportunity for a nuptial kiss, Julianne could not tell. Her hands, still in Simon's large ones, stiffened, as did her arms, holding him away from her in case he thought to lean in. She did not allow herself to look at his face, lest he see it as an invitation, but instead made a study of his hands. Callused. Weathered. A boatman's, perhaps.

Her body remained wooden, rooted to the floor, but inside she felt as though she were being pulled under by a current too strong to fight.

The couples were instructed to leave the church and continue the long journey to the port city of La Rochelle, where their ship waited. The resemblance to the animals being rounded up two by two for Noah's ancient ark was not lost on Julianne.

Near the door, a notary in a black silk robe and white powdered wig bade couples to make their marks on their marriage certificate. "The document will be kept safe in a lockbox on the ship and delivered to the Superior Council on your behalf upon your arrival in Louisiana." He handed a pen to Julianne, who signed her name. That such a proceeding could actually be binding was unthinkable.

Simon scratched an X onto the parchment. "LeGrange," he said. "Our last name is LeGrange." They stepped outside into the courtyard.

No sooner had they left the church than a man was kneeling at Julianne's feet. A cold metal cuff bit her ankle through her thin grey stocking. Another cuff was fitted on Simon's ankle before the blacksmith chained them together. This, on the day of Julianne's so-called freedom. Instead of wedding bells ringing their exit from the church, it was the clang of shackles locking into place.

"Treat us like animals, will they?" The cords in Simon's neck tensed. "Then perhaps animals they will have."

They set off at once for La Rochelle by foot, chains jangling with each step. A few carts remained in their service, carrying provisions and the new clothing, while the rest were returned to Salpêtrière.

Shock muted Julianne as they walked. Only the sharp tug of iron on her ankle kept her from believing this was a dream.

Chapter Three

✤ ✤ ✤

Feel nothing, Julianne told herself. *Be as stone*. But her heart still felt every shard of her shattered expectations and still burned with shame for what was to come.

Rubbish floated in the gutter beside her as they threaded their way west through Paris. Only dimly did she hear the thrumming of the city now. Tears stinging her eyes, she did not look up to see the children begging their mothers for chestnuts or choco-late, or the carriage driver and wagoner lashing each other with insults and whips, or the beggars rattling coins in tin cups, or the woman on the corner offering *café au lait* for two *sous*. Her gaze was riveted on the shadows sliding over the road before her, shaped by her figure next to Simon's. The flat grey forms joined together as one and then separated in turns, wrinkling over ruts full of last night's rain and leaping upon the backs of anyone in their path.

By the time the shackled brides and grooms reached the country-side, they still had not eaten or had any opportunity for rest. Julianne was nearly breathless from the building pressure she felt with every step.

Finally, she said, "Wait."

Simon stopped and turned toward her. She could barely bring

herself to meet his eyes. "I must . . ." She bit her lip for a moment, loathing her predicament. "I'm so sorry, but I need to relieve myself." Humiliation scorched her face.

"Don't be sorry." He pointed to a linden tree near the side of the road. "Can you make it that far?"

She nodded but held her breath as they crossed over to it. Simon stood with his back to the tree, and with the chain pulled taut between their ankles, Julianne lifted her skirts and squatted behind its trunk. Tears coursed down her dusty cheeks as other couples and guards passed them on the left and sheep grazed in the field to her right. A masculine voice threw a vulgar jeer at her, and Simon shouted back in her defense. Julianne's shoulders shook with furious sobs.

"You all right?" Simon asked without looking at her.

Standing, she wiped her damp cheeks. "I'm not hurt, if that's what you mean." She stepped closer to his side.

"The devil you're not." His blue eyes roved from her bonnet to her shackle.

A half smile bent her lips as they headed back onto the road.

Simon ran his hand through his short hair, and it stood on end with dust and dirt. "Tell me, how did you come to be at Salpêtrière? You have too much modesty to be a woman of the night and too much mettle to be an orphan."

Julianne sighed. "Sentenced for a crime I didn't commit."

Simon arched his brows. "Remarkable. Would you believe everyone in my prison was innocent too?" He grinned broadly, but she did not return it. "If you're not guilty, you didn't deserve to be jailed in the first place, and you certainly don't deserve exile."

"What are you saying?"

He looked ahead and behind him before leaning in and whispering, "I'm saying we should fight. Take a stand. I've seen the way you look at the guards. The way you look at our chains.

You hate what we've become just as much as I do. Put that hatred to work. I will."

Julianne turned a bewildered stare on him. "Have you weapons, Simon? Beyond your rage? What can you have that will give you an advantage in this?"

In answer, Simon curled his hands into massive fists, then slowly opened them, palms to the heavens, his fingers bent toward the sky like claws. "Have men not been slaying men with no more than these since ancient times?"

Julianne's breath skittered across her lips. "Was that your crime, then?" *Murder?*

"Salt smuggling." He dropped his hands, and she released a breath. Of all the crimes she could imagine, salt smuggling was almost virtuous. The monarchy used its monopoly on the sale of salt to charge extravagant prices, and salt smugglers sold it to the common people at lower rates. "I fight against injustice, Julianne. I hope that when the time comes, you'll join me. I'll be fighting on behalf of every one of these chained souls. Including you."

Julianne shook her head. "I wanted to go, just not like—"

"Not like this," Simon finished for her. Behind him, sunlight glinted on a gently waving field of wheat ready for harvest.

"There is nothing left for me here. Don't you want to leave all this behind? Begin anew?" She searched his face for some hint he understood.

His eyelids flared. Lips parted in seeming disbelief. "In Louisiana? Are you in earnest?"

"But Picard said—"

"Lies. The Company of the Indies is desperate for colonists. Louisiana is a wasteland, cut off from France so effectively that once we are there, we'll live more like the natives than Frenchmen, and always with the threat of Indian attacks. Have you heard how a scalping is performed? This is what you have to

36

look forward to from your precious Louisiana. Not gold and silver, game and fertile soil. It is a land of despair, where the disappointment alone can kill you."

"Stop, please stop," Julianne gasped. "My brother is there."

His gait hitched for a moment before resuming his pace. "Your brother?"

"He's a soldier stationed somewhere in Louisiana, last I heard. I will find him if it's the last thing I do. He's the only family I have left."

Simon bent down and snatched up a rock the size of an egg, tossed it in the air, and caught it. "I'm your family now."

⚜ ⚜ ⚜

As the sun dipped to the horizon, dread twisted Julianne's stomach.

Mounted guards pounded up and down the road where the couples trudged. "We stop at the inn at the top of this hill," one of them shouted. "Some of you will sleep in the common room, some in the stable, and some outside. Those who sleep outside will have a turn indoors tomorrow night. In five days, we'll be in La Rochelle, where you will all have shelter."

When Julianne and Simon neared the inn, they were each handed a lump of black bread and one thin blanket to share.

"You two will retire to the stable for the night, where you will consummate your marriage."

Sweat beaded along Julianne's hairline almost instantly. She and Simon were splashed with mud and coated with dust, like every other new colonist. The strongest smells of city and countryside clung to their skin like leeches. She covered her mouth with her hand to choke back both fear and revulsion. Gathering her composure, she clutched her bread with both hands. "I can't," she whispered.

The guard's mustache twitched. "He'll help you." He jerked his thumb at Simon.

Julianne shook her head and clenched her teeth against the bitterness backing up her throat.

"Now listen here, you little wench." The guard shoved his finger in her face. "You were purchased for one reason—to populate. You're good and married, and you will consummate that marriage on this, your wedding night. We have ways of putting you in the mood, if that's what troubles you." He tapped his musket. "That's right. We'll be watching the lot of you."

Julianne doubled over and retched on the ground. Terror crashed over her, swirled around her. Sinking to her knees, she gasped for air as she wiped the sick from her chin and rubbed her hand on the coarse grass. Warmth draped her shoulders and back as Simon covered her with the blanket. Her fingers fumbled for the edges, then pulled it tightly in front of her chest.

"May we wash?" Julianne's voice barely topped a whisper.

"Whatever for?" The guard sneered. "Swine have always managed to mate just fine, covered in—"

"Pierre!" Another guard approached, this one older. "If you find pleasure in this business, you're not fit for it." He turned and held his hand out to Julianne. So did Simon. Taking both, she rose unsteadily to her feet. "There is a creek just over there. You may wash in it. Pierre, if any others ask for the same allowance, grant it. I'll guard them from a respectable distance myself. They won't run. There's no place they can reach before we catch up with them."

Simon's arm circled Julianne's waist as he guided her toward the line for drinking water. "Eat. Try, at least." He motioned to the ration in her hand.

She broke off a chunk of the bread but found it too hard to chew. Even the thought sent her stomach flipping all over again. "I can't," she said again, slipping the food into her pocket, and

Simon didn't press the matter further. At the front of the line, she sipped as much water as her nerves allowed.

"To the creek?" Simon tucked her hand on his arm as he led her down to the water. Night was falling, and the temperature with it. Knee-high wild grasses tugged at Julianne's skirt as she waded through them. The chain between their ankles scraped dully over the ground, catching on rocks along the way. By the water's edge, she could hear one other couple splash into the creek downstream from where she and Simon stood.

With trembling fingers, she untied her bonnet strings and uncovered her head. "I'm not accustomed to an audience."

"So I gathered." Simon took the bonnet from her and dropped it on the stiff grasses. Mercifully, he made no comment on her shorn hair as he drew the blanket from her shoulders and laid that aside as well.

When he pulled the bottom of his shirt up over his head, she turned away to take off her woolen dress and toss it near the blanket. Clad now only in her linen chemise, goosebumps covered her skin as she untied the ribbons holding up her stockings. She carefully rolled down the grey wool and tugged them from her toes.

Hazarding a glance, she saw that, with no way to remove his breeches because of his shackle, Simon had simply peeled off his own stockings and leather shoes. "Ready?"

Hardly. But Julianne gathered her chemise to her knees and waded into the creek, Simon beside her. Pebbles and sand squished beneath her feet. Silt burned her ankle where the shackle had rubbed the skin away beneath her rough stocking, and she sucked in her breath until the cold water numbed the pain. Closing her eyes for just a moment, she wished for her heart and mind to numb as well.

Twilight stained the sky a deep purple, and a crescent moon hung brightly between pinpricks of light. Gazing at the rippling reflection in the creek, Julianne held her chemise away from her body with one hand, while with the other she rubbed creek water over her legs. She rinsed one arm and then the other, scooped water in her hand and let it spill down her throat and chest, washed the day's travel—and tears—from her face. Pinching her nose, she closed her eyes, bent at the waist, and submerged her head in the creek. Cold sent a shock coursing through her. Standing straight again, she squeezed the water from her short hair with her fingers.

"Finished." Her teeth chattered with cold.

His hair dripping wet, Simon offered his free hand to her as they climbed back onto dry land. Moonlight skimmed his broad shoulders and back as he bent to pull his stockings over his feet and calves, and her face warmed with embarrassment that she should know his form so intimately already. Feeling far too exposed herself, Julianne snatched up her bonnet, filthy though it was, and covered her head before working her stockings back on, coaxing one up between her skin and shackle.

"You're even smaller when you're wet. How old are you, anyway?" Simon plucked the blanket from the grass and wrapped her in it before he had a chance to notice her fleur-de-lys.

"Five and twenty." Considering most girls married by sixteen, she was well along in years. But between raising Benjamin, training to be a midwife, and a father too lost in grief to find his daughter a match, marriage had merely been a dream. "And you?"

"The same. Surprised?" His grin drew faint lines around his eyes and mouth.

"I would have guessed older, but not by much."

"I feel older."

Julianne nodded. "So do I." But not old enough for this.

Now that the challenge of bathing in the creek was behind her, dread filled her empty stomach once again. She had never been with a man, had never even seen one shirtless, aside from her brother. And standing so near Simon right now, she certainly did not feel like his sister.

"Simon, I don't—" Words failed her. She didn't know how in heaven's name she would survive what came next.

"I know." He draped his shirt and her dress over his arm, for there was no use getting fully dressed just yet. "It is beastly. But I won't be."

Under the watchful eyes of dozens of guards, they threaded through couples bedding on the ground outside the inn and joined those already in the stable with the horses and cattle. The eye-watering stench of slop and manure gagged Julianne. Dust danced in the glow of the guards' lanterns. Even the privacy of darkness was stripped away.

Face knotted with disgust, Simon searched for a patch of hay to claim. Julianne followed him, gaze flitting from the saddles and harnesses hanging on the wall to a bird's nest perched atop a beam—anywhere but at the prisoners on the ground. From within and without the stable, wails rose up from the girls of good character, handpicked from Salpêtrière.

Simon pointed to an empty space in the shadows, beneath rafters gauzed with cobwebs. Heart beating frantically, Julianne lowered herself to the floor. *Disappear*, she told herself, but the straw refused to swallow her whole, and she could not imagine herself away. Horses stomped in their stalls. Guards threatened to shoot. Chains jangled. Virgins shrieked. The debauched groaned with pleasure. Some men laughed and slung ribald comments like dung, but not Simon. The very air reeked of livestock and lust, fear and pain.

"Please," she whispered. "I've never—" Straw needled her back as she lay against it, and she hugged the blanket more tightly around her shoulders. Closed her eyes, tears streaming from beneath her lids, and felt Simon lie next to her. "Pretend you love me," she rasped, desperate for gentleness though she was surrounded by brutality. An extravagant ruse, she knew.

Simon turned her face to his and brushed the tears from her cheek with his thumb. "They will pay for this." His hand cradling the nape of her neck, he pressed a kiss to her forehead, her cheek, the tip of her nose. His lips met hers tenderly, almost compassionately.

Hail Mary, full of grace. Our Lord is with thee. Blessed art thou among women, and blessed is the fruit of thy womb, Jesus. Holy Mary, Mother of God, pray for us sinners, now and at the hour of our death. Pray for us. . . .

Chapter Four

⚜ ⚜ ⚜

LA ROCHELLE, FRANCE
JANUARY 1720

A damp wind knifed through Captain Marc-Paul Girard's grey-white uniform coat and the long-sleeved blue waistcoat beneath. Seagulls circled and swooped among the masts bristling in the harbor. At the water's edge, he scanned the imposing height of the centuries-old Saint-Nicolas Tower from below.

"I'd like to inspect the prisoners, Sergeant."

Sergeant Rousseau placed his hand on the hilt of his sword. "They are well provided for, Captain. Divided into several chambers and given soup and bread each day of the four months they've been here. Once you go in there, their stench won't leave your nose for days."

Marc-Paul eyed the young man as church bells chimed in the distance. "Just the same. I will inspect my charges." His assignment in Paris complete, he had come to the port city of La Rochelle to embark on his return voyage to his post in Louisiana. The Company of the Indies had granted him passage on one of its ships in return for his assistance maintaining order with the prisoners they'd purchased for the colony.

Rousseau nodded. "Very well, Captain. I'll join you as soon as I finish paying the cook for their soup and bread."

Marc-Paul stopped at the guardhouse to leave his sword before ascending the dank stairway. He knew better than to meet the new colonists wearing a weapon.

Unwilling colonists, if Marc-Paul wasn't mistaken, and more was the pity. He understood the dire need for Louisiana settlers, but this way of collecting and pairing them was downright dirty. And jailing them in the same tower where the Huguenots had been held when Protestantism had been outlawed—with scant food to eat, at that—certainly didn't endear France to these people. He understood that the Regent, ruling on behalf of nine-year-old King Louis XV, jumped at the opportunity to rid the country's streets of criminals, vagabonds, and orphans. But did John Law suppose they would suddenly become stable, industrious farmers upon being transplanted to the colony, and loyal to the country that treated them with such little care?

Eyes adjusting to the darkness, Marc-Paul's blood ran hotter in his veins with every step. The only thing a group of people like this could produce was more work for him and the rest of the soldiers stationed in the colony. The Superior Council settled disputes on an official level, but it was up to the military to keep order in New Orleans's streets—if one could call them streets at all.

Footfalls echoed behind him, and he turned to find four armed soldiers. They were mere boys, these guards, and looked proud as peacocks. Marc-Paul was not impressed. Youth may look fine in a uniform, but untested courage counted for naught. At age thirty, he had served France for twelve years now. He'd seen boys aplenty come under his command as cocksure as you please, only to run away from hardships. And it was his job to mete out the consequences.

"Open it." Marc-Paul stood aside as one of the young men

unlocked a heavy wooden door. As soon as it groaned open on its iron hinges, the smell of human waste and decaying straw assaulted him. Jaw tense, he swallowed the urge to gag. "Who is responsible for the condition of this chamber?"

"We report to Sergeant Rousseau."

"I've been in stables that were cleaner than this," he growled. "The simplest of minds knows how to muck out a stall."

One of the young men shifted his weight beneath the insult. "These are prisoners, sir."

"They are people. Now, two of you fetch a rake and fresh straw immediately. Go! You other two, remain outside."

Marc-Paul entered the chamber, and shut the door again behind him. As he moved along the perimeter of the room, large eyes set in gaunt faces blinked at him. *Well cared for indeed.* His opinion of Sergeant Rousseau was falling by the minute. By his estimate, forty prisoners occupied the small space, both men and women together, and he remembered that they'd been forced to marry in Paris before they made the journey. *Another grand idea to settle the colony posthaste.* If these prisoners despised every man in French uniform, he would not be surprised.

"Pardon me, officer." A woman approached him, stepping over sleeping forms as she came.

"Captain Marc-Paul Girard. How can I be of service?" Realizing that the chamber's filth would be among her chief concerns, he added, "I've just ordered fresh hay to be delivered immediately. What else concerns you, madame?"

"A delivery of a different sort."

Her eyebrows arched above her intense grey eyes, and Marc-Paul had the unsettling feeling he had met her before. Of course he could not be blamed for not recognizing her if he had. Her hair covered her head in short, honey-colored waves. By the way her gown hung on her frame, she had clearly lost significant weight.

"Captain," she was saying, "one of your prisoners here is with child. It would appear your plan to populate Louisiana is developing just as you hoped."

Marc-Paul wanted to explain that this wasn't his plan, that he had far more sense than the profit-chasers running the Company of the Indies. He would never yoke men and women together like animals and expect them to couple, and he would never plant unmotivated, disillusioned prisoners in New Orleans when what they needed were farmers willing to work. But like a mute, he said nothing, mesmerized by her arresting gaze. *Surely I've seen her before.*

"The longer we languish here in the tower, the more danger she and the baby will be in when it comes time to deliver. I'd much prefer to deliver the child on land. And not, if you please, here in this room. My patient deserves better than that, and so does her wee babe."

Now it was Marc-Paul's turn to lift an eyebrow. "Your patient?" He looked for some hint of a jest.

"Julianne LeGrange. I'm a sworn midwife, trained in Paris."

Recognition flickered, but he could not be sure. He schooled his features to reveal nothing while he absorbed the color of her eyes, the silk of her voice, the smallness of her delicate hands. *It couldn't be. . . .*

She was asking him how long they could expect to be detained here and what sort of supplies would be available on board in the event she should need them for the birth. Somehow he formed a reply that must have satisfied her, because before he knew it, she nodded in acknowledgment and returned to her place on the floor between a woman sitting cross-legged and a snoring man whom Marc-Paul assumed to be Julianne's husband.

The door clanged open, and Sergeant Rousseau strode in, sword swinging in the scabbard at his hip. A nauseating mix of insecurity and bravado billowed behind him. Marc-Paul watched from the side of the room as Julianne's husband jolted upright. By the time the two armed soldiers entered as well and slammed the door shut behind them, LeGrange was on his feet like a mad bull ready to charge.

"Well, Your Majesty, what an honor to have you in our presence!" LeGrange snarled.

Julianne stood beside him and laid a hand on his arm. "Simon."

Shaking her off, LeGrange stormed over to Rousseau. "The bread was moldy. Couldn't eat it. Think we wouldn't notice?"

Rousseau grimaced. "I didn't think your palate was up to distinguishing the difference." Fists on his hips, the sergeant cocked his head and sniffed at the prisoner with an arrogance that galled even Marc-Paul. "However can you taste anything at all with that horrid stench fouling everything in your reach?"

Without hesitation, LeGrange laid his left hand on the sergeant's stomach and with his right drew out Rousseau's sword. Jumping back, he flourished it like a sabre. "Take one more step. I dare you."

Rousseau should have known better than to enter the chamber armed. From the periphery, Marc-Paul watched the sergeant's face flame a livid red as he shouted for the return of his sword. Men who had previously been sleeping now roused and stood, cheering LeGrange on. The soldiers snapped into action, shouldering their muskets and training them on the prisoner. The forty people in the chamber now sat on a powder keg.

Unless Marc-Paul could diffuse it.

⚜ ⚜ ⚜

"Simon, they'll shoot you. You cannot win this fight." Watching her husband's profile, Julianne kept her voice low and controlled, a counterweight to his recklessness. She did not want to see Simon shot, and neither did she want to see a ball miss its mark and wound anyone else.

"If you don't stand with me, wife, you are against me," he shouted, his gaze still riveted on the sergeant and the soldiers.

Pulse trotting, she stepped closer to him. He was putting everyone at risk. "Simon, please, there are women here."

He rounded on her, slashing the air in warning. "Stay back!"

Fire sliced through her upper arm before something warm and wet plastered her woolen sleeve to her skin.

"You're bleeding!" someone gasped.

"He cut his own wife!"

Julianne covered the burn with her hand, and it came away sticky and crimson. She clapped her hand over the wound again, squeezing the separated skin together. For a split second she locked gazes with Simon and read in his eyes that he hadn't meant to harm her. But he'd drawn blood just the same.

The mood shifted in the room, and Simon was no longer hailed by the rest of the prisoners as a hero. Someone pulled Julianne back. Denise, the pregnant prisoner, whispered caution in her ear.

The soldiers stepped forward, waving their flintlock muskets in wide arcs, and the men who had begun surrounding Simon fell back, leaving him exposed.

Rousseau spoke. "Soldiers—"

"Stay your firelocks." Captain Marc-Paul Girard drowned out the sergeant's voice, and Simon pivoted toward the captain.

As Simon swung the sword up over his head, the captain barreled into his chest, knocking him against the wall behind. The air audibly left Simon's lungs, and the sword clanked against stone as he pushed himself away from the wall.

"Drop it," the officer said, but Simon only laughed and raised his arm again, pointing the sword at Captain Girard.

"Go on and take it from me," Simon taunted. He thrust the blade at the officer, and Captain Girard dodged, scattering prisoners out of the way. As the two men circled each other,

Simon's filthy linen shirt flapped open to his chest, contrasting starkly with the well-groomed officer in spotless uniform.

In the corner of Julianne's eye, the soldiers kept their flintlocks trained on her husband. The cocking of hammers amplified in her ears.

"Stay your firelocks!" Captain Girard repeated without taking his eyes from his opponent.

In the split second that Simon shifted his gaze to the muzzles staring him down, the captain lunged, pummeled his fist into Simon's kidney, then grabbed the elbow of his sword arm, shoving it away. Silver flashed as the blade arced through the air and connected with Captain Girard's shoulder, slicing through his coat. With his free arm, Simon landed a blow to the officer's cheekbone.

"Simon, stop!" Julianne screamed. In his desperation, he would cut down an officer and be killed for it just as quickly. Denise hooked her arm through Julianne's and held her fast to the spot where she stood.

"Afraid to fight an even match?" Still holding tight to Simon's elbow, Captain Girard grabbed his wrist as well, immobilizing the sword, and slammed him into the wall again.

"Do I really look that stupid to you?" Simon hissed.

All at once, Captain Girard released Simon's elbow and crashed his fist into Simon's nose, cracking the bridge and knocking his head hard against the stone. His eyes rolling back, Simon groaned and slid to the soiled hay as the officer swiped the sword from his grip. When Simon began struggling to his feet, the captain plowed his fist into his face again, rendering him unconscious.

"Tie him up, soldiers." The captain shook out his hand. "Sergeant Rousseau, expect consequences for losing control of your weapon."

Helplessly, Julianne watched the soldiers bind Simon's wrists.

In the next instant, Captain Girard was at her side, his eyes smoldering like charred pine. His cheek already purpling, he drew a handkerchief from his pocket, and she dropped her hand from her arm. She held her breath as he inspected her cut and waited for him to say something about the fleur-de-lys.

"I'm sorry." She nodded toward the split on his own uniform. "We have been treated very badly, and Simon . . ." But her explanation stalled.

"A scratch" was all the captain said as he tied his bright white linen snuggly around her arm. "You will heal without sutures. You're lucky it wasn't worse." He shook his head, exhaling a sigh that smelled of café au lait.

"Lucky, am I?" Julianne met his brown eyes, silently daring him to lay such a label on her circumstances again.

His lips parted, then closed again. He held her gaze as one in a trance, his dark brows knitting together. Swallowing, he looked away for a moment, regaining his composure. "I leave you with good news. We weigh anchor tomorrow."

Relief flooded her, suspending thoughts of Simon—at least for the moment. "We? You'll take the voyage as well?"

He nodded. "Yes."

Slowly, her thoughts crept away from her injury and gathered somewhere else. "So you're an officer in Louisiana?"

"I am." His gaze roved the chamber as he said it.

"My brother was stationed there as a soldier a few years ago." Julianne touched his sleeve, coaxing his full attention back to her. "I wonder, sir, if you may know him. His name is Benjamin—"

"Pardon me, madame." His tone, suddenly stiff, halted her speech. "You have blood on your hands."

Her mouth went dry. "What did you say?" she whispered, bristling. So he'd seen her mark after all.

"Your hands." The captain produced another snow-white handkerchief from his pocket and offered it to her.

Julianne looked down to find her hands still slick with blood. Flustered, she nodded her thanks and pressed the crisp linen square between her palms. At least this time, the blood on her hands was her own.

⚜ ⚜ ⚜

On the upper deck, Marc-Paul Girard pinched the bridge of his nose, as if that could do anything to relieve the ache beating like a drum against his brow. Yesterday morning, he had overseen the loading of the prisoners onto the ship. Two by two, hands tied behind their backs, they were marched from the Saint-Nicolas Tower around La Rochelle's harbor to the Chain Tower, where they were put on small boats that delivered them to *Le Marianne*, the flute that would sail them all to Louisiana. At least, the ones who survived the voyage. Many of the new colonists were already so frail that the passenger list was sure to shrink along the way.

Also on board, in addition to the carefree crew, were a few dozen German and Swiss peasants, lured from the countryside with the promise of their own land in Louisiana and assurances that their days as serfs were over. That their Lutheran and Calvinist faiths were tolerated by the Catholic French monarchy was one more indicator of France's desperation to settle the colony. These farm laborers, at least, knew how to work the land.

Now that the ship was beyond sight of the French coast, the prisoners had been unbound, with one notable exception. While most of the new colonists were free to move about the space belowdecks, Simon LeGrange remained chained and isolated in the cargo hold indefinitely. It wasn't the thought of LeGrange that bothered Marc-Paul most now, however. It was the frank gaze of his wife with those eyes the color of the winter sky. Eyes he had seen before, set in another young and desperate face.

"What's ailing you, Girard? A touch of the *mal de mer*

already?" In stark contrast to the sober mood of the passengers belowdecks, a sailor laughingly spread his arm toward a sea as smooth as watered silk. Without waiting for an answer, he jumped back into the dancing circle with the rest of the crew, all blissfully apathetic toward the plight of the new colonists they carried. Three violins and two flutes sang lively tunes.

Marc-Paul didn't feel like dancing, and it had nothing to do with the seasickness that normally sent him chasing after ginger water. Ignoring the merriment ringing in his ears, he strode aft and cast his gaze toward the limp sails. Both the revelry on deck and the dead calmness of the sea ran counter to his intemperate mood.

When Julianne LeGrange had asked Marc-Paul about her brother, he'd cut her off before she had a chance to give his surname, but it hadn't taken long to figure it out. With minimal persuasion, the ship captain allowed him to review the marriage certificates for the passengers. She had signed her maiden name next to the notary's recording of Simon LeGrange, just above Simon's X. The ship records also included a list of Salpêtrière girls who had been remitted to Monsieur Nicolas Picard of the Company of the Indies, and *Julianne Chevalier, age twenty-five*, had been on it.

Of course, her name, her occupation as midwife, and those striking grey eyes that were a dead match for Benjamin's could have all been coincidental. But in his gut, he knew that Julianne's brother was Benjamin Chevalier, once a soldier in the company Marc-Paul commanded. The last time he saw Benjamin, prison bars striped the young man's face and figure. Though his betrayal had cut Marc-Paul to his core, still he had offered to send a letter to Benjamin's sister, of whom he had spoken so often, informing her of his fate. *"No,"* the condemned man had said simply. The shame would bring her naught but heartache.

Marc-Paul climbed up to the quarterdeck and leaned against

the mast, his gaze following a sailor scaling the ratlines to the crow's nest. Though fiddle and fife still played below, all he heard was Benjamin's desperate plea for his own life. His grey eyes had glimmered in the torchlight as he begged for pardon. But Marc-Paul's hands were tied just as securely as Benjamin's own. Pardon was not his to grant, even if he wanted to. Which he didn't. Not after what Benjamin had done.

Marc-Paul Girard served God and country. He obeyed the laws. It was the only way to maintain civilization in the wilderness. If Benjamin had only done the same, he would still be alive to greet his beloved sister on the shores of the Mississippi.

Forehead knotting, Marc-Paul paced starboard to the rail and leaned forward to watch a school of dolphins arcing in and out of the glassy ocean. But it was Julianne's face that now surged in his mind. How would she fare in the rough settlement at New Orleans? Would a husband such as Simon care for her even half as well as a brother would have?

A splash, and then another, jerked his attention to the waters starboard of the main deck. A goose, apparently having escaped from below, had waddled overboard, and a crewman with a knife clenched between his teeth had jumped in after it. The music stopped, and laughter soared as the dancers watched the honking bird and the sailor flailing about, trying to catch it. A smile tipped Marc-Paul's lips as he indulged in a moment of distraction. Once he was back in New Orleans, he'd have no time for goose chases of any kind.

And he certainly would have no time to add the welfare of a dead man's sister—and a convict's wife—to his ever-growing list of responsibilities.

⚜ ⚜ ⚜

The damp smells of sea salt, tar, and livestock lined Julianne's nostrils as she knelt on the floor near Simon. While she and the rest of the passengers had been unshackled on the deck above, he was chained by the fetters on his ankles to an iron post in the hold of the ship, surrounded by casks of wine and olive oil, barrels of flour, hens, geese, turkeys, and some cattle.

His eyes blazed. "Have you come to gloat?"

She plucked a piece of straw from the floor and twisted it about her finger. "I came to see how you fare. Which you might have the decency to ask me as well." Her sleeve still flapped open, revealing both her scab and her brand, a double humiliation.

"You got in the way," he growled.

"To spare you this." She motioned to the shackles on his ankles.

"Did you enjoy watching me fail, wife? Did the captain who made a fool of me in front of everyone offer to dress your wounds while I was unconscious on the ground? How very chivalrous of him!"

Heat flashed over her face. "You're impossible." She shook the straw from her skirt, no longer in the mood to make amends.

The ship pitched suddenly, throwing her against Simon and sending them both sliding down the slanted floor. When his chain jerked taut against his shackled ankle, he cried out, adding his protest to those of the squawking hens and groaning cows. She pushed herself away from him and waited for the rocking to calm.

Footfalls thudded overhead. Simon stared at the deck above before returning his icy gaze to Julianne. "Just remember while you roam freely up there that your husband remains with the livestock, chained like an animal himself."

"I'll speak to the captain about it."

An unkind smile tipped his lips. "I wager he'll enjoy that."

"Don't be boorish, Simon!" She swished her skirt at an approaching goose, sending it in another direction.

"I don't expect your love, but I do expect your allegiance. You're supposed to be my partner. You chose me as your groom of your own free will, remember." In the pause that followed, a cow noisily chewed its hay. When Simon spoke again, he kept his gaze on his chains. "I'm quite used to being unwanted. My parents had no use for me, and the nuns at the orphanage grew so weary of me that they likely rejoiced when I ran away. All my life, I never belonged to anyone, and no one ever belonged to me. I thought perhaps you and I . . ."

Julianne held her breath, waiting.

He looked up, eyes hardening. "You're my wife, Julianne, till death. No one—not some foppish captain, not even that long-lost brother of yours—can lay greater claim to you than that. We belong to each other now. And I'll be hanged before you forget it."

The edge in his voice scraped her sympathy away. Skirts in one hand, she made her way to the ladder and climbed the rungs, leaving him alone with the livestock below.

Chapter Five

❧ ❧ ❧

Almost there, Julianne told herself yet again as she tried to pull oxygen from the sweltering, soggy atmosphere. *We're almost there.* Though due to the bald cypress and tupelo gum trees obscuring the view, she had to trust her guide more than her gut. Sunlight struggled through the branches but managed to catch upon the banana spider webs strewn all over Captain Girard's tri-point hat. Shuddering, she dropped her gaze to her steps. For the first time in five months, she relied on her legs to carry her forward, independent of the sea. Unfortunately, her shoes were long since gone.

Yesterday, after disembarking the flute at Mobile, she and the other passengers boarded narrow dugout canoes for the rest of the journey to New Orleans. Those who had survived the voyage, anyway. Dozens of couples were parted by death during the crossing. Half the German and Swiss contingent had died as well.

Julianne, Simon, Captain Girard, and nearly two dozen others had climbed into a pirogue powered by Canadians and rowed westward along the Gulf Coast into wide-open lakes.

The remaining passengers were waiting for their own expertly guided pirogues when Julianne's party had left, and they would be distributed between New Biloxi, New Orleans, Natchez, and places farther north in Illinois Country.

After spending a wretched night on land, slathered with bear grease to keep the mosquitoes from feasting on their flesh, they'd traveled along the cypress-choked Bayou Saint-Jean, where alligators rippled through the water and curtains of moss dripped from the trees. When the pirogue could no longer clear the bottom of the waterway, the passengers cut through the trees on foot while their guide returned to Mobile with the pirogue.

The ground in front of Julianne moved. Before she could place another cautious step, a snake slithered out from under her path, crackling over the fallen leaves.

Captain Girard turned just in time to see her stumble to keep from stepping on it, her hand trapping a scream in her mouth. "See to your wife," he said to Simon, and transferred his satchel from one shoulder to the other. The captain's black hair, tied in a queue at the back of his neck, curled with the humidity.

"What business of yours is my wife?" But Simon cupped her elbow anyway, and she was glad of his support. After what happened at Saint-Nicolas Tower, it had taken no small length of the voyage for them to reconcile to a strained cordiality.

Behind them, Denise Villeroy panted as she labored to carry her unborn child through the swamp. Her husband, Jean, prodded her along with words that matched his fiery red hair. Lisette, a long-haired Salpêtrière orphan of fifteen summers, made no sound at all, while her husband and a young widow hung back with the rest of the group.

The trail emerged from the shade into a marsh thick with head-high river cane and cattails. The ground squelched and sucked at Julianne's feet, as though she walked on a bed of sponges. Waterfowl stirred in the rushes before soaring into an azure sky.

Finally, the air freshened. On the other side of the marsh, they found themselves in a muddy clearing with a smattering of temporary shelters near the river.

Simon stopped short. "This is New Orleans?"

Murmuring from the rest of the group drifted in the sticky air.

"The one and only." Girard kept walking, and as he had promised to lead them to an inn, Julianne gently prodded Simon to follow him.

Yet she couldn't help but agree with Simon's unstated sentiment; the town was so rugged it seemed to mock its namesake, the flamboyant Philippe II, Duke of Orleans and Regent of France. It seemed more a collection of crude huts strewn along muddy paths.

Mosquitoes buzzed around Julianne where her bear grease wore thin. With her bare feet, chapped lips, hair as short as a boy's, and smelling like a wild animal, she knew the rough impression she gave matched that of New Orleans very well. Perhaps she and the settlement were a perfect fit.

"You were expecting Versailles?" Girard called over his shoulder at them, chuckling. "Courtyards, fountains—"

"Buildings, streets," Simon inserted.

Girard nodded as he strode onward. "All of those things will come in time. In fact, we're waiting for an engineer to come from France to design the city's streets and public spaces. No real progress is allowed until he arrives and plans it. In the meantime, we survive. We farm. We befriend the native peoples already inhabiting Louisiana. Failing that—we fight. We live another day, to build something greater than ourselves."

Simon rolled his eyes. "Long live the king, eh?"

Julianne fought the urge to elbow him in the ribs. For whatever reason, Captain Girard was paying attention to their needs.

Maybe later he would pay closer attention to her inquiry about Benjamin. She had no intention of antagonizing the officer now.

"Clearly you think yourself above serving anything other than yourself," the captain muttered, and Simon laughed in brazen agreement before spitting on the ground.

Groaning dramatically, Denise slapped at the insects on her arms and neck. "Pardon me, *messieurs*, but is it very far to the inn?"

Weariness etched Captain Girard's face. "Not far now, madame."

The walk through town took the party past crude cabins made of pilings and thatched roofs. Everyone they saw was on foot.

"Where do you keep your horses?" Jean asked.

"We don't." The captain sighed. "Not generally. There are only nine horses in this settlement, divided between two very wealthy men. When you want to get somewhere, you walk. Or paddle."

"Don't you soldiers have horses?" Jean pressed. "What about the farmers?"

"No. We pull our own cannon. Farmers pull their own plows. We do have thirty-six cows in New Orleans, however. But don't get any ideas of eating beef—it's against the law to kill them."

Jean frowned. "What about pigs? Sheep?"

"Zero." Captain Girard straightened his hat on his head and pointed. "That's the Mississippi River up ahead."

Julianne could smell the fishermen's catch as they neared it. In an open square bordering the river, Indians carried woven baskets and bundles of pelts, which she could only guess they meant to trade. Men in deerskin breeches with red sashes about their waists bellowed laughter and French patois.

"Canadians," explained Captain Girard, nodding in their direction. "Voyageurs and *coureurs des bois*."

"What's the difference?" Julianne asked.

"Voyageurs are legally employed to trap and trade according to colony regulations. *Coureurs des bois* are unlicensed and work independently. Both groups idle in New Orleans between their trapping and trading trips up and down the Mississippi."

"They're not all Canadians," Denise puffed, looking at ebony-skinned men and women being divided into lots and given to Frenchmen in silver-buckled shoes.

"Africans?" Jean asked.

Captain Girard nodded. "The ones who survived the trip from Senegal. Bienville—the governor here and commandant general—wasn't satisfied with using Indian slaves we captured during conflicts because it's so easy for natives to run away back home."

"So you've gone to Africa to make slaves of any you can catch?" Julianne tried not to stare at them. Their expressions varied between mournful and fierce.

"Not me." Girard's tone was emphatic. "But yes. Bienville has taken a cue from the British, who rely on African labor for their tobacco plantations. He's convinced we can and should do the same. Here we are."

He stopped in the shadow of a large structure made from pilings driven into the ground, with some sort of mud paste hardened between them. Close to the ground, the wood seemed to be rotting and splitting. Large chinks in the homemade plaster must have offered welcome ventilation in the summer, Julianne supposed, but surely in winter the wind was not as kind.

"You'll be staying here in the barracks until you can find other accommodations," the captain was saying. "An officer inside will see to you. You three will follow me." He nodded to Julianne, Simon, and Denise.

"Now just wait a minute." The color rose in Jean's ruddy cheeks.

"Do you wish your wife to deliver your child here? I'm taking her to more comfortable lodgings where her midwife may attend her in privacy."

Leaving Jean sputtering in his wake, Captain Girard led Julianne, Simon, and Denise from the barracks. When they reached the two-story St. Jean Inn, he told them to wait outside while he went in search of the proprietor. The half-timber walls were filled in with a white plaster of sorts between the pine posts. Though it would not have graced a French village, it presented itself here as almost refined in comparison to the crude huts.

Minutes later, the captain reappeared with a woman dressed in a cornflower-blue silk gown, the beribboned stomacher broad enough to accommodate her ample waist. Lace topped her heap of silvery blond curls, and a mole patch graced her cheekbone. Startled to see such French style here in this swampy outpost, Julianne felt afresh her own tattered appearance.

"Monsieur and Madame LeGrange, Madame Villeroy, please meet Madame Francoise St. Jean, the owner of this inn." He bent in a half bow to Madame St. Jean, and Julianne and Denise dipped in curtsy. "As Madame Villeroy is soon to deliver, Francoise has agreed to let you ladies lodge with her on credit until your dowry arrives from the ship," Girard explained. "The barracks is no place to give birth. LeGrange, you'll come with me."

"Why should I?"

A muscle worked in Captain Girard's jaw. "Because I might not feel so generous the moment I resume command of my company." With that, the two men marched away.

"*Mes chères.*" Francoise cupped Julianne's and Denise's shoulders in her warm hands. "Captain Girard told me all about you and gave me explicit orders to take care of you. He needn't have worried on that account." A smile warmed Francoise's expertly rouged cheekbones, and her hazel eyes sparkled. "Your journey has been so long. You have come so far and now find yourself in an untamed land—and wed to untamed men. Believe it or not, I know exactly how you feel. You are not the first brides for France." She smelled faintly of jasmine-scented hair pomade. She smelled like Julianne's mother.

"And how would you know how we feel?" Tilting her head, Denise clasped her hands atop her rounded belly. She raised her dark eyebrows above chocolate-brown eyes in an expression that hinted at her aristocratic blood.

"Three times I have been a bride for France. Sent over first in 1704, I married a soldier who died of fever. My second husband, a Canadian trapper and voyageur, never came home from a trip up to Illinois Country one season. Attacked by Indians, his friends said, and I took their word for it. My third husband helped build this inn, and I made it my business from before his death until now. This work"—she gestured to the inn—"allows me to provide for myself. For me and my son, both. Between the inn and the Lord, Laurent and I get along fine. You will too, you'll see."

"Francoise, did you ever—did you love your husbands? Any of them?" Julianne's mind drifted to Simon and struggled to imagine the life that awaited her with him.

A sigh escaped Francoise's rosy lips. "I grew to love one of them more than the others. And I found immense love in my children. Oh yes—I had a daughter too, but she was not strong enough for this rugged life." She fingered the edge of a lace-trimmed handkerchief and shook her head before continuing. "But of course, you are wondering about your own husband. How things will be between the two of you. Only God knows that answer, ma chère. It would be better for you to take up the matter with Him."

Julianne doubted whether the Creator of the universe cared about her troubles. But certainly calling upon divine help could not make things any worse. "I haven't heard a single church bell. Did I miss it?" After attending mass every day for months at Salpêtrière, she felt more like a heathen with every passing week without church. "This is a Catholic colony, isn't it?"

Francoise nodded. "In theory, yes. A Catholic colony for Catholic France, although you'd not suspect it from looking at the settlers here, would you? Even so, there is a Capuchin friar who holds meetings in a very small room every once in a while, but generally, when it comes to matters of faith, we're on our own."

"So no Eucharist?" Denise asked. "No Latin readings? No confession to a priest?"

"Not like you're used to. But that doesn't translate to 'no God.' God is as present here as He is in the cathedral of Notre-Dame. And always, always, we can pray. In fact, I recommend it. Come." Francoise took Julianne and Denise by their hands. "It's time you two had some food, baths, clean sheets, and, if I may say so, new gowns as well."

Denise sighed in obvious relief. "Saints be praised!"

Julianne could scarcely imagine such heaven. "Out of all the new settlers who are arriving today, why lavish such generosity on us?"

"Ah. Excellent question, and I have three excellent answers for you. First, you came to me. Ask, and it shall be given, knock and the door will be opened to you, yes? Second, I'm a very good judge of character, and I judge you to be special. Not unlike myself this side of twenty years ago. Third, and not at all least, Captain Girard told me to. And when he gives an order, it is meant to be followed."

"I didn't realize he commanded anyone but his own company."

"Oh, don't let him fool you." Merriment danced in Francoise's eyes. "Tough and gruff on the outside, but he has a bigger heart than you realize. Otherwise, why would he have troubled to deliver you to me?"

Why indeed? The man was a riddle, but for now Julianne would be content to leave it unsolved. Bath and bed awaited.

⚜ ⚜ ⚜

They should not have been Marc-Paul's concern. And yet he could not talk himself into leaving the LeGranges completely on their own. In truth, Simon he would have happily deposited at the barracks along with everyone else. It was Julianne his conscience would not release. During the voyage, she had busied herself tending the sick women among them—prisoners and paupers and prostitutes—and quieted them with her voice when nothing else could. She proved herself to be every bit as nurturing as Benjamin had claimed his older sister to be. Sometime during the past five months, Marc-Paul had concluded that whatever violence had been pinned on her was a mistake. She no more deserved that wretched fleur-de-lys than he did. And she certainly didn't deserve Simon LeGrange.

Marc-Paul shot a glance at the man walking beside him down the muddy lane. Benjamin would roll in his grave if he could see who had charge of his sister now. Swallowing his own distaste for LeGrange, Marc-Paul followed the only plan he and Francoise had been able to devise.

"Well, LeGrange, you're a fortunate man." He stopped at a lot between town and the cypress swamp, already cleared for building.

"How can you tell?"

"The owner of this lot had everything he needed to build his cabin." He pointed to the pile of cypress pilings and a separate stack of palmetto branches for thatching the roof. Golden-winged dragonflies perched on the fronds.

"How nice for him."

"He died before he could finish. Just yesterday, according to Madame St. Jean."

LeGrange's eyes narrowed. "He has no family?"

Marc-Paul shook his head. "He was a soldier, recently discharged, who had chosen to stay and settle. It's humble beginnings, granted, but enough to start with if you're willing to work. Are you?"

"Is there an alternative?"

Marc-Paul shrugged. "There is always an alternative. Find your own land, procure your own tools, clear the land yourself, cut your lumber, and get started." Or steal from the company warehouse, or turn to pirating the trade routes between New Orleans, Pensacola, Veracruz, and Havana. How the Company of the Indies expected these new colonists—especially those who were not farmers—to forge an honest living from nothing was beyond his imagination. "Do you have any experience with construction? In this sort of environment?"

"I can build my own house, if that's what you mean." LeGrange's tone hardened. "You're not volunteering to help me, are you? I seem to recall a certain officer breaking my nose." He tapped the bump on the bridge of his nose.

"Ah yes. You refer to the day you disarmed a sergeant and attempted to start a riot in Saint-Nicolas Tower."

LeGrange spread his hands. "Being treated like an animal and forced into exile tends to put me in a foul temper."

"Monsieur LeGrange, I may have been your opponent at La Rochelle, but here in the wilderness, you have new enemies—and I am not one of them. I suggest you build a sturdy shelter for yourself and your wife as quickly as possible, and set yourself to the business of farming. Your rations have just run out."

"I'll build when I feel like it."

"You misunderstand. Madame St. Jean has agreed to take in your wife. Not you. You may go to the inn only when you are ready to bring her home. Preferably a furnished home. Nothing fancy, only the bare necessities."

Simon squinted into the sunshine, muttering, before crossing to the cache of tools and sorting through them.

"I trust you have everything you need for the task at hand. Any questions?"

Marc-Paul barely masked his relief when Simon assured him he had none. After nearly a year away, he was more than ready to return to his own home at last. Bidding Simon adieu, he turned to slog through the heat once again.

As he made his way east through the settlement, an egret soared overhead. New Orleans didn't offer the bird much of a view. Just above the river bend that cradled the town's southeastern border, land had been cleared of its trees but was not well developed. The public places—the Company of the Indies' warehouse, the tavern and canteen, the barracks and commissary, and the St. Jean Inn—clustered closest to the river, near the docks and market square. Northwest of them, footpaths meandered between thatched-roof cabins built wherever the colonists pleased. Surrounding the unshaded village, cypress swamps sprawled between ridges that bristled with palmetto, red maple, box elder, southern hackberry, ash, and sycamore trees. Bayous cut like ribbons across the low-lying land, and cattail-striped marshland hugged Lake Pontchartrain. The entire length of the settlement as it paralleled the Mississippi was five hundred feet shy of a full mile. The width, from the riverbank to the swamp forming the northwestern border, was a mere eighteen hundred feet. One day, New Orleans would be a grand city. But today it was no such thing.

Still, it was home. Upon reaching his pine-timbered house minutes later, Marc-Paul headed straight to his bedchamber and rolled up the linen that covered the windows in lieu of glass. The mosquitoes he would deal with later. For now, he needed the breeze to sweep the stale room and the sun to dry the air as it gilded the dust.

With a sigh, he swiped his hat off his head and tossed it on the bed. Opening his satchel, he pulled out his uniform coat—far too warm to wear in Louisiana during summer—and withdrew the Bible that had been pressed into his hands on the voyage by a Swiss peasant. *"Read the twenty-third psalm to me,"* he had begged Marc-Paul, who had complied. *"Keep it,"* the peasant said then, and exhaled his final breath. Marc-Paul turned the Protestant Bible over in his hands. Surely if the authorities allowed the Germans to settle here, owning this could be no crime. Not here. Not anymore. Still, he tucked the Bible into the top drawer of his bureau.

Then he stiffened. Looked out the open window for any sign of movement. Seeing none, he scanned the room. Something was wrong. It was quiet. The stillness was too thick; it wasn't natural.

Deftly, he unfastened the copper buttons on his waistcoat, shrugged it off, and threw it on the bed. With long strides, he searched the rest of his house. From his bedroom to the dining room to the modest salon, he found nothing amiss aside from the unease building in his chest.

"Where are you?" He turned in a circle once more, but no response met his ears.

Marc-Paul strode out the rear of his house. A gust of wind filtered through his linen shirt as he marched through the dappled shade of his ash trees and pounded on the door of his cook's quarters.

None too quickly, Etienne Labuche opened the door, a broad smile creasing his sunburned face.

"I believe you have something of mine?"

"What? You think I'd take anything of yours in your absence, after all we've been through together? I'm hurt!" Etienne clasped his arthritic hands over his chest. "Wounded!"

Blue eyes crinkling at the edges, the Canadian waggled the abbreviated index and middle fingers on his right hand. They had been caught just below their middle knuckles in a steel trap during his voyageur days up north. When Etienne gave up the fur trade to stay in warmer climes in his advancing years, Marc-Paul gained much more than a cook and groundskeeper.

"Come now, old friend." Marc-Paul raised an eyebrow. "You and I both know there is only one thing I own that could possibly arouse your envy. And that one thing is all I seek now. Hand it over, and no further inquiries will be made."

Etienne screwed his mouth to one side. "Break me on the wheel, will you? Put me in the stocks?"

"Nothing of the sort. If you're ready to cooperate."

Silence filled the gap between them. Etienne broke it with a hearty laugh big enough to be heard on the other side of the river. Half turning, he whistled.

Silence.

"Vesuvius!" Marc-Paul shouted, and in the next moment, a small, dense bundle of fawn-colored fur came barreling out the door on four short legs, tongue lolling out one side of its mouth, curly tail rotating back and forth.

Laughing, Marc-Paul bent down and scooped up his ridiculous pug, jerking his head to the side just before Vesuvius released an enthusiastic sneeze.

"Be gone with him now!" Etienne's eyes sparkled. "I've had about enough of his snoring to last me until your next voyage. Quite a greedy little bedfellow too, isn't he? How he manages to spread himself exactly where my legs rightfully belong, well—it *almost* takes the charm off him."

"Almost, eh?" Marc-Paul chuckled as he set the canine back on the ground.

Etienne shrugged. "Well? Did you have a good visit to the Old Country?"

The smile slipped from his face. "I did what I went there to do, and now I'm home."

"Then all is well!"

Looking from Vesuvius's wide-open grin to the clear blue sky above, Marc-Paul was tempted to believe him. But all was never well in New Orleans. It was why he had gone to Paris, and it was why he had come back. As challenging as it was, he would not abandon his post.

Chapter Six

⚜ ⚜ ⚜

Freshly bathed and dressed in apricot silk, Julianne paused in the corridor to wait for Denise. Heat pressed down on them like damp wool, though the day waned. From the dining room down the hall, masculine voices competed to be heard, their words garbled by the food in their mouths.

"You must eat, Denise, no matter the company."

Denise hung back, wearing a look of disdain and a flowing *robe volante*, which modestly draped her condition. "I miss Paris," she muttered.

"Of course. But we do not miss Salpêtrière, do we?" Smiling, Julianne inhaled the scents of the dinner that awaited. "Come now. You must regain your strength." Her stomach groaned in anticipation as she escorted Denise into the dining hall.

Flies buzzed between the platters of food on two long wooden tables. Two dozen men filled the benches, their arms reaching and elbows poking while they grabbed what they pleased. Upon noticing Julianne and Denise, however, they halted their conversations and ogled.

"Well, what do we have here?" A burly man in buckskin gaiters wiped his hands on the red sash about his middle. "Looks like its trapping season in New Orleans!" He slapped his hand on the table.

"Oh no." The man next to him laughed. "Didn't you hear? This shipment of girls isn't for us. They came already hitched. Only I don't see any husbands here. Did the gents make you widows on the voyage?"

"If it's wives you seek, these ain't the type." At the end of one table, a man mopped the perspiration from his bald dome. "If rumor be true, these girls be no salt o' the earth. They be convicts. Look at their hair! Shorn like sheep."

The mark on Julianne's shoulder itched beneath her borrowed gown. She could not be arrested for being branded, but she could most certainly be judged by public opinion on the length of her hair and rumor alone. No matter. She and Denise would eat quickly and leave just as soon.

"Prostitutes, most like. Tavern's that way, girls!" The bald man pointed through the window toward the distant sound of rollicking laughter and slurred song.

"We are no such thing! How dare you!" Denise spat. Julianne's face burned.

"It's a rough place, New Orleans is. The people are rough to go with it." He scraped the last of his food onto his spoon and scooped it into his mouth. "You'll fit right in, I'm sure."

Men whooped and pounded their cups on the table in glee, wine sloshing between the cracks in the boards, until Francoise St. Jean burst into the room, clucking like a mother hen. "All right, you've had quite enough! Out with you now! See Laurent to settle your bill and away you go!" She shooed three of the loudest diners away. Turning to Julianne and Denise, she added, "Please enjoy the food. You'll see we make our bread with cornmeal since wheat flour is so rare. The porridge is called sagamité, and it's made from boiled, husked corn and bean flour. We learned to make it from our native friends, and I do hope you grow to like it. It's quite a staple here." She swished from the room.

A wail erupted from one of the tables, followed by a fatherly scolding. Julianne turned to see a small boy press chubby fists to his eyes. Opposite him, a weary-looking gentleman sopped spilled water from the table while holding a fussy baby on his lap.

"I didn't mean to, Papa!" the child blubbered. "I was helping!"

"Oui, Jacques, you are always helping! Sometimes I could do without quite so much help from you."

Grateful for the distraction, Julianne scooped up a fresh stack of napkins from the sideboard along the wall and took them to the haggard little family. Denise righted the overturned pewter pitcher, and Julianne soaked up the remaining puddles and rivulets quivering between plates and cups. "May we join your dinner party?" She offered the father a sympathetic smile. "You see, I need *lots* of help."

The little boy gaped at her for a moment before sliding over on the bench to make room. As Julianne seated herself, Denise sat next to the father, whose sun-tanned complexion matched his son's. With a few words, the women introduced themselves.

"I am Monsieur Caillot, and if you have just arrived from France, I am rejoiced to see you both."

Denise arched an eyebrow. "Why, pray tell?" She helped herself to roast duck, sorrel salad, cornbread, and a tentative helping of sagamité, then passed the serving dishes to Julianne.

"I'm taking my family back to France on the ship that brought you here. My wife is ill and resting in our room upstairs. But even if she has not recovered by the time the ship sails, we'll be on it."

"New Orleans doesn't suit?" Julianne asked.

"Louisiana doesn't suit. The Company of the Indies brought me and my family out to cultivate tobacco on one of the concessions farther north along the Mississippi River." Monsieur Caillot shifted his baby to his other arm. "The Company wants tobacco to be a major cash crop. But after three years of trying to make it profitable, I'm further in debt than I've ever been. It's time to go home. Whatever has brought you here, I hope you have a better time of it than we did."

"I wish your wife a speedy recovery then, and a safe passage for all of you." Julianne tamped down the thought that she and Denise—indeed, all the colonists just arrived—had no alternative but to stay, no matter how difficult Louisiana might prove to be.

Beside her, Jacques squirmed, clearly bored. At about four years of age, by her estimate, his little legs swung freely as they dangled from the bench. And by the grunt and glower of the diner on his other side, she guessed his kicking feet had found a mark.

"Now, Jacques," she said quickly, "I need some help. I will need to use my napkin while I eat, I'm sure, but I only like napkins that are shaped like triangles. This one is a square. Do you know how to fold it so it becomes a triangle?"

Jacques's eyes lit up. Lips pursed in concentration, he took her napkin and quietly worked at his folding while Monsieur Caillot stared absently at the baby whimpering on his lap.

"You haven't touched your own food, monsieur." Denise nodded at his untouched plate. "And I have had my fill. Allow me?" She reached for the baby, and after only a moment's hesitation, he transferred the infant into her arms. She shoved her plate and cup beyond the baby's reach. The spoon, however, the baby snatched from the table and thrust into her mouth. Nose running, she belted out her discontent, and Julianne caught sight of two tiny pearls pressing up beneath the surface of her lower gums.

"Shh, Agnes, Agnes," Caillot crooned as he pried the spoon

from her dimpled hand. "I know she isn't hungry. She has already eaten as much as her little belly can hold."

"She's miserable, isn't she? Trying to cut her first teeth." Julianne twisted the corner of a napkin, dipped it into her fresh cup of water, and squeezed out the excess. "Here. This will feel better in her wee mouth than that spoon." She offered Agnes the napkin, and the baby took to sucking it right away.

Denise stared at Julianne in wonder. "Why, that was almost magical!"

"Mothers have a special touch. How many children do you have, Madame LeGrange?"

Julianne pushed Jacques's sweat-dampened hair off his brow. "None yet. Someday, God willing."

"You certainly seem to understand Jacques," Monsieur Caillot said.

Julianne laughed. "I raised my little brother. I was eight years old when he was born. Coming up with small diversions for him became quite second nature." How vividly she could recall Benjamin's arms around her neck as she lay him down to rest. When he awakened in the night with frightening dreams, he only called for their father a few times before learning it was Julianne who answered. When he skinned his knees, she dried his tears. When he found a marvel of nature—a frog, a bird's egg, a perfectly round stone—Julianne was the one who joined in the wonder of it. When he was old enough to realize their father blamed him for their mother's death, Julianne had labored to assure him it was not his fault but the doctor's.

"Benjamin?" Denise asked. "The brother who is here in Louisiana?"

Julianne swallowed her bite of food. "Last I heard." She glanced at Monsieur Caillot and found him leaning forward, eyebrows raised. "He enlisted as a soldier a few years ago and was sent here."

"After the war? Strange time to enlist."

It was. Two years before her brother enlisted, France had lost the War of the Spanish Succession, the French king's attempt to join France and Spain into one empire. Thirteen years of fighting had drained France's treasury and the morale of its military. Soldiers had deserted in droves near the end.

"They wouldn't have taken him any earlier. He was fourteen years old when he sailed in 1716." Still a boy. And still mourning the recent passing of their father, whom Benjamin had only ever wanted to please.

"Voilà!" Jacques presented a misshapen triangle napkin to Julianne, who praised him lavishly before suggesting he use his own spoon to trace more shapes into the thin layer of sagamité still left on his plate.

"Your heart must have broken to see Benjamin go." Denise rocked Agnes, now dozing peacefully.

"It did." Especially since she had not even said good-bye. One day, he'd said he had news to tell her, but she was flying out the door to meet Madame Le Brun for a birth. It was the first month of her apprenticeship, and she could not be late. Nor did she leave the birthing chamber for the two days it took that mother to deliver her child. By the time Julianne returned home, the only thing waiting for her was a note explaining that Benjamin had sailed to Louisiana as a soldier for the king. It would be one less mouth for her to feed, he'd written, and assured her he would be fine. *I'll come back*, the note said. But he hadn't.

"Where is he stationed?" Monsieur Caillot asked.

Julianne swallowed a sigh. "That's the trouble. I've no idea. The last I heard from him was in 1717, and he was in Mobile. He wrote that he was about to begin a grand new adventure with the natives, and that if I didn't hear from him for another year or so, not to fear, but that 'disappearing' was part of the plan. At least for a while."

"And you've received no word from him since?" Monsieur Caillot frowned. "Quite a riddle. But then, mail between here and France could have easily been delayed or lost altogether."

Jacques dropped his spoon in his sagamité and laid his hand on her arm. "You lost your boy, madame?" His brow furrowed.

Julianne blinked in surprise. "Oui, *mon ami*. I don't know where he is."

"You will find him though. And then, how happy he will be!"

Tears stung her eyes as she smiled down at him. "Oh, indeed. How happy we both will be."

⚜ ⚜ ⚜

His torso slick with sweat and humidity, Simon pounded another piling into the marshy ground, then dropped his hammer and circled his right arm in a windmill motion to stretch his muscles. After barely exerting himself for five months, his shoulders and biceps burned from the day's work. If he hadn't been fueled by anger as well, he wouldn't have had the strength to complete three outer walls of his home, each about twelve feet in length.

Chest heaving for breath, he leaned against the outer post and cast his gaze at the moon and stars, which had provided light enough to see by thus far. Slate grey clouds now drifted in the sky, veiling the constellations like wraiths.

With bullfrogs twanging in his ears, Simon stiffly lowered himself to the ground. Right on top of yet another fist-sized mud chimney, courtesy of the crayfish who had decided Simon's dirt floor belonged to them. He broke the mud chimney from the ground and cast it as hard as he could toward the swamp behind his lot. He hated crayfish.

Right now, Julianne was no doubt snug in a real bed in the St. Jean Inn, with real food in her belly. And Girard expected

Simon to stay here, day following day, night following night, with nothing?

Rising, he swiped his shirt off the post where he'd left it, slung it over one shoulder, and stalked through the settlement. A gust of wind cooled the sweat on his chest as he made his way past darkened cabins and a tavern overflowing with music, laughter, and the reek of corn liquor. In the jaundiced glow spilling from its windows and open door, women with uncovered heads and barely covered bosoms draped themselves over men. A couple of them looked up as Simon marched by half dressed.

"What's your hurry, handsome?" one called. Another made a lewd gesture.

He ignored them all. On the riverbank, Simon disrobed and splashed into the water, completely unconcerned about who might hear or see him. Down by the docks, small waves lapped rhythmically against the boats anchored among them. He scooped a fistful of sand from the riverbed and scrubbed it over his body until the grains escaped between his fingers, then repeated the process until he felt relatively clean. He slicked his hair back from his forehead as he climbed out and sluiced the Mississippi from his skin the best he could before donning the same filthy clothing he'd been wearing for months. Fleetingly, he considered that he should have worn his clothes into the river and washed them as well. But now was not the time. Right now, laundry wasn't his priority.

Still dripping when he arrived at St. Jean's Inn, Simon beat his fist on the door until Madame St. Jean opened it a few inches.

"We're full."

Before she could shut him out, Simon stuck his arm through the doorway. "I'm not here for a room. I'm here to collect my wife."

Her eyebrows arched. "At this hour? She's sleeping. Surely you can come back in the morning for her."

Simon forced his way into the inn and shut the door behind him. As Madame St. Jean stepped back, he could see from her candlelight that they stood in a large store room, the walls lined with boxes and trunks that likely belonged to the guests. "I'm here now. And I won't leave without her. If you don't fetch Julianne, I will."

He pushed past her and took the stairs two at a time until he reached the next level of the inn. The floor beneath his bare feet was made of smooth planks. Moonbeams fell through windows onto two long tables spotted with wine or tobacco stains. The scents of roasted game, olive oil, and rosemary still lingered in the cooling night air. Instantly, his stomach clenched.

Madame St. Jean appeared at the top of the stairs. "You would yank that girl from the first good night of sleep she's had in months? And for what?" A moth fluttered in her pool of yellow light.

Simon didn't answer her. He didn't answer to anyone but himself. "Julianne!" he called as he walked toward the corridor he assumed led to the guest rooms. "Julianne LeGrange!"

"Shh! Shhh! You'll wake all the boarders!" Madame St. Jean flapped around him, waving her hands in a downward motion, as if that would convince a man to obey a woman who came only to his shoulder.

"Julianne!" he shouted, louder this time.

From somewhere beyond his vision, he heard the distinct creak of a door opening. Footsteps hurried toward him until Julianne appeared in a white nightgown that billowed behind her slight frame, hair sticking up on one side of her head. As she neared, Madame St. Jean murmured an apology to her. No one ever apologized to Simon. For anything.

Hastening past Madame St. Jean, Julianne stood before him. "I'm here, husband." The soft scent of rose oil lifted from her radiant skin. "What is it?"

"I just—" His gaze trailed to her lips, then to the hollow of her throat before returning to her shimmering eyes. She looked scared. It wasn't what he wanted. He sighed, the anger draining out of him. "You're my wife. We have a home. It's not much, but it's ours, and we ought to be together. Come, Julianne. It's time to go home."

He offered his hand and waited.

⚜ ⚜ ⚜

Hesitating, Julianne remembered the first time she had trusted her hand to his in the priory of Saint-Martin-des-Champs. Lifting her gaze to meet his, she searched his eyes for some hint of his heart, just as she had the day she chose him as her groom. For better or for worse, she had chosen him.

A lump bobbed in Simon's throat. "Shackles or not, we are still in this together, husband and wife. It isn't right for us to be apart." His voice was low now, his tone undemanding.

It was one thing to select a man on first sight, and quite another to say yes again, knowing his faults and tempers. But for all the disappointments, and all the walls they had erected between each other so far, Julianne could not find fault in his reasoning. A wife's place was with her husband.

Nodding, she slipped her hand into his and felt a ridge of calluses at the top of his palm. He'd been working on their house all day while she had bathed, and eaten, and rested. He was dripping wet and cleaner than she'd ever seen him, water beading on the floor around his feet. He was trying. So would she.

"Francoise, you have been so kind to me. I will pay what we owe as soon as we have the dowry."

Francoise squeezed her shoulders. "Let me fetch your things." She swept away, taking her flickering light with her. "Take this," she said as soon as she returned. But even in the half-light,

Julianne could see these were not the rags she had worn on the voyage. "My washerwoman laundered your things today. They aren't dry yet. Take this gown instead, and keep the nightdress too. You can return them once your own things arrive."

"Thank you," Julianne whispered. "I do hate to trouble you."

"It's nothing, I assure you."

"I'd like to change into the dress before leaving," Julianne said to Simon. "I may not have much pride left, but I'm not walking through town in a nightdress." A smile tilted a corner of her lips, and he answered it with his own.

Julianne hastened back into her room to change and emerged in the silk gown. The nightdress she draped over one arm.

The way Simon looked at her made it clear it was the first time he'd ever seen her dressed like a lady. She tried to smooth down her uncooperative hair. Just as quickly, she scolded herself for her vanity when her husband stood waiting, looking as famished as he had ever been. Francoise's candlelight highlighted the sharpness of his cheekbones and the lean lines of his once muscular frame.

Julianne approached Francoise. "One last request, if I may be so bold. If you trust us to repay you soon, if there was any food left over from supper, could we take it with us?"

"Why, yes of course!" Francoise's eyes glimmered. "I only wish I had more to offer to help you gain some weight back."

Julianne smiled. "I had it in mind for my husband, actually. Simon, have you eaten?" For a moment, she wondered if he had heard her. "Simon?"

Abruptly, he shook his head. His blue eyes softened.

"Whatever you can spare," Julianne directed to Francoise. "Put it on our account. We will pay as soon as we can."

After the slightest pause, Francoise nodded. "Of course. I'll see what I can find. Wait here." Returning moments later, she placed a knapsack and a rolled animal skin in Simon's arms.

"Oiled deerskin, to sleep on," she explained. "Water won't soak through it."

"*Merci.*" Julianne bussed Francoise's cheeks before leaving with Simon.

Though cold, the duck meat and cornbread were still fragrant through the cheesecloth knapsack. When Simon's stomach growled a few steps from the inn, Julianne took the deerskin from his arms.

"Please." She nodded at the bundle of food.

Without hesitation, Simon untied the corners of the cheesecloth and began eating as they passed an unsteady knot of drunkards on the street. Though thunder rolled and darkness thickened, Julianne could still hear his satisfied sigh and see his shoulders relax. Soon he was tucking the cheesecloth into his breeches pocket and taking the deerskin and nightdress to carry himself.

With no light to guide them, Julianne took Simon's arm just as large, cool drops of rain splashed her skin. The dirt road beneath her feet would turn into mud in no time. With her other hand, she gathered her skirts and hoisted them above her ankles.

"It isn't far now," Simon said.

Suddenly the rain drove down in sheets, as if the underbelly of the clouds had been slit open all at once. Simon quickly handed the nightdress to Julianne and then unfurled the deerskin and held it over their heads as a canopy. His strides lengthened, and she hurried to keep up until, a few minutes later, he halted.

"We're stopping?" She looked around but could see nothing in the rain-drenched darkness.

"We're home." Lightning cracked the sky and illuminated for a fraction of a second three walls of pilings driven into the marshy ground, forming a U-shaped room. There was no flooring but mud, no roof but the sky.

Julianne's heart sank. "Oh."

"You're welcome." Sarcasm edged Simon's voice as rain streamed down his face. "I didn't say the house was done. I said we have a home. Wherever we are together is home." He turned his back on any protest she might have made, leaving her with the deerskin to herself, and stomped away.

Only when lightning flashed did she see what he was doing: Fastening one end of a long willow branch between the tops of two posts. Fixing the other end of the same branch on the opposite wall. Back to the pile of willow branches. Repeat.

Petticoats already sticking to her legs, Julianne wrapped her nightgown in the deerskin and stuffed it into a sprawling stack of palmetto leaves, then ran to help her husband. Rain poured over her bare head like a baptism and spilled down her throat and chest, plastering her chemise to her skin. Blinking water from her eyes, she hurried to the far wall. She reached up, grabbed the loose end of the willow branch Simon held at the opposite end, and wedged it between the pilings. The mud was now up to Julianne's ankles, and she feared Francoise's gown was splattered beyond redemption.

Once they had positioned and secured several more branches as a framework for their roof, Simon grabbed a palmetto branch, scooped a ladder from where it lay half buried in the mud, and leaned it against a wall. Climbing up to the top rung, he placed the spiky, fan-shaped fronds over the willow branches. Julianne ferried more palmettos to him, handing them up one at a time whenever Simon reached down.

Still stinging from wrestling the willow poles into place, her palms prickled from handling the palmetto fronds. The sharp, stiff leaves were lined with tiny hairs that burned the skin until she felt as though she'd been handling hot coals. But as Simon moved the ladder to different posts along the walls, she kept up with him until the willow canes were covered.

Shivering, and as wet as if she had jumped into the river with her clothes on, Julianne waited by the ladder as Simon climbed down.

"Well, that was . . . motivating." He exhaled. "Shall we?"

She agreed. Mud sucked at her feet and pushed between her toes as she walked along the side of their three-walled house. More than once she felt the hard shell or pinchers of a crayfish against her sole. As she neared the gaping maw that was the opening of her home, Simon laid his corded arm across her shoulders. Before she knew what was happening, he slipped his other arm behind her knees and scooped her up.

"You are still my bride, Julianne. And this . . . magnificent chateau is our first house. Might as well do things right."

An amused chuckle bubbled up out of Julianne as he carried her over the threshold into their home. Leaning her drenched head against her husband, the pressure in her chest burst into a laugh so hearty that her shoulders shook. When Simon laughed too, tears of merriment mingled with the rain on her cheeks.

Cloaked in shadows, he lowered her until she stood near the back of the house. Rain dripped through the thatched roof, and some sprayed between the pilings that formed the walls, but the shelter provided more relief than she'd imagined it could.

Gently, Simon took the deerskin from Julianne, handed her the nightdress that had been wrapped safely inside it, and then unrolled the oiled hide and spread it on the muddy floor. "You need to get out of those wet clothes," he told her, then took the nightdress back once more to free her hands.

Though darkness offered all the privacy she could desire, she turned her back to him anyway to unbutton her bodice and untie the strings that held her chemise and skirts in place. Once she had peeled off her sodden dress, she traded it for the nightgown, which was blessedly dry, if not warm, against her skin.

"Sit." Simon's hand found hers, and he led her to rest on the dry side of the waterproof deerskin.

Julianne sat on the edge, knees up under her chin, twisting her nightgown around her legs. "My feet—they're filthy!"

Framed by the sky behind him, Simon pulled his shirt over his head and knelt before her. His rough hand warmed her ankle as he guided her feet one at a time to his lap and used his shirt to wipe the mud from her skin in long, gentle strokes. When he grazed the scar left by the shackle that had bound her to him, he stopped. He traced the jagged ridge with one finger and sighed.

"It is not the marriage any girl would dream of." His voice gentled. "I know."

Between the words, Julianne heard what neither of them needed to say. The forced wedding. His desperation in the Saint-Nicolas Tower, when he cut her arm with the sergeant's sword. The voyage, full of sickness and hunger, taut with tension. Neither of them had expected the turns their lives had taken together.

She tucked her feet under her and wished she could see him better. But even in the dark, his hand found her shoulder, slid up her neck, and cupped the side of her face. With his thumb, he brushed the tears and rain from her skin.

"We can begin again," she whispered, her throat tight with emotion, and caught his hand against her cheek.

Thunder boomed above them. The flash of lightning blinked through the chinks in their shelter, gleaming on Simon's bare chest and shoulders and arms as he knelt in the mud, one hand outstretched for Julianne. His blue-eyed gaze locked with hers before the darkness rushed in again. She squeezed his hand, released it, then made room for him on the deerskin.

Utterly exhausted, she curled on her side just as he lay down behind her. He extended one arm as a pillow beneath her head, and with the other loosely encircled her waist. She couldn't be sure if she felt him press a kiss to her hair or if she had only imagined it. Warmed by his nearness, she drifted to sleep with his heart beating gently against her back.

Chapter Seven

⚜ ⚜ ⚜

Mosquitoes droned in the heavy air. Waving them aside, Marc-Paul could almost smell oranges as he walked between two rows of sun-soaked citrus trees. Grateful for the shade even at this early hour, he stepped into the covered, ground-level gallery and knocked upon the front door of the grand residence of Governor and Commandant General Jean-Baptiste Le Moyne de Bienville. As the seat of government had not yet been constructed, Bienville conducted business from his home, four hundred paces outside New Orleans.

The door opened, revealing a muscular African wearing the garb of a French butler, complete with white ruffles at his throat.

"Hello, Caesar. I've come to see the governor." Marc-Paul removed his hat. "He'll want to hear my report."

Nodding, Caesar widened the door, allowing Marc-Paul to pass. "He is breaking his fast. This way." Caesar's Senegalese accent thickened the French on his tongue as he led Marc-Paul to the dining room, where the smell of eggs and warm bread with blackberry jam permeated the air.

"Sir," Marc-Paul said as he entered. "You wanted to see me as soon as I returned."

Bienville looked up, his furrowed brow framed by his wig

of white curls. "So. We have a fresh batch of convict colonists then, do we? Already married and ready to populate?"

"The flute also carried Germans and Swiss, eager to farm real food and with the skills to yield a harvest, God grant it." The tobacco crops the Company of the Indies insisted upon did nothing to relieve the colony's hunger.

"And how many disembarked?"

Marc-Paul poked one corner of his tricorn hat into his palm. "A dozen farmers, plus about one hundred fifty convicts. Fever and malnourishment exacted a heavy toll. Of those who survived, dozens are being transported to other settlements along the coast and in Illinois Country. The French settling in New Orleans are lodging at the barracks until they can build their own cabins here, and the Germans and Swiss will soon go upriver to farm the land west of here."

Bienville shook his head. "Aside from those who can work the land, the rest will be a drain on us, not a help. I'd rather they just ran away. Speaking of which, while you were away, three sergeants and five soldiers deserted Mobile, convinced two-thirds of the garrison at Fort Toulouse to join their revolt, seized and bound their officers, and made a dash for Carolina."

Marc-Paul's cravat felt suddenly tight around his throat.

"The officers escaped their bindings, however, and enlisted two hundred fifty Alibamon to capture and kill the deserters."

"And they were successful?"

A grim smile curled Bienville's lips. "I have their scalps to prove it."

"French scalps," Marc-Paul clarified. His stomach doubled over even as he straightened his spine.

"Deserters' scalps. This happened right around the time we were recapturing Pensacola from the Spaniards. Desertion cannot, *will* not be tolerated. I know you agree."

Of course he did.

"Well, what news from France? Did you manage a tête-à-tête with the Regent?"

"I did."

"And?" Bienville leaned forward. "Was he convinced?"

"He won't break his twenty-five-year contract with Law's company. Reminded me that the war drained his resources, so he can spare no more provisions for the colony."

"Confound him!" Bienville's chair scraped the floor as he rose and began pacing the room. His disproportionately large head in full wig resembled that of a lion. "Before the war, France had the largest military in Europe. Now look at us! Shameful. He wants Louisiana riches to refill his empty coffers, to be for France what Mexico is for Spain, but he gives us none of the tools we need."

Marc-Paul waited, spinning his hat in his hands, while the stymied founder of New Orleans simmered. Clearly this village, where Bienville had ceremoniously broken the first river cane two years ago, was not developing as he had planned. At Bienville's request, Marc-Paul had personally met with the Regent to explain the detrimental effects of having prostitutes, convicts, and deserters continually dumped on the shores of Louisiana. No letter even hinting at such sentiments would have made it to the monarchy. The Company of the Indies stationed agents at every French port to confiscate all letters carried by those coming from Louisiana in order to manage public opinion of the colony.

"And did you ask for more troops? More provisions for the garrisons? More flour for the colonists?" Bienville prodded.

"I did more than ask, sir. I made our case so . . . assertively, let's say, that I came near to being thrown out of court on my ear."

Bienville glowered. "And?"

"I was informed that all that could be spared was already being sent."

"While the monarchy was feeding you that line, I had nothing to feed our soldiers!" the commandant sputtered. "I suppose I already know the answer to your request for one hundred thousand livres' worth of merchandise."

"Denied."

The Canadian shot Marc-Paul a look that should have been reserved for the Duke of Orleans. Understandably so. The merchandise was needed for the continuous gift-giving between the French and the Indians. In all of Louisiana there were fewer than two thousand French settlers, spanning from the Gulf of Mexico to the Great Lakes, and from the Rocky Mountains to the Appalachians. The number of Indians in French-occupied lands was estimated at two hundred thousand. Gift-giving and smoking the calumet cemented friendly relations.

"What does the Regent suppose will happen to Louisiana if we fail to supply gifts to our Indian allies?" The governor's voice lowered. "We are at war, Captain Girard. Did you know?"

"With Britain by proxy, you mean. Correct?" Since the peace treaty ending the War of the Spanish Succession six years ago, Europeans in North America had attacked each other through their Indian allies. Spain was now France's ally, and Pensacola was in French possession, so Florida was no threat to the Mississippi Valley. But the British continued equipping Chickasaw warriors, just as the French supplied the Choctaw. For the last five years, Bienville had punished the Chickasaw for refusing to cease trade relations with the British by hiring Choctaw to ambush pack trains on the Trader's Path, a wilderness trail from Carolina's Charles Town to Chickasaw villages in the interior.

"You are only partially correct. We are now at war with the

Chickasaw." Bienville walked to the window and folded his hands behind his back.

Marc-Paul followed him, dismay mounting. "Directly?" The French would be wiped off the map.

"Of course not. We use our allies. I'll spill Choctaw blood before our own." The governor turned to face the captain. "While you were sailing across the Atlantic this spring, the Chickasaw accused a French fur trader of being a spy and executed him. They have tired of our 'silent war' on the Trader's Path. They wish to fight more openly, and I oblige."

"By using Choctaw mercenaries."

"Who are only too happy to be paid for killing their own enemies. It is the Chickasaw—incited by British slave traders—who have killed Choctaw and sold them as slaves for the Caribbean Islands for the last ten years. We're merely equipping our allies for revenge."

"As you say." Marc-Paul cleared his throat. He knew better than to point out that if the British and French left the natives in peace, there would be far less revenge to exact.

"So now you see why the Regent's refusal to grant us more supplies puts us in an even more precarious position. I pay the Choctaw to attack Chickasaw villages, but results are minimal. Meanwhile, Chickasaw retaliate successfully on both Choctaw villages and new French settlements up north, on the Yazoo River. If the Chickasaw are not checked, if they interrupt French traffic on the Mississippi . . ."

"I understand." The settlements would be cut off from one another—from food, supplies, and reinforcements. Isolated and vulnerable. France's only defense was the Choctaw. And the Choctaw's only motivation was payment.

"Go to the commissary and conduct a complete inventory of our stores. Don't trust the ledger. I want a fresh count of all we have."

With a wave of Bienville's hand, Marc-Paul was dismissed. He saluted his superior officer, replaced his hat on his head, and took his leave.

⚜ ⚜ ⚜

Beyond the absent wall of Julianne's three-walled cabin, champagne clouds tufted the morning sky. She stiffly pulled on her steaming silk gown, but smoothing the wrinkles from her mud-splattered skirt proved as useless as taming the waves in her chin-length hair. Since Simon was fishing for their breakfast, she would go to town to collect their dowry herself.

The soft ground gave way like a sponge as she followed a faint footpath unspooling toward the river. Rain-sharpened scents of earth and wood spiced the air. The gradual slope uphill took her past other cabins, outside of which men stirred their fires and women ground pestles in wooden mortars. Their voices mingled pleasantly with the laughter of their children. Julianne wished them good day, and they returned the greeting, but their gazes rested overlong on her cropped hair.

The settlement was a study of brown and green: muddy trails spiked with weeds, rust-colored cypress dwellings topped with palmetto thatch, the grey-green moss dangling from trees in the swamp behind her home. Even the river burnished more bronze than blue beneath the blazing sun. While Paris on the Seine was fragrant with café au lait, fresh bread, leather, straw, and wine, New Orleans here by the Mississippi smelled of fish, coffee, corn, bear grease, and *eau-de-vie*, a cheap variety of brandy.

During the brief walk from her home, humidity licked Julianne's skin, and the breeze did nothing to cool it. Her dress, still damp from last night's storm, stuck uncomfortably to her body. As she passed the tavern, she noticed it leaned slightly off-kilter, most likely due to sinking ground, which gave a fitting drunken air to the building. Completing the impression, its thatched roof sat rakishly atop the whole, like a cap pulled at a slant across a brow. Beyond it, the barracks reeked of last night's liquor. Shamelessly, a man relieved himself just outside the crude building.

Quickly averting her gaze, Julianne crossed the open square to the Company of the Indies' warehouse and ducked inside. The door scraped against the wood floor as she shut it behind her and waited for her eyes to adjust to the relative darkness. A handful of men with skirted waistcoats swinging at their hips and frilled jabots ruffling at their throats seemed to be inventorying the supplies lining the walls. Shelves bore all manner of goods for sale: bolts of silk, pots of bear oil, brandy, muskets, corn. Smells of sawdust and alcohol permeated the air.

A small, bespectacled man stepped out from behind his polished walnut desk. At the sight of his voluminous powdered wig, Julianne's hand flew up to smooth down her hair.

"I am Monsieur Godefroy, company clerk. State your business, if you please." He pulled from his waistcoat a gold pocket watch and checked the time. Tapped the toe of his silver-buckled, high-heeled shoe.

She swallowed. "The dowries from the flute that arrived yesterday should be here by now. I've come to retrieve mine."

Godefroy raked Julianne with a scrutinizing gaze. "Dowries?"

This should not be news to the company clerk. "In Paris, Monsieur Nicolas Picard forced us to marry and compensated each couple with a dowry, which was to be delivered to us upon arrival here." She cleared her throat and attempted a smile. "We're here."

"As I see." The clerk's nose wrinkled. "But I'm afraid I've seen nothing in the inventory about any such thing."

Suspicion prickled her neck. "There were individual bundles of clothing—trousseaus—and three hundred livres per couple. I saw the packages loaded into the cargo hold with my own eyes. If they aren't in the warehouse and the ship has been emptied, how do you explain this?"

Godefroy returned to his desk and sat. Leaning his elbows on the green felt topper, he tented his fingers. "It's not my concern."

"If they were stolen . . ." Julianne could not think how to finish. Of course they were stolen.

"That's a serious charge, madame." But Godefroy's expression remained calm. Apathetic. "Unfortunately, it's not within my purview to investigate."

Heat flooded Julianne's limbs. "Surely this isn't the end of the matter?"

Godefroy shrugged. "If there ever were any dowries in the first place—and I'm not conceding that there were—they've likely been divided up and sold already. To be frank, I'm not convinced you would have made good use of the resources anyway. Good day."

Stunned, Julianne struggled to maintain her composure as she turned and left the warehouse. Leaning against the outside wall of the building, she closed her eyes and released an exasperated sigh. What were the new colonists to do? Were they all reduced to beggary, debt, or thievery? She opened her eyes and reminded herself that at least she was not in Salpêtrière.

But the freedom Louisiana offered was a distorted version of the portrait painted by Nicolas Picard in Paris. Hemmed in by river and swamps, and suffocatingly small at less than one square mile, New Orleans's entire population could fit in Salpêtrière's Saint-Louis Church twenty times over. And though she wore no shackle on her ankle, arriving on the convicts' ship had marked her as clearly as the brand beneath her sleeve. She could only hope that as her hair outgrew its telltale length, she too would outgrow the stigma.

A cry pierced the air. Quickly Julianne rounded the corner of the building until she faced the open square beside the barracks. Soldiers and civilians were gathering in a wide circle, facing inward.

"Stop! You can't do this!" A woman's voice climbed higher than all the others. It was coming from inside the circle.

Hurrying over to the crowd, Julianne saw two soldiers wrestle a used-up-looking woman onto a wooden horse. A hank of her hair fell over one eye, and blood smudged her lip. A strip of cheaply made lace had been ripped from her chemise and now dangled from the neckline barely covering her bosoms.

"What's happening?" Julianne asked. Her gaze remained riveted on the beaten woman and the soldier now raising a whip above his head.

"She's a girl of bad character. The soldiers make examples of them to deter others from following her suit."

Screams ripped from the woman's throat as the whip sliced through her dress and the flesh beneath it. A tavern girl falling out of her bodice clawed at a soldier's arm, shrieking, but he shook her off.

"Why, what has she done?"

"She's a prostitute, but that's common enough. She's being punished for stealing from her customer while he slept. We must have order, you know."

"She is publicly flogged for this? What of the police, can they not handle the matter themselves?" Julianne raised her voice to be heard over the piteous cries of the woman.

The man turned to look at her for the first time, and recognition flashed in his eyes as he took in her short hair. "We have no police in New Orleans," he snarled. "And no lawyers, either, by order of the king. We police ourselves, and the soldiers mete out our judgment, with a little help from a whip and a wooden horse. Try and stop it, and you'll be next."

Julianne stepped back, the woman's screams clamoring in her ears. Whatever notions of liberty she had attached to this wild place were slipping away like sand.

Chapter Eight

Back in the settlement, sharp, successive tugs on Marc-Paul's sleeve pulled his attention from the commissary looming ten paces ahead of him. A little native boy grinned up at him. Bending to the child's level, Marc-Paul spoke in the native tongue. "Why, this can't be Walking Wolf! You're so much taller than the boy I remember!"

"Yes I am!" The little boy produced two brown eggs. "For you! Very fresh, very good. Already cooked in the shell."

"Ah, beautiful!" Marc-Paul's stomach growled at the sight. He carefully took the eggs in one hand. "Tell me, have you seen Red Bird here today?"

The boy shook his head.

Marc-Paul straightened. "Next time you see him, please tell him Captain Girard is back from France and eager to hear from him." He withdrew a few colored glass beads from the pocket of his waistcoat and offered them to his little friend. "Many thanks."

Walking Wolf's eyes sparkled as he accepted the trade and scampered away. As Marc-Paul watched him dart across the square, between other natives who had come to trade or gossip, he prayed the message would reach Red Bird without delay. If Red Bird was still alive to receive it.

Turning back to the business at hand, he marched into the commissary and straight to the clerk's desk. "Your ledger, please."

"Yes, sir." The thin private spun the book around so Marc-Paul could inspect it. He turned to the records of goods earmarked as gifts for the Choctaw and traced with his finger the column of text:

Limbourg cloth, blue and red
White blankets
Striped blankets
Regular trade shirts, for men, as long in front as in back
Ordinary trade muskets
Gunpowder
Pieces of scarlet-colored woolen ribbon
Rough vermillion in one-pound sacks and in barrels of
    100 and 50 pounds
Red lead
Blue and white drinking glasses, assorted sizes
Woodcutter knives
Musket flints
Trade scissors
Flintlocks
Awls
Mirrors in cases

Quantities were marked in columns of black ink beside the goods. If the ledger was accurate, Bienville had a little more than twenty thousand livres' worth of merchandise. It was enough to distribute during the next four-week ceremony with tribal leaders in Mobile, but could it possibly stretch to fund this war?

With a word of explanation to the clerk, Marc-Paul took the ledger and walked the commissary aisles, matching the written quantity with the actual number of goods on hand. Some of the numbers matched. But those that didn't sent suspicion spiraling through his middle.

Carefully, he flipped to the ledger pages that recorded inventories for the garrison. If numbers in any of these columns jumped by the same deficiency he noted on the gift-giving side, he could trust that the missing items had simply been stocked in the wrong section of the commissary.

But he found no such tidy solution. After searching every shelf in the warehouse, Marc-Paul returned the ledger to the clerk. "The numbers are wrong." His tone was flat.

"I beg your pardon, sir?" The clerk sat up straighter, spreading his hands possessively over the ledger.

"There are fewer gifts in stock than your book indicates."

"Fewer gifts? Of what nature?" He turned the pages in the ledger until he found the list he was looking for.

"Ten muskets, ten pounds of gunpowder, twenty pounds of balls. Gun flints too." These same gifts that brought peace could also fund war between native peoples, a tactic used increasingly by both France and Britain to secure their own interests.

The clerk paled. "Surely there's been some mistake."

"Surely, indeed." But Marc-Paul had a sinking feeling that the missing weapons were not lost by mistake but spirited away by someone whose foremost interest was not the good of France. Someone, he suspected, who would grow rich and fat at his country's expense. He could only imagine how Bienville would react to the news.

"I'm sure I have no idea what caused the discrepancy."

Marc-Paul would order a double guard stationed here, day

and night. "You've not seen anything unusual, then?" he pressed. "Is there another clerk I should question?"

"I'm the only one." Sweat glistened on his face. "The only time I haven't personally been here was when I was ill with the fever. Officer Dupree took my place while I recovered."

"Dupree, you say?" Marc-Paul frowned. Surely it couldn't be. "I don't believe it."

Marc-Paul swiveled toward the voice. "Pascal Dupree!"

Pascal gripped his hand and pulled him close enough to clap him heartily on the back. His trademark grin exposed the dimple in his sun-bronzed cheek, belying his thirty-two years. "I've been waiting for your return! Come, let's walk by the river."

Marc-Paul followed him outside, where they passed from the slanting shade between the commissary and the barracks into the glaring sun. "I thought you were at Mobile."

"What sort of greeting is that, old friend? After all these years, you could at least feign some pleasure at our reunion." Pascal's green eyes twinkled as they walked along the top of the levee.

Marc-Paul chuckled. "Of course, I'm pleased to see you're in good health, but you cannot blame me for being surprised. Or preoccupied. I've only just now learned of our war with the Chickasaw." He pulled the two eggs from his pocket and handed one to Pascal.

"You mean the Choctaw's war with the Chickasaw. Don't be dour. You certainly didn't learn that from me." Pascal cracked his egg on his elbow. Marc-Paul did the same. "To your question, then. I was at Mobile, right where you left me. But I transferred to New Orleans to take command of your men in your absence."

"You commanded my men?"

"Someone had to." Pascal slowed his gait and looked over his shoulder toward the barracks. "Rascals."

"Indeed. Likely more so with you in the lead." Marc-Paul raised his eyebrow as he peeled the shell from his slippery egg. "Unless you've changed?"

A laugh erupted from Pascal, deep and throaty. His hand squeezed the back of Marc-Paul's neck in an older-brother gesture, though he was but two years the senior. "Lucky for you, I'm the same friend who looked out for you when you first arrived in Mobile. The same friend, need I remind you, who saved your life."

As if on cue, an alligator rippled through the river below, and Marc-Paul stood riveted as he watched its spiny back slide through the water, its eyes two knobs protruding just above the surface. It opened its massive jaws, scooped up some unseen prey, raised its head and snout, and gulped it down.

A shudder passed through him. He had seen those teeth up close once. He and Pascal had been paddling a pirogue of supplies between two forts soon after Marc-Paul had arrived in Louisiana. When a barrel of gunpowder had tumbled overboard, he jumped in after it, knowing Pascal couldn't swim and thinking to retrieve it before the water spoiled it all. But a female alligator whose young were on the nearby bank interpreted the action as a threat. If Pascal hadn't shot the twelve-foot reptile when he did, Marc-Paul's saga in Louisiana would have come to an abrupt—and excruciating—end. Little wonder that he'd been fond of Pascal's company. For a time.

"I remember quite well." He brushed the eggshell from his fingertips and bit into his egg, relishing the flavor as he swallowed. "Pascal, some of the supplies in the commissary are missing. The clerk said you were the only other person who has been in charge of the ledger, while he was ill. Do you know what happened to the guns set aside for the Choctaw?"

Pascal cringed, then popped his entire egg into his mouth at once. Tucking some of it into the pocket of his cheek, he spoke around his food. "Don't be cross now. I'll restore what I owe as soon as I can."

Marc-Paul narrowed his eyes. "What have you done?"

"Lost!" he blurted. "I've lost, Marc-Paul, a great deal, and to the wrong sort of card player, if you know what I mean. If I didn't pay him off, it would have been the end of me. You've seen the sort of colonists France sends over here. They're no gentlemen, you know that."

"I also know that gambling is forbidden among soldiers, including officers." He sighed and scanned the river again, too frustrated with Pascal to hold his pleading gaze. Huge limbs broken from trees somewhere upstream floated by, their branches clutching at the sky.

"I couldn't say no to this character—if you had seen him, you'd have done anything he told you to do too! There is no law in New Orleans."

"On the contrary." Marc-Paul faced him again, anger simmering in his veins. "As officers in the king's army, we are the law. Or at least, we are charged with maintaining it. Your choice to gamble cannot be blamed on your opponent." The sun beat down upon his black felt hat. Sweat itched across his neck beneath his queue.

Pascal held up his hands, palms facing out. "I'll pay it back. There is no scheduled gift-giving ceremony any time soon. I'll get the guns back to the commissary well before they're needed."

"And the powder."

"Yes, yes. Everything, just the way it was before. No one needs to know about this, mon ami. I'd consider it a favor if you allow me the time to fix this."

"You'll fix it, Pascal. Before you return to your own post." God grant that it might be soon.

"This is my post now." A grin chased the worry from Pascal's face. "Grand, isn't it? Together again, just like old times."

Slapping a mosquito on his neck, Marc-Paul turned back toward the settlement. There was nothing grand about their "old times." The last thing he wanted to do was repeat them.

⚜ ⚜ ⚜

Julianne sat on the deerskin in the fractured shade of her thatched roof. With lace fluttering at her low, square neckline and at the ends of her elbow-length sleeves, she braided wild grass in her silk-covered lap. Wind sighed through the pilings and palmettos. As she worked the spindly stalks into the beginning of a woven mat for her floor, she rehearsed how she would tell her husband their dowry had been stolen.

Footsteps sounded on the path outside her home, bringing Simon back to her, but he stood taller, straighter than she had ever seen him before. Two canteens and a musket swung from his shoulder, and in one hand he held a string of enough fish to feed them both for the day. But it was his smile that made her discard her work.

"I see you caught more than fish!" Smiling, she rose to greet him with a kiss on his cheek. Rays of light wrapped her in velvety warmth.

"You have no idea." He looped his string of fish over a piling before hanging his musket likewise over the top of the wall. "Thirsty?" He handed her a canteen.

Julianne nodded, grateful to finally slake her thirst. "How did you get all of this? I hate to tell you this, but if you've obtained it on credit—there is no dowry. For any of us."

His face darkened. "What do you mean?"

"I went to the warehouse, and the clerk knew nothing about it. Or so he said."

Simon grunted. "We should have expected as much. When has the Company of the Indies ever treated us fairly? But you mustn't worry. I have something better." His broad, rough hands enveloped hers. "Employment. All of this is advanced payment."

Her heart skipped a beat. "Please tell me—you're not smuggling already, are you?"

Miraculously, he laughed. "No, ma chère. This time it is honest work for honest wages. But I never would have been fit for it had I not been a smuggler first." He winked, then dropped her hands and drank from his own canteen.

Julianne followed suit. "Is it a secret, then, this honest work?"

"I am to be a boatman again, plying the waters between here and other Louisiana ports—Natchez, Mobile, even Fort Toulouse, which is even farther east than Pensacola but north of it. They need men to power barques and pirogues, to carry trade items or official correspondence between military forts. Fifteen livres a month. I warrant I'll be able to drive a higher wage once I prove myself, though. There's fighting going on, they say, between French soldiers and a nation of Indians. They need us boatmen now more than ever."

Julianne frowned. "Will you be traveling to where the fighting is?"

"Hard to predict." Simon shrugged. "But if smuggling taught me anything, it was how to sneak around. I was only caught but once. I'll be fine."

Hanging his canteen and hers from the pilings, he motioned to her to follow him as he ambled behind the cabin and plucked from the ground sticks that had blown in during last night's storm. Julianne gathered kindling alongside him.

Though his back was to her, she could hear the smile in his voice. "There are a few forts west of the river, in Arkansas, that I won't be traveling to. And the boats bound for Illinois Country don't leave until August or September for the three- to four-month journey upstream, so we'll determine later whether I'll row for one of those."

She straightened. Holding her branches away from her gown lest they snag Francoise's silk, she carried them to the fire ring Simon had formed and dropped them beside it. "These warring Indians—are they anywhere close to New Orleans?"

"Hundreds of miles away, they say. My guess is it won't affect you at all." Simon joined Julianne at the fire ring and knelt on one knee, arranging the wood to allow air to flow between the sticks. "My one concern is that you'll be lonely. I'll be gone for weeks at a time, maybe longer."

Julianne nodded. She had already considered this. "I'll get along on my own in your absences." Wind sashayed between them, light and sweet, and flirted with the tender flame flickering from the kindling.

Simon cupped the small flame with his hands for a moment before standing. His blue eyes twinkled as he smoothed her hair back from her face. "Are you so ready to be rid of me, wife?" His lips curved in a teasing grin, and when he bent to kiss her, she did not pull away even though he smelled of the morning's catch.

"I meant no such thing, and you know it." She swatted at a band of mosquitoes. "But Simon, think of this. In all those places you visit, you'll be able to look for Benjamin, ask those you see if they know of his whereabouts. Surely we'll find him now!"

The light dimmed in his eyes. "Your brother."

Julianne's hands dropped to her sides and were immediately swallowed up by the folds of her green silk skirt. "Yes, my brother. He's the only family I have left."

"No, he isn't." Simon held her gaze, clenching his jaw. His lips pressed flat and tight.

Unnerved by his sudden hardness, she looked away for a moment before responding. "Yes, husband, you and I have each other." She fought to keep frustration from her voice. "But this isn't about us. Surely you can understand that I love my brother." Her throat closed around the words. How could she explain that their bond still held despite the time and distance that had come between them? "Please try. It would cost you so little and reward me so much."

Exhaling, Simon hooked one of her curls behind her ear. "I'll find out what I can. But if I come up empty, don't be surprised. Louisiana is enormous. Finding Benjamin is as unlikely as coming close to any fighting."

"But you'll try." Hope caught in Julianne's chest as she threw her arms around his neck. "Thank you," she whispered in his ear, and kissed him.

⚜ ⚜ ⚜

Day's end down by the river brought the vibrato of bullfrogs and a chorus of crickets' song to Julianne's ears, overpowered on occasion by the crescendo of laughter surging inside the tavern. Eager to check on Denise, she let herself into St. Jean Inn and crossed through the storeroom on her way to the stairs. Her hand touched the railing, and she froze. She cocked her head. Listened. There it was again.

Screaming. A woman was screaming. *Denise?*

Julianne fisted her skirt and took the stairs two at a time. It didn't take more than a moment to reach the room from which the shrieking came. Finding the door unlatched, Julianne pushed inside and came face-to-face with Lisette, the orphan who had shadowed her and Denise during the voyage.

"Julianne!" The girl's freckles stood in stark relief against her pale complexion. "Saints be praised!"

"I heard screaming—" She looked past Lisette and saw Denise drenched in sweat, her face screwed tight with pain. A sheet draped her rounded middle.

"I came to visit Denise and found her like this. She asked for you. I didn't know where to find you." Lisette's words came in short, breathless bursts.

She asked for you. The last woman to do so was Marguerite, and now she was dead. Julianne's confidence faltered. But Denise was older than poor Marguerite was, and not as narrow. There should be no danger if the baby was positioned right. And this time, she would not allow the patient to be bled during the delivery.

"Well, I'm here now. Please find anyone who works here. Tell them we need wine and lard or oil. Plenty of water, clean cloths, scissors. An apron." Julianne crossed to the washbasin and scrubbed her hands clean.

With a nod, Lisette scurried from the room.

"My husband is at the tavern. He doesn't know." Denise's short brown hair was matted against her head. "Jean doesn't even believe the child is his. But it is. You must believe me. My father had me imprisoned for rejecting his match for me, but I was no libertine. This child is my husband's."

"Of course it is." Julianne rubbed Denise's belly in soothing, circular strokes before probing the thin wall in search of the baby's rope of spine. It wasn't there. Instead, she felt a bulge, not hard enough to be the head, and too round and large to be an elbow or knee.

Malpresentation. Again. Fear cycled up her spine. A voice, soft and malicious, licked in her ear: *Denise will die under your hands as well.* She gritted her teeth.

Lisette burst back into the room, blond hair straggling from the bun at her neck. Rags draped her arms, a bottle of wine and a cup filled her hands, and behind her Francoise carried a pot of oil.

"Francoise." Julianne twisted her hands together. "Please, is there a doctor you could fetch?" She would not give quarter to her pride. She would not repeat the mistake she'd made before.

Gravely, Francoise shook her head.

"Julianne. You are a midwife, are you not?" Denise panted for breath, her gaze as sharp as daggers.

"I am not." She tied an apron over her skirt just the same. "I was. It is not the same thing."

"Delivered almost three hundred babies in Paris, you said. Were you lying?"

"No, no, of course not. I just want to take every precaution. Having a doctor here would be prudent, if possible." If she had done the same for Marguerite, the girl's blood would not be on her hands.

"Well, it isn't. *You* will deliver me, as you promised you would." Denise's eyes glazed before she squeezed them shut at another contraction. The cords of her neck grew tight as she arched her neck and her back off the bed.

"We are really on our own?" Julianne whispered to Francoise.

"Never." The older woman closed her eyes. "Heavenly Father, we beseech thee to have mercy on us, your children. Guide Julianne's hands as she guides this baby safely from its mother's womb. Protect them, Lord. Amen."

Throat tight, Julianne nodded her thanks and set about her work. The scent of bear oil filled the room as she lifted the lid. The movement of greasing her hands shifted something in her heart and mind. Everything she had learned under Madame Le Brun, all that she was taught by the surgeons in the charnel house outside Saint-Côme church, every piece of it gathered to the front of her mind, waiting to be put to good use. Energy coursed through her. The miracle of life was at hand. So was the possibility of death.

Sitting on the stool at the end of the bed, Julianne instructed Lisette to help Denise take some wine and for Francoise to lay cloths beneath her hips. Keeping her eyes on Denise's face, Julianne began her tactile examination beneath the sheet. The neck

of the womb had opened, the bag of waters had already ruptured. But as she'd suspected, the baby's head had not crowned.

"Denise, I must put my hand inside you. I need to feel where
the baby is." *This is not Marguerite*, she told herself. *The out-
come need not be the same.*

Instinctively, Francoise and Lisette flanked Denise and held
her hands as Julianne slipped her hand into the womb. All three
faces watching her were tight with determination. Francoise's
lips moved in silent prayer while Lisette reminded Denise to
breathe.

Julianne felt the crack in the baby's soft bottom, then up
higher, the fold of a thigh. Refraining from probing any further
for fear of releasing the tar-like meconium, she gently followed
the curve of the baby's knee, then the line of his lower leg,
and firmly pulled a foot down into the birth passage. Quickly,
she reached back in for the other foot, but the muscled walls
of the womb clamped down. Francoise and Lisette murmured
encouragement until Denise drowned them out with her cries.

The muscles eased. Arm tingling from the pressure, Julianne
coaxed the other foot down into the passage.

"Push," she urged, and Denise struggled to obey. Exhaustion
circled the mother's eyes, and her hair coiled darkly against her
temples. Her lips had lost their color.

Slowly, evenly, Julianne pulled the feet out into the world. Ten
little toes pointed heavenward, and she wrapped them with a
clean cloth to keep a firm grip. Once the knees emerged as well,
she rotated the body so his jaw would not catch.

"Francoise." Julianne glanced at the older woman for help
but saw she had paled whiter than alabaster and leaned on the
bed for support. "Lisette."

Without a word, Lisette hurried to her side. She was no
younger than Julianne had been when she'd first begun attending births.

"The feet."

As Lisette held the half-born child, Julianne reached in and straightened the baby's arms, and the delivery proceeded into Lisette's steady hands.

"A girl," Julianne announced. "Well done, Mama." But the baby was weak. After tying the navel string in two places, she cut between the knots.

Still, the baby didn't stir.

"Why isn't she crying?" Denise pushed up on her elbows. "Is something wrong with her?"

Julianne didn't answer. *The baby will die in my hands.*

"What do you need?" Francoise, beside her, quietly jolted her back to the moment.

"Cloths soaked in strong wine or eau-de-vie. Crushed onions. A bath for the baby of lukewarm wine and water." *Lord, help. Let not this little one pass.*

She focused on clearing out the baby's nose and mouth, then dropped a tiny amount of wine into her mouth. Turned her over onto her arm and thumped her back to dislodge anything that may be blocking the flow of oxygen to her lungs. The baby breathed, but faintly.

Francoise brought what Julianne had requested, and together they wrapped the cloths around the baby's head, chest, and stomach. Julianne held the crushed onions beneath the baby's nostrils long enough for her own eyes to water. "Come, little one. Wake up for us now."

The baby's eyes opened, and she let out a wail.

Tears thickened in Julianne's throat. "Thank you, Lord," she whispered, then smiled at Denise. "She's fine. She's perfect."

"She's a miracle," Lisette whispered. "What have you named her?"

"Angelique," Denise breathed. She pushed herself up on her pillows.

While Julianne tended the delivery of the afterbirth, Lisette and Francoise bathed the infant and wrapped her in clean cloths.

Exhaling relief, Julianne shuddered to think how things may have concluded if such a delivery were attempted on a rolling, pitching ship. "She knew exactly when to make her entrance, didn't she, Denise?"

"A lady always does." Tears tracing her cheeks and gathering beneath her chin, Denise stretched out her arms for her baby and hugged the tiny bundle to her chest. "Look at her nose! Look at her mouth! Look at her hair!"

Julianne laughed. "She has erased all doubt as to who her father is, hasn't she?" After washing her own hands and arms up to her elbows, she untied the apron and came to admire Angelique in her mother's arms.

Denise clutched Julianne's hand. "Thank you." Her voice strained with emotion. "Do not pretend this was a simple birth. Thank you. If you hadn't been here—"

"But she was." Francoise bent and kissed Denise's temple and then the baby's velvety head. "And so was God, who faithfully guided her." She spoke a simple prayer of thanksgiving in that easy way of hers, then beamed at Julianne and Lisette before tenderly cradling Angelique's head in her palm. "Remember this, mes chères: There is no person so small that the Lord cannot see her, no voice so quiet that He cannot hear it."

A sacred quiet surrounded the women as they marveled at the delicate child, stirred only by Angelique herself.

Denise wiped tears from her cheeks. "My mother will never see her." She sniffed. "Nor my sisters. I always thought—well, whenever I dreamed of becoming a mother and pictured myself having a baby, they were in the room with me. Sharing the pain and the joy as if it were their own." Her watery eyes were rimmed with red.

Francoise bent to stroke Denise's brow. "If I may speak for all of us, it is an honor to stand in for your family."

Her heart full to overflowing, Julianne nodded, unable to squeeze words past the lump in her throat. Lisette smiled broadly for the first time, revealing a narrow gap between her two front teeth.

Pounding shook the door from the other side, shattering the tenderness of the moment. "Denise! Why would you lock out your husband? Denise!"

After dabbing her eyes, Julianne opened the door, and Jean Villeroy's eyebrows plunged. "I was expecting to see one woman in my room. Not four."

"Try five," Denise called, smiling. "But this tiny one here is the only one who has your hair."

His hand flew to his head. "What the devil do you "

"Shush! Watch your language around our daughter."

Jean's eyes flared wide. The new father moved to his wife's side and knelt by the bed. "Is she—can I touch her? Will I hurt her?"

Laughing, Denise assured him it was safe. With one finger, Jean traced the slight indentation in Angelique's chin, then smoothed the dark red hair over her pulsing fontanel. "My daughter," he whispered. "She is mine, isn't she?" Amazement cracked his voice.

Julianne beckoned Lisette and Francoise out into the hall to give the happy family their privacy. Francoise wiped a tear from beneath her eye. "A baby changes everything."

A longing swelled in Julianne that she had not allowed herself to feel in years. She folded her arms across her waist, yet they ached with an emptiness so heavy, she labored to carry the burden.

Chapter Nine

✣ ✣ ✣

MISSISSIPPI RIVER
JULY 1720

Suffocating heat wrapped around Simon, wringing perspiration from his pores. Feet planted firmly as he stood inside the sharp-bowed vessel, he paddled against the Mississippi River's current along with nineteen other rowers. Pine trees scrubbing the shoreline released sweet perfume into air that teemed with mosquitoes and midges.

In addition to hauling supplies for French colonials, the flat-bottomed boat carried items earmarked for the Natchez Indians, whose villages were eighty-eight leagues upstream from New Orleans. Gunpowder, balls, guns, limbourg fabric of red and blue, vermillion, awls, combs, and horn-handled knives would be given to the Natchez on credit. In return, the Natchez would hunt deer, dress their hides this fall and winter, and present them to the company trading post next spring so they could be transported back to New Orleans and sold for shipment to Europe.

"Keen eyes, men. Keen eyes." The captain kept his voice low, and the four armed soldiers also on board were as alert as Simon had ever seen men be. Sunlight flashed on their bayonets.

"What are we looking for, exactly?" Jean Villeroy dared to ask as he rowed directly in front of Simon.

"English agents, maybe. But savages are the main concern," the captain clarified.

"Excepting we won't see them until we've got an arrow or tomahawk in our chest," offered another rower, and Simon shuddered inwardly.

"Enough," the captain growled. "Just keep your mouths shut and your eyes open."

Obediently, Simon combed his surroundings with his gaze. On the east bank of the river, he spied an alligator sunning itself, about nineteen feet long. Further on, a family of ducks bobbed in the water, ripples circling outward from their swimming feet. But after a while, the rhythmic stroking of his paddle lulled his mind away from possible lurking danger. His thoughts nested with Julianne instead.

By the time he left her for this trip, their home was much better situated. The cabin now had a door made of canes lashed together with leather thongs, and there were even some crude furnishings inside. A rope bed with mattress, blanket, and pillow. Two chairs and a table. A chimney so she could cook indoors. A kettle, a pan, mortar and pestle, corn and salt pork. The debt of credit would have to be paid as soon as he was. Cringing, he owned that he had already spent more than the fifteen livres he would earn for the month. At the company warehouse, one watermelon cost three livres. A single pot of bear oil was twelve. He'd had no idea when he accepted this job how little a livre could purchase in Louisiana.

Still, he was committed to earning honest wages, however paltry, for Julianne's sake. Guilt coated him as he considered how he'd resisted her request to look for Benjamin. It was selfish of him and irrational. Truly, he didn't want to lose her. Many of the couples who had been forced to marry in Paris were now seeking divorces from the Superior Council in New Orleans, and the Council was granting them. That little blond waif Lisette Dumont had shed herself of her debauched husband as soon as she learned how, and Simon didn't fault her. But the ease with which it was done had stunned him. Simon had thought marriage was for life. If it wasn't, well, he didn't want to give Julianne any reasons to end their union.

"Take. For you."

Simon snapped from his reverie. Standing at his side was Running Deer, the Indian slave sent along by the Company of the Indies to both serve and interpret at the trading post. His long, loose hair shone like obsidian in the sun, and the few turkey feathers he had woven into it fluttered in the breeze. Wearing nothing but his breechcloth, moccasins, and a shell necklace against his tattooed chest, he offered Simon his fourth and final ration of alcohol for the day. After downing the bittersweet rum, Simon nodded his thanks and handed the empty cup back to Running Deer. Next, the Indian gave him salt beef, boiled rice, and a biscuit. Dinner on the move.

Steadily, Simon rowed upstream for the final stretch of the day until the sun sank in the west, bathing the sky with fire. Mosquitoes hummed in his ears as the rowers found a place to camp for the night and tied the boat securely to some tree trunks. While several men drew lots to determine who should stay on guard for the first watch, Simon went about the task of gathering long reeds and sticking both ends in the ground to form a row of arches. With bearskins for mattresses and cloth topping the reeds for canopies, the boatmen had the best protection they could manage against biting insects while they slept.

Muscles burning, he crawled into his makeshift abode, and

Jean crept in after him. The heat in the airless space proved as dense and unforgiving as the darkness, and yet it was still preferable to being eaten alive by midges and deerflies.

Groaning, Simon turned onto his side and glared at his bed-fellow. If Jean's sour body odor wasn't strong enough to alert any nearby Indians of their presence, his raucous snoring certainly would.

Simon rolled to his back and raked his hand through his hair, trying to shut out Jean's crude presence and shove aside any thoughts of savages waiting in the shadows. How he ached to be lying beside Julianne instead.

A single thought curled around him. If she was so happy just because he agreed to look for Benjamin, what would she do if he were actually able to find him?

✤ ✤ ✤

Julianne's nerves thrummed as Captain Girard led her between the sweet-smelling orange trees outside the settlement. Standing at the door of Bienville's country residence, she reminded herself that the governor needed a woman with her skills. The colony needed her.

Girard rapped on the door, the picture of confidence in his deep blue waistcoat lined with yellow trim. An African the captain greeted as Caesar answered the door and ushered them to the commandant's office. Before Bienville looked up, the captain tucked his tricorn hat under one arm and swiped his hand over his black hair from his brow to the queue at his neck.

Setting down his quill, the commandant rose from his upholstered chair and circled his walnut writing desk, deserting the half-written page behind him. His slave followed him, fanning him with a large palmetto branch. Though he was not a large man, Bienville's bearing commanded respect. The white curls of his wig cascaded over the shoulders of his grey brocade coat patterned with fleur-de-lys. A paisley-covered waistcoat beneath resembled any French gentleman's typical taste. Covered from the tips of his buckled shoes to the silk cravat wrapping his neck, no one would have guessed that—if rumors were true— his chest was heavily tattooed with the Virgin Mary, the infant Jesus, Constantine's cross, and Indian symbols.

"So this is the girl?" Bienville asked.

Julianne made no sign of being insulted at the rough greeting as she curtsied. If Bienville's mother had raised him with any manners, she certainly hadn't had much time. The captain had told her that Bienville joined the French colonial navy at the age of twelve. "Julianne LeGrange, monsieur." Her honey-colored hair was pinned in coils to her head so that, covered with a lace cap as it was, the short length of it remained disguised.

"And you're a midwife, Captain Girard tells me."

"I am. Just delivered a brand-new colonist last week at Madame St. Jean's Inn. A baby girl. It was a footling breech delivery, but both mother and daughter are doing fine." Too late, she wondered if her words smacked of pride or arrogance, when all she intended was to demonstrate her credentials.

When Bienville studied her eyes overlong, her gaze slipped beyond him to a map-covered table behind his desk. Vaguely, she could make out the sweeping lines that symbolized the Gulf Coast, the Mississippi River, and the Great Lakes, which bordered New France to the north. Truly a vast territory, and wild. No wonder populating it remained such a concern.

Captain Girard cleared his throat. "She was trained in Paris, sir. Started attending births when she was fifteen, formally apprenticed for the requisite three years, and passed with honors her examination from the faculty at the College of Surgery."

Surprised at the clarity of his memory, Julianne stole a glance at the officer beside her. Had she really told him all of that in the course of their conversations?

"I haven't seen you before. You came with the convicts? Rough company for you, I'm afraid. Blasted idea, sending worthless souls over here," Bienville muttered, and Julianne flushed despite Caesar's efforts to create a breeze. "At least someone was thinking when they recruited a midwife to make the crossing too. We need our French women to survive child-birth as many times as possible so they can continue bearing children for France. Every French baby is a vital asset to the colony, you understand."

Her fingers played in and out of the pleats in her skirt. "I do understand. Every life is precious."

Bienville wagged his finger. "I said every French baby, and I mean full-blooded French, is important for the success of Loui-siana. You mustn't misunderstand. We need a colony midwife *for the colony.*"

Her hands stilled at her sides. "I understand that, monsieur. But your colony includes women who aren't French, does it not? I am quite prepared to tend all mothers."

"Are you quite prepared to follow orders?" Bienville crossed his arms and puffed out a breath that smelled of coffee. "I'm going to speak plainly, madame, and you best listen well. For years Louisiana has been composed of primarily French men. When they needed to slake their thirst for women, they found it easy enough to do so with willing native girls. Some of the men even professed to love the Indian women they slept with."

Beside her, Girard tugged his cravat away from his throat.

"But half-French is not French. Aha, let me put it this way." Bienville pivoted on his high-heeled shoe, picked up a glass of water and a cup of coffee from his desk, and held them both aloft. He poured some of the coffee into the water glass, and the brown liquid plunged and swirled until the water took on a shade of its color. "You see? No longer pure. Water does not make coffee clean and clear. On the contrary, coffee muddies the water." He set the drinking vessels back down. "Half-Indian babies will not preserve French culture. Half-breed children are far more savage than they are civilized. It can only ever be this way. It is simply the law of nature." He spread his hands innocently. "My job—and should I hire you as the colony midwife, your job—is to care for the interests of France. Do I make myself clear?"

Julianne swallowed. "Abundantly."

Bienville nodded. "Done. You shall be given a stipend of six hundred livres a year." He dabbed his handkerchief to his brow, then returned to his chair at his writing desk. Caesar followed him.

Captain Girard set his hat back on his head and saluted his commanding officer. As Julianne curtsied once more, her mind spun. Six hundred livres a year! It was more than three times Simon's salary, saints be praised!

"One more thing." Bienville did not trouble himself to look up from his correspondence this time. "As part of your duties, you will tend the ill among the soldiers."

"Pardon me?" She glanced from the governor to Girard, who raised his shoulders in an unhelpful shrug.

"We have no doctor. You will care for the garrison's health. Or your pay will be reduced by half."

"Monsieur, with respect." Julianne paused to master her composure. "The health of the mothers and babies is my utmost concern. If I expose myself to your ill men, I compromise the health of the women in my charge." Her voice grew stronger with every syllable.

Bienville squinted at her, and she returned it with a hard stare. If he was unaccustomed to being opposed, so much the pity.

"Surely you understand my dilemma," she went on. "I could

carry disease into the birthing chambers. Certainly this is not what you want."

"I want a midwife. And a doctor." His razor-sharp tone sliced through the tension in the air.

Julianne spread her hands. "I'm no doctor. I know birthing, and that is the extent of it!"

"Then I suggest you learn." Bienville glowered at Girard, a clear sign they had been dismissed.

Lightly, the captain touched Julianne's elbow and led her from the room.

Once outside, she strode away from the residence as if she could not be shed of it fast enough. The sun beat mercilessly down on them, but a light breeze ruffled the edge of her cap and the lace at her sleeves.

"Outrageous!" She nearly spat the word. "Tell me, Captain Girard, if your wife was about to give birth, would you allow her to be tended by someone who surrounds herself with contagious diseases?"

"I—I have no wife."

She pursed her lips. "But if you did. You would want to protect her, wouldn't you?"

"With my life."

"And if you had a slave woman who was ready to deliver, would you allow a midwife to help ensure the mother and baby's safety?"

"It would be my duty."

Slowing her hasty pace, Julianne shook her head. An apologetic smile slanted her lips. "Forgive me, Captain. You are not on trial here, after all." But her smile stiffened and drooped into a worried line. Halfway between Bienville's home and the edge of the city, she came to a complete stop.

From their position on the high ground, they could see the Mississippi glittering in the sun, could hear the boatmen yelling to each other as they anchored by the docks, could smell the fishermen's catch. But all of that fell away when Julianne looked at Captain Girard. She had to know.

"Captain." The wind teased a curl from its pin, and it bounced against her cheek. "I never told you I started attending births when I was fifteen."

He looked everywhere but into her eyes. "Didn't you?" he murmured.

"Please. The truth." Her hand fluttered up and lighted upon his forearm.

"Benjamin must have told me, then. He spoke of you often, and with great affection."

Hope sparked. "You know my brother?"

He looked down at her hand on his sleeve. "I knew him. Quite well, in fact. He had a special talent for languages. As soon as I noticed, I taught him as much of some of the tribal tongues as I knew, until he surpassed even my own ability. I recommended to Bienville that he be embedded in a Choctaw village to learn about them by immersion. He agreed, and Benjamin was thrilled at the opportunity. You must understand, this practice has precedent in Louisiana. Certain boys of Benjamin's age—he was fifteen at the time—are handpicked to leave the garrison and live with a native tribe to become our expert in that people's language, customs, and religion. We wanted to learn their ways of farming, tracking, fishing, hunting, cooking, and warfare. Sending one nonthreatening boy with a keen mind has proven to be the best way to do it. Benjamin was only too eager for the challenge."

Julianne inhaled sharply as Benjamin's last letter scrolled through her memory. *A grand new adventure with the natives*, he had written. This must have been it. "But for how long? A year? Surely you wouldn't just abandon a fifteen-year-old boy for a year?"

"No one abandoned your brother, I vow. As I said, he wanted

to do it, and we checked on him at regular intervals. Each time, he was well and faring better than the rest of the soldiers. He spent fourteen months in a Choctaw village north of Lake Pontchartrain."

Fourteen months. He would have been sixteen years old by the end of his sojourn. "And then he came back to the garrison?" She knew Benjamin had a particular capacity for languages. Knowing she couldn't understand him, at times he would speak in Latin or Italian just to taunt her. But she could not imagine her little brother living as a Choctaw as he grew into a man.

"He did. But he was weakened by a recurring fever that plagued him. Still, whenever men in my company went on foraging expeditions or as armed protection for traders, he was there, eager to practice the language with the natives. When there were calumet ceremonies—when chiefs and big-men came from different tribes to smoke a peace pipe with Bienville—Benjamin was always close at hand. He was a skilled and useful interpreter, and imparted much knowledge to us about native ways of living. You have reason to be proud." A sad smile curved on Girard's face. He looked toward the sun-spangled river below.

Julianne followed his gaze until the brilliance bounced off the water and flashed painfully into her eyes. Sweat prickled her skin as she stood rooted to her spot of earth, but she could not move, not to seek shade, nor even to release the captain's arm, until she knew the rest of the story. "What happened?"

"He was so young." Girard's voice trailed off. "I was genuinely fond of him." He rubbed the small copper buttons on his waistcoat with his thumb.

Julianne tightened her grip on his arm. Wind tugged at her skirt as she searched Girard's tense face. A muscle bunched in his jaw. "Where is he now? Do you know?" She caught his other arm, slid her hands down until they rested in his. Her hands were unreasonably cold, while his were burning hot. "Is he well?"

Girard's eyes softened as they finally met hers.

"Or perhaps you don't know."

"I know." He said nothing more. He didn't need to.

Julianne stepped back from him unsteadily. Dread went to her head like cheap brandy until she was dizzy with it. A profound ache soon took its place. "Oh." She pressed her fingertips to her temples. "He's not well."

"Madame, I would to God I could say otherwise." The captain stepped toward her.

"But at least he isn't dead. He recovered from that fever. You're not telling me my little brother is dead." She backed up again, as though she could distance herself from the horrible fact she refused to believe. A crayfish chimney tripped her heel, and she stumbled. Girard caught her by her shoulders. *No. No. He lives.*

Unable to bear the finality of the captain's grave expression, she squeezed her eyes shut. Instantly visions of Benjamin surged. After their mother died, he'd become her purpose and her joy. Then the mischievous tot grew into a little boy who longed for his father's approval and received only blame instead. In vain, Julianne tried to conjure up an image of him at sixteen, in a military uniform or Choctaw breechcloth. Instead, she saw him lying alone on a pallet, soaked with fever. Without her.

She covered her face with trembling hands. If only she hadn't asked, she could go on believing she'd see Benjamin again, that he was off hunting deer or alligator, or exploring unmapped regions of the territory. Was there any harm in that? Tears spilled down her cheeks. The truth was so much harder than hope.

Girard's voice was hoarse when he spoke again. "I would spare you this pain if I could."

When Julianne's knees buckled, Girard cinched his arm around her waist and caught her to his chest. She made no sound as she sobbed.

✤ ✤ ✤

NATCHEZ, LOUISIANA

With the vessel unloaded and the merchandise safely stored in the trading post outside Fort Rosalie, Simon lingered outside the fort's palisade walls. No one he had spoken with today knew anything about Benjamin Chevalier. Here on the outside bend of the Mississippi, and on a bluff about one hundred eighty feet above it, Simon could see a mile in each direction—and all he saw was the gold-brown river curving between the white cliffs that guided its path. Wind whispered through wild grasses that undulated like the sea. Simon had never seen anything like it.

Popping the last piece of dried deer meat into his mouth, he ambled north along the river into an area he'd not explored yet. Strange, he mused, that he should sense such peace in an area filled with savages. *Natchez,* he corrected himself. They certainly looked fierce enough as they helped the boat dock at the landing, with black and red tattoos decorating their sinewy bodies in dots and stripes. The men's short black hair covered their heads like bowls, except for circles they shaved around topknots that held feathers sticking straight up from their heads. The women's hair, from what he had heard, fell in waves down to their bare feet. But they grew tobacco just like the French colonists did and traded with the settlers for European-made goods, including shirts some men wore above their breechcloths. The Natchez weren't as "savage" as Simon thought they'd be.

His shadow fell to his side, and the bluffs flared purple and russet in the lowering sun. If his fellow boatmen were true to their word, they'd be looking for willing Natchez girls to bed down with for the night right about now. He had his doubts about Jean Villeroy, however. Simon suspected he would stay true to his wife, Denise, just as Simon would stay true to Julianne. In any case, Simon wasn't ready to sleep yet.

Squinting at the fiery sun, he judged he had plenty of time to venture farther north before night dropped its curtain. Come morning, he'd be rowing all day. Now was the time to stretch his legs.

Slung over his shoulder, his *Fusil de Chasse* tapped his leather breeches with every step, reassuring him he was prepared for danger. The Natchez were a peaceful people, anyway, with deer as their primary prey. It took twenty neatly tanned deerskins to trade for a French gun, according to the commissary clerk, and more for balls and powder. The Indians who took a gun on credit this summer would stay quite busy using it to pay off the debt by spring. *If anyone is hunting in the half-light, it's deer they want*, Simon told himself. *Not me.*

By the time he had put a few miles between himself and Fort Rosalie, fireflies throbbed in the air, the warm yellow blinking a silent summer lullaby. The river shushed between the bluffs like a mother soothing her babe. Unbidden, thoughts of Julianne with child emerged in his mind, and his heart quickened. One day he'd have a baby of his own, an eternal soul that would bind him and Julianne forever. The family he never had.

A branch snapped. Simon turned, scanning the land behind him. Other than a few pine trees standing sentry, he saw nothing. Adjusting the leather strap of his gun across his chest, he pressed forward with roving gaze and tingling ears.

Another snap. *A trick of the wind*, he told himself, but he took the musket off his back and carried it in his hands all the same.

Up ahead, smoke spiraled heavenward in grey columns. *Natchez huts.* Perhaps there were Frenchmen or Canadian voyageurs there who hadn't yet taken their pick of native daughters to share their bearskins. As he approached, he slung his gun back over his shoulder so as not to appear hostile.

Behind one of the huts, a packhorse grazed, obscuring its rider, who stood on the opposite side of the beast, talking to another man. One of them wore tall black boots. The other was brown and wore moccasins. Unable to see their faces, Simon strained to decipher their words.

"You have the scalps?" The language was French, but a foreign accent reshaped the syllables. "How many this time?"

Simon stopped. This was no ordinary bartering for deerskins or glass beads. Suspicion kindled in his gut. Jaw tense, he soundlessly moved closer.

"Ten Choctaw." Clear native French, although the way the name of the Choctaw tribe was spoken indicated the speaker had mastered native intonations better than most. "You have ten guns for me? And powder, balls?"

Simon looked closer at the Indian's legs as the two obscured men presumably made their trade. Conspicuously absent were the dotted tattoos he'd seen on every other native today. This native was no Natchez.

"And do the survivors believe it to be the work of the Chickasaw? Or the French?"

"There were no survivors." The Frenchman, again.

Simon's mind spun. What sort of briar patch had he stumbled into now? Pitting Indian tribes against one another was more than enough reason for war, as far as he could reckon. And whoever was behind that horse was not like to believe Simon was just out for an evening stroll and not an enemy spy. His heart throbbed against the strap holding his gun to his back. If he moved to shoulder his weapon, would they hear it? Would he find an arrow in his chest before he even had time to load a single shot?

The voices switched to a tongue Simon couldn't understand,

but the Indian voice, now speaking a native language, sounded remarkably familiar. Simon peered again at the Indian's moccasins. Didn't natives go barefoot except when traveling? He squinted until he was convinced he recognized them. Relief rushed through him. It was Running Deer.

With one more glance behind him, Simon boldly approached the pair. Now that shadows were unfurling, he did not fancy the hike back to the camp in the dark, wondering if he was still being followed, imagining what an arrow would feel like in his back. Whatever the conversation had been about, Simon was not privy to the extenuating circumstances. If Running Deer was part of it, surely it could be nothing too nefarious.

When he was close enough to be heard, Simon spoke Running Deer's name. "It's me. Simon LeGrange, one of the rowers."

A violent shift took place across Running Deer's features, from surprise and anger to a complete absence of emotion. Then, "You this far should not be. Not safe."

Something was wrong. This broken, halting French was a dramatic change from the fluency Simon had just heard Running Deer speak to his companion. Palms sweating, he kept his observation to himself. "Care to keep me safe on the way back?"

Running Deer's eyes burned with intelligence. His mouth remained a tight, flat line.

"How rude of me." Simon thrust his hand out to the Frenchman, who soundly ignored it. "I'm Simon LeGrange. Just came up from New Orleans with a Company boat. Couldn't help but overhear you speak French. Maybe you can help me. I'm looking for a young man—my wife's brother, actually, whom she hasn't seen in years. She believes he may still be in Louisiana somewhere. Have you any information on the whereabouts of a—"

The young man looked at Simon with eyes the color of gunmetal. They were Julianne's eyes. The reddish-brown hair, the scar above his right eye—the exact shape of the tip of a spoon, just like Julianne had said. He looked about twenty years old, but the wilderness aged one so much, he could actually be younger. He could be eighteen. He could be Benjamin Chevalier.

"What did you say?" the young man asked, and Simon realized he'd breathed the name aloud.

"Benjamin? Your sister is Julianne? Now twenty-six years of age, a midwife from Paris . . ."

Running Deer cut short his inquiry with a splintering tone. Benjamin held up his hand to halt the interruption, and Running Deer backed away from view. Benjamin's fingers were long and slender, like Julianne's.

I've found him. Simon could scarcely believe his good fortune.

"Who are you again?" Benjamin whispered.

"Like I said, I'm your brother-in-law."

Benjamin shook his head as if to clear it. Raked Simon with his gaze from head to toe. "Julianne is here, in Louisiana?"

"New Orleans."

Suddenly, both air and time stretched taut. Simon felt the atmosphere parting behind him, the whirring of metal rushing at him, end over end. Heard the thud that cracked his spine and drove him to the earth. Numbness and agony crashed together. Blood filled his mouth, trickled from his lips. Simon tried to breathe through suffocating terror but only gurgled and rattled instead. *God in heaven, save me.*

Simon's body was losing its tenuous grip on his soul. As his blood watered the grass, he slipped further from one life to the next. Dangling between, he saw himself broken on the ground. Saw Running Deer plant his foot on Simon's back, wrench his tomahawk free, wipe the blade on the grass.

Benjamin rolled Simon over and peered into his dimming eyes, resignation and regret chasing across the young man's features. "I'm sorry."

Voices churned, distant and muffled, as though underwater. Simon was sinking.

"No one can know you live, Many Tongues."

"But my sister . . ."

"No one."

A brown hand seized Simon's hair at the front of his scalp, and he shed the bonds that fettered him to his mortality.

Chapter Ten

❖ ❖ ❖

NEW ORLEANS, LOUISIANA
AUGUST 1720

"Shhhh, it's all right. I'm here."

Kneeling on the hard-packed dirt floor, Julianne dipped her sponge into a bowl of water, squeezed out the excess, and bathed a young soldier's face. The air thick and sour inside the broiling barracks, her chest strained against her stays as she inhaled, yet she could scarcely draw a satisfying breath. Still, there was no place she would rather be at this moment than tending her delirious fever patient, a young man named Joseph surely no older than seventeen.

Nursing the garrison was not the work she'd had in mind when she traded Salpêtrière for Louisiana. But healing was a life-giving practice too, if she could only master the art of it. There were a scant forty soldiers stationed in New Orleans, eight officers, and no fort. Any reduction of the garrison through illness or death courted danger. The entire settlement was at risk when soldiers were too ill to defend against potential attack. Though branded for murder, Julianne was here to preserve lives—whether they were mothers, babies, or soldiers. Such a fulfilling occupation would please not only herself but the governor, the Regent, and most importantly, the King of Kings who ruled over them all.

She'd requested a number of medicines from the warehouse, but while she waited for the Superior Council to approve them, she decided to visit the ill with what she could put together on her own. There were fewer than sixty French women in New Orleans—less than half the number of men—and none of them approaching full term, so any risk resulting from exposure to sick soldiers would be limited to her own person.

How odd, she mused, that the very thing she had so resisted when Bienville had demanded it of her would be the working out of her own grief. For in nursing this soldier, she did for him what she gladly would have done for Benjamin when it was he who suffered fever. She could not have foreseen, that morning in the governor's house, the significance this role would take on.

"Mother? Mother, you've come at last." Joseph grasped her hand, and she started at his scorching-hot touch. His glassy gaze did not fix upon her shamefully short hair but instead seemed to cling to her eyes, where she hoped he found the compassion she felt. She saw no reason to tell him they'd never met before this day. Let him believe her ministering hands were those of the woman who loved him most in the world. Surely his mother would want him to think she was there to comfort him. How Julianne wished she had been at Benjamin's side at the end, in spirit if not in body!

"I'm here. Now please rest," she whispered and gave his hand a light squeeze before placing it back down at his side.

He shifted on his pallet, and the dried Spanish moss crackled beneath his weight. After swiping her sponge over the thin wall of his bare chest, she laid upon it a poultice of roasted onions and crushed mustard seeds. She prayed such a remedy would be enough to break his fever—and the fevers of the five other soldiers she would tend after Joseph.

Julianne took her bowl and sponge to the next suffering soul. Lowering herself to the ground beside her patient, she nestled the bowl on her aproned lap and wet the sponge once again. Leaning over the young man, she brushed his hair from his brow. His eyes opened, slightly yellowed, and he sighed in relief as she cooled his skin with gentle strokes. *Heal him, Lord. Restore them all to health.* What she could not do for her brother, she would do for another woman's son.

Dusty sunbeams spilled through the gaps between the pilings, and mosquitoes dipped in and out, tormenting those who hadn't the strength or sense to swat them away. Red welts spotted the next patient Julianne tended, so after bathing him from the waist up and applying a poultice to his chest, she mixed a mud paste to smear on the itching sores. Tenderly, she dabbed the rustic balm on the man's face, neck, arms, and chest.

He stirred, blinking at her.

"Does this feel better, soldier?" she murmured.

"Much." Through half-lidded eyes, he examined her. "I'd ask if you're an angel, but I know for sure we're not in heaven." He wrinkled his nose, apparently smelling the illness pervading the atmosphere.

She smiled. "You're still in New Orleans, right where you should be. I'm Julianne LeGrange, and I aim to keep you out of heaven as long as I can."

An eyebrow raised, albeit slightly, on his brow. "That so?" His lips began to curve in a smile, but they were so dry, she was afraid they would split and bleed. She reached into her apron pocket and drew out a small jar of olive oil, dipped her finger into it, and applied it to his lips. His sigh bespoke his gratitude. "You must call me Matthieu."

Julianne fit the lid back onto her jar and slid it back into her pocket. "Very well. How are you feeling, Matthieu?"

"Better now that you're here." His voice was weak and low,

so she leaned in to hear him. "I haven't seen such a beauty in ages. But you came on the convict couples' ship?"

He was certainly lucid. She cleared her throat as she sat back on her heels. "Some call it so. But I would be pleased if my husband and I, and our friends, were no longer identified by our pasts. We're no longer prisoners. As you see." She hoped her smile softened the edge she felt in her words. Had she been a fool to suppose that as long as her brand remained hidden, she'd be free of its stigma?

"I'm not squeamish." He paused for breath. "You've nothing to be ashamed of in my presence."

Matthieu was more right than he knew on that point.

"You don't speak like one scooped up from the streets for beggary. So what was your crime?" Drawing a deep breath, his lips glistened with the olive oil as he regarded her. "Prostitution?"

She winced. "Heavens, no." She laid the back of her hand on his forehead. "Your fever seems to have broken." She rose, abruptly perhaps.

Matthieu brushed her skirt with his fingers. "Don't go."

"My work here is done. I'll be sure to check on you again soon. In the meantime, don't overexert yourself while your strength returns." Encouraged by his prospects for recovery, she moved on.

⚜ ⚜ ⚜

Clouds billowed like sails against the deep blue sky. Sweat beaded on Marc-Paul's brow as he marched east, out of New Orleans. Squinting, he scanned the edge of the swamp that pressed the boundaries of their settlement, looking for some sign of movement. All he detected, however, was a pair of squirrels chasing each other around a tree trunk.

"Marc-Paul."

With a start, he turned to find Red Bird right behind him.

"Greetings!" He should not have been surprised to find the Choctaw had noiselessly appeared, wearing nothing but a breechcloth and the moccasins he wore when not at home. Red Bird was a scout, a tracker, and a hunter. Fortunately, he was also an ally. Relief poured through Marc-Paul to find him still alive.

"I heard you were back." The flawless French that came from Red Bird's lips was a tribute to his teacher. Benjamin would have been proud, and rightfully so.

"I heard about the Chickasaw war. Have you—" But there was no need to finish the question. One glance at the leather thong tied around Red Bird's waist supplied the answer.

Red Bird patted the scalps hanging at his hip. "Eighteen this time. But not all of these are mine. I'm here to collect on behalf of my friends as well."

Marc-Paul swallowed, suddenly aware of the unpleasant odor. "I understand you'll be paid at the commissary."

Crossing his arms over his bare chest, Red Bird nodded. "I lost nine relatives to Chickasaw raiders years ago. Now I've taken twice as many of them. This is a good trade." A rare smile tipped one corner of his lips. "And you? I heard you brought more settlers to New Orleans." For the name of the French settlement, he used the Choctaw word *Balabanjer*: "town of strangers."

"As it happens, not all of them are complete strangers. Benjamin Chevalier's sister is here."

Red Bird's eyebrows rose. "Does she know?" The wind blew his long black hair over his muscled shoulders, revealing the large copper spools swinging in his earlobes.

"She knows he is dead." Marc-Paul lowered his voice and switched to the Choctaw language. "But she doesn't know exactly how it came to pass, and I'd just as soon leave those details veiled. They'd do her no good."

The Choctaw's lips pressed together resolutely. "If I had

known your chief had no mercy, I would not have tracked Many Tongues down."

Marc-Paul swallowed a sigh. He'd often wondered what Benjamin's death had meant to Red Bird, given that it was his family who'd taken the youth in for fourteen months. "How does your village fare?"

Red Bird peered toward the swamp for a moment, his bronze profile marked by the flattened forehead customary of all Choctaw males. He steered Marc-Paul toward the riverbank, where they could see anyone who might be approaching.

"So far, the Chickasaw have not reached us. But some of my people grow weary of fighting. Especially when their own fields suffer from their absence. They say they should receive larger payment. In other villages too there is unrest regarding our French alliance. Those who waver in their loyalties say France has not enough supplies, trade goods, or presents because you lost all your ships to the English and were defeated in Queen Anne's War. They say only the British can supply us properly."

"We will supply you properly." Even as he heard his own promise, Marc-Paul wondered how he would keep it.

"See that you do, for your own sake. We can fire British muskets as well as French." Red Bird's expression shifted. "Someone comes. I am away." He headed toward the settlement, presumably to collect payment for his scalps.

Pascal Dupree hailed Marc-Paul after he passed by Red Bird. "Who was that you were speaking with just now?" he panted.

"One of our allies, giving me an update."

"Choctaw?" Pascal removed his hat and fanned himself with it. "What did he say?"

"He said they need more guns."

"Same old story, eh?" Pascal clapped Marc-Paul on the shoulder. "Escort me home. We'll have a drink."

Marc-Paul unbuttoned his waistcoat, peeled it off, and threw it over his arm as he walked. "It was you I was coming to see, anyway. The guns and powder you said you'd replace in the commissary—unless you've come from there directly, it hasn't been done. You gave me your word, Pascal. It's been two months." Time enough, and then some.

"Ah, that." Pascal rubbed the back of his neck. "I couldn't get the guns, but I paid my debt in blankets."

"Blankets?" Marc-Paul gaped. "Blankets will not arm the Choctaw for war."

"For some mysterious reason, I've been unable to find any guns anyone is willing to part with." Sarcasm dripped from Pascal's voice.

"You should have considered that before you took them from the commissary to begin with. Blankets are an unacceptable substitute."

"And what would you accept?"

"Guns!"

Pascal expelled a sigh. "I regret that you are disappointed. But that is the best I could do."

"Where are the guns you took to pay off the card player? Does he still have them?"

Pascal looked straight ahead. "Didn't ask. He's not the sort of fellow who takes kindly to questions. Remember Le Gris? How volatile and paranoid he was in Mobile, and how eager he was to squeeze the trigger in any direction? Imagine him, but add about fifty pounds and take away one front tooth, and you'll see what I'm dealing with here."

"Fifty pounds heavier than Le Gris. A missing front tooth. It seems I'd have noticed such a character about the settlement." Marc-Paul raised an eyebrow.

Pascal shrugged. "I'd not be surprised if he's taken to pirating. May he never return to New Orleans!"

"Why you ever took him for an opponent is beyond all logic."

Marc-Paul simmered as they stepped into the shade of Pascal's gallery. "Fine house you have here." He couldn't help but wonder if Pascal had gambled for the money to pay for it.

"Thank you. It's ghastly hot, but worse inside, no doubt. Allow me to get those drinks."

"Water's fine."

Pascal laughed. "Surely you jest. I can understand giving up brandy for Lent, but not for life."

"You don't have to understand it." But Marc-Paul's aversion to strong drink should be no surprise to Pascal, of all people.

The door slammed behind Pascal as he went inside, and Marc-Paul laid his waistcoat over the back of one of the two chairs. Sitting, he snatched his hat off his head and set it on his knee. He pulled his cravat loose and unwound it from his neck. Ghastly hot, indeed. Soldiers were dropping with fever now almost daily.

"Here we are." With one boot, Pascal kicked open the door and let it thud behind him as he handed Marc-Paul a glass of water. He too had shed his waistcoat. "I had hoped the breeze would carry some refreshment today. Dancing Brook! Running Deer!" he bellowed as he sat in the other chair.

Running Deer appeared, gazing at the ground in submission. Marc-Paul could tell he was Chitimacha, a nation formerly at war with the French colonials until they brought the calumet and brokered peace in 1718. Though all French captives had been released, Bienville insisted that the French would keep the Chitimacha slaves as their own.

"There you are," Pascal said. "Fetch Dancing Brook; tell her to bring the palmettos."

Running Deer bowed in acknowledgment and disappeared again, and Pascal took a swig from his cup.

"I thought he was owned by the Company of the Indies." Marc-Paul took a long drink of water, grateful for the cool relief.

"I own him. I rent him to the Company when it suits me.

And it usually suits the Company to have a savage on board when they go upstream." Pascal's breath soured the air with the odor of eau-de-vie.

Marc-Paul traced his finger through the condensation on the outside of his glass in a pattern that matched the tattoo on Running Deer's chest. "Was he with the party that just went to Fort Rosalie?"

"He was."

"Successful trip?" With two more gulps, he downed the last of his water.

"Quite." Pascal's smile broadened, dimples deepened. "Ah! There you are. Stir up a breeze for me, would you?"

Dancing Brook, also Chitimacha, lifted her palmetto branch and began fanning Pascal. She was young, of no more than fourteen summers by Marc-Paul's guess. Unlike other Indian women, who wore their hair in two plaits, her tresses hung loose to her waist. Her deerskin dress, decorated with scarlet woodpecker scalps in a double row across the chest, pulled snugly across her rounded middle.

Pascal caught Marc-Paul's gaze and raised an eyebrow. "Exquisite, isn't she? Do you have your own 'Dancing Brook' awaiting your return?"

Marc-Paul tucked his guilt behind his disgust and set his glass on the floor. "You haven't changed at all, and more's the pity."

"Oh, this is too much! You're not about to persuade me to holy chastity now, are you? Remember, this is me you're talking to. I know you. Even if you don't."

Old sins, though long repented, reared up in Marc-Paul's conscience, towering and formidable, until he could not see his way past them. Rising, he snatched up his cravat and waistcoat and placed his hat back on his head. "You must replace those guns you took."

Pascal looked stricken. "Come now. We resolved that matter."

"The matter will be resolved when the inventory matches the ledger again."

"What's a minor discrepancy between friends?"

"It isn't minor." And their friendship wasn't what it used to be. With a hasty adieu, Marc-Paul stormed away.

By the time he reached his own home, a pounding headache had gathered between his temples. He tossed his hat on the hall table and headed straight for his bedroom. Sighing, he dropped his waistcoat on the chair, unbuttoned his gaiters and peeled them off, along with his shoes, and stretched out on the bed. Eyes closed, he shut out the world.

Moments later, the bed shook. The sound of heavy breathing filled the humid air. And then the licking began. Marc-Paul opened one eye to see Vesuvius the pug licking his own nose, over and over, his fist-shaped head jerking into the air each time. *Ridiculous dog.* Marc-Paul sank his fingers into the rolls around the pug's neck and gave him a sound scratching. Vesuvius rewarded him with a sloppy, face-splitting smile and gyrating tail.

"All right, Vesuvius," Marc-Paul muttered, and the dog's black ears twitched forward, creating the trademark wrinkles on his face. "That's enough now." He folded his hands on his stomach, and Vesuvius turned in three circles on the bed before wedging his stout body against Marc-Paul's side.

In minutes the dog began snoring, and Marc-Paul envied his slumber. This afternoon he'd share Red Bird's report with Bienville. He could put those troubles out of his mind until then, at least.

Pascal's words about Dancing Brook, however, still nettled him. Memories, long buried, resurrected.

Images drew themselves on the backs of Marc-Paul's eyelids, flaying the last seven years from his life. A gaunt, twenty-three-year-old version of himself, wearing animal skins he'd been forced to fashion for himself when his uniform disintegrated.

Staring out at the Gulf of Mexico for relief that never came. Hunger had gnawed at him, as it gnawed at all the French soldiers in Mobile. Louisiana was an infant colony in 1713, totally dependent on its mother country. Without any developed resources or system of cultivation, the colony relied upon supplies from France. But war raged in Europe, and shipments had dwindled, then disappeared. There were only sixty soldiers serving in Louisiana that year, just one-third the total from nine years earlier. Marc-Paul and the others might have been as lost as castaways on a deserted island if it hadn't been for Bienville's command to the greatly diminished garrison.

Following orders, Marc-Paul and Pascal had dispersed into the woods to live by hunting with friendly Indians and lodging with them over the winter. The Mobilian Indians took them in with generous hospitality, offering them sagamité and cakes of dried deer meet, and bearskin beds by fires kept burning through the night.

Unwelcome memories assaulted Marc-Paul. Flames licking the air, twisting and dancing together promiscuously. His belly burning with too much brandy. The taste of tobacco smoke still in his mouth. Soft fur beneath him. Long, smooth black hair entangled in his fingers. The crushing guilt when he woke up the next morning beside her.

Pascal never understood Marc-Paul's regret. But then, Pascal had never fully subscribed to the teachings of the church. Marc-Paul, on the other hand, was devoted to both church and country. Not that he had a choice. Not that any of them did. To be French was to be Catholic. That was the law, by edict of King Louis XIV, for whom Louisiana was named. And Marc-Paul Girard obeyed the law, whether handed down by God or king.

Except for the times he didn't.

⚜ ⚜ ⚜

Curled on her bed, Julianne pressed her hand against her stomach to still the pitching and yawing within. She'd already emptied it three times today. Surely there was nothing left. She closed her eyes and kept as still as possible, lest any hint of movement capsize her stomach.

Alone in her cabin, as she had been since falling ill, Julianne had ample time to measure her loss. How strange, she thought, that even though she had not seen Benjamin for four years, his absence grated on her with unseemly clarity.

Footfalls sounded outside, preceding a knock on the door. "Julianne?" A quiet voice. "It's Lisette. I've brought Francoise."

"Just a moment." The ropes stretching beneath her bedtick creaked as she slowly slid her legs over the edge and stood on the warm dirt floor. She crossed to the door to unlatch it, relieved that her stomach did not protest. The storm inside her seemed to have calmed, at least for the moment.

Upon opening the door, Francoise took Julianne's elbow and led her immediately back to the bed. "I came as soon as I could get away." Her cheeks were rouged, her mole placed perfectly near her eye, as usual. "Lisette tells me you're ill?"

Standing beside the bed, Lisette twisted the end of her flaxen braid around one finger as she looked earnestly at Julianne. The sun had darkened her freckles into a fine sprinkling of cinnamon across her nose. "I know you said you didn't want visitors, Julianne, but I couldn't just leave you alone."

"I don't want you to get sick too," Julianne said. If she had caught the illness from the soldiers, certainly anyone near her was exposed as well.

"You think it's the fever?" Francoise placed the back of her hand on Julianne's brow. Frowned. "You don't feel overly warm to me."

"I don't know what it is. I haven't been able to keep food in its place. As for fever, who can say when I'm constantly sweating from this heat!"

Francoise stood back, folding her hands in front of her waist. "Is your pulse weak? Do you have chills?"

Julianne shook her head.

"Headaches?"

"No, just the vomiting. Ever since I returned from the garrison."

Francoise pulled a wooden chair near the bed and lowered herself onto it, embroidered skirts fanning out from her stomacher. "I see. Does your body ache? Your joints, bones, muscles?"

"None of that, but—" Words disappeared. Julianne's eyes grew wide. She pressed her hands to her heart's strong, steady beat. Her breasts were tender. *How could I have missed it?* She looked from Francoise's knowing smile to Lisette's worried eyes.

"What is it?" Lisette breathed. "What's wrong?"

Julianne shook her head. "Nothing." Reverent wonder wrapped around her. Something cracked open inside her and joy gushed forth, filling her completely, from her fingertips to her toes, until she almost feared she might burst from its pressure. She could only imagine how Simon would react upon learning he would be a father. Visions of him cradling a wee babe in his muscled arm danced in her mind.

Francoise clapped her hands twice before clasping them and looking heavenward. "Praise be."

"Lisette," Julianne whispered through her tears, "I think— I am very like to be with child."

"A baby!" Her blue eyes sparkling, the young woman beamed, the tiny space between her two front teeth rendering her smile all the more endearing.

Shadows darkened the doorway. Julianne struggled to her feet when she saw Denise and two-month-old Angelique.

"May we come in?" Denise asked, the baby in her arms swatting at a loose strand of her hair.

"Yes, yes, there is no danger to you. I'm not ill. Except for what is very natural among those expecting a gift in six or seven months' time." The news burst from her before she considered that Simon should not be the last to know.

Denise blanched. "Oh! Do you mean—"

Unable to contain herself, Julianne kissed Angelique's cheek. "I mean a gift rather like this little sack of sugar here."

"How—how very wonderful for you. You must take care of yourself, you know." A tear spilled down Denise's cheek as she laughed. "Of course you know. You must be your own best, most cooperative patient. Won't you?"

Jean Villeroy appeared in the doorway then, his face ashen. His knuckles grew white on the barrel of his gun.

"Jean!" Julianne gestured for him to come inside. "Welcome home! Is Simon on his way too?" She craned her neck to look past Jean's frame.

"Um, no. He isn't. Not in the way you think." His footsteps fell heavily as he crossed to the far wall and hung his gun upon the pegs. *No, Simon's gun.*

Denise shook her head, her mouth screwed to one side. "Sit down." She handed Angelique to Lisette and sat beside Julianne on the edge of the bed, crushing the dried moss inside the mattress.

The hair rose on the back of Julianne's neck. Dreadful news, unspoken, dangled in the air. She could feel it.

Denise looked to Jean, but his splayed hand obscured his face. She drew a deep breath, swallowed. "I'm afraid there's been an accident, ma chère."

Bitterness filled Julianne's mouth, and her mind scrambled to distance herself from whatever was banking up in the quiet hesitation. Her gaze focused determinedly on the lace frothing at Denise's elbows. Was it Venetian? Or was it made by the lace makers in Normandy's Alençon, who had grown famous for their imitation? In the imperfect light, she squinted to see the hexagonal mesh and the bouquets of sunflowers fluttering whenever Denise moved.

"At Natchez." Jean's words yanked Julianne back into the frontier territory she now called home. His eyes were shot through with red. "Simon wandered too far from camp one night. I don't know what he was looking for."

Benjamin. He was looking for Benjamin. Julianne had no doubt of it. "And?"

"And he went too far."

"I—I don't understand what that means. Too far for what? Please, please speak plainly to me."

Jean tugged his deerskin shirt away from his thick neck. "The Indian slave who was with our group found his body."

The cabin spun. Denise wrapped her arm around Julianne's shoulders, but numbness trickled through her until she couldn't feel a thing. *Dead? No.* She shook her head, found herself staring again at the lace trimming Denise's robe volante.

"He'd been tomahawked in the back and scalped. We don't know why."

"Was it the war? With the Chickasaw?"

"There was no Chickasaw-Choctaw fighting in the area. He was the only one killed." Jean dropped to his knees before her. "Forgive me, Julianne! I would have stopped him from going alone if I had seen him leave!" His face wrenched.

Gasps sucked the air from the room, hands reached out to touch her arm, her knee, her cheek. A searing pain sliced through Julianne's chest, as sharp as the blade that had killed Simon. Was there a more horrifying way to die? She covered her mouth with a trembling hand. Her eyes squeezed shut, but images of her husband's murder splashed brightly across her mind. *Was he alive when the Indian scalped him?* Her lips refused to frame such words. Instead, "Did he suffer?"

Jean's grip tightened on his knees. "The wound in his back

would have killed him pretty quickly. Maybe—maybe he didn't have enough time to know what was happening."

Or maybe he did. Maybe his last moments were filled with terror and agony as he died alone in a strange place. Arms folded over her stomach, Julianne bent her head and rocked on the edge of the bed she would never share with her husband again.

"He's at peace now, Julianne. Rest in that." Francoise dabbed her handkerchief to Julianne's tears, though she was crying too. "Believe me, imagining his end will do you no good."

A baby's cry resounded in Julianne's ears. Lisette swayed with Angelique, her expression twisted in sympathy, but Julianne heard her own baby crying from her womb. Loss stacked upon loss and settled on her chest. Breath could scarcely squeeze past its weight. Her baby would be fatherless because Simon went looking for Benjamin, who was already dead.

Because she had begged him to.

Chapter Eleven

❧ ❧ ❧

Since time had refused to halt while the boat delivered Simon from Natchez, no more of it was wasted in laying his body to rest. Surrounded by Francoise, Lisette, and the Villeroys, Julianne stood outside the settlement on the natural levee of the Mississippi River, the only ground high enough above the water table to accept the dead. Running Deer was there too, as well as the captain, crew, and soldiers who'd been on Simon's boat. Beneath the blistering sun, the priest finished his prayer and made the sign of the cross.

Julianne stared at the lid nailed tight to the coffin as men lowered it into the earth. Jean had advised her not to view the body before he'd been shut away forever. And so she would never see Simon again, save for in her mind.

Rocks clunked on the lid, and Julianne sent a questioning look to Francoise beside her.

"To weigh it down."

Cringing, Julianne struggled not to picture water rising around and inside the coffin. The merciful numbness of her shock was beginning to give way to raw grief. Dirt sprayed and thudded on the pine board top until Simon was completely swallowed up by soil, buried in land he had never wanted to tread, let alone call

145

his home. Now he could never be free of it. She rested her hands on her middle as she felt the tug of ties binding her to this place as well. For in this levee were the brother she had come to find and the husband who died while searching.

"I'm sorry, madame."

With a jolt, Julianne realized the mourners were dispersing and coming to pay their respects. She nodded and thanked each one as they came, until Running Deer stood before her.

"You found his body, didn't you?" Julianne searched his dark eyes.

"Yes."

"Was he already—did he say anything before he passed?" She kept her voice low but could tell others were leaning in to catch the answer as well.

"Sorry. Too late, I found. Too late." Running Deer dipped his head, then went silently away.

Waiting until everyone else had filed by, Denise, Jean, Lisette, and Francoise murmured tearful condolences.

"Let us walk you home," Jean offered while Denise adjusted Angelique's bonnet to better shield the baby from the sun.

Julianne shook her head. "I think—I'm not ready to leave. Just yet."

"Do you want me to stay with you?" Lisette placed her hand on Julianne's arm. She had never said that she knew how it felt to be alone, but the empathy in the orphan's blue eyes and soft manner held earnestness beyond measure.

"No, thank you." She smiled, hoping Lisette would understand. "I'm quite prepared to be alone for now."

"I'll go to your cabin and prepare you a meal, then. If that's all right with you."

Julianne had not even thought of food. Had no appetite whatsoever, between the baby and her grief. But she should try to eat. For her baby—Simon's baby—she would try. "Oui, merci."

As her friends quietly departed, she turned back to her husband's grave. Though the sun beat down on her back, she knelt on the ground and laid her hand on the dirt that covered him. Absently, she rolled the warm, damp grains between her fingers, inhaling the tangy scent of fresh-turned earth. From below the levee, the river added its own distinctive smell. Julianne's stomach complained, but she ignored it. The skin on the back of her neck was being scorched by the sun, but she would not yet seek shade. She had things she needed to say.

She wanted to tell Simon she was sorry for urging him to search for Benjamin, but she hadn't known her brother was already dead. She wanted to tell him he was going to be a father, and that he would be a good one. She wanted to say they would learn how to be parents together, and that this baby was the greatest gift anyone had ever given her. She wanted to say that he was enough for her.

But it was too late for Simon to hear. So she held all these things in her heart, tamping them down ever deeper with every pat she gave the mound of soil beside her.

⚜ ⚜ ⚜

Cursing the meeting that had gone overlong with Bienville, Marc-Paul took long strides as he climbed the levee, determined to pay his respects to Julianne, if she should still be there. Part of him hoped the report he'd heard in the square of Simon LeGrange's death and burial was a simple case of misinformation. Maybe Julianne and LeGrange were home in their cabin even now, and he was puffing up the bank for nothing.

Then he saw her. She seemed so small, sitting on her heels, her blue gown fanned about her, her hand on the fresh grave, and he reconsidered the prudence of his plan. This was a private moment, almost sacred. It would be boorish to disturb.

He could not guess how much time passed before she rose, clapped the dirt from her hands, and turned. He strode toward her.

"I'm so sorry. If there is anything I can do. . . ." But as they neared each other, he saw accusation in her eyes. They met on the slope of the riverbank.

"He died because he was looking for Benjamin." There was venom in her words.

"Your husband was—what did you say? Looking for Benjamin?"

"He rowed to Natchez, and while he was there, he searched for my brother. Because I told him to. Because I didn't know Benjamin was already dead."

Because Marc-Paul hadn't told her soon enough. Another man she loved, another protector, dead. Because of him.

"Why didn't you tell me you knew he was dead right away?" She spat the words at his feet. "If I had known, I never would have told Simon to make inquiries! He would not have left camp; he would still be alive!" She beat her fists on his chest. "If you had just told me from the beginning!"

Marc-Paul caught her wrists before she struck him again. "I've done wrong. I should not have kept the truth from you for any reason, including my intention to spare you pain."

"Spare me!" She laughed and tried jerking free of his hold. "If that was your plan, you failed miserably!"

He set his jaw. "I agree." That he was the source of so much of her pain was unbearable.

She stilled, and her eyes filled with tears. He released her, and she rubbed her wrists. *God in heaven, if I left a mark on this woman . . .* "Did I hurt you?"

She shook her head. "I'm sorry," she whispered. "I lost my composure."

"Understandable." Words failed him so wretchedly. He could

not think of a single comfort to offer her. "Did you love him?" He bit his tongue for letting such a personal question escape.

Sighing, Julianne looked past him for a moment before returning his steadfast gaze. "I loved him the best I could."

He nodded. "What will you do now?"

She turned her face, and he traced the delicate line of her profile with his gaze. "I'm still a midwife—thanks to you. And a nurse. I have my friends. I have—" Her hand went to her stomach. "I have reasons to go on."

Mustering all his self-control, Marc-Paul did not closely examine her middle to measure its roundness. *It's my imagination. She can't mean she's with child.* But maybe she was. A widowed bride with a baby on the way. Because he had not told her the truth. His gut recoiled at the thought that her child would be fatherless.

"You will marry again, of course." Unintentionally, his voice had assumed the tone he used with his troops.

Julianne's eyebrows arched high in her forehead. "This is what you say to a widow at the grave of her late husband?" She began marching down the riverbank, back toward the settlement.

Marc-Paul accompanied her, kicking up dirt that clouded his white canvas gaiters. "Forgive my insensitive timing."

"You have much to be forgiven," she muttered without looking at him.

Granted. "But this is a matter of practicality, a matter of your safety. This is not Paris, where you can live comfortably in the upper apartment with neighbors who will keep track of you, whether from goodwill or for gossip. Let's suppose you come home one day to find a scoundrel lying in wait for you in your cabin. Who would hear you if you screamed?" He paused to measure whether his warning created any reaction in Julianne whatsoever. But her face was stone. Would he need to describe every sort of unsavory character that populated the village and its outskirts? "New Orleans is no place for a single woman of virtue without a protector."

"Lisette is a single woman again."

"Lisette Dumont?" He sidestepped a crayfish chimney and almost set his heel on a sunning lizard. "Francoise told me she is staying at her inn indefinitely and has been hired to work in the kitchen to pay for it. She is safe at night. She is not alone."

They reached the bottom of the riverbank, and Julianne stopped. She turned to him with weary eyes and one fist on her hip. "Have you really never learned how to do this?"

Suddenly feeling exposed, he tugged his hat down over his forehead. "How to do what, madame?"

"Condolences. It is customary, in our culture, to offer sympathy at the graveside, not make the bereaved tally her losses or fear for her future. Or have you been in the wilderness so long you've forgotten?"

Her reproof stung as if she'd slapped him.

"I have been forced to marry before, recall. I'll not be forced into it again. Good day to you."

This time Marc-Paul did not follow her as she hastened from his side.

PART TWO

Currents

"If the Choctaws who serve as a rampart for us should once happen to be destroyed, we should be in a very insecure position."

—Sieur Jean-Baptiste Le Moyne de Bienville, 1711

Chapter Twelve

⚜ ⚜ ⚜

The last burning days of summer curled away like dried corn husks. That month, between sun-soaked days and rain-drenched nights, Julianne delivered two babies safely into the colony, and then there were no more unborn children in New Orleans that she knew of, save her own.

Which was not to say there were no more pregnant women in the settlement. Julianne suspected there were several. She had knocked on each of the cabins scattered about New Orleans, introducing herself as the sworn midwife should anyone in the household ever need her services. Of the four to five dozen women she had met, not everyone was convinced midwifery was even necessary, and of the few dozen female slaves and servants registered with the Superior Council, Julianne had only seen a handful.

What she had seen in abundance, however, were men, more than half of them unmarried. Canadians idling between trapping seasons. Deserters whose sentences to the galleys had been commuted to exile in Louisiana. Reckless young men sent by their fathers to New Orleans by lettres de cachet. Gamblers who had crossed the ocean to outrun their debts. Fishermen. A few warehouse clerks, coopers, carpenters. Convicts like her. In her quest to reach the female population of New Orleans, she had unwittingly introduced herself to every bachelor in want of a wife. Julianne had been as impressed with them as the matrons in New Orleans had been with her.

Dragonflies winging above her, she slowly walked to the barracks, wading through the oppressive humidity that had laid low so many soldiers. At least she could count on being of service there. With a basket of herbs and poultices over her elbow, she passed her hand over her barely rounded belly, measuring her growth by the spread of her fingers. So far, it wasn't much. But if her reckoning was accurate, she was still at least five months before full term. Plenty of time for the baby to grow. And plenty of time for her to be useful still.

Nearing the barracks, she noticed Captain Girard and a few of his men tearing out rotten posts from the corner of the structure. Without his waistcoat, and with his shirt-sleeves rolled to his elbows, he appeared far less stuffy than usual. Julianne raised an eyebrow at seeing the captain lower himself to labor unbefitting an officer of his rank. He looked up as she passed, his hat slightly askew, and spared her but a curt nod before returning his attention to his work.

A guard let her into the barracks, and shade offered some relief, but moisture still thickened the air insufferably. With no chimney inside this temporary structure, the air trapped inside did not circulate. Little wonder so many of the men fell ill and struggled to recover.

"Bonjour, madame! You grace us with your beauty and compassion. I only wish we were better equipped to receive such an honored guest."

Julianne turned to find Officer Pascal Dupree at her side, dimples deep in his sun-bronzed cheeks. She suspected that with his green eyes and even smile, he was accustomed to charming and disarming many fair maidens. But Julianne was not here to be flattered.

"Any illness other than fever today, Officer?" She scanned the room while her eyes adjusted to the dimmer lighting. Sour smells of sweat, body odor, and illness churned her gut. Dipping into her basket, she drew out a peppermint leaf and tore it in half. After rubbing the pieces between her thumb and fingers to release its scent, she brought them to her nose to inhale until her turbulent stomach began to settle.

"Some scurvy, ghastly cases. But unless you have limes or oranges in your basket, you may as well steer clear of them." With a bowl of water and sponge in hand, Officer Dupree followed Julianne as she came alongside the first feverish patient. "Allow me." He took the basket from her arm as he handed her the bowl, and she set about her typical routine of bathing the patient's face, arms, and chest before applying an onion and mustard seed poultice.

Matthieu sidled up beside her, not unlike an eager puppy. "Almost wish I was sick again."

"And I wish the rest of the garrison were as healthy as you."

"Dreadful idea. That would mean your visits would stop, wouldn't it? Unless you had a different reason to drop by." He waggled his eyebrows, and Julianne laughed as Dupree ordered him outside.

For the soldier with a blinding headache, she crushed another leaf of peppermint and laid it on his brow, then drove the oil deep into his skin by topping it with a wet cloth.

"I have need of boiling water, Officer. Could you assist me with this?"

"With this, and anything else."

Ignoring the flirtatious tone in Dupree's voice, she handed him some willow bark. "Please steep this in the water once it has boiled, and when it has cooled enough, we'll remove the bark and give him the tea."

For the soldier who'd been careless near the fire, she offered a comfrey salve. For the one who complained of indigestion, a dose of syrup of licorice. To the patient with bowels in distress, Julianne administered syrup of chicory.

"You are a wonder," Officer Dupree said when he returned with the willow bark tea.

She shook her head. "The Superior Council approved the order for me to obtain these medicines, and many more I don't know the use of, from the Company of the Indies' warehouse. The trouble is, once these stores run out, there's no telling how long it will be before more provisions arrive from France. Some of these I can find here easily enough. But what other treasures of healing does nature offer us in this environment?"

"I'm afraid that is quite beyond my area of expertise."

Julianne bent to help her patient drink his tea, then stood and surveyed the pitiful condition of the barracks. "If I am to promote the health and well-being of the colony—with mothers, babies, or soldiers—I need to know how to make use of the herbs grown right here." An idea sparked in her mind. At once, she arrested Dupree with her gaze. "I need a native. That is, I need to speak with a native, to learn how best to use nature's bounty. Do you know of someone who may be willing to teach me?"

A smile crept across his face. "It just so happens I do."

⚜ ⚜ ⚜

Squinting at his work, Marc-Paul rubbed the knots from the muscles in his lower back. Whether the culprit was spring flooding or relentless humidity, the barracks were in perpetual disrepair. Just as he was about to kick the new pilings to test their sturdiness, Julianne emerged from the barracks, the heat-laden breeze flirting with a loose tendril of her hair.

She was smiling.

Marc-Paul frowned. Mopping his brow with his handkerchief, he straightened his hat and stopped her before she stepped out of the building's shade. "You're smiling." He bit his tongue, but too late.

"Against regulation, is it, Captain?" But her lips curved in amusement as he snatched up his waistcoat and tugged it over his work-rumpled shirt.

"It's not the expression one commonly observes on the face of one leaving the ill. But they weren't all ill inside the barracks today, were they?"

Julianne shifted her basket to her other hip, and he tried not to notice her growing softness. She was not obviously with child, but she had lost the sharp angles worn by all who made the crossing from France last winter. *Just in time to be starved on land during this one.* He chided himself for his pessimism. Not every winter was destined to be desperate.

Her grey eyes flashed. "Officer Dupree was extremely helpful, if that's who you refer to."

Marc-Paul crossed his arms. "In what way, pray tell?"

"I mentioned I'd benefit from learning from a native how to use the healing herbs grown in this area, and he offered his slave Dancing Brook for the purpose."

"Dancing Brook."

"That's right. Officer Dupree is going to come for me before the two o'clock meal tomorrow. After dining, I imagine Dancing Brook and I will take a walk along the bayou so she can point out the plants I should know."

Marc-Paul pinched the bridge of his nose and shook his head before responding. "Dancing Brook speaks very little French. And Pascal speaks very little of her tongue."

Her shoulders slumped. "Oh." Shadows darkened her eyes, a sign she understood his meaning. Such an appointment was not like to yield much learning. Pascal only wanted Julianne in his house. And the walk with Dancing Brook would surely be accompanied by Pascal as well, though his interest was not in herbal medicine.

Julianne tilted her head and regarded Marc-Paul. "Do you believe Dancing Brook has something to teach me, if only we could understand one another?"

"Without a doubt. But you can only communicate so much through gestures. She could point to a plant and sign that its fruit is poisonous. You could misinterpret her meaning and believe that plant's fruit should be taken when one is near death, to revive him. You see?" He spread his hands. "An innocent mistake, but a fatal one."

Strangely, she did not seem perturbed in the least by his excellent point. In fact, she nodded, eyes bright. With one slender hand, she tucked a stray lock of honeyed hair behind her ear. "Then it is imperative that you come."

He blinked. "Pardon me?"

"You must join us, Captain Girard, and interpret, for the sake of all those who may be in my care in the future. For the colony. As you said so eloquently yourself, it is a matter of life and death." She smiled, and he was completely taken in by her.

"When you put it that way, Madame Midwife, how could a gentleman refuse?"

Chapter Thirteen

✣ ✣ ✣

Fresh bread melting in his mouth, Marc-Paul covered his smile with a linen napkin at Pascal Dupree's table. It was probably a sin how vastly he had enjoyed the constipated look on Pascal's face when he came for Julianne that afternoon and found she had a chaperone. It rivaled the expression he wore when he told Dancing Brook to set a third place at the table.

Neither had Marc-Paul missed the light dancing in Julianne's eyes when she saw the telling roundness of Dancing Brook's belly. Certainly she was near the fullness of her time. The poor girl looked as though she was quite prepared to be relieved of her burden as she set a buffet of food on the table. Peaches, figs, sorrel, roasted sweet potatoes, and blackberry jam for the bread. Real bread made with wheat flour, not rice or corn.

"It does seem almost criminal, doesn't it, Pascal, to be eating like kings when shortages choke the colony?" Marc-Paul wouldn't be surprised if Pascal had bribed a warehouse clerk to sell him more than his fair share of flour.

"Ah, then it is well that 'seeming criminal,' as you say, is not the same as committing the crime." Pascal lifted his glass of eau-de-vie and flashed his trademark smile. "Cheers!"

Julianne shot Marc-Paul a reprimanding look, and he acquiesced to behave for the rest of the meal.

When the dishes were cleared away, Julianne brightened. "Shall we begin? Officer Dupree, does Dancing Brook know why we are here?"

Pascal licked his lips and sat back in his chair. "Dancing Brook," he called, and the girl trundled in, looking tired from the effort. "You are to tell madame how to use herbs and plants as medicine. In the manner of your people." He spoke loudly and slowly to her.

"She isn't hard of hearing, Pascal." Marc-Paul laughed. "Shouting won't make her understand French."

Julianne covered the hint of a smile with her fingertips before regaining her composure. Pascal reddened to the shade of beets as he made some excuse for taking his leave.

"Now then. Let us try again." Marc-Paul spoke to Dancing Brook in Chitimacha, her own language, and immediately she animated. Interest kindled on her features, and she nodded as he explained their quest. She spoke to him in reply and led them outside.

"What does she say?" Julianne leaned in toward Marc-Paul with her question, and he inhaled her clean scent. He offered his arm, and although she hesitated, she looped her hand through his elbow. "Well?"

He swallowed. "She says she is happy to show us and that there are many ways we French could help ourselves if we only became better acquainted with this country."

Outside, Dancing Brook led them north of Pascal's property, along a sandy trail that wound between the swamp's sentinel trees—bald cypress and tupelo gum—before sloping upward onto a ridge of dry land that bordered a bayou on its opposite side.

Spider-webbed palmetto blades fanned near their footsteps

as Julianne and Marc-Paul followed their native guide. Lichen-encrusted live oak limbs plunged to the ground before bending back up once more.

As Dancing Brook spoke, Marc-Paul translated quietly into Julianne's ear. "She says her people used to come to her father with their sick, and he would go into the woods to find the remedy. There is a perfect match, if one just knows what to look for."

Dancing Brook led them to a fifty-foot-tall elm tree and laid her hand on the brown, fissured exterior bark. It was slippery elm, she said, very important, very useful. She peeled off the bark and gouged out a piece of the soft, white interior bark.

"Helpful in childbirth," Marc-Paul interpreted Dancing Brook's explanation. "A woman in labor may eat some to ease her delivery, and a midwife can lubricate her hands with slippery elm's interior bark mixed with hot water. For babies or convalescents having trouble keeping food down, the white bark can be pounded into a powder and mixed with cold water, a little at a time, to make gruel."

Julianne stepped forward and pulled a piece of the white bark from the tree herself, rubbing it between her fingers before dropping it into her pocket. "Incredible," she whispered. With her index finger she traced the cracks in the exterior bark. Marc-Paul plucked a glossy green leaf from a low-hanging branch and handed it to her. Thanking him quietly, she fingered its serrated borders from stem to point.

"Her people also use it to create balms or salves to heal wounds or burns," he continued. "Chop or grate the interior bark into water, boil for fifteen minutes, then strain and reduce the volume to create an ointment. Taken orally, it soothes sore throats, relieves coughs, and helps with distressed bowels and indigestion."

Next, she pointed out a cluster of tall green straws poking

from the ground and explained how to use them to make a tea to treat blood infections.

With every discovery, Julianne bent to study the plant or tree up close, touching the trunk or branches and leaves. Her lips moved silently as she plucked leaves and added them to her pocket, and Marc-Paul reckoned she was memorizing their names and details. He smiled at her eagerness to learn.

"And all of this is right here." She spread her arms wide. "Perhaps I can find these plants and trees behind my cabin, as well." She turned to Dancing Brook, smiling. "Thank you for sharing your wisdom with me. If there is ever anything I can do for you, I would be honored."

He translated, adding the fact that Julianne was skilled at delivering babies. Regardless of Bienville's instructions, Marc-Paul knew Julianne well enough to know she would not heed the counsel limiting herself to French births. Dancing Brook rested her hands on her swollen middle and said she would be grateful. That she was not sure she'd be ready by the time the baby was.

Julianne nodded as he spoke the words in French. "Captain Girard, I do believe I'll need some language lessons. Unless you want to translate for us in the birthing chamber too."

Marc-Paul swallowed and agreed. If she was anything like her brother, she'd have no trouble at all.

⚜ ⚜ ⚜

Julianne stood before the door of her humble cabin and waited for Captain Girard to take his leave after escorting her home from Officer Dupree's house. Instead, he remained, hat in his hands.

"Say your piece, Captain," she prompted. "The hour is getting on."

"Yes. Exactly. You're eager to go hunting for herbs now, aren't you?" His brown eyes sought hers.

Of course she was. "Why do you ask?"

"I would caution you, madame, against placing yourself in danger."

"Among the herbs?"

"Do not make light of this. I know any counsel I offer may be rejected simply because it comes from my lips and not another's. I know that, aside from my interpreting, you have little use for me, and I cannot blame you for that. But my conscience will not abide this." The firm set of his jaw and the fine lines framing his mouth and eyes confirmed he spoke from conviction.

The breeze pulled a strand of her hair from its pins, and she tucked it back into place. "What, exactly, will your conscience not abide?"

Scanning their surroundings, he stepped toward her and cut his voice low. "I strongly advise you not to leave the settlement alone. You could lose your way or become injured, with no one there to aid you."

Julianne smoothed her skirt down from her stomacher. "I am not so soft-headed as that. I know how to be careful."

"It is not just you who concerns me. You don't know who else may be lurking there, or who may follow you deep into the shade with anything but your best interests in mind."

"Thank you for your concern, Officer, but I'm sure I'll be fine. I can care for my own person. Good day to you." She half turned to unlatch the door to her cabin.

And found herself utterly immobilized. In a fraction of a second, Girard circled her body with his arms from behind, pinning her arms to her sides.

"What are you doing?" she cried.

"I'm learning just how well you can care for your own person." His breath was hot in her ear. Her pulse thrummed as the ground dropped from beneath her feet. As though she were nothing but corn husk, he lifted her and began carrying her away to heaven-knew-where.

"Put me down this instant or I'll scream!"

"Scream then."

She did. Feet flailing, she kicked at his shins and writhed against his chest, wailing until she was spent.

"Look around." He set her back on the ground. "Do you see anyone coming to your aid?"

Julianne's throat stung with humiliation. "Perhaps no one heard me."

"Perhaps. And perhaps someone did. Either way, I could have had my way with you, and so could any other fiend who puts his mind to it."

Heat singed her cheeks and she looked away, chest heaving for breath. "You scared me," she whispered. "I thought—"

"Good."

She whipped around to glare at him. "It was wrong of you. A gentleman doesn't scare a woman so!"

"A gentleman does not allow a woman to invite harm to herself." His eyes burned like coals; his nostrils flared. "My words clearly did not convince you. I needed—*you* needed your fear to do that. Do not suppose, Madame LeGrange, that just because you are virtuous, the men in New Orleans will treat you as such. Some of these rogues consider any woman fair game. But a woman of your beauty would make a choice prize indeed. It brings me no pleasure to persuade you of it." He sighed. "Furthermore, they convince themselves that women who arrived on *Le Marianne* deserve no respect."

"Because we came from Salpêtrière." Self-consciously, her hand covered the brand beneath her sleeve. She wondered what would happen if word spread that her sentence was not for common theft, but murder. She crossed her arms across her swollen stomach and ground her heel on a crayfish chimney. Then she looked up. "Simon's gun. I have a gun."

"Fetch it."

Julianne slipped into the cabin and came out again with Simon's long musket, powder horn, and shot pouch.

"The Fusil de Chasse." Girard took it. "It's a hunting gun. Do you know how to load it?"

"No."

"You will. Let's take a walk, shall we?" He matched his gait to hers and positioned himself to block the sun from striking her face. His simple kindness brought immediate relief to her eyes as they strode into the swamp behind her cabin.

"It takes a minute or so to load this musket, so you want to take careful aim and make your shot count. You may not have time to load again for a second chance. An attacker may be able to catch you while you're busy with the barrel."

Julianne nodded but hoped such a lesson would never be put to the test. A squirrel darted across their path as they penetrated deeper into the trees. Spanish moss draped branches with greenish-grey fringe, and shadows darkened Girard's features.

A breeze whistled through the shade, stirring the smell of decomposing leaves and warm, fallen cypress needles. She looked around, imagining all the places a hunter could hide if she were ever the prey. She shuddered. Such a predator could be anywhere.

"Look here," the captain was saying, and she refocused on the barrel. "You'll remember this better if you do it yourself."

With the walnut stock of the gun on the ground, the five-foot-long Fusil de Chasse was only a few inches shorter than she was. Julianne grasped the barrel and tipped it toward her so she could look into its open mouth.

"Measure the powder into this gold cap, then pour the powder down the barrel," he instructed. "Now comes the paper wadding, and you'll tamp it down with this ramrod."

She drew a piece of folded paper from the shot pouch and dropped it into the barrel, then pulled out the metal stick and rammed it down.

"Next comes the ball, and you'll tamp that down too. And then more wadding."

"And tamp it down," she said as she accomplished the tasks.

"That's right. The order is very important. Remember: powder, wadding, ball, wadding. And tamp down everything but the powder. It's very important," he said again.

Julianne refrained from asking what would happen if she misremembered any of it.

"Last step before you're ready to fire. Hold the gun like this, barrel pointed away from you. Open this little hatch here under the cock, pour a small amount of powder in the pan, then close it again. The flint inside will last several shots before it wears down enough to need replacing. Now lift it to your shoulder." He stood behind her as she did so. "Place your other hand here." His left hand cupped hers and brought it beneath the gun to support its weight. It was seven pounds, she guessed, the same as a healthy newborn baby. He released her hand and quickly stepped away from her.

The flintlock steady against her shoulder, she cast him a sideways glance in time to see the color rising in his complexion.

"Your range is about a hundred yards. There's a bead sight on the tip of the barrel. Line that up on your target, then cock it and squeeze the trigger. You'll feel two explosions—in the pan when the powder ignites, and the ball firing from the barrel. I want you to know how it handles."

Heart hammering, Julianne closed one eye and aimed at a cypress tree in the distance. She rolled her lips between her teeth, held her breath, and fired. As the barrel spewed spark and smoke, the gun recoiled, slamming into her shoulder.

The captain steadied her from behind. While his hands

warmed her waist, embarrassment scorched her cheeks for being knocked off-balance by the blast. Her shoulder throbbed where the pointed corner of the gun's butt had rammed it. She'd not be surprised to find a bruise there. "Well, I won't be doing that again any time soon." She lowered the Fusil de Chasse and peered into the trees, not at all certain she'd hit any of them, let alone the one for which she'd aimed.

"The recoil is powerful, but now you'll know how to better brace yourself for it."

She turned to face him, and only then did he release her from his hold. Heat spread up her neck at the earnestness in his gaze. "You speak as though I'm to make a habit of it."

"You will fire if you need to." His tone leaving no room for debate, Captain Girard's expression sharpened into severity again. "Promise me. You will defend yourself if the need arises, Julianne."

Her breath caught at his intensity. "Is that an order, Officer?"

His lips twitched in a smile, but his eyes remained grave. "It is."

Chapter Fourteen

❧ ❧ ❧

MISSISSIPPI RIVER
LATE SEPTEMBER 1720

The sun's slanting rays beat upon Marc-Paul and bounced off
the river. After wiping his palms on his buckskin breeches, he
switched his paddle to the other side of the pirogue and continued rowing upstream along with Red Bird and the three soldiers
who could be spared from New Orleans. They had joined an
eight-vessel convoy of voyageurs returning north for the winter
in their birchbark canoes but would part ways with them soon.
Marc-Paul's mission was not in Illinois Country or New France
but in Red Bird's Choctaw village, about a hundred miles north
of New Orleans. A few reports had trickled in about Chickasaw
raids on the river, but those had occurred north of where the
Yazoo River met the Mississippi.

Red Bird's ebony hair blew free in the wind. Sunlight
glinted on the copper spools in his earlobes, which hung almost to the gathered shoulders of the French linen trade shirt
he wore. His lips drew thin and tight, an unsettling contrast
to the jaunty verses the voyageurs sang in the pirogues ahead
of them.

"Alouette, gentille alouette, Alouette, je te plumerai. Je te plumerai la tête. . . ." Lark, nice lark, Lark, I will pluck you. I will pluck your head. . . .

The hair on Marc-Paul's neck stood up. Red Bird's warning still resounded in his ears: *"They say only the British can supply us properly. . . . We can fire British muskets as well as French."* His gaze dropped to the canvas-wrapped packages wedged between his knees and the soldier in front of him. The pirogue was loaded with French muskets, powder, game-shot, and balls to trade, among other items such as trade shirts, vermillion, and blankets. Lots of blankets, thanks to Pascal. With this shipment, the soldiers would procure bulk quantities of maize, beans, and pumpkins for the garrison. And the Choctaw would have more munitions for the war.

Up ahead, the French-Canadians grew more boisterous with every round of their song. "I will pluck your wings. And your neck! And your eyes!"

"It's our colony's wings that are being plucked by not growing our own food," Marc-Paul muttered.

Joseph, a young soldier rowing in front of Marc-Paul, tossed a confused look over his shoulder. "Why should we till the soil ourselves when we get everything we need from the Indians by trade? Besides, they need our textiles and weapons too."

"Ah, but do you never wonder if we need the natives more than they need us?"

Joseph just shrugged and joined in the singing with gusto. "I will pluck your tail!" Behind Marc-Paul, the other two soldiers, Andre and Gaspard, laughed and added their voices to the song as well.

"There." With one low word from Red Bird, the soldiers' exuberant singing fell away. The Choctaw pointed to a clearing along the riverbank, the place where they would haul their pirogue ashore. After shouting farewell to the voyageurs ahead of them, Marc-Paul and his soldiers followed Red Bird's directions and steered their vessel toward land.

The river slapped against the pirogue as the men pulled it halfway up on shore. After unloading it, Red Bird and Marc-Paul tied the paddles with leather thongs to the planks that had served as seats. Then they piled rocks into the pirogue, pushed it back into the water, and let it sink to the riverbed so it was completely submerged. Confident it would remain hidden until they came back for it, Marc-Paul distributed the bundles of trade goods to his soldiers. Andre shouldered fifty pounds of powder, Gaspard took fifty pounds of game-shot, and Marc-Paul wore fifty pounds of balls on his back. To Joseph, who was still somewhat weakened by his recurring fever, he gave the lightest load: a package of blankets, trade shirts, and vermillion to wear on his back, and the three muskets for trading to carry by hand. Red Bird carried naught but his bow and a quiver of arrows, a sheathed knife hanging round his neck. The soldiers followed him into a mass of pine trees.

The shade offered respite to Marc-Paul's eyes, which had strained against the river's glare for more than a week. After sitting on the hard wooden bench for thirteen hours a day, walking was a relief to his stiff muscles, even with the burden he carried. Sweet pine sap and the tang of damp soil cloyed in the humidity. Somewhat absently, he kicked a pinecone from his path and wondered if Julianne searched for slippery elm and cat's foot along the bayou during his absence. He prayed she'd taken her gun.

Grunting, Gaspard labored beneath the game-shot on his back. He nodded at Red Bird. "If the savages are so keen to have these muskets, why does he not shoulder one himself?"

"Firing a gun gives one's position away," explained Marc-Paul. "Most Indians attack unseen. And think of how long it takes to load your weapon. Red Bird can launch an arrow in mere seconds." And by the time one saw an enemy in the woods, mere seconds was all one had.

"How far is it to Red Bird's—" Joseph halted. "What is that?"

Red Bird stood before a tree. The bark had been stripped away, and one side of the trunk was painted black. The other side red. The rest of the soldiers gathered around it.

"It means a war party has been here." Marc-Paul met Red Bird's wary gaze. Images burst upon his memory of shaved heads painted red with scalp locks hanging down their backs. Of eyes blinking at him from behind a mask of black paint just before their owner released an arrow from his bow. Of Benjamin, just before he turned his back on Marc-Paul and ran.

"A war party?" Andre repeated and wiped the cuff of his shirt across his brow.

"They spend two or three weeks in hiding, waiting for the perfect chance to strike a good blow," Red Bird said in French. "If there is no such opportunity, they emblazon the tree as a sign they were here and that they will return again soon."

Gaspard spun in a slow circle. "How soon?"

A flash of crimson bloomed at the edge of Marc-Paul's vision. The closer he moved toward it, the tighter his gut twisted. "They've already come back." He pointed to a soiled red sash on the ground.

"The canoe that left a day ahead of us," said Joseph. "They must have stopped here to make camp last night."

The stench of rotting flesh crept into Marc-Paul's nose and throat. As he followed it, the whirring of insects swelled in his ears until he saw them. Facedown in a bloodstained bed of needles sprawled a voyageur and the indentured servant he'd hired to help him bring supplies to Fort Rosalie, near Natchez, on their way north. They'd been stripped naked and scalped. Mosquitoes feasted in the ragged, tomahawk-shaped holes in their backs. Five arrows rose from the men's bodies, and

Marc-Paul cringed to imagine them trying to run, terrified, from their attackers.

He took his bundle from his back and lowered it to the ground. Bending, he pulled each shaft from the flesh, but the arrowheads remained buried in the corpses. The soldiers came close enough to see and then immediately backed away, cursing and covering their noses.

Red Bird scooped up a wooden club on the ground beside the bodies. "Chickasaw." He held out the club for Marc-Paul to examine. The symbols carved on it matched Chickasaw heraldry. This club claimed the deaths as their doing. "And now they have the supplies meant for the French soldiers at Fort Rosalie."

"Are you sure it wasn't Choctaw?" Andre's words were muffled by his hand, which he held over his nose and mouth. "I thought the Chickasaw were much, much farther north."

Red Bird pinned him with his gaze. "Why would we kill the very people who supply us? No. Chickasaw can travel far. They have horses. In fact, they usually exchange French captives for horses, at a ratio of one to one. In this case, I'm sure whoever did this didn't want the trouble of taking two captives across the wilderness to British lines. This could have been the work of just one lone raider."

Red Bird's words sounded far away. Marc-Paul envisioned two scalps flapping against some warrior's breechcloth and wondered if he would keep them for his own glory or take them to the British, who were without a doubt backing the Chickasaw. The thought lodged like a stone in his chest.

By the time he and his soldiers finished burying the bodies and emerged from the woods, the sun was sinking on the horizon. The sky to the west, above the trees, seemed awash with brandy. The soldiers marched in silence the remaining distance to Red Bird's village.

Night fell as they approached, and fireflies pulsed in the

darkness. Marc-Paul could hear the Choctaw before he could see them. Both men and women sang to the rhythm of rattles made from gourds and pebbles.

"We should wait until they are finished before we go any closer," Red Bird said. "It is a ceremonial dance around a sacred fire."

"Do you want to join them?" Marc-Paul studied the smooth planes of Red Bird's face.

"I would not leave you outside, unprotected." Drawing an arrow from his quiver, he peered into the dark. "Not again."

Music filled Marc-Paul's ears from inside the village as he stood in a small circle with Red Bird, Joseph, Andre, and Gaspard. "A life in the wilderness," the Choctaw sang, "with plenty of meat, fish, fowl, and the Turtle Dance, is far better than our old homes, and the corn, and the fruit, and the heart-melting fear of the dreadful Europeans."

"What are they singing?" Joseph whispered.

They are singing that they are better off without us. Instead of translating, however, Marc-Paul simply told him to keep vigil. Soon they'd be home in New Orleans with provisions to share. But for now, they were strangers to be wary of, even among the very allies they had come to supply.

⚜ ⚜ ⚜

New Orleans, Louisiana
October 1720

In a cramped, dim room in the back of the tavern, Julianne soothed her client, who lay on a sagging bed in the corner. She was six months along with child. "The bleeding has stopped. You must stay abed, Yvette, resting, but I believe your baby may yet reach full term."

"Do you—do you have any way of . . . ending it early?" The

prostitute's voice could barely be heard. On the other side of the river cane door, a fiddle played, sharp and frantic, accompanied by out-of-tune voices. The floor shook with the rhythmic pounding of dancing feet not ten yards away.

"Pardon me?" Julianne frowned. A crash sounded, only slightly muted by the door, then a shattering and a roar of laugher. The reek of spilled corn liquor wafted into the room.

"It's no good for business, you know. And what would I do with another mouth to feed, anyway? I'd be a terrible mother, I would. You can't deny it. It would be better if . . ."

It wasn't the first time a woman had requested a miscarriage. "My job is to keep you and the baby healthy until it is safely delivered into this world."

"And what in heaven's name will we do after that?" Tears traced Yvette's rouge-smudged cheeks.

No answer Julianne could think of would suit. There was no house of industry to which she could turn, no orphanage. There was no Salpêtrière. And no family.

"You're right lucky, you know, that you didn't have to pick up this line of work to survive here, like I did. Lucky you have your own job, no need to rely on any man. Lucky no one cares you were branded for murder."

Julianne's heart jolted. "What did you say?"

"Right, then, am I? Helene said as much." Yvette stared at her, unblinking.

Slowly, Julianne released the breath she'd been holding. She'd forgotten how much of her story she'd shared with an orphan named Helene while they made the crossing from France those long five months. Her pulse trotted. The less said about her past, certainly the better.

"Your services are no longer needed." Yvette burrowed down under her thin blanket. "Leave me."

"Well then, I'll check on you tomorrow."

"I said I don't need you."

Pressing her lips together, Julianne simply nodded, shouldered her midwifing satchel, and picked up her lantern. Rather than exiting through the back door, she slipped into the public house to find Helene, who was draped over some man's shoulder.

"You were right to come for me. The baby may still do well, but it's important Yvette keep to bed rest. Could you urge her to stay abed?"

Helene scoffed. "Staying abed is what she does best."

"You understand my meaning perfectly well. One more thing. I'm sure you meant no harm by it, Helene, but please do not mention my criminal case to anyone else. It's difficult enough to overcome the stigma already hovering over me; I can't imagine what would happen if the details came to light."

"You want people to think well of you, is that it? The way they all think so well of me?"

Julianne frowned at the bite in her tone.

"If the nuns who raised me could see me now . . ." A dark chuckle broke from Helene's lips.

"I know. I'm sorry." Julianne truly was. Her head ached, and it wasn't just with the noise and odor stuffing the tavern. The sight of Helene wearing her long hair loose and her stays even looser, when she'd once been a devout and meek girl, was painful to behold.

"You don't know. And you're not sorry."

Julianne gasped. "Helene, I—"

But she had already turned her back to refill someone's drink.

Elbowing her way out of the tavern, Julianne plunged into the night air, grateful to be shed of the place. A welcome breeze cooled her. As stung as she'd been by Helene's prickly words, her concern for Yvette and her baby eclipsed it.

A raccoon crossed her path, startling her from her reverie, and scampered toward the barracks. Taking a deep breath, she gripped her lantern tighter and headed for home. The hour was late—well after midnight. Exhaustion quickly overtook her, but she was less than half a mile from her cabin. She'd be in her own bed soon enough.

Moths and mosquitoes bumped against the casing of the lantern she held out to light her path. Clouds obscured the moon and stars. The farther she walked from the boisterous tavern, the more clearly she could hear the crickets chirping.

And footsteps following.

Julianne turned to look behind her but saw nothing but darkness beyond the pale glow cast by her flickering candle. She turned back to her path and continued, but her ears strained to hear anything other than nature's night sounds.

There it was again. Apprehension prickled her skin as she remembered Captain Girard's words of warning. *It's just him again*, she tried telling herself. *He means to scare me, that's all.* But she knew the captain wouldn't do that, even if he knew she'd be here at this hour. Not in the middle of a moonless night, when she might mistake him for an attacker, when he knew she had a gun.

And certainly not when he had yet to return from his latest mission and was not even in New Orleans.

She whirled around once more. "Hello?" she called. "Is someone there?"

"No one at all." The words slurred together in a voice she didn't recognize. Alarm reverberated through her body. A drunk man was an uninhibited man.

Energy surging through her limbs, she broke into a run, her satchel bouncing against her hip with every step. Footsteps pounded after her. In a flash of clarity, she realized she led him on with her lantern. She flung it aside and ran blindly toward home.

Hardened ruts in the ground threatened to twist her ankles.

Holes and chimneys underfoot threw her off her stride. She should yell for help. But she could not find her voice, could barely find breath as she rehearsed what she had to do. *Get home. Get the gun. Load it. Fire it.* An explosion sounded in her mind as she remembered the loading would normally take a minute. In the dark, how long would it take her? Did she have time before he caught up to her?

Her skirts in her fists, she steered off course to lure him away from her straight path in the hope that he didn't already know where her cabin was. Not many people did.

"I can hear you, but I want to see you!" Was he twenty yards away or twenty feet? Closer? Julianne had lost all ability to measure distance by sound alone.

Nerves on edge, she tiptoed around a cabin and began weaving her way toward home. Without her lantern, her eyes adjusted to the darkness, at least enough to distinguish the outlines of buildings.

Blood roared in her ears. After a moment of silently changing her course again, she darted to her cabin and quietly slipped inside. *Lord, please!* It was all the prayer she could manage, and yet in the next moment, it seemed He had answered.

The clouds passed from in front of the full moon. In the silvery light, she grabbed the Fusil de Chasse from under her bed and the powder horn and shot pouch. Her hands shook as she poured powder into the barrel. *Powder, wadding, ball, wadding*, she chanted in her mind, and remembered to tamp it down between each one. The ramrod trembled in her hand, and it took three tries to fit it into the end of the barrel the first time. Minutes sped by.

Finally, she poured powder into the small pan under the cock, closed it, and burst back outside. She held the gun to her shoulder and strained to catch any movement that would give away the man's position. Her range was one hundred yards. If her aim failed, as it was very like to do, would she hit a neighbor's cabin instead? Harm an innocent person?

Clouds veiled the moon once more, and darkness dropped down like a shroud. Heart thundering, her shoulders and arms began to burn with the weight of the gun. *Oh God*, she prayed, *let this cup pass from me.* She could not bear to fire into the night.

"Come no closer!" she called out. "I'll shoot!"

"I will have you!" It was a growl now.

Julianne spun toward the voice, braced herself for the recoil, and squeezed the trigger. The blast rang in her ears, and the smoke caught in her throat. She heard nothing else. Was he gone? Or just waiting?

She ran back into the cabin and, with fumbling movements, loaded the gun once more. Sitting on the edge of her bed, she stared at her door and waited, her Fusil de Chasse at the ready. Minutes felt like hours, and still no one came. Every noise from outside—the high-pitched bats, a gurgling owl, incessantly humming mosquitoes—plucked at her nerves. Though she shivered with cold, she knew better than to light a fire.

By dawn, however, no attacker had returned. Julianne was alone in her cabin with nothing to show for last night's terror but memories and a gun that was ready to fire.

⚜ ⚜ ⚜

Rain pattered the palmetto roof above Julianne like a thousand tiny feet. Resting her hand on her belly, she thanked God again that last night's scare had not turned tragic. Whoever had followed her home from the tavern was not like to return. Captain Girard had been right in teaching her to use the gun. She'd need to thank him once he returned from his mission.

Sudden cramping seized her, and her hand tightened over her middle. Then it vanished, as suddenly as it came. *It could be nothing*, she told herself. But beads of sweat crowned her brow. Though her heart railed against the idea, in her mind she knew the truth: Even a midwife was not guaranteed a healthy baby.

Pounding jerked her attention to her door. Before she could form a complete thought, her heart leapt into her throat and she scrambled for the gun.

"Madame Midwife? You come for Dancing Brook."

She knew that voice. Exhaling in relief, she replaced the gun beneath her bed, crossed to the door, and opened it. Running Deer filled the frame with his broad shoulders, rain wicking from the fringe on his deerskin cape. He stood there, unblinking, while water streamed from his long hair and dripped from his nose and chin. Spreading her cloak over her shoulders, she snuffed out her candle, grabbed her birthing satchel from its hook, and followed him out into the rain.

"May we stop at the inn to fetch my apprentice?" Julianne asked. When Lisette's work in Francoise's kitchen allowed, she accompanied births as an eager assistant.

"No time."

She bowed her head to the rain and lifted her skirts above the mud sucking at her feet. Running Deer looked behind him only twice to make sure she kept pace.

When they arrived at Pascal Dupree's property east of the settlement, Running Deer took her into the slave quarters, where she found Dancing Brook panting and gasping on a pallet on the floor.

Julianne turned to Running Deer. "Does Officer Dupree know of her condition? Why did he not send for me sooner?"

Running Deer grunted. "He no send for you. Dancing Brook ask for you. He at tavern. He not know."

Dancing Brook pointed to something on the floor beside her, and Julianne saw that she had already collected some slippery elm. A bowl of warm water and a stack of cloths were beside it. Julianne thanked Running Deer and dismissed him from the room before turning back to her patient.

With the few words she had learned from the captain, she tried to speak comfort to the girl as she rubbed her hands with slippery elm and water, then sat on the floor at the end of the pallet. A tactile examination showed the waters had ruptured and the baby's head was already presenting. Julianne smiled and told Dancing Brook to push with the pain.

Dancing Brook's face contorted with the next contraction, but she bore the agony without a sound.

"That's it, you're doing well." Truly, it did not take a midwife's skill to attend this birth. Dancing Brook and the baby were doing all the work. "The baby will be here soon."

As if in sympathy, a spasm claimed Julianne's own stomach. When it released her, she beat back her alarm until it hid behind the present moment. Fear was a distraction she could not allow. Not now.

In three more silent but strong pushes, a perfect baby boy was delivered into her waiting hands. His pale skin surprised her, but the infant was as alert and strong as he could be. Not much later, the afterbirth easily detached and slipped out as well.

After tying off and cutting the navel string, Julianne bathed Dancing Brook's son in wine, wrapped him in a blanket, and handed him to his mother. He let out a lusty wail, and the women laughed approvingly.

"His father will want to know he has a son," Julianne told Dancing Brook. It was a midwife's business to record in her ledger the lineage of every child delivered.

Dancing Brook spoke too quickly. The syllables tumbled over themselves until tears streamed down the broad planes of the girl's cheeks.

"Slow down," Julianne pleaded. "Again, please."

But repeating herself rendered Dancing Brook's speech no

more decipherable. Until one word, sprinkled throughout her speech, rose to the surface, overshadowing everything else. Julianne's heart sank.

"Dupree?" she asked. "Pascal Dupree? Is the father?"

Dancing Brook nodded and clutched her baby tightly to her chest. She said another word then, over and over, as she rocked her newborn babe. Julianne had no idea what it meant.

Chapter Fifteen

❧ ❧ ❧

When the autumn sun was high in the sky the next day, Julianne returned to Officer Dupree's home to check on Dancing Brook and her baby. But before she could knock on the door to the slave quarters, crying filled her ears. Not a baby's cry. A mother's. She was keening.

With a quick rap on the door, Julianne let herself in. Dancing Brook was on the dirt floor, smearing ashes on her face. Dread building, Julianne swept the room with her gaze. "Where's the baby?"

Dancing Brook shook her head. "No baby," she said. "No baby. Dupree. . . ." And then the word again that Julianne didn't understand. But it was enough to ignite a fire in her chest.

Anger leapt over her sorrow and licked through Julianne's veins. She whisked out of the slave cabin and marched to Dupree's front door. She pounded on it, then clasped her hands and bit her lip to check the torrent of words bubbling just beneath the surface. A midwife's reputation could be ruined by a lack of self-control.

Running Deer opened the door. It took all her strength to maintain an even tone as she inquired for his master. But she was rewarded moments later when Pascal Dupree greeted her and invited her in.

"You honor me with your presence!" He took her hand to kiss it, and it was all she could do not to pull away.

"I was present last night too, as it happens."

Officer Dupree's smile drooped. "Is that so?"

She followed him into the salon, where the sun streamed through the wide open windows, infusing the paisley rug with its warmth. He sat in a scarlet brocade armchair near a game table, the skirt of his jacket fanning in thick folds from his waist, and motioned for her to do the same. "Play a hand with me? No? Just as well. I have a habit of winning, you know." He laughed as he slapped the table.

"I delivered Dancing Brook of a fine, healthy boy last night. Yet when I visited the mother a moment ago, all I found was her wailing in mourning and no baby to be seen."

"Ah, well." The officer shuffled a deck of cards, the sound muted by the table's green felt covering. Behind him, an ornate clock ticked the seconds away. "Don't all babies go to heaven? And yet if he'd survived to be raised by a savage, he might have followed his ancestral religion, and his soul be lost forever. So it was merciful that the infant was weak and God took him in the night."

Julianne felt as though she'd been punched. "No." Her voice was hard. "Not that child. I don't believe it. It was the easiest birth I've ever attended. He was eight pounds, by my reckoning, and hearty and hale."

The sparkle in Officer Dupree's eyes vanished, and his dimples retreated. "Are you calling me a liar?"

She was. "I'm telling you the truth, and I expect the same courtesy of you."

Dupree stretched out his legs and crossed them at the ankles, his gaiters dazzlingly white in the sunbeam. "I'm sure it isn't easy for you to hear it, being the midwife, but your patient's baby is dead. And that is the absolute truth."

No. Not that beautiful, perfect, healthy baby. Despite her best efforts not to feel the loss so keenly, tears sprang to her eyes. "My patient's baby," she repeated, anger sharpening her tone. "You mean Dancing Brook's baby. Your son."

He blanched but recovered himself with a laugh. Sitting forward, he leaned two cards against each other on their edges, then added a third, and then a fourth. "How would you know who the father is?" His tone was casual, but the slightest tremor in his hands gave him away.

"She told me. It is a midwife's duty to record each baby's lineage."

"Record? You've written it down?" At once the cards collapsed and he was on his feet.

"What did you do, Officer Dupree?"

"She doesn't even speak French. And even if you could decipher a few words here and there, you can't trust a slave's testimony. It will never stand up."

"But mine will. Or didn't you know that a midwife's word is as trusted as a priest's?"

A laugh burst from him. "You're comparing yourself to a priest now? Oh, this is too much!"

Julianne narrowed her eyes at him, seething with indignation. "And you playact as if you're Bienville himself! How do you think your superior officer will enjoy hearing that you abuse your slave—and her baby?"

Dupree's coloring bloomed a shade to match his upholstery. Her words had found their mark. He grabbed her arm. "How would he enjoy hearing that the colony midwife is a murderer?"

A gasp escaped her.

"That's right. I know what you are. Had a nice little chat with a girl named Helene at the tavern last night."

184

Julianne bristled. So Helene's tongue was as loose as anything else she wore.

"She told me all about your imprisonment at Salpêtrière and how you were condemned for the murder of one of your patients."

His words were daggers, flaying Julianne's confidence clean away. She jerked to break free, but he caught her other arm and pulled her against his chest. When his gaze probed the edge of her square neckline, she fought to control the breath straining against her corset.

"But how do you think the rest of New Orleans will feel about putting our valuable women and babies in your bloodied hands?" Dupree's breath smelled of brandy. "The very one Bienville hired to deliver life delivers death instead? Maybe it was your fault Dancing Brook's baby died."

"Unhand me this instant!"

"If you speak against me, no one will believe you. Not after today. I could tell you, for instance, that I smothered that baby with a pillow as soon as I found it."

Chills spiraled up and down her spine. "You couldn't have. Not your own son." But she was beginning to believe he could. Shock stilled her.

He took a step back from her but still held her arms firmly in his grasp. "We could have used you at the barracks yesterday."

Julianne frowned at the sudden change in conversation.

"One of our men was shot. Matthieu—do you remember him? He was shot in the arm, right here in New Orleans. When I told him I'd fetch you to come tend him, he said it was you who shot him."

She stared at him. "Matthieu?"

"I told him to keep quiet about it, naturally, that there had been some mistake and that we shouldn't malign your name without good cause. Imagine my surprise when Helene filled my ear. How disappointed I was to find your character is already corrupt."

Fear raced through her veins. "Someone followed me home from the tavern. I told him to leave and he didn't. I defended myself!" Her words came in a torrent.

"With a musket ball. Attempted murder. Matthieu is living proof."

Before Julianne knew what was happening, Dupree grabbed the top of her left sleeve and ripped downward, popping the shoulder seam wide open. Her right hand flew to cover her fleur-de-lys, but it was too late.

"Evidence of your character is permanently proclaimed on your skin." He sighed, as if regretful. But his eyes told a different tale. "Your behavior cannot go unanswered."

A memory ricocheted in her mind. A woman's torment on public display. A voice in the crowd to explain. *She's a girl of bad character. We have no police. The soldiers make examples of them to deter others from following her suit. We must have order, you know.*

When Dupree began leading her away, she knew where he was taking her.

⚜ ⚜ ⚜

Rope pinched Julianne's bare wrists as three soldiers wrestled her pregnant body to a wooden horse in the open square by the waterfront. After delivering her to his soldiers, Dupree had taken his leave, saying he had no stomach to watch, though he knew it must be done.

One of her eyelids was swollen shut, thanks to the fist planted there when she fought against the soldiers who ripped off her gown, leaving her only in her chemise and petticoat. Beyond the dozen soldiers waiting impatiently for their turn at her, a circle of onlookers cinched ever tighter. Helene stood at the front of the crowd, her bosoms half exposed in the indecent garb of her trade. Her smile triumphant, she tossed her loose hair over her shoulders before pressing her fists to her hips.

Shame churning her gut, Julianne squeezed her eyes shut and sipped shallow, rapid breaths of air that smelled of spoiled fish. Wind tugged her hair from its pins and whipped it about her face.

"I present to you the colony midwife! At last exposed for what she really is—a convicted felon. Her crime? Murder in the birthing chamber. Attempted murder of the king's soldier, Matthieu Hurlot."

"I knew her in Paris!" Helene cried out. "He speaks the truth!"

Julianne wondered if Matthieu was in attendance as well, but she refused to scan the crowd. Instead, she fixed her eyes on the muddy ground, where boot prints held last night's rain and mosquitoes rose up with a keen, sharp buzzing.

Judgment filleted her. Condemnation buffeted her ears as she hunched over the wooden horse. *This isn't real*, she told herself. *It's a nightmare.*

But then stripes of fire were laid on her back, ripping through linen and flesh both. Over and again, the whip crisscrossed her back until shreds of fabric fell to the ground in ribbons, leaving her bloodied back bare beneath the glowering sun. Relief came only when the whip passed from one soldier's hand to another, so that all may have their share in the exhibition. Darkness crowded her vision. The crowd wavered.

When the whip's tip reached around her side and licked at her belly, she unleashed a scream that could have woken Simon from the dead. *Lord! Have mercy on my baby!* With every bite of the whip, her prayers grew more fervent, if not eloquent. Cramps gripped her where the leather tongue could not reach. *Mercy! Mercy! God, have mercy!*

Prostitutes and drunks laughed at her agony while the soldiers behind the whip seemed bent only on practicing their aim. The ropes rubbed her wrists raw as she jerked and twisted against them. A voice flickered in her ear: *Your judgment is for life. You are forever condemned.* In her mind's eye, Mother Superior's smooth brow puckered into ridges of blame. *The past cannot be undone or outrun.*

Julianne struggled to suck breath from the atmosphere. Anguish blazed on her back and darted across her middle. Fear for her baby carved out every kindness, every gentleness, every fiber of long-suffering she had and replaced them with the white-hot flames of hate. "Stop! *Mon bébé!*" But no one could hear her rasp above the crack of the whip and jeering crowd.

Then a voice boomed above the others, and the leather ceased to rake its teeth through her flesh. Too weak to turn her head, too consumed with pain to want to, she balanced, motionless, on the plank between her legs and teetered on the edge of consciousness.

The din quieted, then fell away from her diminishing hearing. Two hands held her waist and rocked her slowly off the beam until she stood on the ground with violently shaking legs, and still she was supported by the hands.

Julianne knew who it was without glimpsing his face. Too faint to be mortified over her tattered undergarments, she lifted her arm around his neck while he scooped her up beneath her shoulders and knees. She cried out at the pain of being held but knew she couldn't walk. Hammocked against his chest, she surrendered to oblivion, sinking mercifully into its deep.

⚜ ⚜ ⚜

When Julianne awoke, it was to the smell of crushed onions being waved beneath her nose. She jerked her head away from them and immediately winced at the searing pain the sudden movement caused.

"Saints be praised!" Denise Villeroy knelt at her side in a rustle of silk, her celery-colored skirt pooling around her. "*Mon amie*, I'm so sorry! They are monsters who did this to you!" Tears glazed shaky paths down her cheeks as she set a bowl over the onion poultice to contain the odor.

"Where am I?" Vaguely, Julianne registered that she was on her stomach on a feather bed, wearing a clean chemise that must have been cut away in the back, for moist towels smothered her pain. Two candles on the bureau in the corner cast a pale yellow radiance on the bedposts, washstand, and smooth pine planks in the walls and floor.

"We're in the captain's bedchamber. He insisted on ceding it to you until you've recovered."

"I should be home," Julianne whispered. Ache throbbed in a latticework pattern across her back.

"Ma chère, you're not going anywhere. You should be watched over. Captain Girard will be here whenever he's not with his troops, and his servant Etienne is here night and day. Plus, Lisette and I will take shifts with you. Francoise will come too, of course, as she's able. You'll never be alone."

A tear slipped from Julianne's eye. "Denise," she choked out, "my baby. I'm so afraid—" She hadn't the strength to name her fear. She didn't need to.

Denise's face wrinkled with compassion. "We'll keep watch with you." She sniffed. "Do you mind if I pray for you? Francoise has been rubbing off on me, I suppose."

Julianne blew out a breath. "Please. Please pray." She closed her eyes and let Denise's soft voice wash over her as it winged their requests to God in heaven. "Amen," they whispered at last.

Julianne sighed. "Thank you."

"It's funny, isn't it?" Denise lowered her dark lashes. Her curving lips pointed to the beauty patch she'd placed near the corner of her mouth. "In Paris—before Salpêtrière—I went to church every week, and in between when I needed extra appointments with my confessor." Her smile was rueful. "Here, there is no church to go to at all. But this is where I've been learning to pray. Simply, but often and earnestly."

"And does it change things?" Julianne's reputation was ruined, her occupation discredited, and though she knew in her mind that babies did not miscarry from wounds to a mother's skin, her heart was unconvinced that her child had escaped the ordeal unscathed. Would prayer erase the mark from her skin and resurrect her hope?

Denise's brown eyes softened. "Prayer is not a magician's trick. The changes it brings cannot always be seen at first glance. But just as slippery elm soothes inflammation, prayer is a balm for a raw and ragged soul. And isn't your soul in more need of healing than your skin?"

The gullies in Julianne's flesh burned, but no hotter than the hatred leaping up within her when she thought of Pascal Dupree. In time her skin would reach across the channels the whip's tongue had carved away. But she feared wrath may consume her before she reckoned a way to douse its flames.

With her fingertip, Denise traced the raised edges of a rose on her brocaded lap. "Jean and I ran to inspect the commotion just as Captain Girard put a stop to it. He'd just arrived back from a supply mission up the river—and none too soon. The way he scattered that crowd and cradled you in his arms . . ." She lifted her head, gaze roving about the room. "He is sick with worry for you and for your wee babe. But I can tell concern isn't all that troubles him."

Julianne waited for further explanation. When it wasn't forthcoming, she prodded. "What do you mean?"

Denise stood and moved out of Julianne's vision. Cool air rushed at her back as Denise removed a dry cloth and replaced it with a fresh, warm, damp one. "I should think it obvious.

Love ails a man, Julianne. And Captain Girard has a case worse than most."

Her voice floated above Julianne as she closed her eyes and drifted toward slumber, but Denise's words penetrated her heart.

⚜ ⚜ ⚜

Marc-Paul stood outside the door to his bedchamber, listening to Julianne moan in her sleep. Denise had gone home to her husband and baby, and no other woman would come until morning. In his hand he held a cup of laudanum normally used for wounded soldiers. But Julianne's injuries were severe. She needed it.

"Well, are you going to help her or not?" Etienne crossed his arms.

"I don't want to cause her further distress by entering if she is . . . in a state of . . . disarray." She had already been humiliated enough today.

"Bah!" Etienne waved his hand dismissively. "If you're too modest to bring her the tincture, I'll do it myself. The only indecent thing around here would be for you to let her suffer when it's in your power to ease her."

When Etienne reached for the laudanum, Marc-Paul stepped back, gave his trusty servant a salute, and tapped his knuckles on the door. "Julianne?" he called. "I'm coming in with some medicine."

"I'll fetch some more ointment and fresh cloths." Etienne retreated down the hall.

Slowly, Marc-Paul opened the door. Reassured that she was covered with the sheet, he entered. The candles burned low on the bureau. He stopped for a moment at the sight of her in his bed, her hair fanned out on his pillow. The curiosity that had seized him when he first met her had turned into pity and obligation. But somehow, since then it had deepened into something

191

stronger—and more painful. The whips that had torn into her flesh had flogged his heart as well.

Setting the cup on the bureau, he knelt by her side. "Julianne." Marc-Paul brushed her hair off her face and cringed at the lines whittled into her brow. "Julianne, I've brought you medicine to numb the pain."

Her eyelids fluttered and opened, and she took in the sight of him with no hint of alarm.

"If you can drink this, it will help ease you." Taking the cup from the bureau, he offered it to her. When he saw her begin to raise herself up enough to drink, he turned his head away in case the chemise slipped from her shoulders. Felt the cup leave his hand and return to it.

The whispering of her body in the sheets quieted, and she thanked him. "Do you know why they did this to me?" Her voice was so quiet that he leaned in to listen. "Dupree smothered Dancing Brook's baby, and I confronted him. It was his baby. He killed his own son."

The words fell like rocks to the pit of Marc-Paul's stomach. He closed his eyes.

"He said no one would believe me, not now."

Blood boiled in his veins. Marc-Paul may have extended leniency to his old friend over the guns he took from the commissary, but he refused to keep silent now. "I believe you. And I'll report this to Bienville posthaste. Pascal should be punished, not you." The fact that he once saved Marc-Paul's life did not atone for this.

Julianne's brow wrinkled again as she sought his gaze. "But . . . I shot a man. A soldier."

"What did you say?" He watched her lips. Surely his ears had deceived him. He could tell the effort to speak cost her, yet he needed to hear the rest of the story.

"Someone followed me home from the tavern one night." She

paused for breath, and Marc-Paul held his. "He threatened me. I warned him. I fired the gun into the dark to scare him away. I hit Matthieu Hurlot in the arm."

Marc-Paul exhaled. "Well done."

"He says I meant to murder him. He says . . ." She rolled her lips between her teeth, and her nostrils flared.

"Enough. You defended yourself, and rightly so. Speak no more of it now. You must rest. Please, be at ease. You're safe now." He filled his voice with calm reassurance, though fire burned in his belly at the injustices laid upon her.

A quiet knock on the door, and Marc-Paul rose to answer it. Etienne had returned with a fresh jar of slippery elm ointment and a pile of fresh cloths, which changed hands quickly, before Vesuvius could sneak through the open door. The latch sounded, and the pug snorted from the other side.

Marc-Paul turned back to Julianne. "I—I'd like to change your dressings," he offered tentatively. "Would it distress you if I were to perform this task?"

He waited for her response as he spread a thick layer of ointment on one side of a towel. All he heard was her deep, rhythmic breathing. *Thank you, Lord.* She needed the rest.

Pulling the sheet off her back, Marc-Paul saw the fleur-de-lys that marked her as a criminal. Not a common one, but a convict beyond hope of rehabilitation. The symbol of the monarchy on her skin said she belonged to the king to do with as he pleased—and so he had shipped her to Louisiana. He sighed, then clenched his jaw. *A murderer in the birthing chamber. A murderer in the streets!* When he had jumped from the pirogue and left the soldiers to unload the food, the air had been thick with rumors as he'd cut through it to reach her. Now he understood why.

Carefully, he peeled a cloth from her back. When it did not come easily, he added water to the spot, soaking what had dried until the cloth came free without causing any more pain. Bit by bit, the towels were removed in a tedious, painstaking process until her back was completely exposed. Tears bit his eyes at the sight of her ravaged flesh.

"How much judgment shall be heaped upon this soul?" he whispered. For as long as he could remember, his life had been guided by the law. He followed the law, he stayed alive by the law, and he punished those who broke it. But ever since he met Julianne Chevalier, a hunger for something more had grown in him. Grace. He craved grace. For her, and for himself.

He tenderly covered a third of Julianne's back with the ointment-laden towel. Memory triggered. *If I have wronged, I merely ask forgiveness, and grace covers me. My sins are blotted out.* He stared at Julianne's back as the words of his former neighbor, Antoine, jumped over the decades that had parted them.

Marc-Paul was ten years old then and shared hot chocolate at Antoine's table every afternoon that winter. Until he learned that sixteen-year-old Antoine was a Huguenot. Protestantism was illegal in France, and so Marc-Paul had told the police. Antoine and his family had disappeared—whether by flight or execution—because Marc-Paul had followed the law. Just like Benjamin Chevalier had been executed because Marc-Paul had followed the law. But was following the laws of man enough? Did pleasing King Louis please the King of Kings? Lately, he wondered.

Jaw tense with unvoiced doubts, Marc-Paul placed the next towels on Julianne's back and drew the sheet over her shoulders. Slowly, he opened the top drawer of his bureau and felt beneath the linens until his hand closed over the Bible the Swiss peasant had given him on the voyage. He pulled it out and dipped the pages into the flickering light of the candle. They crinkled quietly as he turned them.

In the Apostle Paul's letter to the Romans, he read: "Moreover the law entered, that the offence might abound. But where sin abounded, grace did much more abound." Then, on the next page, "For sin shall not have dominion over you: for ye are not under the law, but under grace."

Incredible. Marc-Paul was intrigued by the apostle for whom he was named. Before Paul was an apostle of Christ's, he too followed the law with what he considered a righteous vengeance. But after his conversion, every letter he wrote to the early churches began and ended with grace. Not the law, but grace.

Marc-Paul thumbed the edges of the fragile pages to see the words again for himself. "Grace be unto you, and peace . . ." "The grace of our Lord Jesus Christ be with you." To the Corinthians, Galatians, Ephesians, Philippians, Colossians, and more. *Everything begins and ends with grace.*

Closing the Bible, Marc-Paul laid it reverently on his bureau. Kneeling at Julianne's side once more, he placed his hand over the black mark on her shoulder. His gaze resting on her face, he whispered the prayer from Paul: "Grace be unto you, and peace, from God our Father, and from the Lord Jesus Christ." *Grace and peace,* ma belle.

Chapter Sixteen

✤ ✤ ✤

"No!" Suddenly ripped from her slumber on her fourth morning in Captain Girard's house, Julianne found herself panting with pain, rocking on her hands and knees. Her sleeveless chemise clung to her shoulders though its back had been cut away. Beneath her petticoat, lifeblood spilled down her thigh. Crying out in dismay, she frantically snatched one of the towels that had fallen from her back and held it between her legs.

Knocking rattled the door.

Without asking who it was, Julianne shouted, "Fetch Francoise and Lisette! I am losing the baby!"

Footsteps pounded away. A door slammed, and the house shuddered. Time slowed as dawn crept between the slats of the shutters. Grey bars of shadow-light loomed across the room, transforming it from sanctuary to prison. Julianne's arms and legs shook as cramping racked her. Unable to lie on her back for the stripes still oozing there, she crawled to the edge of the bed and sat with a mound of towels between her legs, watching their white bloom crimson. It was too much blood, too soon. "Please," she prayed.

By the time another knock beat the door, her head had grown light and cobwebs tangled her thoughts. Before she realized the door had opened, Lisette stood before her, freckles stark against her face, her blond hair plaited down her back from the night before. Beside her was Francoise, her earnest face wiped clean of its usual toilette.

"Tell us what to do." Francoise's voice sounded far away.

"It's too early. The baby is lost," Julianne choked out. "If I stop pushing, Lisette will have to bring it out. And afterward—" The afterbirth would have to come out. But if Lisette pulled too hard on the navel string, the rupture in the womb could be fatal.

"I remember." Lisette's strong voice belied her trembling lips. She turned to Francoise and listed all the things she would need. Francoise hurried to the door and relayed her requests to whoever was in the hall.

Another contraction washed over Julianne, and she squeezed her eyes shut to push with it. She felt the flow of too much blood leaving her body, warming and slicking her thighs.

And then she felt nothing at all.

⚜ ⚜ ⚜

When Julianne awoke, she found that she'd been bathed and dressed in a fresh ankle-length chemise that opened in the back.

A spark of light flared as Francoise lit the candle in the glass hurricane lamp on the bureau. "*Ma foi*, Julianne, you frightened us all to death!" Her tone was thick with worry.

Julianne moaned as she pushed herself up to sit on the edge of the bed. Gripping the mattress, she closed her eyes until the spinning sensation stopped.

"Lisette did well for you. I sent her home to rest. But I—I wanted to be here when you awoke."

"Tell me," Julianne whispered, praying for the strength to hear.

"A son." Francoise sighed. "You had a son yesterday."

Julianne bowed her head beneath her grief. The stripes on her back stretched painfully as her shoulders slumped forward. Loss pressed down on her until her torso formed a hollow arc. How cavernous her womb felt, and how empty her arms! With her finger, she caught a tear from the tip of nose. "Where is he? May I see him?"

Francoise picked up a bundle that was so small—impossibly small—and Julianne's hand flew to her throat.

"His skin is so thin, like the skin of an onion," Francoise began to explain.

Julianne understood the full meaning. He had not been washed in order to leave his skin on his body. Just touching him might disturb it. And yet, how could she not hold her baby?

She took the bundle from Francoise and held it close to her aching chest. Sorrow hardened into shards that pierced her heart. "*Mon bébé,*" she crooned through her tears. His tiny body lay unwrapped on the cloth. She longed to stroke her finger over his cheek, his chest, his little hand! But she could not bear that doing so would peel his skin away.

She lifted him closer to her face. "There you are, my little one. Mama has you." He was only slightly longer than the length of her hand and weighed less than a pound. One fist was curled, with just the thumb extended, and Julianne wondered if he'd been sucking it not so very long ago. "Ah, *mon coeur.*" She kissed the tip of her finger and ever-so-lightly touched her finger to his cold, perfect lips. *You were supposed to grow into the image of your father, with eyes that sparkled like the ocean. I was going to rock you in my arms and sing to you even after you'd drifted to sleep, for the joy of holding you close. You were going to bring me wildflowers and frogs. And I was going to clean your scraped knees and kiss your pain away and tell you not to rip holes in your breeches again. I would never have refused a single sloppy kiss from you.*

Francoise blew her nose into a handkerchief. "What have you named him?"

"Benjamin. For my brother." But in her brother's case, it was the baby who lived and the mother who died. Gladly would Julianne have given her life so that this boy could have brightened the world. Gladly would she join him now, if the Lord's mercy would but summon her.

Tearing her gaze from her son was like ripping nails from a board as Francoise took him back. With all the care his grandmother might have had, the older woman laid him inside a small wooden box.

"Etienne made the box for him. Lined with blue serge, which Captain Girard cut from one of his uniform waistcoats." Tears streaked Francoise's careworn cheeks, and Julianne suspected she cried not just for Benjamin, but for the little daughter she had also laid to rest years ago.

When Francoise fit the lid to the casket, Julianne cried out in pain.

"I don't—" She gasped for breath. "I don't know how to do this. I don't know how to shut him away! How did you manage it, Francoise? I can't—" Sobbing racked her shoulders, sending small cracks through the fresh scabs on her back. It took all her strength to keep from crying out that her baby was suffocating in that closed box. But Julianne was the one who could not get air.

She was not just laying *her* baby to rest, but Simon's. Once little Ben was buried, she would have nothing left of her late husband.

Francoise's skirts rustled as she eased herself onto the bed. Julianne sobbed onto her soft shoulder while Francoise stroked her hair. "I know, ma chère. I would spare you this if such were in my power." The older woman's voice broke with empathy. "But I want you to listen to me. You will survive it. If God wanted you with Him now too, He would have taken you. But here you are. There is more life for you to live. The sun will shine again."

With her hand pressed to her heart, Julianne trapped a groan in her chest. "Does the pain ease?" she whispered.

Francoise sighed. "The pain changes, and you will change with it. The sharp edges wear away in time, but the loss remains. You'll learn how to live with it. There's not a day that goes by that I don't think of my little girl, and I warrant you won't forget your son. Never, as long as you live. And when we get to heaven, our little ones will know their mamas. I believe God Almighty and the Blessed Virgin, who also knows what it is to lose a child, will see to that."

Nodding, Julianne lifted her head and sluiced the tears from her cheeks with trembling hands. "Thank you. And now, please go home to rest. You have done all you can for me, and I thank you."

Slowly, Francoise stood and pinned her lace cap to her curls. "Talk to the Lord, Julianne. Even if you're mad as hornets. If you keep it all bottled up, you'll only end up with a belly full of bee stings." Straightening, she patted her hair before pointing to a chair. "Denise brought a fresh gown for whenever you're ready. But the captain is in no hurry for his bed, so take your time." She bent and kissed Julianne on both tearstained cheeks before taking her leave.

Alone again, save for the tiny coffin, Julianne blew out the candle and returned to bed, where she prayed for a dreamless sleep to cover her, for she could not stomach another wakeful moment.

By the time the first light of day trickled into the room, she was awake again. She raised herself up, walked stiffly to the window, and lifted the linen shade. A cool breeze feathered over her and stirred through the captain's bedchamber. It was the sixth day since she'd been carried here. She could not bear to stay any longer.

At the washstand, Julianne wiped the film of tears and sweat from her face and neck, then crossed to the clothing on the chair and found Denise had remembered to bring a binding towel. Carefully, she slipped her arms out of her chemise, wrapped and pinned the length of muslin around her torso, and pulled the chemise back over her shoulders. As she did so, the stripes on her back rekindled, and her breasts ached for a babe she would never nurse. Though the binding towel helped protect her scabs as she moved, sliding the loose-fitting robe volante over one arm and then the other still made her suck in her breath. Standing ramrod straight, she fitted the buttons in their holes from her chest to her waist, then gathered up the blue silk damask skirt to fasten the rest so she would not need to bend to reach them.

Wincing, Julianne brushed out her hair and pinned it up again. Denise had brought small pots of paste and rouge for her toilette as well, but she skipped these, availing herself only of the roots that freshened one's teeth.

Once she was dressed and coifed, she took up her baby and prepared to emerge from the captain's bedchamber a different woman than when she had been carried in.

⚜ ⚜ ⚜

Marc-Paul sat forward in the chair he'd placed outside his bedchamber. If Julianne called for anything—water, or nourishment, or herbs, or Lisette—he'd hear and fetch it for her. But since Francoise had gone home last night, all had been quiet.

Elbows on his knees and head in his hands, he dipped in and out of prayer for Julianne's physical and emotional recovery. Vesuvius wedged himself between Marc-Paul's right thigh and the arm of the chair and snored, but not loudly enough to drown out the haunting memory of Julianne's cries.

On his voyages to and from Louisiana, Marc-Paul had seen his share of prentice seamen tied to the mast and lashed, then plunged into a barrel of stinging brine. One boatswain was so cruel and so expert with the whip that he laid the blows over and again on exactly the same place until the leather had bitten clear through the muscle to the bone.

This was what came to his mind as he thought of Julianne. Loss had fallen three times upon her, three cruel blows to the same raw heart that had not had time to heal from the last.

The latch sounded on the door to his chamber, and he shot out of his chair. While Vesuvius circled three times on the seat cushion before lying down again, Marc-Paul brushed the fur from his rumpled breeches and looked expectantly at the door as it creaked open.

Stiffly, Julianne backed out of the chamber, one arm bearing the baby's coffin while the other hand pulled the door closed behind her. Turning, she gave a start upon seeing him standing there in the dawn's watery light.

"I didn't mean to startle you," he began, rubbing a hand over his stubbled jaw. "Are you—is there anything I can do for you?" The question sounded as inept as he felt. The sorrow in her eyes seized his heart.

"I wish I could thank you properly for what you've already done. But—forgive me—I barely know what to do from one moment to the next right now," Julianne confessed. "I need to lay my son to rest. At least, his body." She clutched the box to her middle. "I just—I don't know how to let him go." Her voice trailed away, as though she spoke to herself now and not to him.

He touched her elbow, and indeed, she looked surprised to see him still at her side. "Whatever you need, I will supply. If you allow it, I will help you bury him. But, madame, could you not eat something first?"

Her gaze slid to the sunlight gliding slowly across the floor. "Afterwards I will. I'd like to do this before the town is fully awake. If you please."

"Of course." The sooner they went to the levee and back, the fewer people they'd be likely to meet along the way. "Shall I send for Francoise, or Lisette or Denise? The priest?"

Julianne shook her head. "I've taken enough of my friends' time. And the priest would not bless the baby of a branded convict, would he?"

Marc-Paul blew out a frustrated breath. "A different priest would. But the priest we have here is not likely to trouble himself for this. We don't need that man to assure us of your baby's heavenly home." His gaze fell to the casket and her white-knuckled grip on the lid. "There can be no doubt where he is."

"Yes, quite my own thoughts," Julianne whispered and then looked up with red-veined eyes. "Have you a spade, then?"

He assured her he did and excused himself for a moment to change his clothes. When he returned, he was in a fresh uniform: grey-white full-skirted coat with wide blue cuffs over his blue waistcoat, blue breeches, and white gaiters from the tops of his black leather shoes to his lower thighs. Cautiously, he approached her and wordlessly offered to carry her load as they walked to the riverbank.

"Oh no, merci." Julianne stepped back from him. "He will leave my arms soon enough."

With a bow to her wishes, he ushered her out into the cool October morning. After fetching a small shovel from the work shed, he rejoined her and led her toward the river.

The pace was understandably slow, and he wished time and again she would forfeit her burden to him. But she had labored to bring her baby into the world, and she would labor to give him back to the earth. Meanwhile, he gathered rocks from the ground, dropping them quietly into a basket as they walked.

"Here," Julianne said when they came to the whitewashed cross marking Simon's grave. "Please," she added, "at his feet."

Marc-Paul drove his shovel into the earth and dug until the

ground yawned open at the foot of Simon's grave. It did not take long. Finished, he stood back, placed his hat over his heart, and waited.

The smells of damp soil and river water floated on the breeze as the early morning sun doubled itself on the glass of the Mississippi River. Julianne's clutch tightened around the box. "Adieu, *mon amour*," she whispered. "Your papa will take care of you now." She handed the tiny coffin to Marc-Paul to lower into the earth. "I know, more than most, how common it is for babies to die." Her voice trembled. "So I also know how uncommon it is that mine should have such a formal burial. Thank you."

He would do more for her than bury her son, if she would let him. For now, he laid the rocks on the casket, then replaced the dirt and packed it into a neat, smooth mound. *Dust to dust.*

Keeping her back awkwardly straight, Julianne knelt and placed her hands on the dirt, smoothing away any lumps she found, as he imagined she would if she were tucking her son into bed. When she bowed her head, he did the same.

At length, Julianne looked up, and he offered his hand to help her rise. When she turned her palms up to inspect them, he easily read the sentiment shadowing her weary eyes. There should have been a baby in those hands. Not the dirt that covered the child before his lungs had a chance to fill. Slowly, she brushed the grains of earth from her hands and watched them scatter in the wind.

"Marc-Paul," she whispered, and his Christian name on her lips throbbed in his ears. Tears lined her lashes as she looked at him. "I am shipwrecked on these shoals."

His throat tight, he offered his arm, and she clung to it. He would lead her to calmer seas if he could. He'd give her all that he had, and all that he was. He needed to tell her the path that lay ahead of her, according to Bienville, but not now. And as much as he dreaded it, he should clear his conscience and tell her of his role in Benjamin's death. Better sooner rather than later, for secrets festered the longer they were kept. But this was not the moment for that either.

Right now, all he said was, "I'm so sorry." He kissed the top of her hair, warmed by the morning sun, and led her slowly from the graves.

Chapter Seventeen

✦ ✦ ✦

To avoid being rude, Julianne forced herself to eat the food
Etienne had placed before her, though she had no appetite at all.
The food shortage in the colony made Marc-Paul's hospitality
even more precious, and she would hate to insult her host, even
if all he had to offer her was sagamité, salted deer, and dried figs.

"I hate to impose," she tried again. "I'll head home this afternoon. I do thank you for everything." Weak words next to the
care the captain and his servant had provided.

Marc-Paul's silverware clinked on his plate as he laid it to
rest. "In your professional opinion, has the danger for your
health passed?"

Julianne turned her lips up determinedly. "I'm quite well,
thank you. At least, well enough to return home. And I've already proven I'm not afraid to use my gun."

The captain did not return her smile. Sighing, he pushed his
plate away and rested his arms on the table. "Now, madame,
I have news for you." His brown eyes were troubled, his shadowed jawline set.

"Please tell me."

"I've spoken to Bienville on your behalf, to try to wrench

some justice for what happened to you at the hands of Pascal Dupree and his men."

"Justice?"

"I wanted to save your position. As the colony midwife."

"Oh." Her hands fluttered to her napkin, and she dabbed the corners of her mouth with it before smoothing it again in her lap. She did not need to ask how it went. Defeat rested in the furrows of his brow, and by degrees the implications nested within her chest.

"I told him what you told me. He tasked me with lecturing the officers on abusing their slaves but won't punish Pascal without evidence."

A *lecture*. Julianne clenched her teeth.

"The circumstances of your defense against Hurlot cannot be proven either. He said the only evidence he has is the soldier's wound, the ball from your gun, and—"

"My brand," she finished for him. Humiliated, she focused on the yellow trim of his waistcoat. "And he cannot employ a convict."

Marc-Paul folded his hands on the table. Cleared his throat. "He told me to pass along the two options remaining to you. So please understand that what I am about to say comes from Bienville, not from me."

She nodded but dropped her gaze to her napkin, which she folded like a fan and then flattened again, over and over.

"Your passage was paid for by the Company of the Indies with the express intention that you would help settle the colony. But you are not married, and your occupation as a midwife has concluded. The Company cannot sustain you on charity."

She balled her napkin into her fist and fought against narrowing her eyes at the messenger. "And where are these choices you speak of?"

He drank from his pewter cup of water before responding. "There is a ship due soon in New Orleans. When it sails back to France, you may return with it."

Julianne's chair scudded across the floor as she rose from the table, and Vesuvius scampered away. "I'm being exiled from exile?"

Marc-Paul rose from his seat as well. "If I were to speak freely, I'd say you were but a pawn in a political move. Bienville tires of settlers who unsettle the colony, he says. He wants to make a point by sending back 'unsuitable' colonists. But have a care, Julianne. Your brand—"

"Yes, I know full well if I return to France it will not be to practice midwifery. Perhaps a convent would take me. And there is always Salpêtrière." But she could not return there. She'd sooner throw herself overboard than commit herself to that place for life. She stalked out of the dining room, out of doors, and onto the gallery.

Footsteps told her Marc-Paul was close behind. "I meant no offense." He grabbed her hand and turned her to face him. Her pulse quickened at the warmth of his touch. "Is it your desire to leave Louisiana? Do you wish to go back to France, if you could only be assured of your freedom?"

Wind blew through the gallery, swirling his leather and coffee scent about her. "Is it even possible?" she asked.

"If this is what you want above all else, I'll do all in my power to secure your freedom beyond all doubt. Your sentence was already commuted once, and you cannot be tried for the same crime twice." He took her other hand in his, and his eyes smoldered with intensity. "Tell me what you want, Julianne. Would you return to France if you could? Is there some way you could be happy there, if you were free?"

If there was, Julianne could not envision it. She could see nothing beyond the strong lines of Marc-Paul's face, could feel nothing but his hands enveloping hers. Sighing, she looked out over the vegetable garden, where corn and beans and squash grew together in untidy but happy tandem. "I cannot leave. Yet how can I stay?"

"Marry again." His voice was solemn. Earnest.

"Marry again," she repeated. "Is the groom already chosen, or am I to be given a roomful of unwilling bachelors again?"

"Choose a willing partner for yourself. That is, if you yourself are willing."

Pulling free of his hold, Julianne grasped the back of a chair and lowered herself into it. She closed her eyes, and the panic and fear she had felt at the priory of Saint-Martin-des-Champs trickled back to her. Simon's face appeared in her mind. She fingered the lace edging her sleeve but by some trick of memory felt the calluses on his broad palms instead. "I've not been a widow a full three months yet. Surely it wouldn't be decent."

"The rules of marriage are different in the wilderness than they are in Paris. Remarrying would not be a betrayal to Simon's memory. You wouldn't even need to love your new husband." Marc-Paul leaned against one of the gallery's supporting posts. In the autumn sun, his black hair shone like the polished leather of his shoes. "There must be someone you could abide. Someone you could trust to protect you and care for you as you deserve." He held Julianne's gaze for so long she could see tiger flecks in his brown eyes, so long that warmth washed right through her.

But Julianne's heart had been carved up and buried in the riverbank, in three different coffins of wood, weighted with rocks and covered in earth. And Marc-Paul knew it. "How could any man be satisfied with the little I have left to give?"

In an instant he was kneeling before her, taking her hand. He was resplendent in his uniform, the picture of chivalry bent on one knee. "Marry me."

Surely she'd misheard him. "I beg your pardon?"

"I do not force this upon you, Julianne, but I do offer myself to you as an alternative to consider. Marry me, and let me shelter you with my provision. A house, garden, food, clothing. Any need you have will be supplied. You can practice midwifery for the love of your work and for the good of the colony, not for income. Allow me the honor of caring for you."

Shock shuddered through her.

He bowed his head over her hand for a moment before lifting his face once more. "Your brother adored you. He was completely devoted. If he were here, he would have provided for and protected you to the best of his ability. And Simon—you said yourself that if I had only told you the truth about Benjamin as soon as I knew who you were, he would not have gone looking for him, would not have put himself in the danger that took his life. Let me atone for my sins. Allow me to care for you as they no longer can."

He was breathtaking. She pressed her hand against her thundering heartbeat. "You would do this for me?"

"I promise I'll not abuse you, nor take from you what you do not willingly offer. You may sleep in your own bedchamber. Bienville may order you to marry, but he'll not be briefed on what transpires between these walls." He took her other hand and brought them each to his lips in turn. "Gladly would I call you wife if you would only consent to have me. Don't answer me now, on the day you've just buried your son. The ship that would carry you back to France, if you choose, isn't due to arrive in New Orleans for another month. In the meantime, say you'll consider my proposal."

"How very generous," she whispered.

He rose and smiled tenderly. "It would be no sacrifice to be your husband."

⚜ ⚜ ⚜

In her own cabin again at last, fatigue weighted Julianne's limbs. She should feel more than gratitude over Marc-Paul's proposal, but grief for her son blunted all other emotions.

Dusk's rosy glow filled the room. Outside, children shouted as they chased each other. Above her bed, a spider went about spinning a home for itself among the palmetto fronds and willow canes. It was a double cruelty that came with each death— that everything else kept on living, that the world did not pause for even an instant while Julianne slowly picked up the broken pieces of her heart.

Exhausted, she shucked her gown from her body and exchanged her chemise for a nightdress. Wary of disturbing the scabs on her back, she stiffly performed the necessary tasks of her pre-bed routine and eased herself onto the mattress, where she rested on her stomach. Her stripes stung and itched beneath the binding towel she'd kept in place, and she gritted her teeth. Tomorrow she'd ask one of her friends to dress her back again. For now, the only relief at her disposal was sleep.

⚜ ⚜ ⚜

Panting, she lurched from a nightmare and fought to regain her bearings. Darkness enveloped her. She inhaled deeply, then expelled her breath slowly to calm her frantic heartbeat. It was only a dream, she told herself. She was safe at home.

The door creaked, and a thin ribbon of moonlight unspooled toward her. Had she forgotten to latch it? Of course not. Not after Matthieu had followed her home.

Had he returned?

Her heart thumping wildly in her chest, she struggled to hear anything above the sound of her blood rushing in her ears. Lifting her head off the pillow, she scanned the interior of the small cabin. Gossamer threads of pale moonlight hung in the air like cobwebs, but she could barely see a thing by their silvery filament. Her fear, however, cast shadows and footsteps where there were none.

Lord, protect me. Still on her stomach, she dropped her hand to the floor. She searched with her fingers for the musket, expecting at any moment to feel its cool, smooth barrel against her skin. It was already loaded and ready to fire.

But she felt nothing. She reached farther back toward the wall, then up toward the head of the bed, then back down toward the foot until she had traced circles with her fingertips far beyond where the gun should have rested. Panic hammered behind her eyes. The gun was gone. Whoever had stolen her defense could have done so during the previous week, while the cabin was empty, but instead he had waited until she came home to break in. Clearly he wanted her to know how close he could get to her.

How close is he? The dried moss in her mattress seemed to crunch with the volume of snapping twigs as Julianne raised herself up to sit in the corner of her bed. Straining her eyes against the darkness, she saw only what her imagination set before her. Terror rattled her teeth, so she clamped shut her jaw and held her breath, listening intently for the breathing of another, for the creak of a footstep. For the click of the hammer on her own flintlock. For the hiss of an arrow piercing the air, or a tomahawk slicing the night.

⚜ ⚜ ⚜

The next morning, Julianne rose from the sofa as Marc-Paul stepped into his salon, hat in his hand. "I'm sorry to startle you." Aware of her fingers worrying the folds of her skirt, she clasped her hands to still them. "Etienne assured me I could wait for you here."

"I'm glad he did." He tossed his hat onto a side table and crossed the room to stand before her. Questions loomed in his eyes as he neared. "Are you—are you well?"

"My gun is gone," she blurted. "It was there when I went to sleep, but I woke in the night, and when I reached for it, it wasn't there anymore. Someone was in my cabin and took my gun from under my bed while I slept." She bit her lip to halt the rush of words.

Marc-Paul's eyes darkened as he listened. "You're certain?"

"I'm certain." Her heart galloped as she retold the tale, as if the clock had turned back its hands and set her in the dark with a stranger once more. "I sat on my bed and kept vigil until dawn, but I neither saw nor heard anything. Who would have done such a thing? And why?" She ended with a whisper.

His gaze bore into hers. "I don't know what's going on, but I do know one thing." He took her hands and kissed them both. "If anything had happened to you, I—I—" He closed his eyes for a moment. "Not even a day has passed for you to consider my proposal, but say you'll be my wife, Julianne. Let me protect you. Make this house your home, and be safe." He cupped her chin and rested his other hand in the hollow of her waist. "Marry me, for pity's sake," he whispered.

She warmed beneath his touch. "For pity?"

Marc-Paul shook his head, the color rising in his cheeks. His gaze rested on her lips overlong before meeting her eyes once again. "For more than that, if you desire it."

Heart throbbing at his nearness, she blinked back tears. With the slightest nod of her head, his hand slid to the small of her back, and he gently pressed her closer, careful not to touch the places where she'd been lashed. Julianne held his arms as he bent his head and tenderly took her lips.

When his kiss deepened, all doubt dissolved in Julianne's heart. It might have been duty that drove him to propose, but something stronger would bond them as man and wife.

Chapter Eighteen

❧ ❧ ❧

By the time the violin stopped singing and the wedding reception guests stopped twirling over the grass outside Francoise's inn, Marc-Paul was more than ready to be alone with his bride. Their engagement had lasted two weeks, during which Julianne had stayed at the St. Jean Inn. It was time enough for her stripes to heal, for Francoise to prepare this party, and for him to prepare his house and heart for his wife.

It had not been time enough, however, for him to discover who'd stolen her gun while she slept. He searched the barracks and found nothing. He re-inventoried the commissary, to detect whether Pascal had used the stolen weapon to replace one of the guns he'd taken during the summer. But the numbers were off by the same margin they'd been before. If Pascal had managed to get past the double guard and add a gun to the stock, Marc-Paul doubted whether he could identify it, anyway. With a little polish, Simon's barely used gun would look like all the rest. When questioned directly, Pascal had said he was a customer at the tavern all night that night. A short and awkward conversation with a girl named Helene confirmed it.

"Congratulations, Captain!" One of his men, Andre, raised his glass to Marc-Paul, snapping him back to the present moment. "You're a lucky man."

Thanking him, Marc-Paul resolved to put the thief out of his mind, at least for the present, lest the mystery rob him of this moment's joy as well.

A smile curved his lips as he watched Julianne. The violet shades of twilight did not dim her glow as she kissed Denise and four-month-old Angelique on their cheeks to bid them adieu. Jean Villeroy vigorously pumped Marc-Paul's hand before ushering his family away.

"And here I'd lost all hope of you ever settling down." Pascal sauntered over to Marc-Paul, and Julianne immediately broke away—in search of better company, no doubt. "Didn't think you were the type, old friend." He clapped a hand on Marc-Paul's shoulder.

Marc-Paul shrugged it off. "I don't recall inviting you to the party." In fact, he distinctly remembered leaving him off the guest list.

"Oh, I was just here at the inn for dinner. It's a public place, recall. Heard the music on my way out and couldn't help but say hello. I'm hurt you didn't ask me to join your celebration, after all we've been through together. Truly offended."

"*You're* offended?" Marc-Paul shook his head in disbelief at Pascal's nonchalance. "Excuse me."

Julianne beckoned him to join her, and he gladly strode over to her side.

Pascal stayed with him. "I must say, I wouldn't have matched a convict with someone who loves the law so very much. Although, she does have a certain appeal about her, if you ignore her past—and yours." Pascal raked Julianne with a carnal gaze that twisted Marc-Paul's gut.

Julianne's face flamed red, matching Marc-Paul's anger,

which simmered dangerously close to the surface. Taking his bride's elbow, he led her away from Pascal and thanked Françoise, her son, Laurent, and Lisette for their efforts in hosting the reception. After a few more good-byes to soldiers in his company, he walked home with Julianne on his arm and Pascal's words rattling in his ears. If she asked him to explain the cryptic comment, what would he say? Pascal couldn't know that Marc-Paul had sent her brother to his death. But he certainly knew about Willow.

Once they were a musket shot away from the inn, Julianne broke the silence. "I won't ask you what he meant about your past, Marc-Paul. You know my own history, and yet you've chosen to yoke yourself to me just the same. If there is something from your life before I knew you that you're not proud of, don't let that horrid man dangle it in front of you the way he does with me. I'll pay no heed to his taunts. I trust you to tell me the truth about anything I need to know." She laced her fingers in his as they walked along. "I trust you."

Her words counterbalanced his tormented conscience. She was only asking for that which she needed to know. Why would she need to know about the exact nature of Benjamin's death? It was over. She had mourned her loss, and knowing about his dishonor would only sharpen her grief. Learning that Marc-Paul's testimony had sealed the young man's death sentence—he could think of no reason to tell her that.

As for Willow, the young Mobilian woman who kept his bearskin bed warm during his twenty-third winter, she held no claim on his heart. He had confessed his youthful moral lapse to the Almighty and trusted that he was forgiven. Confessing it to Julianne, however, would only hurt her.

Marc-Paul brought her fingers to his lips and kissed them. "Thank you for that. I trust you too. And if there is one person in Louisiana I don't trust, it's Pascal Dupree." It pained him to say it, all the more because he had once trusted the man with his life.

"Oh!" Julianne snapped her fingers. "I never did ask you. After I delivered Dancing Brook of her son, she kept repeating a certain phrase alongside Pascal's name. I may be saying it wrong, but it sounded to me like this." She repeated the native phrase. "Do you know what that means?"

Marc-Paul raised an eyebrow. He knew Pascal used Indian women to satisfy his own lusts. But it was no secret, and not at all uncommon. And it did not account for this. "I should talk to her myself. I need to be certain."

"But what do you think it means?"

Suddenly wary that someone may be watching them, Marc-Paul pulled her close and whispered into her ear: "Two Faces. It's the name she's given him. She calls him Two Faces."

"Because he abused her and killed her baby, and yet pretends to be a gentleman?"

"Likely so." But there could be more to it than that. Marc-Paul intended to find out what.

⚜ ⚜ ⚜

"You're home, Julianne."

Marc-Paul's tender smile as he opened his front door for her should have melted her heart. But once inside, the sound of the latch clicking into place behind her sent her pulse racing instead. Vesuvius ambled over, and she reached down to scratch his ears before he sauntered away.

It was a beautiful home, a real house, where cypress shingles would keep her head dry and polished floors would keep her feet clean. Instead of the smoke of an indoor fire, here the pine walls and thin, oiled linen over the windows would keep the mosquitoes and flies out. She would sleep on a feather bed, not a mattress of dried moss suspended by ropes, and would eat on porcelain rather than tin and wood. The library offered a bounty of books, the salon an array of cushioned sofas. The gallery behind the house looked out over roses, orange trees, vegetables, and herbs for the kitchen and medicine cabinet. It was more than she could have dreamed she could call her own.

Yet this was the place where she had lost her son, and never could she forget it. Knots formed in her middle at the thought of sleeping in that room again, on the same bed where she nearly died.

"Marc-Paul," she said, "your bedchamber . . . it holds such sorrow for me." Her throat grew tight, and she willed him to understand. She could not sleep there and would not make love there when it was haunted by memories of miscarriage, still fresh after only two weeks' time.

"And you never have to enter it again, if that's what you desire." He guided her down the hall until they stopped before another closed door. "How would this suit?"

She opened the door and stepped into a room aglow with candles in glass hurricanes. A glossy walnut bed nestled beneath a counterpane of blue and white toile and bolsters to match. Matching toile curtains draped the windows, softening the room.

"It's lovely! And I confess, more feminine than I imagined your house could be!"

Marc-Paul laughed. "I have a confession of my own to make. The counterpane and curtains are a gift from Francoise. She wanted you to be surprised."

"I am!" Then she spotted the bearskin rug on the floor before the bed and immediately slipped off her shoes to walk upon it. Even through her stockings, she relished the luxurious softness.

A walnut washstand with turned legs, matching the style of

the bedposts, held a pure white china washbasin and pitcher, with an oval mirror hung on the wall above it. There was also a chaise longue in the corner of the room, upholstered in camel-colored silk and brass studs, with a small table beside it.

"Turn around," Marc-Paul prompted, and she did.

On the wall opposite the window, there was a toilette table draped with lace that flounced to the floor and topped with a set of silver pots, brushes, and a silver-plated mirror. The traditional gift from a French groom to his bride, it clearly came directly from the mother country.

"How on earth did you get it here?"

"Are you impressed?" His lips tipped up in a lopsided grin. "Then I should let you go on believing its arrival was nothing short of miraculous. But I'll tell you the truth. All this furniture, including the toilette table, is here because of Vesuvius. So be sure to thank him."

"Your dog?"

"That's right. A concessionaire up the river lost his wife to fever, and he wanted to be rid of everything that reminded him of her: her furniture, her toilette table and jewelry, her gowns— which you'll find waiting for you in the dressing room—and her pug. But as he was too impatient to sell it off piecemeal, he bundled it all together in one package and sold it at auction."

"And you bought all of it?"

"I wanted Vesuvius." He laughed. "And I paid a pretty price for him too. Still a bargain!"

With impeccable timing, Vesuvius waddled into the room and draped himself over Julianne's stocking feet on the bearskin rug. "Does he keep you warm at night too?" Kneeling, she rubbed behind his floppy black ears.

"It's really a case-by-case negotiation. And in this case, he'll keep Etienne company for the night." Marc-Paul scooped up the pug, and Julianne rose as well. "Etienne," he called at the doorway, and the Canadian appeared moments later. "You don't mind having a bedfellow tonight, do you?"

Blue eyes sparkling, Etienne reached out and took Vesuvius, the two missing fingers on his right hand bearing witness to his trapping days. "Why do you look so worried, pug?" His gruff voice was laced with humor. "You'd better get used to that expression, madame," he added. "It's the only face he's got."

"I'm glad of it. I find him charming." Julianne couldn't resist rubbing his velvety ears one last time. "Good night, my handsome fellow."

"I knew she was a good woman," Etienne directed toward Marc-Paul. "Takes a heart of gold to love a wrinkled face." Smiling broadly, lines seamed his own countenance as he turned and retreated down the hall.

Julianne laughed as Marc-Paul closed the door to the bedchamber. When he met her gaze, however, his smile faded. "And now, *ma chérie*, to put you at ease. I almost hate to mention it, but it warrants being addressed. I know what happened on your wedding night with Simon. That you were forced to—the guards told me what they did to you prisoners. It was unconscionable. And I can only think those memories threaten to poison this night as well. So the bed is yours. Completely yours, until you invite me into it. I will not force myself upon you. You will not relive that nightmare."

Tears stung Julianne's eyes as his thoughtfulness clashed with the horror of her wedding night in the stable. In his own way, Simon had been thoughtful then too. Her heart ached with the weight of all it held. She struggled to disentangle the forebodings that wrapped her spirit, but their tendrils clung like ivy to brick. She met her husband's eyes again. "But where would you sleep?"

Marc-Paul pointed to the chaise in the corner and crossed

to it. Taking off his winter uniform coat, he laid it on the back of the chair. His linen shirt gleamed white behind his deep blue waistcoat. "I promise to behave, but I do insist on staying in the room with you after what happened the other night in your cabin. If someone has designs on you, for any reason, I'd never forgive myself if something happened to you under my own roof. That is, our roof. Your well-being is my foremost concern. It has been since the moment I met you."

Julianne's lips parted in surprise, but Marc-Paul wasn't finished.

With a few steps, he went to the small table near the bed and lifted a book from it. A Bible. Reverently, he held it in his hands. "I was an altar boy once." The ghost of a smile softened his chiseled face. "My mother wanted me to be a priest. I grew overfond of robes and rules. I watched myself and others so closely, looking for missteps that needed correcting. It was wrong of me, and it disgusted my father so much that he yanked me from the church and enlisted me in the army." He chuckled. "He was ready for me to become a man and thought soldiering would do it."

"Which it did," she offered.

He smiled. "Yes, but it's not enough. I don't want to be just a man. I want to be a man of faith. I've come back around to this book, Julianne. I'm no priest, and to tell you the truth, the Capuchins here are more interested in politics and status than they are in souls. I've no interest in confessing to them. But I do want this house, our house, to be a house of faith. I want to try to follow these teachings." He thumped his finger on the cover. "I want grace and peace for you and for me. No condemnation. Grace. And peace. From God, and from each other. This is my prayer." Marc-Paul searched her eyes. "How does that sound to you? Have I shocked you with my religion? Or does it sound like blasphemy instead?"

"Grace and peace?" Julianne repeated. "I am marked by condemnation, and in truth, I worry its curse will never leave me. Yet I can think of no better way to live, and no better way to treat each other than with grace and peace." She took the Bible from his hands and ran her finger along the spine before opening it. "I never wanted to be a nun, I confess."

"Why does this not surprise me?"

Julianne warmed beneath his gentle gaze. "But I do want what Francoise has. She prays so easily, and life doesn't scare her. She knows God, which is different than just knowing about Him. That's what I want."

"To know God, and to be known by Him. Yes." His brown eyes glimmered in the candlelight.

She nodded. "And to know His grace and peace, though storms rage and nations fight and food is scarce and France has forgotten us. And though I wear judgment on my very skin."

"You never deserved it."

The pain and guilt of losing Marguerite washed over her afresh. "I'm not innocent, Marc-Paul. I don't claim to be." Mustering her courage, she unveiled to him the bloodstained day that haunted her still. "Maybe it was my sinful pride that kept me from calling for a surgeon right away. If a doctor had been present—" She swallowed the catch in her voice. "I loved Marguerite. She would have lived if Madame Le Brun had not bled her so dangerously, but she also may have lived had I not believed so much in my own capability. Because I failed to prevent her death, her son is motherless, and her husband bereaved. May God forgive me." Her throat closed over the words.

Marc-Paul cupped his hands around her shoulders, covering the fleur-de-lys. "He does forgive you, as far as the east is from the west. He doesn't see that when He looks at you, and neither do I."

Julianne laid the Bible upon the table and looped her arms around his waist. "And what do you see?"

"Don't you know?" A lump bobbed behind his cravat before he smiled, sending warmth to the tips of her toes. "I see my wife."

Chapter Nineteen

⚜ ⚜ ⚜

NOVEMBER 1720

Marc-Paul pulled his paddle through the mat of duckweed covering the bayou, vigilant for alligators. Mist muted both sound and color so that the pirogue floated in eerie quiet. Grey Spanish moss dripped from blackened branches, ghostlike in the fog-bleached air.

Here on the Bayou Saint-Jean, halfway between New Orleans and Lake Pontchartrain, misgiving nipped at him. He'd managed to speak with Dancing Brook, but her observations about Pascal's demeanor and activities brought more questions than answers. Whatever he was up to, Running Deer seemed part of it, from what she'd shared. Since the Chitimacha slave and his master had joined the hunting party this morning, it had been easier to leave Julianne alone in New Orleans.

Still, suspicions dogged Marc-Paul. Perhaps he was too distrustful of his fellow settlers. But ever since Simon's gun had been stolen right out from under Julianne, and because he still couldn't identify the thief, he'd begun to think of New Orleans by its Choctaw name. Town of strangers.

The ache in his neck crept upward until it filled his head as well. He couldn't decide whether it was the constant strain of the Chickasaw war on their resources or merely a casualty of sleeping on the chaise for two weeks while Vesuvius snored beside Julianne.

Red Bird rowed noiselessly in front of him. He'd come to New Orleans to trade more scalps for merchandise on behalf of himself and other Choctaw who knew no French, but his presence on the hunt was a kindness unpaid for by trade goods.

The pirogue emerged from the swamp and into dawn's half-light as they neared the lake. After beaching the vessel, the hunters slung their flintlocks over their shoulders and climbed out.

The rising sun lifted the fog, revealing wild geese—tens of thousands of them, if not more—covering Pontchartrain fifty yards ahead. Marc-Paul's stomach rumbled at the sight. After months of eating corn, the colonists were hungry for meat, and he could almost taste the game. Andre, Gaspard, Jean, and Laurent quietly headed west, keeping their distance from the shoreline until they were ready to move in.

Marc-Paul and Red Bird trailed Pascal and Running Deer. No words passed between them, lest they disturb the waterfowl. The ground became soft and wet beneath their steps as they closed in on the geese.

When he was close enough to the water's edge, Marc-Paul staked his spot in a band of cattails. Pausing, he indulged in the tranquility of the moment. The sun radiated its bloodred glow through the thinning vapors lingering above the water. A great blue heron browsed among the pickerel weed spiking up through the shallows of the lake. Aware that others would be firing their muskets soon, he reached for his powder horn and shot pouch.

"Gaspard!"

Frowning, Marc-Paul turned toward Andre's reedy voice. He was running toward Gaspard, who dropped his gun and fell to his knees.

Then a blood-curdling cry ripped through the mist. A war cry. In the same instant that Marc-Paul whirled around, thousands of geese exploded from the lake behind him, honking and flapping their wings in a cacophony that only added to the bedlam. The hunting party, exposed and backed up against the lake, had become the prey.

Red Bird's neck arced as tight as the bow in his hand as he drew back his arrow and let it fly. "Get down!" he shouted in French, his voice barely audible above the rioting geese filling the sky.

Crouching, Marc-Paul loaded his gun with a ball rather than game shot, cursing the precious seconds ticking by. He looked up. Saw an arrow strike Andre in the leg. The young man's mouth opened, but any cry that issued forth was swallowed up by the geese's frantic clamor. He dragged his leg behind him as he tried to run. Another arrow struck him in the back. Then a third. He was fifty yards from Marc-Paul when he collapsed next to Gaspard.

A native darted from the swamp and across the marsh toward Andre, hair flying behind him as he ran. His tomahawk was in one hand, his scalping knife in the other. Blood rushed in Marc-Paul's ears as he trained his sights on the moving target. He squeezed the trigger, absorbed the recoil in his shoulder, and watched the ball tear through the native's tattooed throat. The knife and hatchet dropped to the ground just before he fell.

"Look out!" Pascal's words drove Marc-Paul to duck just as an arrow sailed over him.

Between geese and guns, he could not untangle the noise between his ears. Shots fired, but were they French or British balls peppering the air? At least one other native fired from between the trees still wreathed in haze, but how many there were, he couldn't guess. Urgency washed over him in a wave of heat. He reached for his powder and shot once more. Sweat slicked his palms. Red Bird had disappeared from view, but Marc-Paul dared not look for him now, lest he spill his powder or drop the wadding into the marsh. The minute it took him to arm the weapon seemed to last an hour.

Someone was shouting. Jean? Laurent? Surely Andre and Gaspard were already gone. Hunched over one bent knee, Marc-Paul scanned the edge of the swamp, musket to his shoulder. A red-painted face flashed between the cypress and tupelo gum trees. Marc-Paul swiveled, his sights trained on the movement, grinding his knee into the chill, wet ground. An impossible shot. He might as well have been aiming for a woodpecker.

The relentless squawking and flapping overhead scraped his ears. Then the native in the swamp drew an arrow from his quiver, and the noise fell away.

A blast sounded from behind, and the thick smell of sulfur choked the air. A scream filled with terror and pain exploded from Pascal. Rattled, Marc-Paul lowered his flintlock for an instant, then suddenly fell backward into the marsh.

Fire combusted inside his chest. Eyes squeezed shut against the white-hot pain, his hand instinctively moved toward it and stopped when it bumped something smooth and hard. Groaning, he opened his eyes and closed his fingers around the dogwood shaft of an arrow rising from his flesh. He stared blankly into the sky above him, where the last of the geese flapped away.

⚜ ⚜ ⚜

Julianne sat at the work table in Etienne's quarters and ground corn into meal while Vesuvius slept on her feet.

"When the captain said to keep an eye on you, I'm quite certain he didn't mean for you to do my work." Etienne wrapped his hands around his cup of coffee, and Julianne winced inwardly at the sight of his swollen knuckles. Surely his arthritis made grinding corn a painful task, though he never complained.

"Nonsense. I enjoy your company, and I enjoy being useful." She let the pestle rest in the mortar and sipped her coffee.

"If the hunting is going as planned, we'll have roast goose for dinner! But in the meantime . . ." Etienne wiped the coffee from his mouth with the back of his hand and went to the fire. With a grunt, he knelt on one knee and stirred among the ashes with a poker until he uncovered four small bundles and rolled them onto the hearth. "A little something your husband taught me. It's called *paluska holbi*. It's the Choctaw's most basic cornbread." He placed them on the table before her, then wiped his hands on his breeches. "Your light repast, madame." His eyes twinkled with accomplishment.

"Merci, monsieur!" Julianne smiled. Each bundle was wrapped tightly in cornhusks and tied with a strip of the same. Taking one, she carefully peeled the husks away to reveal a neat roll of cooked cornbread. "How very clever! Marc-Paul taught you this?"

"He learned it from a young man who lived with the Choctaw for more than a year. Learned everything about them, and brought it back to share with us. Clever, indeed." Etienne beamed.

A lump formed in Julianne's throat. *Merci, Benjamin.* Tears glossed her eyes as she tore off a piece of the steaming bread and placed it in her mouth. It was a connection to her brother, however small, and she was grateful.

Etienne eased himself onto the bench and drummed the three fingers of his right hand on the table. "I do hope the hunt is going as planned." Deep furrows carved his brow.

"You worry?"

Etienne took a slow drink of his coffee. "It's that Pascal Dupree character. I never trust a man with dimples." He shook his head with conviction. "It just doesn't suit."

Julianne chuckled. "There are more substantial reasons not to trust a man than his appearance."

Frowning, Etienne tilted his head. "True, true. But the dimples—the way he flashes them about like a coquet—no self-respecting man does that unless he's up to no good. At least, no Canadian. No offense to you or the captain."

Laughing, Julianne resumed grinding the corn.

Her hand stilled.

Shouts ricocheted between the house and Etienne's quarters. She knew those voices. Jean. Laurent. But Marc-Paul's baritone was not among them.

Dropping her bowl, Julianne leapt up and hastened outside to see her husband stumbling toward the house, supported by Jean. His face contorted in obvious pain, his complexion was the color of death itself. He held the shaft of an arrow steady in his chest.

Gasping, she dashed ahead of them and opened the front door to the house. Everything else in the room blurred, and every sound muted as Jean helped Marc-Paul stumble through the salon, then heaved him up onto the dining table.

Julianne rushed to him, aware of Etienne close behind her, and laid her hand on his brow. His eyes were ringed with dark grey bands.

"It must come out, ma chérie," he rasped. His hand moved, and she grasped it. The cold of his skin seeped into her palms. "Don't pull the shaft or it will release the arrowhead. It will burrow deeper, and you'll have to fish for it. Cut it out. Now."

Shock numbed her. The air stretched thin and tight as she struggled to grasp whether this was actually happening or if it were only a vivid nightmare. The feathers at the top of the arrow's shaft were bold and stiff, a flag of conquest staking its claim. *No. You will not have him.*

"Etienne, set some water to boil, then bring brandy and clean rags." Her voice sounded distant. She gave orders as though she were removed from the patient, as though he were only another ailing soldier at the garrison. As though the arrow in his chest did not pierce her very heart as well.

"What the devil happened out there?" Etienne growled on his way out the door.

"A raid," Jean shot back. "Is he going to make it, Julianne?" His face was blotched with pink and red.

"He's strong. He'll make it." *Show them, mon coeur.*

Etienne burst back in with a bottle of brandy.

"Help him drink it." Julianne hurried from the room, donned her birthing apron, and retrieved her midwifing kit. Scissors, small knife, suturing needle, string, probe. *Help me now, Lord,* she prayed but did not wait for her hands to stop shaking before returning to the dining room.

Shadows drooped beneath Etienne's eyes. "He won't drink."

Julianne stifled a groan. She knew of Marc-Paul's aversion to alcohol but had no idea it precluded medicinal purposes as well. "Hold him fast."

Jean paled but laid his hands on one of Marc-Paul's arms. Etienne held the other.

"You can do this," Marc-Paul whispered, his brown eyes glazed.

Julianne nodded. "It's going to hurt. Please drink the brandy."

"Don't need it. Make the incision wider than the arrowhead." His gaze landed on the feathers at the end of the shaft. "The small feathers mean it's a small arrowhead."

Jean looked away, but Etienne remained steadfast, talking to Marc-Paul to distract him. The Canadian slipped into his French patois as he spoke, and the current of his words kept Julianne moving. After tucking her lace flounces up into her sleeves at her elbows, she cut away his shirt until his entire chest was exposed.

"Julianne," Jean said quietly above Etienne, "if you could bring Angelique from Denise's womb without so much as looking, you can pull an arrowhead from his chest."

Confidence crept cautiously back into place, and she gently probed the wound with her fingers. She needed to know the orientation of the arrowhead before she knew which direction to make the incision. "I'm sorry," she whispered, and slipped her index finger down into the wound until she felt the sharp edges buried there. Dark red rivulets of blood flowed from the open wound and down Marc-Paul's side, and Etienne caught them with rags.

Knife steady in her hand now, Julianne clenched her teeth and incised her husband's skin to make wider the passage. The cords of his neck pulled taut as she separated his flesh, and he groaned between gritted teeth. Then he relaxed, unconscious.

"Enough," she said, and laid down her knife. Once more she reached into his body, this time with her finger and thumb, and more blood seeped out, filling her nostrils with its sweet, metallic smell. Firmly she grasped the slippery arrowhead, and the feathers quivered in response. "Almost there." Slowly, she pulled straight up until the arrow was completely free and laid it on the table at his feet. So narrow a weapon, yet how frail the human body beneath it. "Done," she pronounced, and pressed a rag to stanch the scarlet flow from the wound. "The worst is over, mon amour." Even in his unconscious state, pain lined his handsome face. She pressed a kiss to his brow before straightening.

Etienne exhaled. When he looked up, his blue eyes were glossed with tears. "I was right to worry. Hang it all."

"It happened so fast. Red Bird was with him, and so were Pascal and Running Deer." Jean rubbed his eyes and shook his head.

Julianne met Etienne's troubled gaze before turning back to Jean. "What happened?"

"The fog—we must have paddled right under their noses when we passed through the swamp."

Her heart lodged in her throat. "Here? So close?"

"There were three of them, by my count. Arrows came flying before any of us got a shot off. The commotion set all the geese to flight, and the blasted honking drowned out everything else. I couldn't tell where the raiders were coming from, between the mist and the trees. Laurent and I were farthest from the action. Andre and Gaspard—Marc-Paul's soldiers—they didn't survive."

"You mean—" For a moment, horror snatched Julianne's words. Recovering, she placed Etienne's gnarled hands over the rags on Marc-Paul's chest and threaded her needle. "Please continue."

"I saw one of the savages run toward Andre after he fell, hatchet and knife in hand, but one of our hunting party shot him before he reached the poor lad. Might have been Marc-Paul or Pascal, I couldn't tell."

"What of the other natives? Still at large?" Etienne asked. He stepped aside, and Julianne began stitching Marc-Paul's flesh back together.

"I wasn't witness to the act, but besides the warrior shot by musket, another was full of arrows and lying in his own blood by the end. Maybe Red Bird killed him, maybe Running Deer. I spied Red Bird giving chase after the third native into the swamp."

Julianne focused on the silver flash of her needle as it worked. She heard Etienne inquire after Pascal.

"Pascal lives, but he was badly injured. Running Deer said it was an accident with his musket. I didn't see it happen, nor did I see the gun he blames. Running Deer cast it into the lake. Said it was ruined, anyway." Jean shook his head. "You wouldn't recognize Pascal now, at least on one side of his face."

Two Faces. The name Dancing Brook had called Pascal sprang to mind, sending chills over her skin. Who could have known the name would fit his physical appearance as well? *What sort of accident could do such a thing?*

"Will he make it?" Jean asked again, now daring to look at Marc-Paul.

Julianne's throat tightened. She tied off the silk thread and cut it. She had no idea of the extent of the damage already done to nerves, tissues, and muscle. She could not guess when the bleeding would stop, or if it would continue beneath his skin, unseen, until he died of it. "I've never seen this type of wound before." She looked to Etienne. "But you have, haven't you, during your years in fur trade?"

"Seven times." Etienne's voice was gruff, his nose red. He cursed beneath his breath.

"How many survived?" Jean voiced the question that Julianne was almost afraid to ask.

"Two."

The word struck like a blow, and all breath left her lungs at once. Streaked with Marc-Paul's blood, her hands clenched the rags that she had held against his wound, and something inside her screwed tighter. *Don't take him!* her heart cried out. *Not him too!* Her limbs shook, even as Etienne placed his crooked hand on her back. In her mind, she was at the levee again, heaping rocks and earth upon another grave, with no one else there beside her. The gravity in the room increased, and Julianne bowed her head to its pull.

"*Ma foi,* Julianne!" Lisette's voice sounded suddenly beside Julianne, yanking her from Marc-Paul's future grave. She had not even heard her come in. "I'm so sorry!" Lisette was saying, wisps of blond hair framing blue eyes wide with concern. "Laurent told me what happened. Show me where the water is, and I'll get to work."

The wound sewn shut, Julianne and Lisette did all they knew how to do. Salve. Poultice. Tea. Etienne helped move Marc-Paul into the bed and reluctantly retired to his quarters for the night, long after everyone else had gone home. Marc-Paul's complexion improved from ash grey to a pale shade of his normal self, but he would not be out of danger for some time.

Vesuvius curled up on the bed beside him and nuzzled his stocky head beneath his master's hand. Wrinkles folded the little dog's brow, and he looked at Julianne from between Marc-Paul's fingers with eyes that reflected her own anxiety.

Fire crackled in the hearth, its amber glow chasing shadows to the corners of the room. Arms crossed over her nightdress, Julianne wore a steady circuit over the bearskin rug, but her thoughts looped and twisted like brier canes with thorns that pierced her to the quick.

The fleur-de-lys on her shoulder burned as if the hot iron had singed her skin mere moments ago. Surely it carried a curse. Could there be any other explanation for all this loss? All she wanted was to bring forth life, but ever since she'd been branded, it seemed her life was marked by death. Her brother Benjamin. Simon. Her baby. And now . . . She strode to Marc-Paul's side and laid her hand on his pallid cheek. She bent her ear to his lips to hear him breathe.

Vesuvius licked his hand, and Julianne slid to the floor and stared into the dancing flames. Memory flickered, and she saw Marc-Paul at every key moment from the last ten months: in the Saint-Nicolas Tower in La Rochelle; at the St. Jean Inn on arriving in New Orleans; at Bienville's residence as he recommended her as colony midwife. He was there with her at Simon's grave, had carried her home after she'd been flogged. Marc-Paul had dug her baby's grave. Kissed her. Held her. Married her and made his house her own but did not take her as was his right.

Tears squeezed from the corners of her eyes and spilled down her cheeks. Her husband could die tonight, before she had ever shown him that she loved him. For all the pieces of her heart that she'd already laid to rest, the ache in her chest now consumed her.

Julianne had slippery elm to aid in the healing of wounds. Cat's foot to cleanse the body of poisons. But what was the cure for regret? Was there a tincture, a powder, a root, an herbal brew that could remove it from the soul? Regret was a river like the Mississippi, with depths the eye could not measure. Though her body remained on the soft bearskin rug, her heart was immersed in its dark waters, and she struggled to keep from drowning.

Vesuvius whined, and Julianne turned to see him nudging Marc-Paul's limp hand. Rising, she felt his skin and found it cool to the touch. Terror seized her. She pulled the covers down and laid her ear on his bare chest. His pulse was steady, if not strong, but his body trembled with cold.

After pulling the blankets and counterpane back up to his chin, she stoked the fire and added another log. Circling to the other side of the bed, she slipped under the covers. Pressing her body against the length of his to warm him, she rested her head against his muscled shoulder and carefully placed her arm over his waist.

Gently, she stroked his side, from the bottom of his rib cage to his hip. Until her finger dipped into a hollow. Well practiced in seeing the human body by touch, Julianne traced the length of the groove with one finger. It was a scar. Slightly wider than an arrowhead. Questions exploded in her mind. *Was he struck by an arrow before? When? Why? If Etienne knew, why didn't he mention it?* Then hope rushed to the surface with blinding brilliance. If Marc-Paul had survived one arrow, could he not survive another?

Relief kindled inside her, and she brushed featherlight kisses on Marc-Paul's shoulder, his cheek, his lips. Her fingers memorized his body as she ran her hands over his skin to warm him.

It took an arrow near her husband's heart for Julianne to fully feel hers again. She would not lose him now. She must not.

Chapter Twenty

✣ ✣ ✣

Marc-Paul awoke to searing pain in his chest, Vesuvius sprawled at his feet, and Julianne beside him, radiating warmth. His pulse trotted at the sensation of her bare arm on his waist beneath the covers, and he covered her hand with his own.

Julianne's lashes fluttered on her cheeks until her eyes focused on him. "You're up!" She pushed herself up on one elbow.

Marc-Paul tried to sit up but fell back upon his pillow when an invisible dagger twisted where the arrowhead had nested. "Awake, but not up."

"You will be soon. Let's see how we're doing." Lips curving in a gentle smile, she leaned over him to peek beneath the bandage, her hair curling just above her shoulders. Though the fire in the hearth had guttered, her nearness more than compensated for it.

Marc-Paul winced with both longing and the burning in his chest. As soon as she laid the bandage back in place, he caught her wrists, then circled his thumbs on her palms. "Thank you."

Her eyes brimmed with tears. "You're not leaving me, you know."

His lips tipped up on one side. "I'm not leaving you. I love you." At the slightest tug, she lowered her head to his.

"I know you do. I love you too, Marc-Paul, with every piece of my heart," she whispered. "All I have left, I give to you."

The sharp edges of a lump pressed against his throat as he swallowed. "I could ask for no greater gift."

Gently, he entwined her silken hair around his fingers. Her lips swayed against his in a kiss sweeter than honey, and her hand flattened against the uninjured side of his chest. Drinking in the clean, soft scent of her, he yearned to love her with the strength he had but a day ago.

Before he could draw her closer, she pulled away, nose pink, and slid her hand over the frenetic drumming of his heart. "You'll hurt yourself."

Trapping a moan in his chest, he silently conceded that the fire in his wound sliced deeper with the slightest movement. Exhaling, he stretched out his arm as her pillow instead, and Julianne nestled in beside him once more.

Vesuvius roused himself, snorted, and waddled up the bed on the opposite side of Marc-Paul, fully extinguishing any romance in the air with a succession of sneezes.

Julianne laughed. "He never left your side, you know."

Marc-Paul cupped his hand over the pug's head and scratched behind his ears. "And neither did you."

"I should change your dressings. And Etienne will want to know your condition."

"The dressings can wait a moment, and so can Etienne." He kissed her hair. "My soldiers were killed, both of them." His chest constricted. "I fired too late to save them."

"But they will have a Christian burial."

He understood her to mean that their bodies were not cut to pieces, their organs not spilled on the shore. Neither were their scalps taken, he presumed. Small comfort. He would need to write their families in France. The boys were his responsibility.

Something between anger and sorrow pulled at him. Closing

his eyes, he sank into it and saw the bloody mayhem all over again. Heard the undulating warbles, the honking geese. The shouts. A deafening blast. And that scream. "Who else was hurt?" Defeat weighted his voice.

Julianne adjusted the covers over them both before resting her hand on his bare waist beneath the sheet. "Pascal. Jean said his musket exploded somehow and burned his face."

Had he been aiming for the hostile who shot Marc-Paul when his musket misfired? "He was looking out for me out there, just like he did when I first arrived in this wilderness. Shouted a warning, and I dodged an arrow."

"Only to receive another." Her tone seemed unimpressed. "I don't understand. I thought the Chickasaw warred with the Choctaw."

Marc-Paul stared at the beams of the open ceiling and at the underside of the cypress planks above them, recalling the natives who had attacked. Their war paint and tattoos had been a blur, but he'd seen enough. "They weren't Chickasaw."

Fear slipped into her eyes. "Who, then? Will they come again? New Orleans is not even fortified!"

"I couldn't see them well enough to tell. Raiders like that don't come into towns, though. They pick off small numbers of people isolated from their communities." Ridges formed on his brow. "Where is Red Bird?"

"Jean says he ran after the third raider, the only one who survived. That's all we know." Her smooth hand slid over his waist, igniting a different sort of burning within him. Then her fingers stopped right on top of his scar. "What happened here?"

The irony. Marc-Paul should have known she would ask. He should have prepared an answer.

"It was an arrow, wasn't it?"

Outside, an owl hooted in the span of his hesitation. He was unwilling to tell the tale he had kept secret even from Etienne, whom he had hired shortly after it happened. Still, he nodded.

"What happened?"

Do not lie to her, his conscience demanded, yet he was loathe to tell her the whole truth. It would only hurt her to know the details. "I was searching for someone I thought needed help. But it turned out he didn't want to be followed. The arrow stopped me." *Please don't ask more.*

Julianne raised herself on her elbow again, and questions swam in her eyes. "You were trying to help?"

He sighed. "Yes. I thought he was lost, or sick, or injured."

"One of your soldiers?"

"Yes."

"Did you find him?"

Benjamin haunted Marc-Paul's memory. The young man had watched an arrow strike Marc-Paul and then turned his back and run away, leaving Marc-Paul to bleed while Red Bird fought the Chickasaw warrior ferociously, hand to hand. "Yes, I found him."

Closing his eyes, he volunteered no further information, and Julianne did not drag it from him, though he sensed she wanted to know. Instead she asked, "Are you cursed to be shot twice with arrows? Or blessed to survive them both?"

"I have you, ma chérie. I am blessed."

A fleeting smile lit Julianne's face before her gaze traveled to the Bible on the bureau. "If we had prayed harder for peace, could we have prevented the arrow from touching you?"

"I don't know," Marc-Paul admitted. "Certainly the hand of God could have nudged the arrow off its path—and maybe He did, for it didn't strike my heart or head. But the greater miracle is for us to have peace and grace in our spirits, no matter what the circumstances."

She sighed. "Miraculous, indeed."

"It can only come from trusting God."

"And trusting each other?" Her fingers tapped his scar once more. Was it a signal that she knew he held back? Or was it merely a wife's loving gesture?

Marc-Paul swallowed. "You can trust me, Julianne. I would never betray you or forsake you. And I know I can trust you." This much, he knew, was true.

⚜ ⚜ ⚜

"His coloring is good," Julianne reported to Etienne and Francoise that afternoon. She dropped more cat's foot into Etienne's pot of boiling water. "The wound site looks as well as it possibly can at this stage. I still prefer taking every precaution, so let's keep bringing him these teas and salves."

"Quite right, and I'm relieved to hear it," gushed Francoise. "I'm only sorry I wasn't able to come sooner. But I see the captain has been in very capable hands between the two of you."

Etienne grunted as he leaned over the steaming brew and sniffed. "I don't understand it, and I certainly can't recommend the smell, but if you think it may aid his recovery, I'll not go against you. I don't suppose ol' dimple-faced Dupree is getting such good care."

Julianne bit back her amusement. "I learned all of this from his slave. If anyone can tend his injuries, Dancing Brook can."

"Oui, mon amie, but would she?" Francoise asked gently.

Julianne regarded her friend's knowing hazel eyes and considered the question. Pascal had smothered Dancing Brook's perfect, healthy babe. Wouldn't she be at least tempted to see him suffer? Would she not consider it justice?

"After what Pascal did to her, and to me, the thought of his pain does not much bother me either," Julianne quietly admitted.

"Oh, I count it slightly enjoyable!" Etienne raised his metal cup of coffee in a toast to himself.

Ignoring the Canadian, Francoise slipped her arm around Julianne's waist below the jagged scars that crisscrossed her back. "He has wronged you greatly, and well I know it. But beware that bitterness doesn't poison you, ma chère. If you feed it, it will eat you up instead. Do you know what I would do, if I were you? I would march over to Pascal Dupree's house and offer to tend him myself."

Julianne's heart rate climbed, and her blood ran hot in her veins. "I'm no longer the colony midwife nor the garrison nurse. Thanks to him, I might add."

Francoise shook her head. "Don't do it for duty. Don't do it just for his sake either, but for yours. Love your enemy, Julianne, and that poison in your heart will disappear."

"Love him? How?" Julianne crossed her arms, rebelling against the entire idea.

"You behave like you love him—even if you don't care for him—and your heart will release its bitterness. You practice grace."

Grace. Julianne sighed. She craved it for herself, but she hadn't considered extending it to Pascal Dupree. "I'll visit him," she said at length. "But I am not like to enjoy it."

"Visit Pascal the rascal?" Etienne gaped. "Oh no you don't."

"I would like to see how Dancing Brook fares too."

Etienne rubbed the back of his neck and muttered an unholy oath. "Then I'm going with you. I'll not be having you off alone with that man, even if he is blown to shreds." He jammed his felt hat down over his scraggly grey hair.

Francoise beamed. "I'll stay and keep vigil with the captain. Just tell me when he ought to have this tea."

After mixing up a paste for Pascal's burns, Julianne left instructions with Francoise and headed to Pascal's house with the trusty Canadian at her side. They walked in companionable quiet, the only sound their off-tempo footsteps on the path that edged the swamp. A damp wind flapped Julianne's cape against her skirts and drove dark, low-hanging clouds across a pewter sky.

When they reached Dupree's property, it was Running Deer who answered the door.

"I've come to see the patient." Julianne held up her jar of paste. "To ease his pain. May we come in?"

Running Deer stepped back to allow them inside. "I tell him. You wait."

Moments later, he returned and motioned them to follow as he led them to Pascal's bedchamber. The sickly smell that filled the room was so thick, Etienne brought his hat over his nose. Julianne took shallow sips of air through her lips as she approached her patient's bed.

The right side of Pascal's face resembled raw meat. Eyebrow and eyelashes singed off, it was a blessing his right eyelid remained. His brow, nose, cheek, and chin were a mass of blisters, some of them weeping. In some places, his skin was charred black and curling. The burn traveled down his neck and covered his right shoulder as well.

The green eyes Pascal turned on her were pleading. "Help me," he rasped through cracked and blistered lips.

After signaling to Etienne to fetch brandy from Running Deer, Julianne hurried to open her jar of ointment. She knew without asking that no one had tended these wounds, not even his slaves. She knew Dancing Brook's reasons but wondered if Running Deer had his own for watching his master suffer, or if he merely had not known how to help. Julianne's conscience pricked her. She'd been wrong to believe seeing Pascal like this wouldn't bother her. She still hated what this man had done, but she eked no pleasure from his pain. Bitterness receded, and pity grew in its place.

"Officer Dupree, I have an ointment of comfrey here that will help your skin heal. I'll be as tender as I can as I apply it."

Etienne returned with a bottle and cup, and Julianne urged Pascal to drink it. Brandy dribbled down his stubbled chin, and she dabbed it with a napkin. How handsome he had once been, she mused. How fleeting his charm.

With the utmost delicacy, she bent and dabbed the herbal concoction onto Pascal's raw skin with her fingertip, beginning near his hairline. As she moved further down his face, he began to shake.

"I'm sorry," she whispered, and paused to straighten her aching back.

"Do it," he muttered, and the alcohol on his breath pinched her nose. He groaned as she continued, and veins pulsed on his arched neck.

Oh, the agony she could inflict on him now! Though Francoise's gentle words still echoed in her mind, the stripes on her back tingled as if urging retribution. Despite the pity she felt for him, in the dark corners of her heart, the embers of her hatred still glowed.

Outside, rain suddenly pounded the earth like a steed under spurs. It sprayed in between the window frame and the oiled linen shade, misting Julianne as she worked. Etienne sprang forward and held the shade in place.

"Marc-Paul," Pascal said with ragged voice. "How does he fare?"

Julianne cocked her head, surprised that he should inquire. "He does well, considering."

He pursed his lips and grunted. "I have no ill will toward him, you know. I never did. Did he send you to me today?"

She shook her head.

"Then why come?"

"I told you," she sighed. "To offer relief." She replaced the lid on her jar of ointment. "I'll leave this here so you can apply it again yourself, as needed. Now I'll visit Dancing Brook and then be on my way."

His eyes hardened into cool jade. "No you won't."

"Pardon me?"

Pascal turned his face toward the storm outside. "She's run away."

Julianne's breath hitched. Sadness and hope vied for the upper hand, for while she was sorry she would never see the young woman again, she could only rejoice that Dancing Brook was free and pray for her safe and happy reunion with her family.

Quietly, Julianne bid Pascal adieu, and Etienne escorted her outside onto the gallery. Already she could see water collecting in footprints on the ground. Her mules would be ruined in the mud.

"Just a moment, if you please." Turning her back to Etienne, she sat in one of the chairs and removed her shoes, untied her ribbon garters, and peeled her stockings from her feet. She stuffed them all into her apron pockets, resolved to go barefoot instead.

Just as they were about to step off the gallery, lightning flashed behind Pascal's house.

"Oh! Before we go, Etienne, give me a moment to fetch some more herbs from the woods along the bayou. Dancing Brook showed me right where to get them, and I know I'll need extra for Marc-Paul. Stay here out of the rain, if you like."

"And let you have all the fun playing in the mud? Not at all!" Lightning stabbed the sky once more, illuminating Etienne's grin. "Lead the way."

Julianne pulled the hood of her cape over her head, raised the hem of her skirts, and dashed out into the rain. Sand squished between her toes as she ran along a ridge through the swamp surrounding Pascal's property. The sky was the color of wet stone, and the copper foliage on the bald cypress trees more vivid by contrast. Etienne was close at her heels when she came to a halt on the higher ground bordering the bayou.

"What are we looking for, exactly?" He sat in the crook of a live oak limb to catch his breath.

"Clusters of tall, dark-green straws." Her hair clung to her rain-dampened neck as she stooped to inspect the ground. Overhead, the naked trees shook in the wind. "When taken as a strong tea, it's good for blood infections. I want to keep giving it to Marc-Paul just in case that arrowhead was dipped in poison."

"So it's green straws against poisoned arrows, eh?"

Julianne chuckled as Etienne pushed himself off his perch and slowly paced between dwarf palmettos. "Every precaution, Etienne. Every precaution." Her feet sank deeper into the soft ground as she searched. "Found some!" Squeezing her skirts between her knees, she made a spade of her hand and dug deep under the plant. If she could lift it out with some roots intact, she'd replant it in Etienne's garden. "Voilà!" Triumphant, she presented the plant cupped in her hands.

"Allow me." Etienne took it from her, and she wiped her hands on her apron.

The mud was up to her ankles now. She turned on the ball of her foot to leave, and it pressed down onto something hard. It wasn't a crayfish chimney.

Frowning, she twisted her foot once more and felt it again. A ring of sorts, laid on top of a flat, hard surface. "Something's here."

"Aside from the mud, you mean?"

She dropped to her knees, abandoning her skirts to their fate, and dug through the mud with her hands until her fingers clasped an iron ring. Probing around it, she found unsanded wood. Laying her palm flat, she swept over its rough grain in search of its edges. Confusion rippled through her. "Etienne. It's a door."

"What the devil?" He placed the plant aside and stiffly dropped to the ground beside her. Rain streamed from his tricorn hat as he bent over the space. Together they scooped away the mud until the entire door was uncovered.

Thunder rattled the trees as Etienne pulled up on the ring. The board was four feet by four feet and came off like a lid. He set it on the pile of mud beside him and backed away. "Can you see anything?"

Julianne lay on her stomach and peered into the hole. Lightning flashed. She gasped. "It's a cache of food! Barrels of flour and wine, far more than one person should have. There must be a dozen barrels squirreled away down here, maybe more, while the rest of New Orleans goes hungry. I see sacks of corn too, and beans." Chilled through to her skin, she sat back on her heels. "Is he selling it piecemeal for personal gain, or keeping it for himself?"

"Either way, he's a lying, thieving cheat!"

She was already replacing the lid and covering it over with mud. "Help me. Quickly." But Etienne did not need to be prodded. In no time they had re-hidden the hatch, though Pascal was not like to come outside in his condition, and certainly not in a storm.

"Bienville must know at once." She kept her voice low.

"I'm coming with you." Etienne's tone left no room for argument as he scooped up the plant she had come for.

They clambered back down the bayou's levee, Julianne restraining her pace to match Etienne's as they took the sand ridge through the swamp and threaded their way diagonally through the settlement to the southernmost corner. As they covered the distance between New Orleans and Bienville's residence, the rain that drummed on the Mississippi filled her ears.

Etienne knocked on the door. As Julianne waited for Caesar to answer, she realized with a start the state of her disarray. Sluicing the rain from her cheeks, she then smoothed her hair and pulled her cape more snugly about her shoulders. She hadn't seen Bienville since being dismissed from her position. She prayed he would see her now.

The door opened.

"Hello, Caesar," she began. "We need to see the governor. It's a matter of grave import."

He held the door open, and she and Etienne stepped inside, dripping on the polished wood floor.

"What's all this?" Bienville came around the corner, looking as fierce as he ever had.

"I beg your pardon, monsieur." She curtsied as graciously as she could, while Etienne bowed beside her, and noticed with horror that she stood in a puddle of rainwater with mud-plastered feet. She dropped her skirts and cape back into place.

His face like a gargoyle of Notre-Dame, the governor crossed his arms. "You're the midwife I hired. And dismissed, let it not be forgotten. The criminal. If you're here to beg for your old position, you're wasting your time and mine."

Julianne shook her head, but her mouth was suddenly dry. Pascal had been the one to expose her. Would Bienville not suppose it was pursuit of revenge that brought her here now?

"We've found a cache of hidden food. Thought you might have use for it, seeing as your soldiers are hungry—not to mention the rest of us." Etienne spoke with an ease Julianne did not feel. "Etienne Labuche, manservant for Captain Marc-Paul Girard—and fellow Canadian. At your service." He held her plant behind his back.

Bienville cocked an eyebrow. "How much food?"

Julianne gathered her courage. "Barrels of flour, wine, some bags of corn and beans, and the rest I couldn't see. I regret that this news comes on the heels of the attack at Lake Pontchartrain."

"During which her husband, Captain Girard, was injured," Etienne put in. "If you'll just come with us, we'll take you to the spot."

"And just where is this alleged store?"

"Near the property of Pascal Dupree." Etienne had the good sense not to gloat.

Bienville's face darkened. "Take me at once."

They did.

By the time Julianne, Etienne, Bienville, and Caesar arrived back at the woods along the bayou behind Pascal's home, the rain had stopped. With the shovel Caesar had brought, Etienne scraped the mud from the door and lifted the lid. In the moment Bienville peered down into the hole, fear cycled through Julianne. *It's all gone. He moved it already; we're too late.* But it was still there.

When Bienville looked back at her, his eyes burned into hers. "How came you upon this?" A muscle twitched in his jaw.

She told him.

He turned to Caesar. "Take these stores to the Company of the Indies' warehouse. I have an interrogation to conduct."

Chapter Twenty-one

✤ ✤ ✤

Stunned at the report Julianne and Etienne had just given him, Marc-Paul tried to push himself upright, but the sharp stab in his chest persuaded him to reconsider. Leaning back on his pillows once more, he glanced at the empty cup of tea Francoise had brought him before returning to her inn and wondered how long it would take to ease his pain.

"You didn't happen to see Simon's gun in that hole, did you?" he asked Julianne.

She shook her head. "Just food."

A sigh swelled in his chest before he released it. "Still a crime."

"We were right to report it." Etienne stood with his hat in his hands. Wiry grey hair that had escaped his queue straggled limply at his neck. "You would have done the same."

"You were right. But, mon coeur"—he turned to Julianne— "Pascal must have reckoned it was you who found it and reported it to Bienville."

Julianne straightened her soiled skirts. "Yes. He was already suspicious of my presence at his home. He'll never believe now that my intention truly was only to bring the salve and then to find more healing plants. If I was already his enemy before this, I have only given him more reason to hate me. What will he do? What can he do?"

Marc-Paul cursed the injury that kept him abed. He would stand if he could and wrap her in his arms, heedless of the mud. As it was, he could only reach out and take her cold hand in his. "I'll get an order from Bienville. If anyone lays a finger on you, he'll learn the other end of the whip. Courage, ma chérie."

Etienne excused himself, and Julianne whisked to the dressing room for dry clothes, leaving Marc-Paul alone with his melancholy. He should have known Pascal had not given up gambling. Far from it—he'd only gotten better at hiding the contraband he planned to use to pay any future debts. Marc-Paul groaned. If he'd had the courage of his convictions last summer to report Pascal's theft at the commissary, Julianne would have been left out of this entire mess.

A knock sounded down the hall, followed by the thud of Vesuvius jumping from a chair to the floor and the click of his claws as he ran to the door. At the sound of his barking, Julianne emerged from the dressing room in a fresh gown but still pale.

"Let Etienne see to it." Marc-Paul offered her a smile, and she nodded.

Moments later, Etienne returned to the bedchamber. "The governor to see you."

Julianne's eyes rounded as she looked at Marc-Paul. "You can't receive him in the salon. It's still too soon for you to be up."

"Quite right. Send him in."

Julianne flew to her toilette table and pinned a fresh lace cap over her wet hair. She was standing at the bedside again, spine straight, chin up, when Bienville darkened the doorframe.

"Girard. Don't stay in that bed too long. I've lost enough men this week."

Marc-Paul sensed Julianne bristle beside him. "What news do you bring?"

"I have no proof that cache belonged to Pascal Dupree."

Marc-Paul gritted his teeth. Felt the muscles tensing in his neck.

"That is not to say I believe him to be innocent," Bienville continued. "I have neither the time nor the interest in conducting an investigation. I can't jail him. But I can transfer him. The Yazoo post just lost an officer and six soldiers in a Chickasaw attack. They'll be glad of a replacement. His slave I'm keeping here, to serve the Company of the Indies. Retribution of sorts."

"I thought you said you can't prove he did it," Julianne said.

Bienville smiled grimly. "And he cannot prove he didn't."

Marc-Paul glanced at his wife. The relief in her eyes reflected his own. "Thank you."

Etienne appeared again in the doorway. "Pardon me. Room for another visitor in there? Red Bird."

"Bring him in," Bienville boomed. "I want to hear what he has to say."

Marc-Paul placed his palms on the mattress, ready to push himself up, when he felt Julianne's hand on his shoulder. "Can I trust you to not get up?" she whispered. "If so, I'll let you men hold counsel without me." She slipped out of the room just before Red Bird entered.

"I'm glad to see you well," Marc-Paul began, but the Choctaw looked haggard. No scalps were tied around his chiseled waist. "I take it you did not overtake the raider, then."

"I did."

"And?" Bienville thundered. "Where is his scalp?"

Red Bird turned cool eyes on the governor, his face nearly devoid of emotion. "On his skull, right where I left it."

Dread snaked through Marc-Paul's middle. Surely Red Bird wouldn't betray him. Would he?

"Explain yourself." His eyes dark and threatening, Bienville drew himself up to his full height. "Who is to blame for killing two of my men and injuring two others?"

"Choctaw."

Heat flashed over Marc-Paul's face. "The pro-British faction."

"What?" Bienville's voice was filled with fury. "Did they not receive enough presents? Do they prefer the nation that enslaved their people for years?"

Red Bird appeared unmoved. "They say if it weren't for your policy of attacking Chickasaw and British on the Trader's Path, the Chickasaw would have no reason to attack our villages."

"You refer to my policy of paying Choctaw handsomely to inflict justice on the Chickasaw slave traders. The policy that made your people—at least some of them—rich. That policy?" The edge in Bienville's tone rivaled a saber's. Like a true politician, he left out the real reason he paid mercenaries to attack the traders. He was punishing the Chickasaw for giving their deerskins to Britain instead of to France. "You've been loyal to us all these years, Red Bird. And we have always paid you in kind. Why, then, did you not kill the rebels who killed your French brothers? You must have known I'd have paid you for that as well."

Red Bird turned to Marc-Paul and answered Bienville's question as though it had been his. His dark eyes flashed. "I do not wish you to suffer by the hand of any man. I regret your French brothers were killed." His tone was earnest. Apologetic, almost. "But remember, two Choctaw were slain too. When I caught up to the third and saw who he was, I told him he must never try the same tricks here again, and if he did, that I would kill him myself. Our Choctaw chiefs made a war treaty with our French Father. It is not up to us to go against that. But unlike our French Father, we do not kill a young man for his first offense."

Except for his glinting eyes, the Choctaw's expression remained blank. Marc-Paul understood perfectly well, however, that Red Bird referred to Benjamin.

Exhaustion washed over him, weighting his eyelids and limbs. He had been over this with Red Bird before. Desertion was a plague among French colonial soldiers that Bienville did not tolerate. It was a sickness that could wipe out a garrison just as surely as European smallpox had wiped out some native villages, and it could not go unchecked.

The ache in his wound receded somewhat, and suddenly Marc-Paul could barely stay awake. Soon a soft voice filtered through the room, and he registered that Julianne was gently guiding his guests to end their visit. With one last effort, he bid Bienville and Red Bird adieu, heard the door close behind them, and surrendered to the pull of sleep.

⚜ ⚜ ⚜

Julianne curtsied to Bienville one last time as he strode out the front door. When she raised her head, she found Red Bird before her, staring intensely into her eyes. He was nothing like Running Deer. She'd heard Red Bird speaking perfect French moments ago, and yet there was a wildness to him that could not be disguised by the buckskin leggings and linen trade shirt he wore. Her gaze traveled from the copper hoops in his earlobes to the tattoo above his collar. Marc-Paul had mentioned he wanted her to meet this Choctaw, but surely not like this. She felt exposed. Vulnerable. Especially after all that had transpired in the last several days.

"Your eyes," he said. "So much like Benjamin's."

She flinched. "What did you say?"

"We called him Many Tongues."

Her hand flew to her throat, and she felt her heartbeat pulsing there. "Would you please sit? Do you—do you have the time?

We could take tea together—and *paluska holbi*." Did she sound desperate for him to stay? She was.

"*Paluska holbi*?" Something near to a smile bent his lips as he repeated the words as they were meant to be pronounced.

"Oh! Did he learn how to make it from you?"

"From my mother. Fair Sky."

Tears stung her eyes. It took every ounce of control to keep from reaching out and grabbing his hands. "Please," she whispered. "Please tell me more."

He glanced toward the fire glowing in the salon hearth. She led him there, and he sat cross-legged on the bearskin rug on the floor. With a word to him, she swept outside and found Etienne, who agreed to bring in a tray of tea and the Choctaw bread.

Back in the salon, Julianne joined Red Bird on the rug, her skirts spreading about her in a silken puddle. Her hands clamped together in her lap, and the broad lace trim spilling from her sleeves at her elbows fell to the floor near her hips.

Red Bird's eyes softened. "Many Tongues—Benjamin—was very bright. He was eager to learn our ways and our language, and quick to capture everything to his memory. He also made a patient teacher as he taught me his mother tongue."

"He was so young when he was with you, wasn't he? Did he seem lonely?"

Ridges formed on Red Bird's brow. "At first, yes, of course. But my mother all but made him her own son while he was with us. Even before he knew our language, he knew he was welcome. She gave him many signs."

Julianne's throat tightened. "I'm so grateful. I didn't even know he was coming to Louisiana before he left," she confessed. "I certainly had no idea he was to live in isolation—that is, away from everything he was familiar with."

"Many Tongues was not in isolation."

"Forgive me, I misspoke. Won't you tell me about your village?"

Etienne returned with the tea and a small pile of husk-wrapped cornbread. After placing it on the rug between them, he called to Vesuvius and made his exit.

"Please, eat first," she urged, and did the same.

When the bread was gone, Red Bird tossed the corn husks into the fire and watched them blacken and curl before the flames utterly consumed them. Then he told Julianne of the place Benjamin had called home for fourteen months of his life. Of a village much larger than New Orleans, neatly arranged with houses made of river cane and plaster, as warm and strong as any log cabins would be. He told her of the fields where he and Benjamin had turned the earth together before the women maintained the crops, harvested the corn, and cooked it in more than forty different ways. He talked of fishing with bone hooks, using cornbread dough for bait, and of hunting the white-tailed deer with Benjamin. He described the stickball games, which settled disputes between communities. And he explained how Benjamin helped negotiate trade between the Choctaw and the French.

Every word was a brushstroke in Julianne's mind, painting a picture of her brother she could not have imagined. This was why Marc-Paul had wanted her to meet Red Bird. Her understanding of Benjamin's experience in Louisiana was pale and blurred, like chalk drawings on the sidewalks at Montmartre after being trampled by too many feet. Red Bird sketched it for her with vibrant hues.

Her tea was cold in its cup when he stopped sharing. He rose, and she did the same. Gratitude squeezed her heart. "Thank you," she whispered.

As Red Bird nodded in acknowledgment, a shadow passed over his face. Though he didn't say it, she reckoned she was not the only one who missed Benjamin.

⚜ ⚜ ⚜

In the swamps crowding New Orleans, winter settled in a layer of fog and fallen cypress needles. Fire crackling beneath the kettle, Julianne set her morning rhythm to the thud of her knife on the herbs for Marc-Paul's teas, and its beat became to her the music of restoration. Days of tending her husband melted one into another until the hot red swelling around his stitches faded and the fever stayed away. Five days after the raid, the danger was gone—if not the pain—and Marc-Paul returned to work.

Julianne swallowed her dismay at the exhaustion lining his face after his first day back with the garrison.

"He's gone." His gaze stayed on her as he removed his tricorn hat and set it on the bureau. "Pascal left two days ago for the Yazoo post."

A weight lifted from her, and she filled her lungs with the pleasant woodsmoke scent wafting from the hearth. As she exhaled, tension vacated her body and mind. At last she was rid of Pascal Dupree.

Marc-Paul enfolded her in an embrace, the cold brass buttons of his coat embossing her cheek. "It was Pascal and his wooden horse that first put you into my arms, you know."

Julianne's mind whirred, scarcely able to digest all that had happened since that dreadful day. Stepping back, she slipped her thumbs beneath the lapels of his coat and lifted it off his shoulders. He winced as he shrugged his arms out of the sleeves, a signal that beneath his crisp uniform, the site of his wound was still tender.

"Now that he's gone, you feel safer, don't you?" he asked.

"Much." She untied the cravat at his neck and pulled it off.

"So safe, in fact, that you no longer need my protection?" he teased.

Julianne smiled into his rich brown eyes. "I'd never dismiss your protection." She slid her hand over his chest, the linen soft and warm beneath her fingers. "But I'm far more interested in having your heart."

"You have the whole of it already."

The truth of his declaration was proven in the tenderness of the kiss that followed. Nestled in the confidence of her husband's love, Julianne looked forward to bidding adieu to the year that had wrought so much upheaval in her life.

Chapter Twenty-two

❧ ❧ ❧

JANUARY 1721

While the Choctaw and Chickasaw remained embattled north of Yazoo, the colonists of New Orleans ignored their gnawing hunger with the most determined merrymaking they could muster.

With his wife in his arms and strains of violin and flute in his ears, Marc-Paul waltzed in Bienville's grand hall for the Twelfth Night Ball and shoved those dark thoughts from his mind. Candlelight glittered from the chandeliers and shone on Julianne's swept-up hair. Pearls dipped into the hollow of her creamy throat. Golden silk painted with white flowers traced her figure from her low square neckline to her waist before cascading to the floor. Yes, the people of New Orleans had fashions and music, jewels and lace, perfumes and rouge and wigs. What they did not have, however, was enough food. Pascal's cache, once distributed between New Orleans, Mobile, and New Biloxi, had been quickly consumed. Famine cast its shadow even here at the ball, for those who had the stomach to notice.

The ache in his chest from his hunting injury was but a twinge compared to the emptiness cramping his middle. Surely Julianne felt it too. The ring on her finger spun too easily. Beneath his hand, her corseted waist felt slimmer than ever, and he realized she'd taken in the seams of her gown to fit her narrowing figure when she longed to grow bigger with child. *When the time is right*, she'd told him, *we'll try*. As they whirled among the other dancers, he hung a smile on his face, and her lips curved in response. But the crowd's laughter, as hollow as their bellies, haunted him.

The music ebbed away, the men bowed, and the women curtsied. Just as Julianne raised her head, Marc-Paul felt a tap on his shoulder.

"Pardon the interruption, madame, but if I may borrow your husband for a moment . . ." Bienville stood between them.

"Of course." Julianne quietly slipped away.

"Let's take a walk, Captain." Bienville led Marc-Paul outside and into gardens that mimicked Versailles. The geometric pattern of the walkways between boxwood hedges offered an oasis of order as New Orleans awaited an engineer to plan its streets. The crisp night air breathed a welcome chill over Marc-Paul.

"I have need of you in Biloxi." Bienville looked haggard in the moonlight, almost ghostlike as the brown velvet of his gala costume blended into the night. Louisiana had aged him well past his forty years.

Marc-Paul nodded. "Go on."

"The people there are piling up. The latest report said twelve hundred forty-nine languish there."

Marc-Paul stopped walking. Surely the report was inaccurate. There were only seventy adult civilians, forty-four soldiers, eleven officers, and twenty-two ship captains in New Orleans. Slaves and servants added two hundred more to the population. He could not imagine the need—and the chaos—created by more than one thousand new settlers all in one place. "Sir? Could there be a mistake?"

Bienville grunted. "Indeed, and plenty of them! France sending shiploads of people with so little provisions that they are used up by the time they arrive at Ship Island. That's a mistake. Using ships to ferry more people, but not beasts of burden, and not food enough for the colonists already here. Another mistake. They tell me that in some camps, half of the settlers have already died from hunger or disease. The Company of the Indies has taken the garrison's provisions to feed the settlers who yet live, but barely. 'Borrowing,' they're calling it. The liars."

Marc-Paul resumed walking, hands behind his back. "Just how reduced is the garrison's commissary, then?"

"Corn and beans. And not much of that. The soldiers will starve. Unless . . ."

Marc-Paul sighed. "You want me to ask the Biloxi and Pascagoula to allow the soldiers to winter with them again." And eat their food, and sleep in their homes, with their daughters.

"You're the only one I trust. Just remind the men that they should not expect to marry any dark-skinned maidens, whatever feelings should arise. We are here to settle for France, not to create a generation of half-breeds."

"With respect, regardless of any speech I give the men, if the garrison goes native this winter, half-French babies will be conceived."

"Then those children will stay with their Indian mothers rather than muddy the French population with their uncivilized natures." Bienville's tone was matter-of-fact, albeit slightly impatient, as though Marc-Paul should have realized the due course of these things himself.

He turned his steps to follow the path's curve. Another bend in the semicircle path, and they once again faced the glowing two-story residence. Music and laughter grew louder as they neared but did not eclipse one last concern chafing Marc-Paul's conscience.

"Sir, if our men introduce illness to the natives in their villages, you do realize the Indians will die in droves." Some nations had already been virtually wiped out with European disease and forced to abandon their ghost villages in favor of healthy communities, which sometimes suffered because of it.

Bienville nodded slowly. "I've considered this. But my duty is to my own countrymen. Frenchmen will die if they don't avail themselves of native hospitality. I would to God the case were otherwise. I know I can count on you to follow orders."

"Yes, sir."

"Now, enjoy the rest of the evening. You leave at dawn."

Caesar swung the doors open wide, and Marc-Paul was once again enveloped in warmth and light. When he reached Julianne, he pulled her to his side.

"The time is right," he whispered in her ear and watched the color bloom in her cheeks. If this was to be his last night in New Orleans for some time, there was only one place he wanted to be. It wasn't here.

⚜ ⚜ ⚜

Firelight swayed on the walls of her bedchamber as Julianne counted the weeks since her miscarriage. More than two months had passed. It was time enough.

"I don't want to push you. . . ." Marc-Paul's voice behind her was low, cautious even, as he unclasped the pearls from about her neck and laid them on her toilette table.

She turned to face him, and her breath caught at the longing in his eyes. Her heart hammered against her breast as his gaze trailed from her eyes to her lips to the curves that swelled above her neckline. Julianne lifted her chin, and his warm hands came around her waist as his lips met hers.

Eyes closed, he deepened the kiss, and she melted into him. He pulled the pins from her hair one by one until her locks fell freely about her shoulders. Desire for her husband surged in a way she hadn't known before.

When she slipped her hand around his neck and tugged the ribbon from his queue, he pressed her closer and whispered in her ear, "You're sure?"

Julianne smiled and laid her hand upon his cheek. "If you can see beyond my scars."

With the utmost tenderness, he placed his fingertips upon her back, where ridges still slashed her skin just beneath her silk. "We all have scars, my beautiful one. They make us who we are, and if we let them, they bring us together." His lips curved gently. "Now, let me show you how much I love you."

Tears misted Julianne's eyes as Marc-Paul scooped her up in his strong arms, as he had once before, and carried her to the bed.

PART THREE

Fissures

"Misery reigns always in Louisiana. . . . All is in disorder and misery."
—Sieur Jean-Baptiste Le Moyne de Bienville, 1719

Chapter Twenty-three

⚜ ⚜ ⚜

NEW ORLEANS, LOUISIANA
FEBRUARY 1722

Darkness curtained Julianne's home. In the salon, a fire toasted
the air while Vesuvius warmed her feet. It was Lundi Gras, but
still fatigued from attending a difficult birth the night before,
she only wanted to stay in. Francoise sat across from her, read-
ing aloud from the Gospel of Luke, banishing the silence—at
least for now.

Julianne's concentration slipped, and she pricked her finger
with her large embroidery needle. With a sigh, she set down the
waistcoat and gazed blankly into the flames instead. The fire
hissed and popped, and sparks darted after the smoke.

"Blessed art thou among women, and blessed is the fruit of
thy womb," Francoise read, and Julianne's thoughts turned
inward. It had been sixteen months since her baby Benjamin
had died. Fifteen months since she married Marc-Paul. Absently,
she pressed her hand against the flatness of her belly.

Francoise must have noticed, for she paused and closed the
Bible. "You must not give your disappointment free rein."

"Of course you're right," Julianne conceded, but that did

not ease her aching. Month following month, her courses came and went, and with each failure to conceive another child, she mourned afresh for the son she had lost and for the hope of having another chance at motherhood.

"Your friends miss you, you know," Francoise pressed, and Julianne felt as if a bruise had been touched.

When Denise gave birth a second time, Julianne had attended the delivery and mustered what joy she could for her friend's new baby girl. Then Lisette, who had married Francoise's son, Laurent, grew round with child as well, and envy drove its stake into Julianne's tender heart. Still, she performed the duties of a midwife once more, and Lisette delivered a healthy boy. Self-pity seized Julianne then, twisting her middle as much as the famine ever had. By degrees, a darkness seeped from her broken heart, blackening the edges of her friendships.

"Their babies keep them busy."

"They would be glad of another set of hands, if you have the heart for it."

"Oh, Francoise." Sorrow choked the words from her throat. "Being with them only magnifies the silence of my childless home."

The older woman circled the table between them to sit beside Julianne and pull her into her arms. "Pray for peace."

But Julianne couldn't give up praying for a baby. She was eight and twenty and had delivered babies from girls half her age. Over and over, she begged God for a child, and time and again, He refused her.

"Beware, Julianne. Sorrow breeds isolation, and isolation brings despair."

"I know, and yet I cannot will myself free of it. I feel exiled to disappointment. Everywhere I look, I see mothers with children or pregnant women. New life is all around me, but not in my own womb."

"You're too much alone with your thoughts." Francoise's voice was not unkind.

And fears. But Julianne would not confess it. For during these long absences when duty called Marc-Paul away, her imagination magnified the night sounds to unreasonable proportions. Memory reeled back to the night Matthieu followed her home, and to the night she awoke in the dark to find an intruder had been with her. At least Etienne was close by, and Vesuvius would bark an alarm if warranted. *Maybe.* She wiggled her toes beneath the pug's warm belly, but his snores continued.

"When does the captain come home?"

Julianne turned toward the east-facing windows and imagined Marc-Paul far beyond them, with Bienville at the annual gift-giving ceremony in Mobile, during which Bienville renewed alliances with the Choctaw. "He'll come home in seven weeks."

"Then he'll miss Lent and Holy Week. You must observe Easter with us. I'll not hear otherwise." Francoise's jasmine scent lifted from her hair as she shook her head emphatically.

"I'd be glad to do that, thank you."

Francoise bussed both her cheeks. "And now, I must be getting back. Come visit soon, won't you?"

Julianne agreed and escorted her friend to the door. She could faintly hear the music of celebrations in the settlement.

Unable to think of a reason to stay awake any longer, she returned to the sofa and tucked her embroidery tools back in her *nécessaire.* "Come, pug. Time to take care of business." Scooping up the snoring ball of fur, she took him to the front door, opened it, and tossed him gently to the ground. While she waited for him to do his duty, she leaned against the doorframe, arms crossed over her *robe a la française,* and tilted her head, listening. The music grew louder. The faint glow of torchlight bounced toward her.

Etienne emerged from his quarters and looked from the light to Julianne. "What the devil?"

"Lundi Gras singers," she explained. In Paris, the day before Mardi Gras included carolers in disguise, reveling from house to house. "*C'est bon.*"

"Are you sure, madame? They sound a wee bit tipsy."

"Not at all!" a voice called as they approached the house. "We're just French and merry!"

Julianne laughed, and a group of ten or so singers came prancing up to the house, masquerading in all manner of makeshift costumes, from a shepherdess to a peacock to a pirate, so thorough that she didn't recognize their true identities.

Vesuvius, yapping, barreled into the group.

"Vesuvius!" Julianne called. "Come!"

He ran the opposite direction instead, into the gardens.

Exasperated, she clapped her hands and called again, to no avail. Meanwhile, Etienne ushered the musicians and singers off the property and then headed back to his quarters. "*Bonne nuit*, madame! See you in the morning!"

"*Bonne nuit*, Etienne! Merci!" She waved from the front door, then went inside to slip on her shoes so she could retrieve the ill-trained pug.

Julianne threw open the door once more—and nearly ran headlong into a man holding Vesuvius.

"Looking for this?"

She reared back in surprise, then recovered herself. It was merely a youthful Lundi Gras singer in a pirate costume, delivering her wayward pet. "I thought you'd gone."

He looked at her with one grey eye, the other covered with a patch. "I came back, Julianne. Didn't I tell you I would?"

Her heart lurched into her throat. It couldn't be. She stepped aside, allowing the light to spill around her and onto the young man's features. "What game are you playing?"

"It's me."

A breeze raised the hair on her neck as confusion churned through her. Every sense stood on tiptoe as she fought to gather her wits. Details leapt at her. The scuff of his boot on the doorstep. The smell of tobacco on his breath. That chestnut hair splaying from under his cap with the wildness of a *coureur des bois*. One grey eye, piercing her heart with a saber's point.

"Take off your patch." Julianne heard the shaking in her voice, felt it in her limbs. But it was nonsense. It was madness, and surely he would refuse her request. He was on masquerade, enjoying his anonymity. To reveal himself would spoil his game. He was no one. Surely. Only a fool would think otherwise.

"You are alone?" The stranger's tone held no hint of menace as he peered over her head into the house.

Julianne nodded, for she was no longer able to form a single word.

"Make no sound," he whispered, then slowly removed his hat and pulled the disguise from his head. And there it was. The V-shaped scar above his eyebrow, still visible twenty years after the doctor used spoons to pull him into the world.

With trembling hand, Julianne reached up and feathered its groove with her fingertip. Shock stole all speech. Had she lost her mind? Was she dreaming? He was a dead man. A ghost. He was Lazarus, back from the dead. *Impossible!*

Without waiting for her to speak, he guided her back into her house, then closed and locked the door behind them both. Vesuvius jumped from his arm and trotted away, sneezing. "Surprised to see me, aren't you?"

"Benjamin," she breathed at last. "Is it really you?" She gripped his arms and looked at him across the distance of the last six years. The softness of boyhood had melted away, revealing the lean angles and planes of a young man's jaw and cheekbones. His shoulders were broader. He stood a head taller than he had at fourteen. But it was him.

Benjamin pulled her to himself, wrapped his arms around her. She clutched him with the irrational fear that he might slip away again if she didn't make him stay. Tears squeezed past the shock, and she stood back to look at him once more.

Smiling, he wiped the tears from her cheeks with his handkerchief. "Please don't cry."

"I thought you were dead!"

He nodded. "And deeply do I regret the pain it caused you. If there were another way . . ."

Julianne flinched. "You knew? You let me believe I'd lost you? But why? And how did you know you'd find me here?" Other questions rushed to mind with the crush of a tidal wave. *What have you been doing? Why is there a grave for you if you're still alive? How did you find me?* They frothed and swirled together, roaring between her ears.

Benjamin guided her to the sofa. "You've suffered a terrible shock. Nothing I say may account for it right now."

A log crumbled in the fireplace as she sank onto the cushions and drank in the sight of the grown man sitting beside her. The clock on the mantel chimed, and she realized this moment would not last forever. The minutes marched on with no regard for her inability to keep up. Furtively, she clasped his hand in both of hers.

"Am I now your captive, sister?" He chuckled, but a softness in his eyes belied his casual tone. "Be at ease. I won't disappear quite yet."

"Yet?" The single word cut through all other questions in her mind, driving them in one direction like a river carving a canyon. "Will you not stay?"

"I'd love nothing more than to sit at your knee and exchange stories as we did when we were children. I missed you more than you'll ever know." His voice suddenly hoarse, he raised her hands and brushed a kiss to her knuckles. Then his gaze fixed upon her wedding ring. "But I mustn't tarry."

"Marc-Paul would rejoice to see you again!"

"He's not here, though, is he?" Alarm laced Benjamin's whisper.

She shook her head, and the lines in his face relaxed.

"No. No, Julianne, on this we must agree. You must not speak of me to anyone. Especially to your husband."

She released Benjamin's hands, felt her palms grow damp as they rested on the oriental pattern of her gown. "How is it you know of my marriage? And why should he not know you are well? He speaks so fondly of you."

"Does he? Then he hasn't told you everything. A master of secrets, that one." Benjamin twirled the eyepatch on its string around his finger.

"And so are you, I see." Julianne chafed her arms, suddenly cold. She watched silently as Benjamin knelt to add a log to the fire. "You'd better explain yourself."

"Captain Girard thinks I'm dead because his testimony against me resulted in a death sentence. Your husband wants me dead, Julianne."

"What?" she gasped. A headache swelled beneath her skull, throbbing with every pulse.

"You can see why he must never know I'm still alive. He'll kill me. He'll say it's simply carrying out orders, but he'd as soon murder me in my sleep and call it lawful." He remained on one knee for a moment, gazing in the fire.

"No. No." Julianne pressed her cool fingers to her temples. "How dare you come into my house and say such wretched things! You, who have kept me in grief for you all this time— is that not deception? How do I know you're not lying to me now?" But why would he?

"It's no lie. I vow it's the truth." Brushing his hands on his breeches, he returned to her side and sat.

"Then what did you do to prompt such condemning testimony in the first place?" Her brother was charming but no saint, this much she knew.

Benjamin held her gaze. "It's not what I did that matters, but what he *says* I did."

She licked her lips. "Then what did he say?"

"That I deserted."

Julianne leaned back against the cushions. The conditions the troops faced were horrid indeed, but running from duty and country was dishonorable. Shameful. And punishable by death. "Did you? Desert?"

Benjamin pulled a toothpick from his pocket and stuck it between his lips, chewing the end of it as he had as a child, though she had urged him not to. The quiet sound of his teeth on the narrow stick grated on her ears.

"Tell me." She fought to keep the scold from her tone, but having raised him herself, she couldn't help but feel like his mother as much as his sister.

"I would spare you the details."

"You would keep secret the details. Have a care, *mon frère*. For all my love for you, Marc-Paul is my husband now."

Benjamin crunched the toothpick in one corner of his lips. "What did he tell you about me?"

"He said you were intelligent and quick to learn native tongues. He said he taught you all he knew until your knowledge rivaled or surpassed his own."

Mercifully, he took the toothpick from his mouth, broke it in half with two fingers, and tossed it into the fire. "And that is the crux of it. Have you ever seen, dear sister, what jealousy can do?"

Julianne kept her face a mask. But in her mind, she saw

Adelaide Le Brun, the midwife she had surpassed in both skill and reputation, and poor Marguerite's still body. "Yes." Her chest constricted, and the heat from the fire suddenly grew intolerable. "I have seen what jealousy can do. But I beg you, speak no ill of my husband."

"Then I will say no more." Benjamin stood and wandered about the salon, observing the patterns on the rug, the clock and candlesticks on the mantelpiece, as if he were in a museum. Then he stepped into the adjoining dining room and headed for the sideboard. "You don't mind, do you?" he said as he lifted a pewter pitcher of water and poured himself a cup.

She narrowed her eyes at him as he drank.

"Will you tell me how you came to be here? In New Orleans?" he asked. "Married to the captain?"

Bewildered and exhausted as she was, Julianne relayed to him the scaffolding of events that had led her there. She added the epilogue to John Law's colonizing scheme she had learned last summer. "It finally collapsed, his investors ruined. Law disguised himself as a woman to flee France with his life."

Benjamin's eyebrows raised. "Serves him right. And how does New Orleans fare now?"

"We've had few new colonists since the forced immigration stopped. The worst of the famine ended when a few ships finally arrived with provisions, but the Company of the Indies abandoned the colony, and many concessionaires likewise abandoned their plantations, freed their indentured slaves, then left them here while they returned to France."

"Did they?" His eyes gleamed strangely.

She frowned. "Where have you been that all of this is news to you?"

"Never mind that. Tell me, are you happy now?" His voice gentled as he asked it. "You, above all others, deserve every joy life can bring."

Julianne's thoughts flew to her baby, named for her brother, in the tiny coffin in the levee. She considered her empty womb and the healthy babies given to Denise, Lisette, and prostitutes, servants, and slaves. *Happy?* It would be glib to say she was.

Vesuvius ambled back into the salon, and she reached down, holding her hand out so he would trot to her. He nuzzled his velvet face into her palm.

"What are you doing here, Benjamin? Why have you come back to me? Why now, especially if you cannot stay? Will you stay in the shadows for the rest of your days?"

He smiled, obviously keen to her diversion. "It's in the shadows where I can be of most help to my country."

"I don't understand." Struggling to orient herself, Julianne nestled back once again on the sofa while the pug sat on the hem of her skirt.

"You don't need to. Where is the captain?"

"Mobile," she answered. "The annual gift-giving ceremony with the leaders of the Choctaw villages."

"That's right." Benjamin nodded as if he should have already known this. "Very important, with the war on, eh? Remind me, what is the rate for each Chickasaw scalp? Something like one gun, one pound of powder, and one pound of balls for each?"

"No, two pounds of balls, plus the gun and a pound of powder," Julianne corrected. "And eighty livres of merchandise for each Chickasaw slave."

Benjamin's eyes glimmered as he swirled the water in his cup. "Yes, that's what it was."

She rose and walked toward him, the better to read his features. But before she could ask any more questions, he downed the last of his drink and replaced the cup on the sideboard, then wrapped his arm around her shoulders.

"I've missed you, Julianne. I love you." He released her and tugged the eye patch back over his head. "But I must away."

"When will I see you again?" She grazed his sleeve with her fingertips, then dropped her hand behind the pleats of her gown.

"When it's time. Do not look for me. And remember, you mustn't breathe a word to anyone—not to Girard, not to anyone—that you've seen me. Either they will believe you, and I'm a dead man, or they'll label you insane as well as criminal." He pressed a kiss to her cheek. "Bring me to God in your prayers, *ma sœur*. Perhaps He will listen to you."

Chapter Twenty-four

❧ ❧ ❧

MOBILE, LOUISIANA
APRIL 1722

Outside Mobile, sunrise dazzled the gulf waters as Marc-Paul
and Caesar finished loading the flat-bottomed barque with
the canvas that had been their tents for the last several weeks.
The spring breeze skimming his skin smelled and tasted of
the ocean. After seemingly endless gift-giving while Bienville
smoked the calumet of peace with Choctaw leaders, Marc-Paul
was as grateful for their alliance as he was ready to return to
Julianne.

He hated being away from her, but relations with the Choctaw were more critical now than ever. The Chickasaw had been
attacking French and Canadian boatmen on the Mississippi
already this spring. If it continued, the wheat harvests in Illinois
Country wouldn't get down to the coastal settlements, and
Mobile and New Orleans wouldn't be able to get provisions
and ammunition to the posts up north, near the fighting. If
the attacks worsened, they would block the flow of furs and
deerskins, Louisiana's only major export. Ironic, Marc-Paul
mused, since it was Bienville's jealousy of British trade that
sparked this war in the first place.

Bienville marched double-quick down to the shoreline. "Ready."

"Yes, sir." Marc-Paul chafed the salt from his hands and arms where the gulf waters had splashed him and prepared to follow the commandant into the boat.

"Stop!"

Bienville groaned, and Marc-Paul turned and shaded his eyes with his hand, in search of the voice's owner. "I'll see what he wants."

Leaving Bienville and Caesar in the boat, he approached the tawny figure in leather breechcloth and leggings striding toward him, half dragging a little girl by her upper arm.

"Peace, friend," Marc-Paul said in Mobilian. A sense of urgency propelled his steps over the sand until he was close enough to see the beads and shells woven into the man's long black hair.

"They told me you were here." He shoved the girl at Marc-Paul with a scowl. "Take her."

Marc-Paul had seen this man before. The broad span of his chest and shoulders, his tapered waist, even his frown rang familiar. Frantically, he scrolled through his memory until recognition sliced through him. "Standing Bear." Marc-Paul and Pascal had wintered in his family's home. With his younger sister, Willow.

"Willow is dead. Now her burden is yours. As it should be. She's your daughter." He turned and walked away.

"What? Standing Bear, wait!"

Standing Bear laid his hand on his tomahawk and slowly swiveled on his bare feet. "You French. You say 'friend,' but you are no friend to us. We deprive ourselves of grain, of game, and of fish so that you may survive. You need us to live, you need us to fight your wars, but what need do we have of you?" He pounded his chest with his fist. "Is it your guns we need? We lived on bow and arrow before we'd ever seen one, and never lacked. Is it the blankets of red, blue, and white that we cannot live without? We are warmer with animal skins. Before you came, we were men who knew what to do. Now we walk like slaves to do your wishes. You are no friend of my people. Take the fruit of your seed and be gone." He flicked his hand toward the child crouching behind Marc-Paul's leg. "The sight of her pale skin makes me sick." Standing Bear strode away, his black hair swaying freely across his back.

"Girard," Bienville called from the boat, "we mustn't tarry."

The words barely registered. Stunned, he knelt in the sugar-white sand beside the girl. If she was indeed conceived during the winter he'd spent with Willow's family, her age would be about eight years. Head bowed, she sniffed, and he wondered if she was crying behind that curtain of dark hair. *Say something*, he told himself. But what could words do? What could he possibly say?

"Please don't take me back," she whispered in Mobilian. "He hates me." With one thin hand, she parted her hair and looked Marc-Paul full in the face. Bruises mottled her arm.

"He did this to you?"

"He is very strong. I displeased him. I always do, somehow, but it was worse after my mother died. I tried not to anger him, but my skin . . ." She peered thoughtfully at the backs of her hands. "My name is Lily, for the white flower."

The flower of France, the fleur-de-lys, was a lily, Marc-Paul mused, and he wondered if her name was one more reason Standing Bear could not abide her presence.

"Captain, we must away." Bienville's voice inserted itself again. "Leave the half-breed. She'll find her way back."

Marc-Paul waved toward the boat in acknowledgment but could not take his eyes from Lily.

"I tried staining my skin darker with coffee beans and tobacco juice, but he didn't like that either." She glanced slyly at Marc-

Paul's hands, then laid one of her own across his, comparing their coloring. She tilted her head and met his eyes. "Are you really my father?"

Bewilderment unmoored him. With Bienville's call dimly echoing in his ears, compassion and denial both tugged his heart. Lily was half-French, marked clearly enough by her complexion and the sharper angles of her features, but how could he know if she was his? And yet the instinct to protect her overtook him. Would he abandon her here on the gulf shore if he knew beyond a doubt her father was some other Frenchman?

He studied her beautiful face. Her brown eyes, sparkling with tears, stared expectantly back at him. Waiting for his answer.

⚜ ⚜ ⚜

"Congratulations, monsieur." Julianne smiled at the new father, a wigmaker from Paris, as she held open the door to his bedroom so he could see his wife and newborn twins. "You see, good things come to those who wait."

It had taken two days, but the babies and mother fared well, an exhilarating accomplishment for both midwife and mother. After witnessing such dangerous labor, Julianne's own longing for a child bowed to the grim reality that every birth also opened the door for death. She would not wish the pain of bereavement upon anyone.

After giving instructions to the parents and a promise to visit later, she took her leave. Since the French engineer, Adrien de Pauger, had finally come to New Orleans, the settlement now boasted a grid of streets with names like Iberville, Bienville, Chartres, and Royal. Decatur Street took Julianne toward home.

Just over the levee, the Mississippi churned around its crescent turn toward the gulf. Dragonflies glittered between gossamer wings. As Julianne covered a yawn with her hand, her own words floated back to her on the roar of the swollen river. *Good things come to those who wait. . . .*

In truth, waiting only suited her when the birthing process required it. And yet waiting was all she seemed to do of late. Wait for a baby. Wait for Marc-Paul to return home. Wait for Benjamin to appear again. Wait for a client to call her for a birth. Between deliveries, the days wore out and fell away, and Julianne was wearing out with them.

As she approached the center of town, the noise of activity buoyed her. Children chased each other in the cleared space called the Place d'Armes. Between the barracks and the levee, soldiers on barrels slapped cards and knees and snuck sips of eau-de-vie. Julianne could not see them without thinking of Benjamin and Marc-Paul.

In the weeks since she'd sworn to keep her brother's life hidden from her husband, the secret had burrowed into her soul like a crayfish slowly working its way through a levee. Quietly. Treacherously. It scared her. For as one crayfish's path created a fissure that would eventually break apart the embankment and flood the town, couldn't one secret allow a trickle of distrust that could grow and destroy a marriage? This was the question that raked its teeth through her mind.

The end of Decatur Street brought the end of New Orleans, and Julianne's path curved, following the river's bend, until she saw the house that had been Pascal Dupree's. Turning left, she took the footpath past it and away from the Mississippi, skirting the swamp that separated Pascal's home from her own. A little more than half a mile later, her house came into view.

Marc-Paul emerged, shielding his eyes from the shimmering sun. His body was taut with purpose, his movements pulled between staying and searching. He was looking for her.

Julianne's skirts billowed out in front of her as the wind

fairly pushed her toward him, and with long strides he strode to meet her.

"Ah, mon amour," he murmured as he neared, "how I've missed you."

Before she could reply, he drew her into a fierce embrace. She dropped her midwife's satchel at her feet and circled his waist with her arms. He smelled of the ocean and sun and tobacco. Gently, he tipped her chin up. His brown eyes were as warm and deep as velvet.

"Welcome home, husband." Julianne exhaled, pulse quickening.

The intensity of his gaze heated her cheeks. He smiled as he twirled a ringlet of her hair around his finger. "*Ma belle*," he said, as if she were the most beautiful woman in King Louis's court and not a bedraggled midwife coming home from two days' work. When his lips met hers, she allowed herself to melt against his chest, to be enveloped by his strength, his scent, his love. Benjamin's defaming words dissolved in the heat of her husband's kiss.

"Come." Marc-Paul took her hand and slung her satchel over his shoulder. "Let's get you home." Once they were standing on the gallery before the front door, however, he paused. "Before we go in, I must tell you. We have a guest."

Julianne blinked. "A guest?"

"A little girl, eight years old. I do hope you're not displeased. She had no other place to go, you see. Her mother died."

"And her father?" she asked. "Where is he?"

He dropped his gaze and rubbed the back of his neck before looking up again. "Lily is half-French. Half-Indian."

Comprehension filtered through Julianne's fatigue. Of the babies she had delivered of Indian slave women, none who were mixed race were cherished by their fathers. None were even claimed by them. "You found her in Mobile?"

A lump shifted in his throat. "Her uncle brought her to me. The bruises on Lily's arms are from him. He was only too eager to be rid of her. I realize it's a terrible shock, but I—I would like her to stay with us."

"Until?"

Marc-Paul lowered her satchel to the floor before returning her gaze. "Indefinitely. Permanently."

Julianne tried to keep up. "As our house servant?"

"No, ma chérie, as a member of the family."

Her eyebrows hiked in surprise.

"Would you sit down please?"

Fatigue pressed down on her, and she drooped into a chair. Something was building inside her husband. With bated breath, she waited for it to rise higher, higher, until finally it spilled out into the open.

"I might know who her father is." He winced.

"What?"

"I can explain. I vow I have never loved another woman as I love you." Marc-Paul paced the gallery as he spoke. "You must believe that. When I wintered with Willow's family, I was twenty-three years old. On the brink of starving or freezing to death, whichever would have come first. They took me in, sheltered me, fed me—"

"Gave you a bed," Julianne whispered and watched him flounder in his own memories.

"I resisted her overtures. I was meant to be a man of the cloth before my father enlisted me—I know God's rules about fornication, cultural customs notwithstanding. I had no desire to break my vow of abstinence before marriage." He marched away from her, then back again.

"Then what happened?"

Marc-Paul's nostrils flared as he exhaled. His jaw bunched. "Her father made me her bedfellow that winter, and I shared her bed. She understood I wanted only sleep. Then one night I drank. Too much, apparently, for whatever I imbibed over-powered me."

"Your inhibitions?"

"Perhaps. My memory, certainly." Three paces away. Three paces back.

"You speak in riddles. Be still. Be clear."

Brow creased, he stopped before her. "When I awoke the next morning, I had no recollection of the night before. Pas-cal Dupree, who slept in a nearby cabin with her brothers and father, told me that he heard Willow and I—" He looked away. "It's his word against the gap in my memory."

"I see." A wave of heat scorched Julianne's face. She rose and strode to one end of the gallery. A songbird trilled in the quiet that yawned between them. "You don't remember it, truly?"

Marc-Paul didn't follow her. "I remember Willow . . . offer-ing. But I don't remember accepting. The fact that Lily was con-ceived during the winter I was there doesn't prove she is mine."

"But you also can't prove she isn't." It was the same logic that had condemned Pascal to the front lines of the war. Julianne rubbed her eyes with the heels of her hands.

"You're exhausted. Forgive my insensitive timing. Forgive me if I've hurt you. But, mon coeur, it happened almost nine years ago. No matter who her father is, she needs a home. I want her to stay." Compassion filled his voice.

Desperately, she picked at the snarls of jealousy in her mind until her thoughts untangled. She might cringe at the thought of him with another woman, but how could she condemn him for taking Lily, when so many men refused responsibility for children they knew were theirs?

His eyes pleaded as he crossed to her and grasped her hands. "One day, God grant it, we'll welcome our own baby into the family. But in the meantime, is your heart not big enough to love Lily too?"

Julianne's thoughts shifted dramatically from Marc-Paul's past to the future now stretching out before them. A child in the home, so suddenly! It nearly took her breath away. "Of course," she whispered, overcome. "Introduce us, if you please."

⚜ ⚜ ⚜

"She's inside." Marc-Paul ushered Julianne through the door.

Without bothering to remove her lace cap, she swept past him and into the house.

"I told her my old bedchamber could be hers now."

Julianne's back straightened, as if braced against his words. Only then did he realize that room would have been almost sacred to her. The only place she had held her son before they put him in the ground. "I'm sorry." He reached to touch her, but she raised her hand, and he dropped his arm to his side.

"It was empty," she said, nodding, and he heard the pain in her admission. "I understand." When she turned toward him, her nose was pink, and her eyes glimmered like grey pearls.

Marc-Paul ached with her disappointment. "I know it's not what we had in mind. . . ." Julianne's life was measured by the births of other women's babies. She deserved a husband who would give her children—and not like this. But he could not bring himself to admit as much aloud for fear of her resounding agreement.

Shame burned in his gut and heated his blood. Turning from his wife, he led the way to Lily's chamber and knocked quietly at the door.

"Lily, I'd like you to meet my wife." He spoke first in Mobilian and then repeated the sentence in French before entering.

Lily's eyes rounded, and she backed away, her shell necklace swinging against her bare chest. The unbrushed mass of her hair overwhelmed her small face as she bowed her head and sank to the floor. She hugged her deerskin skirt to her legs as she pulled her knees to her chin.

"*Enchantée.*" Julianne dropped a curtsy, then looked imploringly at Marc-Paul. "What do I say?" She lowered herself to the floor as well, and her gown pooled around her. Marc-Paul told her the words of greeting, and she repeated them awkwardly.

Lily blinked at Julianne, then reached out and touched her silk hem. Suddenly the child recoiled and pushed herself farther away. "I miss my mother," she wailed. "I want my mother! I don't belong here!"

Julianne's hand trembled as she touched her lips. "What? What did she say?"

Hesitantly, Marc-Paul told her the truth and watched the color drain from his wife's face. After a moment, she rose silently. When he murmured to Lily, Julianne faded from the room.

⚜ ⚜ ⚜

A week after returning from Mobile, Marc-Paul shoveled earth from the ditch he was digging in preparation for the inevitable spring flood. All along Decatur Street, his soldiers were tasked with the same assignment. Their laughter told him they were taking a break. Again. Their laziness grated his patience.

Straightening, he thrust his shovel like a pike into the ground and marched toward Matthieu Hurlot and Raphael Le Comte, who stood a full head taller than almost every other soldier in the garrison. "Your idleness is a disgrace," he growled. "Have I truly been gone so long that you don't remember how to string two hours of labor together?" He should not need to point out that these canals were mandatory and critical. The Mississippi, already swelling with melted snow from the north, rushed around its crescent bend even now.

The two soldiers glanced at each other and then back at him, amusement twinkling in their eyes.

Frustration needled Marc-Paul. "Discipline yourselves, or I'll do it for you. You'll not be laughing after a few weeks behind bars." He hated that threatening jail time was the only way to extinguish their smirks. "If I can't trust you to follow these simple orders, how can I trust you to follow my command should New Orleans be attacked? Prove that you're worthy to be a soldier of the king."

Raphael nodded, the broad expanse of his face suddenly serious, while Matthieu only looked to be holding his breath.

"No more breaks until I say so. Understood? We work until this is done." Marc-Paul turned and strode back to his shovel.

"Well, he's in a fine temper!" Matthieu said loudly enough to be heard.

"Can you blame him?" Raphael countered. "When the cat was away, how his mouse did play! I feel sorry for him, really."

Marc-Paul about-faced and hiked back to the soldiers. "What did you say?"

Raphael gripped his shovel. "Your trouble at home, sir. It's not your fault, and you have our sympathies. Unless—perhaps you've worked it out already, in which case—congratulations." His frame strained the seams of his uniform as he began digging.

"What trouble at home? What rumors have bent your ear?"

"No rumors, sir," Matthieu said. "We've been very quiet about it, haven't we, Le Comte?"

Marc-Paul held up his hands to stop their work. "The mouse at play. You can't be referring to my wife." He should walk away now. He should not listen to whatever these fools had to say. But neither could he let them slander Julianne.

Matthieu shrugged. "You were gone a long time. That is, your wife was home alone for a long time."

Suspicion flowed coldly through Marc-Paul. "Exactly what are you saying?" When answers were not forthcoming, he added, "I order you to speak plainly."

Raphael glanced at Matthieu, who offered nothing. "We—we went singing with a group of other soldiers and sailors for Lundi Gras. We went to your house."

Marc-Paul stepped closer. "And?"

"Your wife came out to hear us, and then we moved on after our song was over."

"So what's the problem?"

Matthieu cut his voice low. "When she went back inside, she wasn't alone."

"What the devil do you mean?"

"One of the singers had slipped away from the group," Raphael explained. "When we looked back, he was going inside your house. With your wife. They closed the door in a hurry, but it sure looked to me like they knew each other."

"Who?" Fire burned through Marc-Paul's limbs as he snapped his gaze to Matthieu. "Was it you? So help me, if you attacked my wife in my absence—"

"It wasn't me!" Matthieu cried, rubbing at the arm she had shot. "If it was, do you think we'd tell you about it?"

Marc-Paul stared at him, then at Raphael, gauging their expressions. "You're lying."

"Don't you think she gets lonely, waiting for you to come home? No children to keep her busy . . ."

The words pummeled him. She'd said she missed him, he knew she longed for children, but Julianne would never be unfaithful to him. "Were you drinking? Before you went out singing—were you intoxicated?"

Both soldiers colored. "Captain," Raphael tried, "be reasonable. Who doesn't drink during Lundi Gras? That doesn't discredit our report."

Marc-Paul disagreed. But he'd play along. "Then who went inside my house? Could it have been Etienne that you saw?"

"Your manservant? The one shorter than me?" Matthieu laughed. "No, this fellow was taller. He wore a pirate costume. I don't know who he was. A widower of some woman who died in childbirth, perhaps? A rogue sent here by lettre de cachet? Look around, Captain—we've plenty of bachelors to choose from. And she does bear a mark that—"

"If there were a thousand princes at her door, she'd never let one in," Marc-Paul said, cutting him off. "I trust my wife, and that's the end of it. Not another word against her character. Do you hear me?"

"Yes, sir," they both replied at once.

"Now dig this ditch, and don't let me hear your voices again."

Marc-Paul stormed back to his own post along the road, wrenched his shovel from the ground, and drove it into the ditch with renewed vigor. The accusation against Julianne was so baseless that he wouldn't even bother mentioning it to her. Doing so would only distress her when she was already fatigued with trying to parent a little girl she didn't understand. A girl who may have been born from Marc-Paul's own sin. That in itself was surely more than enough to handle. Soil sprayed the side of the road as Marc-Paul tossed it from the trench.

But why would Matthieu and Raphael invent such a story when they knew he was already cross enough to toss them both in jail? The question dug into his mind even after the ditch was complete. *They are fools*, he told himself, and buried his doubt down deep.

Chapter Twenty-five

❖ ❖ ❖

Lily felt better as soon as her bare feet hit the sand. Houses were fine for sleeping in, if she had to, but days should be spent outside. Now that the sun had lifted the morning fog, she closed her eyes and raised her arms toward the sky, forming a funnel to catch all the rays she could. Warmth and light soaked her skin. But not enough of it.

She looked down at the French dress Madame made her wear, then glanced back at the house. Saw no one. As she scampered along the ridge, she unfastened her buttons down to her waist and peeled the fabric off her arms and chest, letting it flap against her skirt as she ran. The familiar bounce of her mother's shell necklace on her bare skin brought comfort and ache all at once. Just weeks ago, she was in her old village, where girls and women wore only deerskin skirts. She wondered what her friends were doing today.

"Lily!" Madame Girard's voice was far away.

Lily ran deeper into the swamp before pausing to catch her breath. She looked up. The trees towering up out of the water were enormous. Masses of matching cones pushed up through the water at the bases of their trunks, like little worshipers paying homage to their tree-god. Bright green feathers sprouted from the tips of their branches. Their limbs were hung with pale grey tendrils that swayed in the wind like witches' hair. Arching her back, Lily held out her arms, looked way up at the tops of the trees, and rocked side to side, smiling as her hair brushed against her naked back.

It was easier to be a tree than a Lily these days. Sighing, she draped herself over a large fallen limb covered with furry green moss and rested her head on her arms. Faintly, she heard Madame calling for her again, but Lily was exhausted. She had to learn how to eat at the table, how to dress French, and now she was learning how to draw lines and curves that made sounds. "Letters," Madame called them. Lily even surrendered to taking a bath in a giant bowl instead of in the river. The French soap smelled horrible, though, and when she pushed it away, she could tell Madame Girard was unhappy. Papa seemed to understand her, and she loved him for that and for his kindness. Talking to him eased her.

Drowsily, Lily watched a snow-white egret wade through tiny green dots that covered the water and spotted its spindly legs. It thrust its beak into the water and came up with a frog. The bird worked it backward in its blade-like bill until the frog became a huge lump in the egret's slender throat. Nearby, a mother duck paddled with eight fluffy ducklings behind her.

Lily's throat grew tight around a knot that felt as big as the frog in the egret's neck. She envied those baby ducks, who still had their mama. They looked so much alike; there was no mistaking they belonged together.

Once more, Madame's voice sounded, but it was even more distant this time. Ignoring her, Lily let her arm drop down and gently stroked the shell of a napping turtle. Madame was kind, but she couldn't speak a word of Mobilian. Trying to understand and please her only made Lily miss her mother more. At least in the swamp, with the turtles and the trees and the birds and the wind, she never felt like she didn't belong.

A sunbeam flickered. Lying as still as she could, Lily's gaze darted toward the faint sound of rustling leaves. A man in deer-skin breeches and a linen shirt threaded through the trees in the distance, a gun strapped to his back. His skin was nearly as tan as a native's, but the cypress-colored hair tied at his neck told her he must be French. Languidly, she raised her head and watched as the hunter walked away from her, wondering if he searched for alligator or something else.

"Lily!" Madame called again from some unseen place, and Lily flattened once more upon the limb.

A moment later, she looked up again. The hunter she had seen was gone.

⚜ ⚜ ⚜

Julianne's heart pumped faster as she whirled around. *Where is she?* Standing on a narrow sand beach among a forest of cypress and gum trees, she looked at the swamp and saw only danger. *Please, Lord, keep her safe.*

"Li—" A hand clapped over her mouth from behind and yanked her backward against a hard chest. Panic burst open inside her.

"Shhhh!"

The hiss in her ear ignited her, and she stomped as hard as she could on his instep.

"Stop it!" he whispered harshly. "It's me!" His arms relaxed enough for her to spin around.

"Benjamin!" she gasped.

"You could have hurt me if you had shoes on." He smiled roguishly.

"I meant to hurt you!" She pressed her hand over her frantic heart to calm it. "I didn't see you coming!"

"Forgive me." But he laughed under his breath. "How have you been since I saw you last? You look beautiful, as always."

Pulse still racing, she fought the urge to box his ears. "Did you learn to track and hunt from Red Bird?"

Faint lines fanned from his eyes as he looked down at her, so weathered by sun and wind was his face. A yellow-throated warbler flashed behind him, singing a tune as bright as its feathers. "What do you know of Red Bird?"

"I know you lived with his family. He speaks fondly of you, Benjamin."

"You spoke to him? You didn't tell him I live, did you?" His tone pleaded.

"Of course not. But if you are working for the good of France, we are all on the same side."

"We are not—" He stopped himself, seeming to gather his thoughts. "I already explained this to you. I've been condemned to death already. If you tell anyone about me, I die. Now, what can you tell me about your husband's next mission? For the good of the empire."

Frustration expanded in her chest. "I don't know anything about his next mission. I'm not even certain he does, until Bienville gives him orders. How would this information be of use to you?"

"Hundreds of miles away, there is a war, in case you forgot. Communications between here and there are increasingly interrupted by hostile native raiders."

"So you're a courier?"

He hooked a thumb under the strap that looped his gun over his shoulder. "Yes, a courier. I need to know the state of things."

A splash turned her head. But it was only a muskrat plopping from a cypress knee into the water. "The state of things," she repeated, and waited for him to clarify.

"How many soldiers are in New Orleans?" Sunlight slanted

in shafts through branches that trembled in the wind, painting bright, quivering stripes across his body.

"Around fifty-five, I think, including officers."

"What about at Fort Rosalie near Natchez? The Yazoo post?"

"Saints alive, I have no idea!" She didn't care that impatience clipped her tone. "I'm not one of Bienville's troops."

"But you married one. You must know more than you realize. For example, how are the supplies holding out—guns, powder, balls? Are you able to pay the Choctaw what you owe them for fighting the Chickasaw?"

Julianne's mind whirred. "I don't know." Sand itched across her bare feet, and she rubbed one on top of the other to brush it off. Chafing at so many questions, she took a step back, away from her brother.

"Then find out, please. It's important. But be prudent. Arouse no suspi—" His gaze shifted. Narrowed. "Don't move." Slowly, he reached for the hatchet slung at his hip, his eyes fixed on the ground, where a rattling sounded.

Holding her breath, she looked down to see a snake coiled by her bare feet. Its jaws were open, its tail flicking vigorously in the fallen leaves. The hair rose on her neck and arms.

In one lightning-fast strike, Benjamin's blade sailed into the reptile and separated its head from the rest of its writhing body.

Julianne's voice returned in a cry as she watched her brother wrest his weapon out of the ground, wipe it clean, and thrust it back into its place at his hip. She dashed away from the dead animal.

Benjamin draped his arm around her shoulders and squeezed. "I'd never let harm come to you while I'm around. But would you consider, for your next outing into the swamp, a pair of shoes? And perhaps some caution. Stepping on a venomous snake is not recommended." He smiled teasingly, then kissed the top of her head and let her go.

Thoughts of Lily, barefoot and prone to wandering, rushed back at her. "Benjamin, I need to go."

"Ah yes, looking for someone named Lily, aren't you? A little girl about this tall? Who perhaps enjoys disrobing in the swamp?"

"Where? Where is she?"

"Be at ease, sister. I'll help you find her. Watch your step." He winked.

Turning, he led the way through swarms of flying insects, between lichen-encrusted trunks, and by woodpeckers drilling into the trees above shallow pools of water. Lifting her skirts a bit higher, she tiptoed through dozens of spiky brown globes dropped from the sweet gum tree overhead.

And almost ran into her brother's back. He held his hand up to stop her. He crouched low, and she did the same, feeling ridiculous in her painted silk dress.

"I'll turn around here," he whispered, "but she's lying on a limb over there. Look for the yellow color of her skirt."

Relieved, she squeezed Benjamin's arm. "Thank you."

"Who is she?"

"Our daughter," she replied without hesitation. "We're raising her."

Benjamin's eyebrows arched. "She's Indian?"

"Half."

Tenderness swept into his grey eyes as he angled to catch one more glimpse of the child before facing Julianne again. His smile brought an ache to her heart. "If you raise her half so well as you raised me, she will be most fortunate indeed."

And yet here he was, crouching in a swamp, afraid for his life. She pushed the thought away. "Benjamin, when you lived with the Choctaw, how did Fair Sky do it? How did she make you feel loved even when you couldn't speak her language?"

His nose pinked as he looked down at his moccasins for a

moment. When he lifted his head, tears misted his eyes. "She wasn't afraid to touch me, for one. I can still feel her hand on my cheek sometimes when I sleep. She talked to me though she knew I missed most of it at first. She didn't give up on me. But in the beginning, she didn't push me either. When I needed to be alone, she didn't grab me and pull me back." He shrugged. "You'll know what to do, Julianne. You always do. If I haven't said it before—thank you."

She wrapped her arms around his neck and kissed him lightly on both cheeks. "You have always been a gift to me."

"Lily can be a gift to you too. Give her time." He reached into his pocket with a smile. "Speaking of gifts, hold out your hand."

She did. Benjamin placed two silver hair combs in her palm. It took her only a moment to recognize them. "I thought I lost them! You had them all this time?"

"I took them with me when I left Paris for the army. They were all I had to remember you—all three of you—by."

She turned the combs over and read the engraving etched into one of them: *Devotedly yours.* Her father's words. Her mother's combs. The ones Julianne had worn so often to feel close to her after she died.

"They are yours again, at last. I always intended to return them, you know." Leaving the precious gift in her hands, Benjamin rose, touched her shoulder in farewell, and with a few muted footsteps, disappeared among the trees.

Thunder rumbled in the distance. As shadows disappeared beneath a full-bellied sky, Julianne traced the combs with her finger and tucked them into the pocket of her gown. Images of Fair Sky and Benjamin, and her own two parents, swirled in her mind as she watched Lily relaxing on a fallen limb, wearing Willow's shell necklace.

Hand in her pocket, clutching the only link she had to her own mother, Julianne waited until the first raindrops of the afternoon storm pattered through the foliage and Lily climbed down from her perch. Only then did Julianne meet her along the path with a smile and an outstretched hand. She pulled from a nearby shrub a sprig of white, star-shaped flowers and offered it to the little girl. Lily cupped it in her palm and watched water bead on the petals. Blinking the rain from her eyes, she peered up at Julianne and grinned.

It was a start.

⚜ ⚜ ⚜

Marc-Paul paused in the doorway to his bedchamber, wishing Julianne were here to see this too. He wondered if he should scold Lily but whisked the thought away, too curious to stop her.

The little girl sat before Julianne's toilette table, eyes aglow at the bounty of silver pots before her. Tentatively, she reached for a small pot of rouge, smeared her finger in it, and drew pink circles on her cheeks. Tilting her head, she gazed at her reflection with one eyebrow raised, drawing a smile to Marc-Paul's lips. The art of cosmetics remained beyond her, but that expression was the very image of Julianne.

Savage, indeed, Marc-Paul thought, recalling Bienville's words during their most recent confrontation. Since Lily came to New Orleans, the governor had made no effort to disguise his disapproval. And for the first time in memory, Marc-Paul didn't care that his superior officer found fault with him. Not for this. His conscience in this matter was clear. His heart full.

Lily coiled the braid that hung down her back and pinned it to her head, then inserted two silver combs in her hair. Beaming, she peered into the trifold mirror to inspect her handiwork.

"Ah, mademoiselle!" Marc-Paul entered the room, and Lily covered her giggle with her hand. "You're growing up so fast, ma belle! Before I know it, you'll have suitors!"

"Oh no, Papa!" she laughed. "It's just for play."

"And do you suppose you should be playing with Madame's things?"

Her lashes lowered over her too-bright cheeks. "Are you cross?"

Marc-Paul knelt on one knee to look into her eyes. "No. But let's put these things away. Next time you want to use them, ask Madame to help you, yes?"

Nodding, she tidied the toilette table while Marc-Paul unclipped the pin from her raven hair and drew the silver combs out as well. The combs winked at him from his palm. Frowning, he held them up to examine them further. He'd never seen these before. Tastefully engraved but not loaded with gemstones, they were simpler than the rest of the ornaments on the table and more elegant. Why had he never seen them grace Julianne's hair?

He turned them over. The inscription seized him. *The man who came to her on Lundi Gras. He gave these to her. Of course she'd never wear them around you.* Wild imaginings. The fears of an oft-absent husband. He pushed them aside and swallowed.

"Where did you get these, Lily?"

"I found them."

His shoulders relaxed. No wonder he'd never seen them before. "You didn't steal them, did you?"

"No, no. They fell from the pocket of Madame's gown when I moved it to sit down." She pointed to the discarded dress Julianne had shed in her haste to don more serviceable attire for midwifing.

"She kept them in her pocket?" An ache swelled behind his forehead. Suspicion banged against his mind.

Lily shrugged, took the combs, and placed them in the silver box with the other ornaments. "I keep my treasures there too." She pulled an oyster shell from her pocket and held it aloft. "See? No cracks. It's perfect."

"I see!" Marc-Paul forced a smile. Were these combs a treasure to Julianne as well? Why? "It's getting late. Off to bed with you."

After Lily changed into her nightdress, washed the rouge from her cheeks, and brushed her teeth, Marc-Paul brought her a glass of water and sat on the edge of her bed. While he told her a story, he heard Julianne come home. Questions burned on the tip of his tongue until he finished the story, bade Lily good-night, and sought his wife.

He found her in her nightdress in their bedchamber, searching the pockets of the crumpled gown. "Looking for something?"

She startled at the sound of his voice. Then, recovering, she folded the gown over her arm. "The birth went well."

"I'm glad of it." He spoke over the whisper in his head that suggested perhaps she was not at a birth at all but visiting the man who gave her the combs, the man who came here when Marc-Paul was away.

But it was madness to leap to such conclusions. He chided himself for bowing to his fear. "Lily played at your toilette table this evening," he told her. Lifting the lid of the silver box, he drew out the combs. "She found these."

She laid her gown in a basket and took the combs from his hand. "Ah, thank you." She tucked them back inside the box and closed the lid.

"I don't recognize them. Are they new?" His voice was calm despite his rippling doubts.

"And do you keep an inventory of all the ornaments that came with this set?" But her smile was flat, her gaze dim. "I'm exhausted, mon coeur. The day has been long."

Seating herself at her toilette table, Julianne brushed her hair while Marc-Paul stood rooted behind her. Was she hiding something? Or was he only seeing monsters in the shadows like a frightened child? Combs in her pocket. The word of two drunken soldiers. It could mean nothing. And yet he could not coax the unease from his heart. "Is there—anything we should discuss?"

Her hand stilled, then she set her brush on the table before swiveling to face him. Her eyes flashed. "Yes. I think there is."

He steeled his spine, bracing himself. "I'm listening."

Julianne shook her head. "I'd much rather listen to you."

Marc-Paul frowned, unable to guess what she meant.

"My brother," she breathed at last. "You never told me how he died."

Her words crashed over him like water bursting its dam. "You never asked."

"You let me believe it was fever. I'm asking now. For the truth." She folded her hands on her lap.

Marc-Paul trapped a groan in his chest. "Even if it hurts you?"

"Tell me."

Exhaling, he sat on the foot of the bed and pinched the bridge of his nose. What were two silver combs compared to this? "I've never lied to you, Julianne. But since you're asking, I'll fill in the missing pieces. I once told you about a time one of my soldiers went missing."

"Benjamin."

He met her gaze. "Yes. He did have a fever when we brought him back to the garrison, and we nursed him back to health. But he never adjusted back to soldiering very well. It was a hard enough life as it was, I suppose, but the transition from the Choctaw village to the garrison—" He rubbed at a muscle in his neck. "It didn't suit him. When he went missing somewhere around Mobile, I was genuinely worried. Red Bird helped me find him. But as soon as we did, war cries rent the night air, and we found ourselves battling Chickasaw. We were outnumbered, but by how many, we couldn't tell. I was struck by one of their arrows. Your brother watched me fall and ran from the fight."

"He didn't." Julianne rose, indignation filling her voice.

Before she could walk away, Marc-Paul was on his feet. He pulled his shirt hem from his breeches, grabbed her hand, and pressed it to the scar on his side. "You asked for the truth, and I'm telling you. I bear the proof." He drew her hand to the back of his waist until it covered the groove where the arrow had been wrenched from his flesh.

With her other hand, Julianne pushed against his chest to be free of him, but he caught that hand too. Slid her palm over the ridge beneath his linen where she once dug out an arrowhead. She tried to pull away, but he held her fast against his body.

"I have enemies, Julianne. Benjamin was one of them."

She looked at him with pleading in her eyes, as though he could change the truth by sheer force of will. "You still haven't told me how he died," she whispered.

Marc-Paul released her. She stood back and waited for him to speak. Dread stalled the words in his chest before he began.

"Red Bird tracked and captured Benjamin. Honoring the Choctaw alliance with France, he returned him to Bienville, bringing with him the scalps of the Chickasaw who were lending him aid. Red Bird tried persuading the governor to give Benjamin a reprieve, especially since your brother had previously been so helpful in our understanding of our allies. Bienville asked for my testimony, and I gave it to him. The punishment for desertion is death, Julianne. His fate was out of my hands, out of Red Bird's. Benjamin knew the risk. I visited him in prison and asked if he wanted to write you a letter, telling you good-bye. He said no. His end was too disgraceful, he said. He didn't want you to think ill of him. So I respected his wishes. He didn't want you to know. You cannot think I rejoiced over his death, ma chérie. I would to God he was still here for you. You have lost so much." Marc-Paul looped his arms behind her waist and slowly pulled her to him. "I'm sorry."

Weak words for such a powerful confession.

Julianne's composure crumbled, and she squeezed her eyes shut. As Marc-Paul cradled her head against his shoulder, he couldn't help but think that he'd just given his wife one more reason to seek solace in another man's arms.

PART FOUR

Flood

"It is most disagreeable for an officer in charge of a colony to have nothing more for its defense than a bunch of deserters, contraband salt dealers, and rogues who are always ready not only to desert you but also to turn against you."

—Sieur Jean-Baptiste Le Moyne de Bienville, 1719

Chapter Twenty-six

❧ ❧ ❧

NEW ORLEANS, LOUISIANA
APRIL 1722

Spring rain drove into the ground like arrows, pockmarking the mud and stippling puddles. In his garden, Marc-Paul looked down at the pools flooding the vegetables, and rainwater channeled from his hat as though from a gutter's spout. New Orleans was about to learn if all the canals the colonists had dug at the behest of the city engineer would be enough to prevent another flood.

Though he could not see it from where he stood, the swollen Mississippi roared around its bend. It was too fast. Too strong.

"Etienne," Marc-Paul called, "grab your ropes. I have a feeling we're going fishing."

Muttering, Etienne ducked inside his cabin and came out with two coils of rope. After handing one to Marc-Paul, the men looped them over their shoulders and marched through the rain toward town.

Just as he had suspected, the ditches along Decatur Street had already overflowed. River water, dark grey beneath the sunless sky, charged over and through the embankments. Soon the cold water spilled over the tops of Marc-Paul's boots, weighting his every sodden step. Fish swam in the streets. But this was not what he wanted to catch.

"Here we go. You know what to do."

Marc-Paul made a lasso of his rope. Etienne caught the pine box floating toward them, guided it into the rope's ring, and Marc-Paul cinched it tight around its middle. A quick glance at the lid confirmed that the owner's name had been carved into it. Good. More would come.

In the spring, the river rose and pushed against the levees, into every pocket of air, every fissure created by burrowing crayfish. This time, the pressure had built until the coffins buried there were pushed from their earthen cradles and drifted on the floodwaters into the streets.

Etienne squinted at a streak of light cracking open the clouds overhead. "Rain's stopping."

"Not that it will help," Marc-Paul said. Snowmelt at the north end of the Mississippi added volume to the river, which only compounded as it flowed south. The river strained its banks from Illinois Country on down, so by the time it reached New Orleans, a break in the rain could do nothing to slow its churning rapids.

Marc-Paul and Etienne pulled the floating coffin to the barracks, where they stacked it on some poor private's bunk and prayed it was high enough off the ground to stay dry until the river receded back into its banks. At Marc-Paul's order, a dozen soldiers geared up to wade the streets as well, fishing for coffins that had been dislodged from the levee. Those soldiers remaining at the barracks were tasked with receiving and organizing whatever the "fishermen" brought back. The garrison would be in charge of draining each coffin and replacing it once the graveyard section of the levee was repaired. They'd need to match the coffins with the correct markers as well, assuming the markers were also recovered.

"Why bury these poor souls in the levee at all when we know flooding might knock them loose again?" Raphael shouted across the barracks.

"It has only happened once before," Marc-Paul replied. "The water table in the ground between New Orleans and Lake Pontchartrain is too high to accept the bodies. The levee is the highest land for miles around."

"Clearly this isn't working either!" Raphael swore as he stood in the doorway of the barracks, watching.

Marc-Paul could not deny it. Odors oozed from the floodwaters that rushed between and around his tall boots, so foul he breathed shallowly through his mouth. The coffins that came into his hands sloshed with water and human remains. The soldiers wading through Decatur Street cursed among themselves as they followed Marc-Paul's orders. Not for the first time, they scorned Bienville's choice for Louisiana's capital.

Nearly every coffin contained someone Marc-Paul had known. As they were lassoed and shuttled to the barracks, memories bobbed to the surface. Men killed by arrow, tomahawk, musket ball, or drink. Mothers who did not survive childbirth. Germans who starved, Frenchmen who burned up with fever. Prostitutes taken by disease. Colonists had only come to New Orleans four years ago, but the death rate far exceeded the births.

Shades of brown and grey laced together in the flowing water. Sunlight perforated the clouds. Large branches shivering with leaves came rushing toward them, along with rotten tree stumps floating on their sides, exposing their gnarled roots. As Etienne reached for the coffin headed his way, Marc-Paul formed his noose, ready to secure the box.

Etienne grunted as he stopped the floating cargo against his legs. "Simon LeGrange," he read from the lid, and the name struck Marc-Paul in the chest.

The convict forced to colonize, Julianne's first husband, and the largest presence in any room, he now floated helplessly like flotsam through the streets of a land he never wanted to begin with. And now New Orleans had spit him out, rejecting him and all the others who had been buried here. Though Marc-Paul didn't consider himself superstitious, he could almost believe, between famine and flood, that this land fought against settlement. And that this land would win.

Solemnly, he cinched the rope around Simon's coffin, and Etienne dragged it to the barracks.

Oh no. A sickening thought rolled Marc-Paul's stomach. *The baby.* Julianne's tiny son, Benjamin, had been buried at Simon's feet. His box had surely come unmoored along with Simon's, but where was it? Marc-Paul turned in a full circle. Land and river and sky crashed together. He squinted against the sunlight reflecting off the water.

"Men!" he called to his soldiers. "Be on the lookout for a small one, about this long." He held his hands about a foot apart. Such a small span of space, and yet what emptiness it represented in Julianne's heart. "It . . . it is my wife's son." If it were not found, if her baby's body were lost into the sea . . . A dull ache consumed him. *Please, Lord, not this. Not this as well.* He knew the wee babe was now in heaven and had no need for his earthly tent. Julianne knew this full well herself. But what mourning heart did not long for a place to quietly sow one's tears?

The barracks at his back, Etienne shook his head, jowls quivering, as he rubbed his swollen knuckles. His eyes misted beneath his craggy brows. "Blast this place. Blast it." He threw his head back and stared at the heavens, lips moving silently, before surveying the waters around him.

The river ruffled around Marc-Paul's long strides. A cursory glance confirmed that the soldiers were performing their unpleasant duties, so he waded downstream to search for the baby.

His heart felt as heavy as his legs pulling through the water. *I'm sorry*, he could hear himself saying to Julianne. Again. How many times had he said it? His jaw tensed. Despite his misgivings about his marriage, he still could not bear Julianne having more pain to endure.

"Marc-Paul! There!" Etienne's voice whirled Marc-Paul's attention to a mass of tangled roots coming at him. Nesting inside was a small wooden box.

Energy flooded Marc-Paul. He formed his lasso and threw it at the trunk. The rope caught, and the line pulled taut. Etienne threw his rope as well to help fight against the current. Together they closed the distance until Marc-Paul was able to free the tiny coffin from its trap.

While Etienne unhooked the ropes from the roots, Marc-Paul bowed his head over baby Benjamin. *Thank you*, he prayed. Relief and gratitude poured into him as he carried his wife's baby to the barracks.

A soldier met him at the door and reached for the box, but Marc-Paul brushed past him. He wanted to lay the baby with his father once more. And after the levees were repaired, he'd lay them both to rest in the earth again, where they would stay until the next flood.

✣ ✣ ✣

That night, after Marc-Paul had assessed the minimal damage to his own property, he scrubbed the filth from his skin and fell into bed, exhausted. Julianne climbed under the covers, and though he was aware of her warm body against his, he could only think of sleep. With a chaste kiss to her cheek, he bade her good night.

In the half-conscious state between wakefulness and slumber, scenes from the day's work drifted back to him. Above Julianne's rhythmic breathing, he could still hear the rush of the flood and feel the river water soaking his skin. Images and smells he'd experienced hours before lapped at his mind. At least he'd found Benjamin's coffin. For that, he could rest securely.

Marc-Paul's eyes popped open. He stared into the dark. *Benjamin's coffin.* Benjamin Chevalier. He hadn't seen Julianne's brother's coffin. *Did I miss it?* His forehead ached, and he pressed his fingers to the ridge between his eyes. An owl hooted in the still of the night.

And suddenly, Marc-Paul wrenched wide awake. He had surveyed the men's work in the barracks before he and Etienne had come home. Closing his eyes, he reeled that memory back until he saw himself counting the coffins and inspecting them to find the names. They were in no particular order, of course, but if he had seen Benjamin Chevalier's at any point, he certainly would have remembered it.

Julianne hadn't asked about it either. Why, when she was so eager to hear about Simon's and her baby's, did she neglect to ask after her brother's remains? He should have been fresh on her mind from their recent conversation. And why had she been suddenly so curious about Benjamin's end when she hadn't bothered to ask since that first visit to Bienville's home?

If Benjamin Chevalier's coffin hadn't come out with the rest, where was it?

The riddle burned in his mind until he could remain in bed no longer. Careful not to wake Julianne, he rose, dressed, and put on his tall boots once more, though they were still wet. Quietly, he stole from the house, plucked a shovel from the gardening shed, and set out.

Fireflies blinked beneath the star-studded sky. Mosquitoes swarmed around him, but he was barely aware of their incessant buzzing as he squelched through the ankle-deep mud. Moonlight glowed dimly on the graveyard levee, now a ruined mess. He could see where the river had cut through it. The earth sagged in the gaps where the coffins had once been. Except for one lone spot where Benjamin Chevalier had been buried. The marker had been washed away, but Marc-Paul knew in his gut the coffin remained.

Using the shovel as a walking stick, he sank deep into the mud as he made his way to Benjamin's resting place. The air was thick with stench, and he muscled back a gag. Overhead, bats flapped erratically in the sky, swooping as they feasted on mosquitoes. With their high-pitched chirping in his ears, he thrust the shovel into the wet soil and heaved it away in sodden clumps, feeling like a grave robber.

A thud announced he'd hit the top of Benjamin's coffin. *He's there. Leave him in peace*, a voice whispered in Marc-Paul. But there had to be a reason this one coffin was not washed away. He intended to find out what it was.

He cleared the mud from the lid. Benjamin had been dead for two years. Looking inside was bound to be unpleasant. Bracing himself, Marc-Paul inserted the edge of his shovel between the warping lid and the box. He pushed down on the handle and heard the squeaking of the nails as they pulled free.

He held his breath. Blood throbbed inside his skull like a clapper vibrating inside a bell. He tore off the lid and waited for a cloud to pass from in front of the moon. Slowly, by degrees, the moon shone its light into the open coffin.

It was full to the top with rocks.

Breath whooshed from him, and air rushed back in to fill his lungs. His heart beat a tattoo against his ribs as he used the handle of the shovel to probe and stir inside the coffin. Perhaps the body was buried beneath them, a precaution taken by the original gravedigger to keep it securely in place. If that was the plan, it had worked.

But aside from the rocks, the coffin was empty. Benjamin's body was gone. *Don't be a fool*, Marc-Paul told himself. *His body was never there.* He speared his shovel into the soggy ground and leaned on the handle. Shock shuddered through his limbs as the wind chilled the sweat on his skin.

Benjamin was alive.

While he put the empty coffin back in its place, the gears of his mind felt rusty as they turned. All the way home, and as he washed the mud and stink from his skin, he could not rinse away his alarm. He had no idea what to make of his discovery. And until he did, he wasn't ready to share the news with Julianne.

He slipped back into bed beside her, but sleep was not likely to come.

⚜ ⚜ ⚜

In the dark of night, Julianne stirred awake. Wind moaned outside the window, and she wondered if it would bring more rain. Then she startled with recognition. That was no wind she heard. It was coming from inside the house. Pushing herself up on one elbow, she strained her ears. There it was again. Lily was weeping in her room.

Julianne sat upright and flipped her braid over her shoulder, but Marc-Paul stayed her with his hand.

"I'll go," he whispered, and was gone.

Pulling her knees up under her chin, Julianne crossed her arms around her ankles and listened to her husband's rich velvet voice soothe a little girl's fear or sorrow. Julianne would not have been able to offer such comfort, not without speaking Mobilian. So she remained, useless and alone, while the bed grew cold around her.

As the sun rose, Marc-Paul returned to dress, only to leave again without a word.

When he came home for dinner hours later, he was so aloof that Julianne's appetite vanished. Lily played outside as soon as she was done eating, but Julianne remained at the table across from her husband, waiting for him to address her directly for the first time all day. Her fingers pleated the napkin in her lap, first one way, then the other. Finally, he caught her gaze with shadow-ringed eyes.

"Didn't sleep well last night?" she ventured.

Marc-Paul shook his head. "Lily had nightmares. I meant to stay in her room only until she slept again, but I ended up drifting off on the floor. Still paying for it too." He rolled his head from side to side, wincing.

Julianne nodded. "You look exhausted."

"Well." He sipped his coffee. "Losing sleep will do that."

"Next time I'll go to her so you can rest."

"She wanted me."

The words stung. With a nod, she let the matter drop. But in her heart, she wondered why Lily would ever want her when she had Marc-Paul already.

Three days later, she found him packing in their room. Morning mist shrouded the house in a thick blanket of white, muffling the world outside.

"I'm leaving again. A new mission." He studied her as he told her. Fog's lacy veil spilled in through the open window and hovered between them.

Julianne leaned against the bureau, her heart dividing. One portion was lonely for him already, while the other portion felt only relief. Benjamin had grown bolder of late, finding her at home when Marc-Paul was in town. The secret ballooned inside her marriage, pushing her ever further from her husband.

"How long this time?"

"Of course. You want to know how much time you have." He set his jaw as he stuffed a linen shirt into his leather valise.

The hardness in his face startled her. Vapor dampened the air and filmed her skin. "What do you mean?"

He stopped packing to face her fully. "Is there someone else?"

Dread rippled through her. "How could you ask such a thing?"

"You're hiding something. You haven't been yourself since I returned from Mobile. At first I thought it was just the strain of adding a child to the family, but then I heard a man came to visit you on Lundi Gras, and you let him into the house."

The room spun, and Julianne pressed back against the bureau, its brass handles stamping into her spine. Her mouth went dry.

"I didn't listen at first, couldn't imagine you would do such a thing. I know I'm gone for long periods of time, but I trusted you."

"Marc-Paul!" A sob strangled her voice.

"You want a child of your own, and I'm not giving that to you, but I never dreamed—" He stared at the bed they shared. "My worst fear is that I'll come home and find you miraculously pregnant."

"How dare you!" she cried, aghast. "I would never do that!" The bureau rocked as she shoved away from it, and the glass hurricane tumbled from its top and shattered on the floor.

Shaking, Julianne sank to her knees. Marc-Paul knelt on the other side of the glittering mess she'd made and pulled the myrtle wax taper and candlestick holder out of the broken glass, setting them aside. She reached to pluck the larger pieces from the floor, but he held out his hand to stop her.

"You cannot fix this." The edge in his tone told her he spoke about more than just the glass. His words sliced at her heart.

Silently, he took the broom and shovel from the fireplace and swept the shards away. Once the mess was cleared, he leaned both arms on the bed, bowing over his half-packed bag while the room grew thick with fog.

"Someone else saw you with a man. Said that you embraced him. Kissed him." He looked at the broken glass in the shovel on the hearth, his voice gruff.

316

It's not what you think! But if she told him it was Benjamin, what then? "Who said this?" she whispered, pushing herself up from the floor. The witness must have been someone he trusted. Etienne? Red Bird? Lily? If it was Red Bird who'd seen Benjamin, was his life already at risk?

Marc-Paul shook his head, dismissing her question. The anger receded from his eyes, leaving only raw sorrow behind. "Have you given your heart to another? Who is he? I'm asking you plainly."

But nothing was plain, nothing clear. Julianne clenched her teeth lest a lie—or the truth—slip free. In her hesitation, his lips parted and his shoulders slumped slightly, as if her silence were a confession. *What have I done?* The truth about Benjamin would absolve her, but was that worth her brother's life? The two men she loved most hung in the balance, and she could not bring herself to tip to either side.

She stepped through the mist toward her husband. "Mon coeur—I am faithful to you! I vow, I have not taken a lover!" The words burst from her as she grasped his cold hands in hers. "You insult me by believing this slander!"

"Why would they say these things, if there were not at least an element of truth?"

Desperately, she considered blaming her mark for her maligned reputation. But she could not pretend, even to herself, that the fleur-de-lys had opened this chasm that yawned between them. Instead, all she said was, "You must believe me. I've given myself to none but you. I love you."

Marc-Paul did not squeeze her hands, or dry her tears, or smooth her hair back from her face. He merely returned to his packing, ignoring Julianne until she fled the room.

Chapter Twenty-seven

❧ ❧ ❧

With a heavy heart, Lily watched her papa strap his gun over his back. Its silver glinted in the sun that soaked into her hair until it nearly burned her scalp. Tugging her dress away from her sticky skin, she sidled closer to Papa, who was also wearing too many clothes for the weather. But she had learned that arguing the point was useless. "Do you really have to go away?" she asked him.

"I really do. But I'll come back."

In the corner of her eye, Lily noticed Madame Girard standing quietly apart from the two of them. Her eyes wore the dull look of one who didn't understand. Lily knew exactly how she felt. When her papa was not around to interpret, Lily hadn't understood much when she first arrived here either. But she'd been learning. French words felt so thick in her mouth, like a wooden spoon that swelled on the tongue, or like corn boiled in water too long. She was too embarrassed to try to speak them to anyone but Papa.

"Is it a hunting party?" Lily wanted to know.

"I'm hunting for a good place along the Riviere de la Madelaine to build a new fort. Does that count?" He chucked Lily under the chin, but he still didn't look at Madame. Lily cast a glance in the woman's direction, hoping he'd follow her gaze and speak a French word or two to her.

Instead, Papa reached down and scratched behind the ears of the dog whose name Lily could never pronounce. She'd renamed the animal Fist Face, because it looked like he'd been punched in the nose. Fist Face wagged his tail so hard his entire back end moved from side to side. Lily giggled. Fist Face was easy to understand.

"I must leave now." Papa pulled Lily in for a hug and kissed the top of her head in the space where her hair parted down the middle. "Be good for Madame. Just try."

"Oui, Papa." Lily grinned at the smile this drew to his face.

Her smile wilted, however, as Lily watched him go. He'd forgotten to kiss Madame.

Madame turned as white as the flower for which Lily was named. Lily tucked her hands behind the skirt Madame had sewn for her from one of her old dresses. Maybe if Lily could say something to her, something Madame could understand, then Madame would smile. But she could not think fast enough to do it properly. Madame was already slipping back inside.

That night, Lily lay on the floor of her room, for even the bed was too hot. The rug being rolled away for the summer, she spread herself out on the smooth wood floor, arms and legs open wide. Staring at the open window, she begged a breeze to come swishing through its gaping mouth, to sweep the sweat from her skin and give her goose bumps instead. *I am a water lily*, she told herself, and her lips tipped up with amusement at her own game. *The lake is my bed, and I float, flat, on its cool surface.* Drowsily, she brushed her fingertips along the floorboards, pretending they trailed in water. When she felt mosquitoes land on her skin, she told herself that little fish mistook her fingers for worms and nibbled at her flesh.

The click of claws on wood alerted her that Fist Face was

approaching. Before she could think of what role he might play in her game, he sneezed on her face and broke the spell.

With a squeal, Lily sat up and wiped the dog's spittle from her cheek, then went to her washstand and rinsed her face clean. She gazed at the water in the basin and at the mosquitoes and midges dimpling its silver skin. She wrinkled her nose. Most people wrinkled their nose at Lily's skin too. Papa didn't though. He said Madame didn't either, even though it was harder to tell with her. He said she had helped some half-Indian, half-French babies to come safely out of their mamas, and when one of them died once, she cried and cried. So she must not hate Lily for her skin. Papa said that Madame had a baby once, but the baby didn't live, and her heart hadn't healed from that yet. Lily knew what that was like too. She still missed her mother something fierce. The missionary who taught her mama about the French Jesus-God said she'd be waiting for Lily in heaven. But that was little comfort. A daughter had more need of her mother on earth.

Lily lifted her gaze to the cross-shaped shadow on the wall above the washstand. Papa had called it a crucifix, an impossible word to say. But she'd looked upon it often enough that she could see it in her mind through the darkness. Her fingers walked up the wall to touch the silver metal at the bottom of the cross, for she could reach no higher than that. The missionary who had come to her village carried a similar crucifix. He told them about the God who created the entire world—the sun, the water, the land, the animals and people—everything. And then that same God sent His son Jesus to walk the earth so people would listen to Him, even though they hung Him on that cross to die. The people had a hard time believing He was who He said He was, that He loved them and had a purpose for everything. So God had sent signs to show them that He had everything worked out, and they just needed to believe.

Lily tried hard to believe. She prayed to the French Jesus-God—since the missionary said He wasn't actually on the cross anymore, but in heaven—and she asked Him to send her a sign too. Because pretending to be somewhere else was a lot easier than really living where she was.

Crossing to the open window, she leaned on the sill. She thrust out her arm as far as it would reach and wiggled her fingers just to feel the air kiss her skin with its hot summer breath. She pulled her arm back inside. If she listened carefully enough, she could hear beyond the thrumming mosquitoes to the chirping crickets, the gurgling owls, the vibrating tones of the frogs. She could hear . . . crying.

It was Madame. She was weeping. Lily imagined the sound as a long purple ribbon floating out of Madame's window and fluttering inside Lily's, a fragile bridge connecting them.

Carefully, she lit a candle in its glass chimney. The flame flared tall for a moment, then settled back down and bobbed agreeably on its wick. Lily smiled. The light was a small glowing head, nodding *Oui, oui, mademoiselle, we should go see what the trouble is.* She left Fist Face to snore where he was.

The light pushed back the darkness, one step at a time, until she reached the doorway to Madame's chamber. Timidly, she knocked on the frame, then pushed open the door.

Immediately, Madame muffled her cries, likely startled by the sudden appearance of light out of the abyss. Lily wondered if she resembled a ghost. She should speak, or Madame would be frightened more. But in French.

Lily licked her lips nervously. "*C'est moi*, Lily."

Madame's eyes grew large. They were silver with her tears. "Lily? I'm sorry I woke you." She wiped the wetness from her cheeks, looking ashamed. "That was excellent French, by the way. Very good. *Très bien.*" She was nodding now, like Lily's tiny flame.

Lily pursed her lips. She wasn't sure how to say, *I was not asleep, don't be sorry.* So she merely shook her head, probed further into the room, and placed her light on the bureau. She was afraid she might drop it by accident and cause a fire.

Two mosquitoes looped and dipped in the space between Lily and Madame. But when Lily looked beyond them, she noticed the thick gold-brown rope hanging over Madame's shoulder. A smile spread slowly on Lily's face as she pointed approvingly to Madame's braid, and then to her own dark plaits.

"Ah, oui! We both wear braids, don't we?" Madame smiled too, but her eyes were rimmed with red, her lids swollen.

Lily moved closer until she stood at the edge of the bed, where Madame sat against her pillows. "Madame," Lily began. Her voice shook with concentration. She wanted to say something important. But it had to be simple, or she'd never manage to get it out.

"Oui?"

"Madame, I—I—see—you." Hesitantly, Lily reached out and laid her hand on Madame's back. "I see you. I hear you."

Madame's lips trembled, and another tear spilled down her cheek.

Lily wiped it away with one finger, then patted Madame's white cheek. "I see you," she said again. Lily pointed to her own heart and then to Madame's. "I know. It hurts."

Madame's face cleared like the sky rinsed clean by the rain. She cupped Lily's shoulders in her hands. Candlelight sparkled in her soft grey eyes. "Lily, ma belle, I see you too. And I want to hear more from you." She raised her eyebrows. "Please? Shall we try?"

Lily grinned. "Oui, oui, Madame!"

Smiling, Madame patted the bed beside her. When Lily climbed up, Madame folded her in a warm embrace, rocking gently, as a mother might. Her braid tickled Lily's nose, but Lily didn't mind. When Madame placed her hand on Lily's head, her faint rose scent enveloped her. Lily sank into it, eyes closed, and did not imagine herself anywhere else.

When sweat dampened the nightgowns between them, Lily leaned back and noticed something dark beneath the lace trim on Madame's short sleeve. Gently, Lily touched a fingertip to the scar and lifted her questioning gaze to Madame. "What is it?"

Madame pulled her sleeve up to her shoulder, revealing a black brand shaped like a flower. But not just any flower. Wonder filled Lily as she traced the ragged edges on Madame's skin. "Lily? My name! You have my name on your shoulder!"

Madame's lips parted in surprise. "So I do!"

"You wear my name!" Lily repeated, just in case her French wasn't clear on her first attempt.

It must mean I belong here, she wanted to say, but could not find the right words. Instead, she only pointed delightedly at herself and then touched her fingertips to Madame's mark. She did not need to ask where it came from. Lily knew it was there for her.

Merci, Jésus. She need not be afraid, for she was exactly where she was meant to be.

⚜ ⚜ ⚜

While Marc-Paul was gone, spring bubbled and simmered until the full boil of a Louisiana summer took its place. With Lily's hand hot and damp in her own, Julianne shielded her eyes from the morning sun and gazed at the St. Jean Inn as they approached. A childish squeal drifted to her ears.

"Angelique is here," she said to Lily and led her around to the back of the inn.

"Bonjour!" Lily skipped over to the redheaded two-year-old splashing in a pan of water on the ground.

"Bonjour, Lily and Julianne!" Francoise rose from her wooden chair on the gallery and kissed them both on their cheeks in turn. The scent of her jasmine hair pomade wafted behind her. Denise sat on the gallery with her skirts full of peas. "Join us?" Francoise tossed an apron to Julianne.

Knotting the apron strings behind her waist, Julianne bent to kiss Denise on her rouged cheek, then grabbed a mess of beans and settled into a chair in the shade. Blue-bodied dragonflies darted through the heavy air, the glassy panes of their wings glinting with rainbows.

"It's good to see you, Julianne," Denise offered with a smile. "And Lily." Her tone held no judgment, though Julianne knew she had stayed away too long. "Lisette will be sorry she missed you, I'm sure."

Julianne nodded. "She isn't ill, is she?" Fever had come along with the summer and had already laid more than a few colonists low.

"No, she's with a client. Laurent is watching their baby and mine."

"Ah. Good." Humidity coiled the hair at Julianne's temples and neck. Spun between the gallery's overhang and the wooden post that supported it, a spider web glistened with dewdrops. Each strand of silk thread had become a necklace of glass beads overnight.

Peas tapped into pails and hulls pattered into piles on the ground while Julianne and Denise worked, a calming background to the gleeful chatter between Lily and Angelique. "They understand each other's French," Julianne said, and laughter rippled through the women.

Francoise perched on the edge of her chair, scooped softened corn kernels from a basket, and poured them into her mortar. "Where would we be without corn?" she murmured with a shake of her head as she began grinding with her pestle.

Denise sighed, swiping the back of her hand across her brow.

She squinted into the sun, where Angelique and Lily played. "But do you think there will be enough? After the flood?"

No one responded. Julianne didn't want to think of another famine, not after the one that just ended last fall with the arrival of a few ships from France. Over the sound of children playing, she could hear boatmen shouting to each other on the river a block away. They were bringing more Africans or more colonists or both. If they weren't to settle in New Orleans, they would certainly clog the settlement, as they always did, until enough boats could be found to carry them away. They more than doubled the number of hungry bellies in New Orleans while they sojourned, and they brought nothing with them to contribute.

The lull in conversation amplified the rhythmic grinding of Francoise's pestle against the kernels. "France will send another shipload of flour," she said. The flour sent from Illinois was never enough.

Denise arched one dark eyebrow at Julianne, as if to say, *But when?*

A stifling breeze blew Julianne's hair against her neck. The lace edging her sleeves at her elbows swayed as she ran her thumb along the inside of a pod, sending eight small peas into her apron. Weightless on her lap, they seemed so insignificant. It would take so many to fill the bucket. To fill a belly. After shelling a handful more, Julianne made a funnel of her apron and tipped the peas into the pail at her feet.

Oblivious to the hunger pawing at the colony, Lily planted herself on her knees and pushed a piece of bark across the pan of water. Angelique caught it and shook it above her bare head, sprinkling herself and Lily with their very own rain. Laughter soared from the little girls' mouths. "Bravo!" Lily patted Angelique's curls.

"Angelique!" Denise called out. "You put that hat back on

your head this instant! Look at her. Beet red already. She'll burn to a crisp."

Lily glanced at Denise, then lifted Angelique's straw hat from where it dangled by its ribbon behind her back. Smiling broadly, she set it—just so—on the toddler's head and waved victoriously back at Denise.

"Merci, Lily!" Denise blew her a kiss.

"Your Lily has bloomed." Francoise smiled as she tipped her ground corn into an earthenware jar and scooped more kernels into the mortar. "She looks happy, ma chère."

"She saw my brand." Julianne looked up from her peas to see if they understood. "She saw her name in it."

"Of course! The fleur-de-lys!" Denise chuckled, hands momentarily suspended above her apron.

Julianne smiled. "And she hasn't been the same since. Every day she drinks in more French, and she soaks up any attention I give her. In truth, it's been good for us that Marc-Paul has been gone. She gravitates toward him, and he does her no good by coddling her. But now she and I share a connection of our own." She still marveled that God had taken her mark of judgment and used it as an instrument of grace.

Denise turned a frank gaze on Julianne. "So how are you? Really?"

Julianne twisted the ring on her finger, unsticking the metal from her skin. "Marc-Paul questions my fidelity. And now he's gone for so many weeks, and there's no way to repair it. Likely, the longer he's gone, the more he will doubt."

Denise's brown eyes flashed. "Why in heaven's name would he suspect you?"

Julianne thumbed another row of peas into her lap. Gazed at Lily, who was drawing pictures in the dirt with a stick. "People talk." She shrugged, unwilling to confess that there *was* another man, even if that man was not a lover.

"Does he have reason to mistrust you?" Francoise's voice was gentle but firm. "Have you been honest with him in all things?"

"I'm faithful to my husband. I've told him so." But she would not broach with her friends the subject of her brother's desertion and her husband's role in his execution. Biting her lip, she fixed her gaze on the peas growing blurry between her fingers. Not even her friends could know that Benjamin lived. The secret was a boulder on her chest. "He's pulling away from me. I don't know what else I can do if he won't believe I'm true. I fear there is no bridge long enough to breach the gap between us now."

"You must try to reconcile, whatever that requires," Denise said. "You tended Pascal Dupree's burns after all that he did. Surely you can do what is required for healing in your own marriage."

"He won't believe the truth." At least, not the piece of it she had told him. A sigh shuddered over her lips. "I don't know if I can fix this."

"You can't." Francoise smiled. "But God can, through you. Ask Him."

Chapter Twenty-eight

❖ ❖ ❖

AUGUST 1722

At the market between Decatur and Chartres Streets, Julianne held tightly to Lily's hand in case she tried to wander off. Wearing a brown silk dress, the little girl tugged first one way and then another, according to whatever caught her eye. The Place d'Armes thronged with activity in the open space surrounding the barracks.

Germans from upriver came with peas, spinach, peppers, and cabbage. Houma and Acolapissa natives brought chickens, maize, and beans. Indian women bore baskets on their backs by leather straps circling their foreheads. Their half-dressed children darted with handfuls of wampum between silk-clad colonists. Choctaw entered the commissary with clutches of Chickasaw scalps and emerged with guns and powder. A fisherman slapped a catfish on a table five feet from where she stood. With opaque eyes, the fish seemed to stare at Julianne while the fisherman cut fillets from either side of its spine and ran his blade along the length of it, separating skin from flesh.

She followed Lily's gaze to the African families being marched in from the docks and parceled out to French and German farmers. When she had first arrived in New Orleans, most of the population was French. Now French colonists were far outnumbered by the Africans they had snatched from sunny shores and enslaved for the purpose of growing the French empire, in the manner of the British growing theirs. It was overwhelming, even to Julianne.

After weaving their way to a German woman with florid cheeks, Julianne paid fifty *sous* and carefully laid a dozen eggs into the basket at her hip. "And now," she said to Lily, "how would you like to spend the day with Madame St. Jean and her grandbaby? Lisette and I have some clients to attend." Clients who also happened to be tavern girls in need of their yearly examinations. It was no place for a child.

"Oh yes!" Lily clapped her hands. "I'm very good with babies, you know. The ones already born."

"I understand." Laughing, they threaded back through the crowd.

Shouts pierced the din of the market. Slowly, people siphoned from the docks and sale stalls and toward the wooden horse. Acid churned Julianne's gut as she craned her neck. A woman, stripped naked, hair draping her face, was already tied there for all the town to see.

"Let's hurry." Julianne picked up her pace and delivered Lily to Francoise before the whipping began.

Lisette was ready to go when they arrived at the inn. Crossing back to the tavern was much easier now that so many people had gone to see the girl on the wooden horse. Summer's heat became unbearable as it beat upon the shadeless square.

Julianne could not ignore the woman's heartrending screams. "Here." She transferred her basket of eggs to Lisette. "Take these to the girls. I'll join you as soon as I can."

Wariness framed Lisette's clear blue eyes. "What are you going to do?"

"I can't do nothing." She turned back toward the sound.

As she elbowed her way through the circle of onlookers, she could almost feel the leather lash through her skin once more. Was this girl as innocent as she had been? Then the young woman raised her head and locked her desperate gaze on Julianne. Helene, the tavern girl whose loose tongue had exposed Julianne's brand to Pascal, was now being flogged herself.

Julianne waited for a sense of vindication to wash over her. Sorrow rushed in instead for the devout orphan girl Helene had once been. How very far she'd fallen.

"Stop!" she cried. "Stop at once!" She fought her way up to the soldier who held the whip. "Why, Joseph!" She clutched the arm of the young soldier she had once nursed through a fever. "This isn't justice, it is base diversion."

The crowd jeered at her and urged Joseph on, like a swarm of Romans bent on seeing blood spilled for sport. When he paused, another soldier ripped the whip from his hand and laid the lash on the woman's back again.

Julianne lunged for him, but Joseph caught her, pinning her arms to her sides. "Do not cross him, Madame Girard. Not him. He would have you on the horse next, and I'd not have the strength to stop him."

Helplessness boiled in her chest. Blood streamed from Helene's back, and Julianne felt that fire raging across her own flesh all over again. She couldn't bring herself to watch this torture, but neither could she walk away from it. Helene's body slumped and slipped off-balance, half hanging from the horse. She'd lost consciousness.

Slowly, Joseph relaxed his grip, and Julianne sprang from his arms. "You've done enough. She is scarred for life!"

"Like you are, you mean!" A voice in the crowd assaulted her. "It's the marked midwife! Watch out, or she'll shoot you in the dark like she shot Matthieu Hurlot!"

"I've heard about you," sneered the soldier with the whip. "Always wondered if it was true." In one violent move, he grabbed her sleeve and yanked, popping the seam and ripping the fabric down to expose her brand. Out of the corner of her eye, she noticed three brave women rush up to Helene and untie her limp form. Circling the whipmaster, Julianne drew his attention away from it—and unwittingly exposed her mark to the crowd.

"The fleur-de-lys!"

"Didn't you hear? She's a murderer sent from the jails of Paris."

Like a scab torn away, the fresh taunts reopened her wounded reputation. She absorbed the taunts as long as she could while Helene's friends spirited her to safety. The whipmaster looked over his shoulder at them before turning back to Julianne. Evidently, the whip was reserved only for conscious victims. Like her.

Another voice in the crowd rose up. "Such a pretty face. You'd never know the schemes lurking behind it, would you?"

"Bloody her!"

Julianne's heart raced. She'd stayed long enough.

The whipmaster lunged for her, leering, just as one of Marc-Paul's men, Raphael, blocked his path with his towering bulk. "You will not touch Captain Girard's wife."

As Raphael and the whipmaster faced off, Joseph took her hand and pulled her away. "Time to go."

He walked behind her through the crowd but could not protect her from the fist that flew at her from the side. "Get back!" he shouted as she tasted blood. "Where can I take you?"

With a shaking hand, she touched her fingertip to her split lip. "I'm fine, Joseph." She tried to believe it. "My friend is waiting for me in the tavern."

A moment later, she was inside the dim building and at Lisette's side.

"*Ma foi*," she whispered. "Your gown!"

"It's nothing. I can repair it."

"What's that?" A tavern girl named Claude pointed to Julianne's shoulder. Her eyes narrowed. "Don't touch me."

"Claude—" Lisette's soothing voice was cut off.

"No. You can tend me just fine, and the other girls too. We don't want her here."

A few other nodding heads confirmed the consensus.

"I'm sorry," Lisette whispered.

"You needn't be." Julianne forced a smile. Lisette had a special rapport with the tavern girls, anyway. She was an orphan at Salpêtrière because her mother had been held there for prostitution when she was born. She must have let these girls know it, because her presence was always welcome. "I'll just collect Lily and go home."

"Why don't you rest a while? I'll bring her back to you later."

Blood pulsed in Julianne's lip as she nodded. It would not suit for her daughter to see her this way.

⚜ ⚜ ⚜

Once home, Julianne went straight to her chamber to see her swollen lip in the glass above the washstand.

"The door was unlocked. Didn't think you'd mind." Benjamin's reflection stared back at her over her shoulder.

"Benjamin!" She rounded on him. "Did anyone see you come in? You must be more careful!"

His expression shifted from easy confidence to fury. His eyes were sharp grey slits as he scanned from her injured mouth to her flapping sleeve. "Who did this to you?" Muttering a word he'd never been allowed to say as a child, he circled his thumb over her brand, and she flinched from the heat of his touch. "The mark of the king, indelibly on your skin." His tone was ice, but his face was flushed well past his normal ruddy hue.

Julianne laid her wrist on his brow, and alarm poured into her. His skin was scalding hot. "You're ill!"

"Just the fever. It comes and goes."

"To bed," she ordered, then saw that he had been lying in it already as he waited for her to return. His gun was propped in the corner of the room with his hatchet and moccasins on the floor beside it. "We need to bring your temperature down. Shirt off."

"Ah, my sister takes such good care of me." Benjamin pulled his linen shirt over his head, revealing a pattern of tattoos tracing his chest. They were different from Red Bird's markings.

"Is this the fever you had at the end of your time at the Choctaw village?"

"Yes."

So that much of the story, at least, had been true. "How near did it come to claiming your life?"

"Very near."

And it had returned. Turning back to the washstand, Julianne poured fresh water into the basin, plunged two cloths into the water, and wrung out the excess. Back at Benjamin's side, she folded one wet cloth and laid it on his forehead. She felt his gaze on her as she used the other cloth to sponge the perspiration from his face, neck, and shoulders. His chest rose and fell with every breath as she swiped the cloth over his tattooed skin.

"So we are both marked, I see." She tried on a smile.

His eyes blazed, but blankly. He was sinking fast.

"You need cinchona tea. I'll get it."

When she returned with the concoction, she held his head and brought the cup to his lips so he could drink.

Benjamin grimaced. "It tastes terrible."

"You don't have to like it," Julianne murmured, taking the empty cup from his trembling hand. "A poultice," she said at once. "I'll make a poultice to draw the fever out."

He grabbed her wrist as she moved to leave. "Stay. Talk to me."

She lingered at his side. His eyes closed, but he slid his hand down and clasped hers. When was the last time she'd held her brother's hand?

"Girard is gone again."

She blinked. "Yes."

"Where did he go?"

Sighing, she sat on the bed beside him and held his hand in her lap. She doubted he would even remember anything she said right now. "Bienville sent him on a brig to the Riviere de la Madelaine, with food and munitions, soldiers and workmen. Very far west of here."

Benjamin's eyelids fluttered. "To do what?"

"They were to travel upstream and establish a fort on the riverbank. That's all I know."

"Mmm." He stilled, then began shivering. "So—so cold. Can we not have a fire to take off the chill? Please."

A fire. In August. But she slipped from the bed, tucked the counterpane snugly around him, and kindled a small flame in the hearth. Soon his deep breathing told her he'd fallen asleep.

All day he slept, and she was glad of it. After Lisette brought Lily home, and once the little girl was snug in her room for the night, Julianne returned to her chamber to find him still there. As the last light of day hung in the room, she saw in his face the little boy she had grown up mothering, and her heart squeezed.

Her gaze shifted to the gun and hatchet in the corner, stark reminders that he'd grown into a man. Then something triggered inside her. She moved closer and knelt on the floor. His gun wasn't like Simon's or Marc-Paul's. She frowned as she brushed her fingertips over the barrel and stock. Benjamin's gun wasn't French.

Her middle flipped. Sitting on her heels, she clasped her trembling hands in her lap and stared at it. Surely there was a reasonable explanation. When he awoke, she would ask him. In the meantime, she climbed onto the chaise in the corner, where Marc-Paul had slept for the first two weeks of their marriage. Her eyelids drooped, and she nestled deeper in the brocade upholstery, wishing it was her husband, and not his chair, who held her.

In the morning, Julianne awoke to find her brother's things absent from their corner and the counterpane drawn up over the empty bed. Benjamin was gone.

Chapter Twenty-nine

⚜ ⚜ ⚜

Aside from Vesuvius's enthusiastic greeting at the door, the house was quiet when Marc-Paul arrived home. Lily was already in bed for the night, and judging from the rose-scented steam wafting into the bedchamber, Julianne was in the bath.

The bed groaned when he sat.

"Marc-Paul?" Julianne's voice floated to him. "I'll be right there."

Was she disappointed that he'd returned? Steeling himself for their reunion, he peeled off his gaiters and shoes, removed his waistcoat, and set his tricorn hat on the bureau. With a glance at the Bible resting there, he uttered a silent prayer for peace as he stretched out on the bed and closed his eyes, for even his marriage had become a battleground over the last several months. Truth and deception warred, and he couldn't guess which would triumph. But there was only one answer that fit all the riddles in his mind.

Julianne stepped, barefoot, into the room, her damp hair falling in waves over her linen nightdress. As Marc-Paul raised himself up to sit on the edge of the mattress, longing stirred within him. He ached to draw her into his arms and into his bed, to indulge in her fragrant skin, her soft lips—but doubt and suspicion held him back.

She sat on the chaise in the corner of the room. Dust hung between them in the fading light of evening. "How was your mission?" A polite question. Or a probe for intelligence.

Head pounding, Marc-Paul leaned forward, elbows on his knees, and rubbed at the calluses on his palms. "There will be no French fort on the Riviere de la Madelaine." He sighed. "We met a strong party of natives twenty leagues upstream. I told them we came in peace, that the French were here to be their friends and to bring them the conveniences of life."

"And?"

"They said no. They told us they were satisfied with their condition and wished to live free and off to themselves, without taking any other nation among them. Bienville will be furious." He studied her for a moment. "Did you know this would happen?"

A ridge formed between her grey eyes. Eyes the very color of her brother's. "How would I know such a thing?" She pulled her feet up under her, burrowed further back into the chair.

"The natives were ready for us, Julianne. As if they'd been told of our arrival and had been persuaded against an alliance with France." He kept his voice calmer than he felt. "They knew about our trouble paying our allies. They didn't trust us. Meanwhile, Britain's colonies continue to grow."

Her eyes grew wide. "Will Louisiana survive?" she whispered.

The stillness that followed was thick and heavy, broken only by a pair of white-winged moths fluttering among the open beams above her head. At length, Marc-Paul quietly added his voice. "I don't know. We are in danger of extinction in this land, more than Bienville cares to admit. Is that what you want? For the French to cede to the British? Or is it merely what your brother wants?"

Julianne froze, her pulse visible in the hollow of her throat. "My brother?"

Tension banked up in the silence. Blood rushed in his ears as pressure mounted between them, a swelling tide that would not be turned back.

"I found his grave." Quiet words, but a breaker pounding the surf. "Your brother's grave. His coffin did not come out with the rest during the flood. So I dug it up."

Julianne reeled back, the color draining from her face. She sat unmoving save for the tears rolling down her cheeks and gathering beneath her chin.

"Why do you cry? It can't be in mourning for Benjamin. You already know that the coffin I opened was empty, don't you? How long have you known? How long have you kept this from me?"

Julianne pressed her lips together, her eyes bright with tears.

"Of course, he swore you to secrecy." Disappointment thickened Marc-Paul's voice. "No doubt he was none too pleased to find you've made me his brother-in-law."

Pushing herself from the chaise, she crossed the room and stood before him, clasping his hands. "You don't understand."

"Then tell me." He stood as well. "The man who came to you on Lundi Gras—that was Benjamin, wasn't it?"

She nodded. "It was the first time he came to me. I was so unhappy, so alone, and he—it was like he'd been resurrected from the dead to bring me comfort."

"So unhappy," he repeated dully.

"Yes." Sighing, she released his hands. She brushed her hair over one shoulder and braided it into a loose rope, her fingers trembling. "I was unhappy, for reasons you already know."

She was lonely, and he couldn't be with her. She wanted a child, and Marc-Paul wasn't man enough to give that to her. Yes, he remembered. The breeze that swept through the window failed to cool the shame that singed him even now. He walked to her toilette table. Flipping the lid from the silver box of ornaments, he stirred his finger in it until he found what he was looking for. "All those weeks and months, I thought I was losing you to another man." He held up the silver combs and recited the inscription that had been burned onto his mind since he first read it. "Devotedly yours."

"A gift from my father to my mother," Julianne breathed. "Benjamin kept them as a remembrance and gave them to me."

Nodding, Marc-Paul tossed the combs back into the open box. "I was right to suspect you were hiding something. I was only wrong to assume it was adultery. Still, I lost you to another man just the same, didn't I?" The young man who betrayed Marc-Paul's friendship had turned Julianne against him as well.

"That's unfair." Her nightdress whispered across the floor as she came and stood between him and the mirrors on the table. "My long-lost brother came back to me and said you would kill him if you knew."

"I am no murderer." But he did not say what they both understood. Judgment had already been cast. If Benjamin was caught and the law upheld, the order to execute must be carried out. If not by Marc-Paul, by another.

"Tell me, Marc-Paul, what was I to think? You let me believe Benjamin died of fever—"

"To spare you pain!"

"But it was a lie! You kept the truth hidden when we'd said no secrets should ever come between us! And let's not forget about Lily—"

"I told you Lily could be mine the very day I brought her home!"

"She was another secret, Marc-Paul. I love her, and I know you do too, and I even concede that her existence was a surprise to you as well. But trust is a fragile thing, and twice I've been shocked when something in your past dramatically entered my life."

Marc-Paul's cravat tightened around his neck as he fought to maintain his composure. "Are you forgetting that Benjamin left me to die when he attempted to desert? Yet it seems I'm the only one on trial here. What is my crime, exactly?" He unwound the linen from his neck and cast it to the floor.

When Julianne started to turn away from him, he grasped her shoulders. "Forgive me, for I am guilty. Of loving you when France and New Orleans had abused you and cast you aside. I love you in spite of your brand, in spite of what your brother did, both to me and to the colony. I love you so much I was willing to bear that burden alone, because I could not bear to lay one more heartache upon you. And for this, you condemn me? Now that you know Benjamin is alive, do you prefer him so completely over me?"

Julianne pressed her fingers to her temples. "Must I choose between the little brother I raised and the husband I love?" Her voice cracked beneath her question. This was exactly the pain Marc-Paul did not want her to carry.

"Have you not made your choice already?" he asked, smoothing a crease from her brow with his thumb.

Tentatively, she rested her hands on his waist, and he wondered if she knew her fingers touched one of his scars through his linen. "You must believe that if his intention has been to injure Louisiana, I was not aware of it. Until . . ." Her gaze shifted sideways.

"Until what?" he prompted, careful to keep the urgency from sharpening his tone. He took her hands in his. "Tell me."

She bit her lip. "After you left, he came to me with a fever. I noticed some strange markings on his chest. They looked native. I've seen some tattoos on Red Bird and Running Deer, but these weren't the same."

"Describe them."

She did, then peered up at him for the verdict.

A knot tightened in his gut. "You're quite certain? You got a good look at them?"

Julianne nodded. "Why? What do they mean?"

"Those are Chickasaw markings."

She squeezed her eyes shut. For a long, tense moment, the only sound in the room was the chirping of the crickets beyond the window. "Marc-Paul, his gun. I think it was British." She choked on the words.

A great sigh rose in Marc-Paul's chest before he wearily released it. "I wish I could say I'm surprised, but I am only grieved. Benjamin is in far too deep, and he's trying to pull you in with him. But if you truly desire to join him, I'll let you go. A quiet divorce."

Her gaze flew up to his.

"I'm sorry, Julianne, but you cannot be devoted to both of us."

"I know," she whispered. A lump bobbed in her throat. "But would you still have me, after all of this?"

Hope glimmered, however dim. "I would have you, wife." He cupped her cheek in his hand. "But you must choose, and be certain. This is not a decision to be made in haste."

Chapter Thirty

⚜ ⚜ ⚜

A week later, Marc-Paul left again, this time without telling Julianne—or the soldiers remaining in New Orleans, for that matter—his destination. Hours after his departure, shimmering, sweltering heat beat down upon the settlement. The air was so thick with humidity that Julianne felt as though she were wrapped in steaming flannel. On afternoons like this, she could think of nothing but napping like the Spanish. Lily too had taken to her room, most likely to splay herself over the floor.

Shuttered light striped the room with hot gold bars. As she peeled the layers of her gown from her body, Julianne caught the reflection of the fleur-de-lys in the looking glass at her toilette table. *My name! On your skin!* The thrill in Lily's voice still rang in her ears. So too did the taunts of the crowd gathered at the wooden horse. *Murderer! Bloody her!* Shuddering, she pulled her mother's silver combs from her hair and laid them in front of the mirror.

In nothing but her chemise and petticoat, Julianne sagged onto her bed and spread her hand over the dip in the mattress beside her. The scent of Marc-Paul—leather and clean linen and the coffee he preferred to brandy—enveloped her. Her thoughts rolled back to the circuit in her mind. To choose between her brother and her husband seemed a cruel decision. Fear of losing either one of them marched beside the love she held for both, pounding her bruised and weary heart.

Questions hounded her. Why would Benjamin side with France's enemies? Could Marc-Paul be mistaken about her brother's tattoos? Perhaps she hadn't described them correctly. Her head ached as she struggled to grasp what she was loathe to admit. At some point after his arrival in Louisiana, Benjamin had taken a dreadfully wrong turn.

Rolling onto her side, Julianne hugged Marc-Paul's pillow to her chest. Did he miss her, wherever he was? Or was he only relieved to leave the palpable tension in their home? As she drifted off to sleep, it was her husband's face she longed to see again in her dreams.

Then a thud sounded from somewhere else in the house. Julianne held her breath, listening. Footsteps fell. They did not belong to Lily.

Etienne? Julianne slipped from her bed and threw her robe volante over her body. Careful not to disturb Lily's rest, she quietly went in search of him.

She followed the sound of rustling papers to the library across the hall. But the man whose back was turned to her, hunched over the desk, was not her Canadian friend. Her frown deepened as she silently watched him rifle through Marc-Paul's things.

"I see you've recovered." Julianne kept her voice low.

Her brother whirled around. "I didn't want to bother you."

"You came into my house without so much as a knock, and you're rummaging in my husband's desk. That bothers me."

Benjamin shrugged. "The window was open."

"It's customary to use doors. After knocking. After being invited in." She crossed her arms over her gown.

"I knew Girard was gone. What, aren't you happy to see me?"

Julianne raised an eyebrow. "It would seem I'm not the one

you came to see." She nodded at the mess on Marc-Paul's desk. "Wondering how his mission went to establish a fort on that river?"

"Heard it went badly." He did not seem displeased.

"Heard from whom?"

"Another courier."

"Would this be the courier you sent to the natives along the river to warn them of a French contingent headed their way? The courier who advised them against an alliance?"

"I won't bore you with the details." But he didn't deny her insinuation. He certainly didn't seem shocked. "What can you tell me about where your husband is now?"

She gritted her teeth. "Nothing. He didn't brief me."

"Don't be coy, Julianne. Tell me what you know. You just have to trust me."

But trust was a luxury she no longer possessed. "No, I don't."

His eyes flashed like silver saber points. "Tell me. I would not ask if it wasn't important. Where is he now?" His voice ratcheted up in both volume and pitch.

She narrowed her eyes at her younger brother. Rarely had he taken that tone with her growing up. Never, not once, had it persuaded her to give him what he wanted. "Exactly what business is that of yours?"

Benjamin's determined gaze matched Julianne's. He ran a thin hand over his face. "My business is the good of the country. I vow." Sweat glittered on his brow.

She stepped closer to him. "Which one?"

"Pardon?"

"Which country, Benjamin?" She swallowed, willing him to deny her suspicions. "Which king do you now serve?"

He straightened, as if at attention and ready to salute. "The one who serves me back."

Releasing her breath, Julianne gripped the back of Marc-

Paul's chair, fingernails digging into its crimson brocade. "How could you?" Her voice quavered.

"*Ma foi,* Julianne, how can you wonder at this? You, of all people? France exiled you in the name of Louisiana, but did the king or his regent trouble themselves to see that you had enough to eat? Of course not. They did not even care to clothe their own soldiers, let alone send food. How can you serve a country that doesn't serve its people? You've had no choice, perhaps, but Captain Girard—" Benjamin shook his head. "His loyalty to the crown borders on the blind faith a sheep has in its shepherd. I've seen him suffer for France. I've seen him haunted by some of Bienville's policies toward the native peoples. And yet he remains. Following orders. Obeying rules. As if he had no mind of his own."

Julianne stepped back and leaned against the doorframe as Benjamin's words crashed over her. This was treason. This was a death sentence. "Marc-Paul serves a cause bigger than himself. You were a soldier once. You should understand."

"I understand that he is a fool not to cut his losses."

"And turn his coat?"

"Strategically realign himself."

Traitor. Julianne felt the scales fall from her eyes. Marc-Paul had not testified falsely against Benjamin. Benjamin had condemned himself with his actions. And now again, with his reckless words.

"Julianne, come with me."

What? She was too stunned to speak.

"Start over in Carolina. There are many, many French in Charles Town. Huguenot exiles. They've formed a community and thrive as merchants and farmers. You have no idea what a colony can be. You should see how the British live, while here it's all you can do to survive."

Her head spun. "I'm married," she sputtered.

"To a soldier. Soldiers die."

The look in his eyes sliced through her. "What are you say-ing?" A whisper, for her voice had gone.

"Dangers are everywhere. A snakebite can kill a man. An alligator certainly would. Not to mention a stray musket ball, or arrow, or tomahawk."

Memory triggered. Her first husband brought home from Natchez, his body so altered by tomahawk and scalping knife she was not even allowed to look at him to say good-bye. "Simon."

"I'm sorry, Julianne. Truly. If there was any other way . . ." He pursed his lips, cutting off his confession.

She swallowed. "Sorry for what?" She looked at him with new eyes, daring him to admit some role in Simon's death, and in the same instant, silently begging him not to.

Benjamin opened his mouth, then shut it for a moment, clearly thinking better of his reply. "Louisiana is a dangerous place. And I genuinely regret your heartaches."

But she knew. Her little brother was dangerous too. *Oh, what have you done?*

"You have no children by Girard," Benjamin barreled on. "Surely you don't prefer an impotent husband. You had a baby with Simon, after all. Come to Carolina, remarry, and have the desire of your heart: a baby of your own. Why stay, when a better life awaits? Abandon this godforsaken place. King Louis already has."

"You go too far—"

"Your mark would mean nothing to the Huguenots, who have their own reasons to reject the king and country who put it there. Aside from your marriage, which is tenuous, what ties you here?" His face was bright with persuasion and possibil-ity. "We'll take Lily with us. What's left? Do you even midwife anymore, or has your brand exiled you beyond the settlement's borders?"

"I am not in *exile*," she spat. "I'm still a midwife." She would not tell him that her brand had reduced her from official colony midwife to a volunteer. Nor that Lisette was almost as skilled as Julianne by now. She certainly wouldn't tell him that her greatest recent professional victory was that Helene had softened toward her since she'd interceded at the wooden horse, and had convinced the other tavern girls to allow Julianne to tend them again.

Why stay? The question curled around her. *A better life. A baby of your own. Your mark would mean nothing.* Like a vine, the words climbed, winding their way about her in a breathless embrace.

"Come with me," he whispered, and it sounded like a serpent's hiss in her ear. "Please."

Her gaze snapped to his, and the uncertainty that had bound her shriveled away. She made her choice. "I will not leave Marc-Paul."

Benjamin's jaw tightened as he looked at her. "At least tell me where he is."

Silence.

He swore under his breath, then sighed. "Once I leave, you'll never see me again if you don't come too."

She bit her lip to keep from crying but made no sound.

A sadness flowed into his eyes and hung there a moment. "If you tell anyone I was here, I'm a dead man. Adieu, *ma sœur.* I trust you'll keep this to yourself." He kissed her cheek and climbed back out of the window.

Julianne sank to the floor.

⚜ ⚜ ⚜

Lily wasn't really taking a nap. She was doing what she did best—staying invisible. And listening to the angry voices coming from Papa's library. There was a man in there with Madame, and he was making her upset. He spoke so quickly, and Lily couldn't understand his French. But there was no mistaking that whatever he'd said had made Madame cry. Again.

She watched him slide from the window and recognized him as the man she'd seen twice before. He was the hunter from the swamp and had come to talk to Madame at the house while Papa was away. But when Lily told Papa about him the night he came to soothe away her nightmares, he'd seemed so upset she tried to take it back. *"Maybe I didn't see anyone after all,"* she'd said, desperate to smooth the creases from Papa's brow. *"Maybe I only dreamed it."*

Maybe she'd been wrong to try to cover it up. This man who spoke French but stole around like a Chickasaw—he was up to no good.

Lily's legs ached to run after him. And so she did. Her feet made no sound as they landed on the ground outside her own window, as they carried her off toward the swamp. She would trail him like a real hunter. Wouldn't Papa and Madame both be proud? Arms and legs pumping, she smiled as her braids swished and bounced behind her back. *I am the wind, an invisible sigh.* And the wind could never be caught.

Sand sprayed her calves beneath her skirt as she ran along the ridge between cypress and gum trees. Moccasin prints on the path ahead of her pulled her along. When a branch barred the path, she planted her hands on its mossy bark and vaulted over it, eyes keen on the man's trail. Clearly he hadn't thought he would be followed, or else he would have walked in the water instead. Lily smiled at her sharp wits.

Then she stopped. Frowning, she looked behind her. Her own footprints were just as easy to spot as his, since she had been pounding the ground so hard. If someone wanted to follow *her* trail, she'd made it far too easy. With only a moment's hesitation, Lily stepped into the shallow pool where turtles waded beside the sand. She took long, steady strides, and satisfaction filled her chest. She'd made her trail disappear.

Mud squished under her feet as she traveled beside the sandy ridge, keeping one eye on the moccasin prints and the other eye on the water, where fish swirled about her ankles. More than once, she stepped in a hole and lost her balance, nearly falling headlong into the water. Still, she trudged on.

Until a hand clapped over her mouth and her feet lifted out of the mud. An arm cinched around her waist and carried her farther from Papa's house.

Shock coursed through her. She kicked, but he squeezed her harder, until she needed all her strength just to breathe. Unable to see his face, she looked down at his feet instead. He wore black leather boots with square heels. This was not the man she'd tracked.

"Bonjour, little spy," he hissed in her ear.

Chapter Thirty-one

✤ ✤ ✤

Benjamin's exit still stinging, Julianne drew a fortifying breath and went to Lily's room. Surely she would have heard the shouting and would be wondering what had happened.

"Lily?" Julianne stepped inside the room. The bed was empty. The floor was clear. Quickly, she looked under the bed.

Lily was gone.

Dismay drummed in Julianne's chest as she hastened from room to room, calling her name. *Did she run away? Or did she only wander again?* They were the wrong questions for the moment. The only things that mattered were where Lily might be and if she was safe.

Julianne ran from the house and found Etienne in the garden. "She's gone," she cried breathlessly. "The river—the current is so fast—"

Etienne hurried to the shed, grabbed a coil of rope, and looped it over his shoulder. "Just in case," he said.

"I'll check the swamp," Julianne said above the pounding of her heart, for the settlement held no charm for Lily.

Fistfuls of silk grew damp in her hands as she held her gown above the ground and ran toward the steaming shadows of the swamp. Blackbirds exploded from a tree, peppering the sky with their flight. "Lily!" she called, heart in her throat. The far-off crackle of dead leaves amplified in her ears as she entered the shade. A snake? A possum? A child?

A branch snagged her hair, for she'd left without bothering to cover it. Her pins came loose, and the curls that had topped her head tumbled free while mosquitoes needled her skin.

There. Lily's footprints had left a trail on the sand. Julianne chased them along the ridge—until suddenly they disappeared. Helplessly, she scanned between the trunks for some sign the girl had been here. *Oh, Lily, where did you go?* At her back, the sun was beginning to set. If Lily was lost here after dark, not even the moonlight would penetrate the canopy overhead to show her the way home. If home was where she wanted to go.

Spider silk webbed Julianne's nose and eyelashes. With a shudder, she swiped it away and wiped her fingers on her skirt. The deeper into the swamp she wandered, the more lost she felt herself, but as long as she could see light, she'd be able to find her way out again. She glanced over her shoulder to mark the sun's rays and found them fading. Receding.

Lost. The word scraped like a razor through her mind. Lily was missing. Benjamin was a traitor. Marc-Paul was in harm's way. And she could do nothing about any of it.

But there was someone who could.

Twigs snapped beneath her feet as Julianne scrambled through the trees and headed straight for Pascal Dupree's house. Though he was in Yazoo, his slave remained in New Orleans. She didn't know where he lived with Pascal gone, but Pascal's house was the first place she'd check. Her hair streamed behind her as she ran through the last of the light.

Sharply, she rapped on Pascal's front door. When Running Deer opened it, her knees nearly buckled with relief. "Running Deer!" she panted. "Lily's gone. I need your help. Can you track her?"

Pascal Dupree appeared behind the man, and Julianne gasped at the sight of him.

"Happy to see me?" He lifted one side of his mouth in what might have been a smile, but his dimples remained hidden. The skin on the right side of his face had contracted, pulling his right eye open a little wider than his left. The scars were webbed and pale pink, a marked contrast to the tanned, smooth complexion just on the other side of his nose. "You'll understand why I cannot say the same for you. I must say, the change of pace in Yazoo was invigorating. Nothing to get a man's heart pumping like the threat of an arrow—or a musket ball—right through it."

"When did you—I didn't know you were—" But she could scarcely breathe, let alone speak. And it didn't matter when he'd returned. All that mattered was that he was here now, and so was she.

"I've only come for Running Deer, if you can spare him."

"Please do come in. I insist."

"No. I need to find Lily."

"And what if I told you she'd already been found?"

Hope flared. "Is she here? Is she all right?"

"Please. Come and see her for yourself."

Julianne brushed past both men until she stood in the salon. "Lily?" She rounded on Pascal. "Where is she?"

A small form appeared from the hallway.

Julianne ran to her. In an instant, she was on her knees in front of the child, arms thrown around her.

"I'm sorry, Madame!" Lily said in a rush. "I heard you crying, and I only wanted to find the man who made you sad! I wanted to track him to see what he was doing!"

"Are you hurt?" Julianne smoothed the hair back from Lily's face, her gaze quickly skimming from the girl's head to her toes.

Pascal laughed, then poured himself a cup of eau-de-vie.

"She's fine. A charming, talkative girl. She told me all about her mother, and you, and her dear Papa. Her French is coming along nicely."

Unease filled Julianne. She rose, taking Lily by the hand. "We'll be going now."

"No, madame. You won't." Pascal set down his cup and motioned to Running Deer, who grabbed Lily by the arm and started to pull her away.

"Where are you taking her?" Julianne cried out, lunging after them, but Pascal grabbed her by the waist and pulled her back.

"I don't want to go! I want to stay with Madame!" Lily screamed, arms and legs flailing, until Running Deer picked her up and carried her over his shoulder, absorbing the blows from her heels and fists with every step.

Squirming out of Pascal's grip, Julianne stumbled toward them, but she was too late. Running Deer and Lily had already gone, and Pascal dashed around her and to the door as soon as it closed. He locked it and pocketed the key.

"You and I have a little business to attend." His hot breath reeked of alcohol.

"I have no business with you."

"I want her." Pascal's fingers dug into Julianne's sides.

"What?"

"Lily. Name your price."

"She's not for sale! You cannot have her!" Julianne grabbed his hands to uncurl his fingers, but he held her fast.

"Think clearly now. I need a slave, now that Dancing Brook has left me. You are not likely to miss the child your husband sired with another woman."

"And you think Marc-Paul would agree to this arrangement?" He was mad. "Out of the question. Let go of me." She twisted out of his hands and hastened to the other side of the room. "She is not a slave. She is not a servant. Lily is our daughter."

Pascal's head dipped, his green eyes on Julianne, a predator crouching before its prey. "That's your argument?"

"Of course it is."

"What if she wasn't? Your daughter, I mean. What if she was just someone else's child that you were stuck with because your husband has a penchant for strays? What if she was . . ."

Your child. Understanding crept like spider legs over her skin.

With slow, fluid movements, Pascal neared her. Circled her. Stalked her. "I mean, really, what are the chances that on a single night of drunken indiscretion, Girard, the boy destined for the priesthood were it not for his father's intervention, would have actually managed to impregnate Willow, when you're still childless after nearly two years of marriage? Or is it unreasonable to assume he's at least been trying with you?"

"How dare you!" Her cheeks flamed red. The sand in her shoes ground into her feet as she backed away from him.

Pascal moved closer, his eyes fixed on her in an unnerving stare. He clucked his tongue. "It's a crime, really. You were purchased by the crown to settle the colony for France. Only you're not holding up your end of the bargain. You're barely midwifing anymore, and you haven't produced a single baby to help populate the empire."

"You stay away from me." Sweat filmed Julianne's face, her neck. Her bodice stuck to her skin.

"A baby of your own. Isn't that all you really want?" He blocked her path to the door, pinning her against the wall. He turned his head in a way she suspected he'd practiced in the looking glass, so that all she saw was his unblemished side. "Everyone knows it. The women of the town—or at least the tavern—seem to think you're cursed to a barren womb. Wouldn't it be nice to prove them wrong?"

She turned her face away from his sour breath. Pascal leaned into her. His lips brushed her ear as he whispered, "You'll never be able to do that with your husband. And yet, if you did bear a child, he would surely love you more. Find you irresistible." He nibbled her earlobe.

"Stop." Her throat was a desert. Her voice a mere croak.

"For what man can resist a woman who swells with the fruit of his seed?" Pascal splayed his fingers over Julianne's stomacher, and she knocked his hand away. Spit in his face. But fear stole the words from her mouth.

With a grimace, he yanked a handful of her hair and used it to wipe his cheek. "You know, the wenches at the tavern don't find me attractive anymore. Now I understand what it is to be judged by my skin. Like you. And I have you to thank for that."

Julianne swallowed. Her blood thrummed in her ears. "I don't know what you're talking about."

"Was it a deliberate trap, or just the foolish method of a woman, that you loaded your gun before you had any plans to fire it?"

Acid churned in her gut. Memory flashed to the night she'd awoken in her cabin to find her gun had vanished.

"If it was deliberate, I give you marks for cleverness. You must have known anyone who stole it would have loaded it with his own ammunition. That it would explode in his face as soon as he pulled the trigger. The question I've been dying to ask, however—did you know it would be me?"

Comprehension sliced through Julianne. "You took Simon's gun on the hunt with Marc-Paul?"

He shrugged. "I stashed it in the cache for a while, but I thought it vastly amusing to have the object of his search right under his nose. No one could have known it was Simon's but me. There was nothing to distinguish his Fusil de Chasse from any other from the Company of the Indies. I never could have guessed that I'd burn half my face off while trying to defend Marc-Paul. That's the thanks I get for my friendship."

Julianne's mind whirred to keep up.

"Ironic, isn't it?" he was saying. "Now we are both marked. We share a bond in this commonality, especially given the fact that you caused my injuries. If revenge was your aim, for exposing you on the wooden horse, I'd say you overshot the mark."

She fought against the rising tide of panic in her chest. Pascal was out of his mind.

"If you won't give me Lily, I'll have you instead—and you'll thank me for it when you carry my child. So will Bienville. You'll see."

"No!" A scream ripped from Julianne's throat. She thrashed against him, but he caught her wrists and pinned them against the wall behind her. Ground his body against hers.

She rammed her knee into his groin. He recoiled, just enough for her to wriggle free of his trap, and she lunged away, frantic to find Lily and escape.

Pascal caught the hem of Julianne's skirt and wrenched her backward. Threw her to the ground. Straddled her.

⚜ ⚜ ⚜

Lily curled into a tight ball outside the house, while Running Deer stood guarding her. She rocked back and forth in the twilight shades of ocean blue. *I am a shrimp, or a crab in its shell, swayed only by the current,* she told herself. *No one can see me. I am nothing worth seeing. I am invisible.*

Running Deer squatted before her. Cautiously, she peered over her knees at his glittering black eyes and wondered if he too would wrinkle his nose at the color of her skin.

He didn't.

"I had a daughter," he said. "White men took her while I was away. They made her their slave, I'm sure."

"Who?" Lily wanted to know. "Who took her? Did they give her back?"

Running Deer gave a short jerk of his head, almost like a twitch. Lily guessed he meant no, she didn't come back.

"It is not your fault that a Frenchman took your mother to his bed. You did not ask to be born half in one world, half in another. You can only span the chasm so long before you fall in between."

Lily frowned with the effort of understanding his meaning. "What will happen to me?"

Running Deer stared off into the night. "I wonder if my family would forgive me if they knew what I have become. I hate the French. And I hate the British. Monsieur Dupree, in a way, is both." He sat beside her and held his tomahawk in his lap. With his thumb, he felt the blade. "Did you know that my people will often divide scalps into two and get paid from both sides for one head?"

Lily shuddered and ducked her forehead back down onto her knees. Her hands covered her head to stop the tingling now crawling beneath her hair.

"White men are cowards. They get red men to fight their battles for them. I weary of stirring violence among them when the natives grow too peaceful to bring the white men gain."

Lily didn't understand any of this. But she heard Madame's cry and understood that perfectly well. She twisted toward the sound, but Running Deer pulled her back down. "He's hurting Madame. He's hurting her! What will you do?"

A long pause stretched out between them, and Lily tried not to ask her question again. She watched his long fingers slide over the broad side of his blade. Her gaze fell to her lap, and she picked at a stain between the pleats in her skirt. Wondered if Madame would ever be able to wash it free. But Madame was in trouble now, and Lily's belly jumped up and down with every sound she heard.

Finally, he said, "Are you good at hiding? If I help you find just the right place, could you keep silent all night long? Invisible?" Running Deer's hand tightened over his weapon.

Solemnly, Lily nodded. "I am a drop of water in the river." No one would find her, even if they were looking right at her. "But—what about Madame?"

⚜ ⚜ ⚜

Julianne's spine dug into the floor as she writhed beneath Pascal. *Oh God, not this!* She cried out, but would anyone hear? She curled her fingers into claws and slashed at him.

Enraged, Pascal struck her, banging her head against the floor. A hand-shaped burn scorched her cheek. Ache throbbed inside her skull.

"You've done enough damage to my face, ma belle, wouldn't you agree?" His hand cinched around her throat, squeezing ever tighter, siphoning the strength from her limbs.

Darkness spotted the edges of Julianne's vision. She was sinking. She fought to stay conscious.

Pascal released his grip, and she labored to pull air through her windpipe. His half-burned face hung above her as his hands groped roughly over her curves. She couldn't breathe. Couldn't fight, couldn't run. Bile rose in her throat as she felt the hem of her skirt rise higher, higher.

Footsteps thundered across the room. "Leave her!" a voice boomed, and Pascal jerked in surprise.

Julianne turned her head just as Benjamin slammed his fist into Pascal's jaw, knocking him off-balance. Julianne rolled to her side, coughing, gasping for breath. Shock rippled over her as her brother helped her off the floor and over to an armchair. Hand to her throat, she crumpled onto the seat.

Pushing himself up from his knees, Pascal touched the tip of his tongue to the blood trickling from his lip. "You fool."

Benjamin's hand was hot upon Julianne's shoulder. "You were never supposed to touch my sister."

"And *she* was never supposed to see us together. You reckless idiot. I was only having a bit of fun. No harm would have come to her. But now . . . we can't let her go. You know that."

Disbelief coursed through her. She barely trusted her senses. With trembling hands, she pushed her hair aside and tucked it behind her ears.

"She need not die," Benjamin said.

Pascal laughed. "And will you now tell me she will work for Britain? No, not her. She may be your blood, Chevalier, but she will not follow our suit."

"You two work together?" Julianne rasped.

Pascal dropped into a chair and sighed. "Shall you explain, or shall I?"

Benjamin flushed. He pierced Julianne with his gaze. "I was condemned to execution, as you know. Dupree here was tasked with carrying out the order. We worked out an arrangement. As you can see."

"Oh, you've left out all the good parts!" Pascal grimaced as he rubbed his jaw. "You should have seen your little brother beg for his life. Said he had a sister he loved so dearly, and that if he were to die, she'd have no other relation in the world. It was so pitiful, I own I was affected by it. But then, in a stroke of genius, he devised a plan. He could work for the British and send me a share of the profits for letting him live."

"What kind of work?" Julianne dared to ask.

Pascal tented his fingers and looked at the ceiling. "Collecting intelligence and selling it to the British, stealing French supplies, inciting unrest among the French-allied natives . . . the usual." He grinned, his bloodied lip garishly red.

She leveled her gaze at her brother. "How could you? After living so long with Red Bird's family and village?"

"I hated soldiering. I saw no point in our being here, since France didn't see fit to support us. When I tried to leave, it was the Chickasaw who aided my flight. Or tried to. And it was Red Bird who captured me and took me to Bienville. How could he have done that? He was like a brother to me! The Chickasaw and the British were only too happy to have me."

Pascal ran his hand over the smooth side of his face. "Now we must kill your sister, for she won't stay silent. And never forget, Chevalier, when you weep for her loss, it was your doing tonight that killed her."

Surely Julianne's ears deceived her. "You can't mean—"

Benjamin silenced her with a glare. "We leave tonight, if the men are ready to desert. Correct?"

"They are. The time is now, while Bienville and the others are away. There will be no one to stop us."

"Is that why you were so adamant to know where Marc-Paul is?" Julianne ventured to guess. "To make sure you don't cross paths during your flight?"

Benjamin nodded, then angled toward Pascal. "We'll take Julianne with us. She'll never make it back to New Orleans on her own. She'll be no danger to us in Carolina."

Julianne's heart banged against her ribs. Her breath burned inside her swollen throat. Without looking overlong at the door, she rehearsed in her mind making a dash to escape. *But where is Lily?* She could not leave without her.

Pascal regarded her with one raised eyebrow. Cocked his head. "That may be best. Running away while Marc-Paul's on his mission—very tidy. And believable. Write a note, Julianne, so he doesn't come looking when he finds you gone. I'll send Running Deer to plant it." Pascal looked at her as if he would flay the skin from her face to see her thoughts. "You will cooperate."

Julianne swallowed the rage that would have leapt out of her mouth if only given the chance.

"I plan to take Lily too," Pascal added with calm assurance. He pulled a knife from his boot and held it loosely, a casual threat. "So just say in your note that you've taken her with you."

"It's for the best, *ma sœur*." Benjamin reached for her hand, and she let him take it but would not return his squeeze. "You'll be happy in Carolina. Just as we discussed. Whatever your heart desires, you'll find it there. We'll be together, at long last."

His smile was a barb to her heart. Did he not realize it was kidnapping all the same? Had he so long rebelled against his conscience that he didn't notice the hatred blazing just beneath her skin?

Time flowed backward in Julianne's mind. *"Must I choose between the little brother I raised and the husband I love?"* she heard herself ask, followed by Marc-Paul's response: *"You cannot be devoted to both of us. I would have you, wife. But you must choose. . . ."*

Now her husband would have her answer. And every word of it would be a lie.

Chapter Thirty-two

✦ ✦ ✦

Disoriented, Julianne opened her eyes to find herself curled up on the floor. Benjamin sat on a barrel across from her. Rope bit into her wrists and ankles. Head spinning, she righted herself. "You drugged me." Hazily, she wondered if it was the same stuff Pascal had once given Marc-Paul, for she had no recollection of the time since she took it. No wonder her husband had sworn off strong drink.

"For your own good. And I made sure Dupree didn't touch you while you slept."

Small comfort. The cobwebs slowly cleared from her mind, and her eyes adjusted to the darkness. Barrels crowded the space behind Benjamin. Dozens of them, maybe hundreds. The floor creaked and tilted. The damp air smelled of—tar and salt? *Oh no.*

"What have you done?"

"You'll thank me once we're in Carolina, I vow. Look, Running Deer packed some of your clothing for you and even brought your midwife bag." He nodded toward the leather satchel in a crate just beyond her reach.

But it was what she didn't see that sent her stomach rolling. "Where is Lily?"

"In the wind. Maybe she and Running Deer ran off together."

"What?"

"She vanished." Benjamin chewed on a piece of straw as he spoke. "No trace of her. After Running Deer brought your things, Dupree sent him out to track her, but he never returned, and we couldn't wait."

Julianne scarcely knew what to think. *Lord, protect her. Be her light in the darkness.* She had to get back home. Pascal was not the only Frenchman who would turn the girl into a slave. *Please, let Etienne find her first.* As she prayed, Julianne fastened her gaze on the floor between Benjamin's boots. It was dusted with fine white powder.

"This ship. Isn't it the one that just arrived in New Orleans from France? The colony needs this flour! Women and children are hungry!"

Feet firmly planted on the floor, Benjamin crossed his arms. "They need to abandon the colony. The sooner they reach that conclusion, the better off they will all be. Louisiana is not the land of promise the crown insisted it was. Mark my words, the Chickasaw will block traffic on the Mississippi in a matter of months, and then they'll learn what hunger really is."

Julianne couldn't see his face to measure how convinced he was by his own logic. His voice came from the shadows.

"How long will they rely on France to feed them before they die? Better to relocate to a land made for farming," he went on. "Be independent of King Louis—and the colony that bears his name—for good."

Julianne didn't respond. While Benjamin sat on a barrel of stolen flour, preening himself with sleek self-assurance over the merits of his cause, her stomach flexed weakly, and darkness seeped through her veins. She was her brother's prisoner.

After a silence broken only by the lapping of water against the hull, the slide of crates across the listing floor, and the scratch of rope on her skin, Benjamin spoke again. "The ropes were Pascal's idea. I'm sorry. Merely precautionary, you understand."

She didn't.

As footfalls clambered over the deck above them, memory came swimming back to Julianne. *"We leave tonight, if the men are ready to desert."*

"How many did you persuade to come with you?"

"Persuade? These soldiers were only too eager for the opportunity. They didn't want to risk being sent up to Yazoo to be scalped by the Chickasaw. If it's numbers that concern you—only a handful. The rest went with Bienville and your husband to—wherever they are now."

The ship pitched to one side, and Julianne banged her head on the corner of a crate beside her. Wincing, she returned his stormy gaze. "You used me. When you knew I wouldn't approve."

"Because you wouldn't understand."

The floor rocked violently. Benjamin sprawled but caught himself, while Julianne rolled and smashed helplessly into a barrel with the small of her back. "Free me," she groaned.

"I'm sorry." Benjamin pushed himself to his knees, paused until the ship leveled, then stood and walked away, leaving Julianne alone in the hold.

Time had no measure beyond the scant meals that were delivered to her, and even those were not regular. She was no more certain of the hour or the day than she was of ever seeing Lily or Marc-Paul again.

When sleep took her in its fitful grip, Julianne dreamed the ship that rocked her was *Le Marianne*. Hair shorn, she wore the thin grey uniform of Salpêtrière, the dirt of the Saint-Nicolas Tower still under her nails, and she was sailing to New Orleans for the first time. Buoyed by the hope of finding her brother despite the marriage so recently forced upon her.

But when she woke on the stolen frigate, reality returned like a sour taste in her mouth. Julianne had found Benjamin in Louisiana after all. And now she was deserting the family she'd grown to love, just as her brother had deserted France.

⚜ ⚜ ⚜

The sea was calm. Horribly so, Marc-Paul thought as he gripped the brig's rail and scanned the horizon off the stern. They'd managed to sail away from the Florida coast just before winds gusted to fifteen knots and the seas rose to twelve feet. Now the gulf was once again a smooth surface of watered silk.

As he looked east toward Pensacola, the smell of burning timber and thatch still lingered in his nose and mouth. The mission had not been a pleasant one. A peace treaty signed across the Atlantic dictated Pensacola's return to Spain after three years of French occupation. But first—and the reason for this voyage to the barrier island—Bienville had commanded that Pensacola be burned before they abandoned it to the Spaniards. Now that it was out of French control, it would surely become a magnet for French deserters once again, which was the reason this trip had been kept secret from the rest of the garrison. No need to court temptation.

As Marc-Paul leaned on his elbows and gazed at the gulf waters, it was Julianne he saw. Was she thinking of him now? Would she have an answer for him upon his return? He prayed for the grace and strength to bear up under whatever the future held.

The wind snatched his hat and sent it cartwheeling south, over the larboard side of the ship. Straightening, he watched it disappear into a wall of fog. It was not a good sign. The wind was restless, shifting from quadrant to quadrant all afternoon. At first it came from the southeast. An hour later from south-southwest. Now it came from due north. And the pressure in the air was steadily sliding down an invisible slope.

A storm was coming. So was evening.

The wind strengthened, and crewmen swarmed up the rat-lines to take in the sails and secure them fast to the spars, their queues like flying ropes behind them. Marc-Paul inspected the deck, double-checking every cleat and line. The last thing they needed was a loose cannon in high wind.

A shout rang out from the deck above. "Sail! Off the starboard quarter. Headed this way."

Marc-Paul set the spyglass to his eye. Frowned. *Les Deux Sœurs.* "French supply ship." *Why is it sailing back now, ahead of schedule?* His skirted coat flapped against his breeches as he continued observing through the glass. A few sailors dotted the decks, but none climbed the ratlines. The sails, fully unfurled, quivered and snapped on the masts. No one hurried to secure the decks.

Marc-Paul marched fore, joining Bienville. "Signal her," the governor shouted over the wind, one hand keeping his hat securely atop his white powdered wig.

Armistead, the brig's captain, had already given the order. But *Les Deux Sœurs* made no response.

Marc-Paul looked through his spyglass again. "She's veering south by southeast. She's running." Or trying to.

"Deserters," Bienville muttered, and Marc-Paul promptly agreed. The queasiness that always accompanied him at sea was quickly doused with something stronger. Fury licked through his veins and burned in his belly. Would the interests of France always be undermined by her own men?

The brig was half the size of the 216-foot supply frigate, and faster. If the weather was fair, Armistead would have pursued *Les Deux Sœurs*, disabled her if necessary, and boarded the vessel. But thunder pounded the skies like a galloping, nettle-fed mare. If those who had commandeered the frigate didn't know enough—or have crew enough—to take their sails in during a storm, the seas would thrash her far more than any cannon could. The seas would thrash them all.

And then it hit.

Whether the brig entered the storm, or the storm suddenly materialized from nothing, the change was as instant as stepping from one room to another. The sea was the marbled grey of spoiled meat. Winds close to forty knots parted through the rigging with a scream. Swells mounded up chaotically, ominously. Eight-foot waves grew to twelve-foot, fifteen-foot seas. Twenty-foot. Within five minutes, a forty-foot wave broke over the brig. The rigging caught Marc-Paul like a net, and he clung fast to the ropes to keep from being washed overboard while the brig recovered.

"Get below, sir!" he called to Bienville. Louisiana would not survive its governor being lost at sea.

While Bienville made his way to his cabin, sea spray raked Marc-Paul, and his stomach heaved. Stumbling on the rolling decks awash with foaming seawater, he crashed belowdecks while the brig took the seas head-on, straining up the swells, struggling to maintain steerageway, then plunging back down the other side. Wind moaned as it sheared through the rigging.

Even if he had been above decks, the frigate would have been lost to sight, but Marc-Paul could imagine its plight. Unless it had turned about to head into the swells, they were going downsea, which was far worse. A ship headed downsea would be lifted on a wave, which would then just drop out from beneath it, and the frigate would fall back to the sea.

The soldiers belowdecks doused the lanterns to prevent fire. Darkness engulfed them as they collided with the floor and each other. The brig lifted on a swell and leaned dangerously starboard. No one said anything. There was nothing to say. If the vessel broached, turning broadside to the waves, they would roll and find themselves upside down in the water.

Back down they dove, and the smell of vomit and alcohol grew thick in the blackness belowdecks. Sea slammed over the stern, again and again, and the ship listed dangerously.

Even in the dark, Marc-Paul could tell the gulf waters were confused. Mountains of water converged, diverged, and piled up on themselves from every direction. If the brig buried its bow in the trough between waves, they would flip. If a hatch cover tore loose, they'd have one minute, maybe two, before the hold filled with water.

"It's only a storm. We've weathered storms before," said a voice.

"No," came another. "Not like this."

⚜ ⚜ ⚜

Water streamed through the cracks in the deck above Julianne. Standing, she pressed herself against the partition behind her, but the ship rolled, and she rolled with it. Wrists and ankles still bound, she tumbled into the water already sloshing over the floor. Pascal might leave her to her fate, but Benjamin, at least, would come for her. Surely her brother would come.

He didn't. No one did.

Seawater swirled around Julianne before she could raise herself up again. Her chemise was plastered to her skin, and her skirts billowed around her. Unable to swim with her limbs tied, she would drown in the cargo hold. She would be dead within the hour, and no one would ever know. At home, on dry land, where sunshine squeezed sweat from his pores, Marc-Paul would read the note she had been forced to leave him, and she would never be able to explain her final lie. She would be buried with secrets in the deep, between nations.

Shouting for help would be in vain; her voice was lost the moment it left her throat. Wind moaned, waves crashed, and the ship creaked in distress.

All was blackness. As water climbed up her body, she was buoyed up from the floor. She felt her hair fan out about her head, like eels floating on the water. Barrels of ruined flour rammed against her as the frigate was tossed about in the sea.

Suddenly, Julianne was somersaulting under the water, skirts over her head, with no idea which way was up. She held her breath, but she'd had no warning, no time to fill her lungs.

Something smooth and round and narrow nudged into her hand. The handle of her midwife's bag. She grasped at it blindly, even as her chest burned for air.

Another roll of the ship, and water cascaded down over her shoulders. She gasped and sputtered, vomiting seawater into the dark. But her bag was still in her hand, bobbing in the water. *Please, Lord.* With clumsy fingers, she unclasped the satchel and reached inside with both hands. Water had filled it, and darkness concealed it, but didn't she know how to see with her hands?

There. The scissors for cutting a baby's navel string. Her fingers curled tightly over them and let all else float away.

The ship lurched and lifted higher. Julianne flew backward, banging her head against the partition, but she held her twin blades fast. Braced herself for what she knew would follow.

The ship dropped freely from the sky back into the sea. Julianne's head knocked the ceiling before she plunged back down into the churning water that now reached to her chest. Blood trickled warmly from her temple.

The scissors were still in her hand. Awkwardly, she opened them, gulped a lungful of air, and dove under the surface to saw back and forth against the ropes binding her ankles. Over and again the frigate rolled, but still she kept blade to rope until her legs could snap the remaining fibers.

Kicking wildly against her skirts, Julianne emerged from the water and caught her breath. Wasted no time in cutting through the rope at her wrists. Finally, her arms were free.

But the weight of her sodden gown still pulled at Julianne. While water splashed at her face and seaweed tangled between her fingers, she cut the heavy embroidered silk from her body, leaving only her full-length chemise to cover her.

Her heart should have been racing, she thought, but it was honey-slow when she needed to think and act with lightning speed. In the belly of the frigate, she was three levels below the upper deck, maybe four. She needed to escape all of them, and she needed to do it in the dark.

Lord, be my light. Vaguely, Julianne remembered the layout of the flute on which she had sailed from La Rochelle almost three years earlier and wondered if it could be similar to the frigate on which she now sailed. Images sparked in her mind, of Simon in the hold and of the path she'd taken to reach him belowdecks for a visit. If she could only get her bearings . . .

Violently, the ship rocked, but whether it was larboard, starboard, aft, or fore, Julianne could not tell. She was thrown like a rag doll. Pain sliced through her when she landed. Water streamed down from above.

"Julianne!" A shout came down with the water. "Julianne!" It was Benjamin.

She spewed salt from her mouth before answering. "I'm here!" She pushed back her hair and turned toward his muffled voice.

"We need to get you out of there. Can you climb?"

The ladder. The rungs dug into her back. "Yes!" Turning, she clenched the wood and pulled herself through the abyss, toward the sound of her brother's calls.

When her hands slid over Benjamin's boots, he reached under her arms and lifted her to stand on the next deck. His stubble scratched her face as he pressed a hurried kiss to her cheek. "Here" was all he said, and Julianne felt a rope snake around her waist and pinch her skin through her chemise. Felt the tug of a knot being tightened. "Quickly now. Up we go."

Blindly, Julianne followed the rope's pull, stumbling over a deck that jerked and lunged. She tripped, and her hands grew warm and sticky as her tether ripped through her palms. Salt burned in the channels freshly carved from her flesh. Kelp caught between her toes.

"Two more decks to go," Benjamin called over his shoulder.

"And then what?"

But he only pulled her harder, faster, up toward the raging sea.

Chapter Thirty-three

✤ ✤ ✤

NEW ORLEANS, LOUISIANA

Wind roared through the swamp where Lily hid, cracking trees in half with the force and sound of French cannons. Running Deer had told her to stay tucked away as long as possible, but it couldn't be safe to stay here.

Darkness poured down upon her, cold and wet, until she was drenched with night and rain, though it should be day. Treetops bowed beneath an iron grey sky, their branches whipping sideways. A tangle of Spanish moss tore from its limb and caught on Lily's head, and she clawed the wet strands from her face.

The sand beneath her feet spread and loosened as she turned around, desperate to find her way home. The howling wind knocked her over, and she struggled on hands and knees. *Which way? Which way?* Fallen limbs and broken tree trunks barred the ridge she no longer recognized.

Panic beat in her chest. Papa was gone. Madame was lost. Lily couldn't even hear her own scream. Rain-pocked water lapped at her feet and wrists as she crawled to the base of a cypress tree. Nearly paralyzed by wind and fear, she clung to its ribs, terrified she would blow away like the Spanish moss. Another crash sounded, and the top of her tree tore off and smashed to the ground.

Wailing, she hugged the trunk of her tree and prayed to the Jesus-God who made the wind and the rain and the trees, begging Him to calm the storm, to bring her home, and to bring Papa and Madame back to her again.

Hands covered her shoulders from behind. With a start, she turned. Red Bird, Papa's friend, crouched before her, hair lashing about his face.

Throwing herself into his arms, she wrapped her legs around his waist. Without a word, he stood, holding her securely against his chest, and carried her away as the storm buffeted them both.

Thank you, Jesus-God, Lily prayed as she clung to Red Bird's neck.

When they emerged from the swamp, Papa's house came into view. Shingles ripped from the roof and flew through the air with dangerous speed. She ducked her head against Red Bird's shoulder as he hurried inside and wrestled the door shut behind them.

"Lily!" Etienne's voice sounded above the storm as Red Bird set her on her feet.

"Where are you?" she called, for all was darkness between the shuddering walls.

She heard the old man's knees thud to the ground just before she felt his arms fold around her. "Merci, merci!" he was shouting. "Where is Madame?"

"Taken!" she yelled in his ear. "On a ship!" At least, that was what Running Deer had said.

"What?"

The door burst open again, banging wildly against the house until the wind snapped it from its hinges and launched it far away. Leaves and bark and branches rushed into the salon on gusts that scraped Lily's face with sand.

Red Bird's hand went beneath her elbow. "To the fireplace!" he called, and she scrambled over the hearth to huddle in the small cave. Screaming filled the chimney over her head. She covered her ears but could not block out the noise.

"Where is Fist Face?" Lily cried, but no one seemed to hear her.

Her gaze desperately probed the room for the little dog. Papa's books flung from a table onto the floor and blew open, the pages flapping against the rain. Chairs toppled and hurled across the salon while blowing dirt and grass caught on the damp rug. But Fist Face was nowhere she could see.

Etienne fought to hold a plank over a window while Red Bird drove a nail into one end. But the storm's grip was stronger than Etienne's and tore the board from his hands. After several more tries, the one plank Red Bird managed to pound into place ripped free almost as quickly. Giving up, the men joined Lily in the fireplace.

"Can't we light a candle?" she pleaded. "I can't see Fist Face!"

"No flames," Red Bird shouted over the shrieking wind. "Too dangerous. The wind could throw something against it and start a fire."

"What about Madame Girard?" Etienne asked. "What ship?"

"A bad man took her! I don't know where they went! Can you search?"

Red Bird gravely shook his head. "If they are on the water—"

His words disappeared in the moaning wind, and perhaps that was just as well. Fear and guilt knotted Lily's stomach. If she hadn't run away, Madame would not have been caught either.

The storm shook the house in rage, and the frame around the missing door splintered into jagged spears of wood that sliced through the air. In the next instant, Fist Face yelped and bounded from the place one of the shards had landed.

"Fist Face!" Lily called, reaching for him.

He turned in circles, his tail tucked between his legs, searching for her.

A sound like cannon boomed over the wind, a signal that another tree had broken. With a deafening crash, it smashed through Papa's roof and right into the salon. Etienne and Red Bird crept out of the fireplace, shielding their eyes with their hands as they looked up at the ruined roof.

Near the door, Fist Face squeezed out from beneath a fallen limb—and didn't stop. When he ran outside, Lily launched herself through the wreckage of the salon and after him, praying one more time for Madame, who had chased after her.

⚜ ⚜ ⚜

THE GULF OF MEXICO

Minutes had dragged like hours while Benjamin resurrected Julianne from the depths of the ship. She now huddled with the rest of the deserters just below the main deck. The pounding of water over the bow seemed to pummel her chest as well. Foam slipped between the cracks above and rained down upon them.

Julianne gripped Benjamin's wet hand and pressed her other hand against the porthole as she peered out. Lightning split a black sky over an obsidian sea. Streaked with white froth, the waves convulsed and seized.

The frigate lifted in the air and slowly turned broadside on its way down the backside of the wave. Now *Les Deux Sœurs* lay sideways in the trough so that she could clearly see the wall of water rearing up before her. Thirty-five feet high, forty feet, fifty feet. Taller.

Benjamin cursed. "We are lost."

The wave picked up the frigate and rolled it.

And then the ship was upside down. Julianne tumbled and spun, the rope cinching around her middle while saltwater rushed in and lapped at her chin. They were sinking into the deep. In a pocket of air, she raised her palms and found the deck not one foot above her head.

"Swim down to the ladder!" she shouted, clutching Benjamin's arm. "Or you'll go down with the ship!" She released her brother and dove underwater.

Someone pulled her back, and she bobbed to the surface, sputtering.

"I can't swim!" Pascal's voice pealed desperately in her ears.

"I'll help you." Benjamin this time. "Julianne, go!"

She gathered as much air as her lungs would hold, then propelled herself through the dark water, hands groping for the ladder as she went. It wasn't where she thought it would be. Frantically, she waved her arms and hands through the deep while precious seconds ticked by. *How long can one hold one's breath? A minute? Ninety seconds? How long has it already been?*

Finally her hand brushed something, and she grabbed it— someone's arm. Whoever it was took hold of her, yanking until her hand hit the ladder. While her lungs urged her to surge upward like a buoy, her mind contradicted. *Down the ladder, to reach the upper deck*, she told herself. *Down, and then out and up.* One rung at a time, she pushed herself further down, escaped through the hatch, and felt her way along the upside-down deck. There was the mast pointing down, there was the rigging. And all of it cloaked in black.

Julianne's breath built inside her chest until the pressure was a vice around her middle, screwing tighter, tighter, until she thought her sternum and her spinal column must break. At last, she felt her way to the rail, pushed herself over the edge, and mustered all the strength she had into making swift, long strokes toward what she hoped was the surface.

Then a yank from below, and she was being jerked further down into darker, colder waters. She kicked at whoever was pulling her before realizing the rope was still tied to her waist—and still tied to whatever anchor Benjamin had used before he'd descended to the cargo hold to find her. She was leashed to a sinking ship.

Stunned at her oversight, and with an explosion building in her lungs, Julianne tore at the knot with fingers that scarcely cooperated until the rope loosened enough for her to wiggle from its noose.

Blackness crowded her mind, blurring her thoughts. The pressure in her chest disappeared. Muscles cramping, she surged away from the falling frigate.

When she broke through the surface of the rolling waters, she gasped for air and inhaled rain and the splashing sea. A long wooden plank bobbed near her, and with a final heave, she swam to it. There was so much water in the air, and so much air in the water, that without the plank keeping her afloat, it would have been impossible to tell where the sea ended and the atmosphere began. Raphael had surfaced too, and two other men she couldn't recognize.

Air refueled Julianne's lungs, and fear came rushing with it. "Benjamin!" she shouted, scanning the waters.

Beyond her reach, two heads came sputtering up to the surface, rasping to pull oxygen from the rain-drenched sky.

"Stop! You're pulling me under!" Benjamin's voice carried over the water.

"I will not drown a mile from shore!" Pascal, in a panicked scream.

Lightning blinked in the churning sky just long enough for

Julianne to see Pascal pushing down on Benjamin's shoulders, as though the young man were a life raft Pascal could mount.

"Pascal, stop!" she cried over the wind. "You'll drown him!"

Darkness again. Dread poured through her as she realized Benjamin had stopped fighting back.

"Help! Help! I can't swim!"

"Where's Benjamin?" Julianne shouted.

"Gone!" Pascal gurgled and thrashed.

Her heart turned to ice. Taking the plank with her, she swam toward Pascal and shoved the wood beneath his arms so he would not take her down too.

A swell lifted them, but they kept their heads above the surface. The black sky faded to gunmetal grey. Still menacing, but at least Julianne could see.

Still grasping the plank supporting Pascal, she swirled around, calling for Benjamin. His name caught in her throat. For there, within swimming distance, two arms latched around a bale of silk. Relief washed through Julianne as she released the plank and swam over to her brother.

"Hold on," she told him when she was near enough to be heard.

"Julianne. You made it." But Benjamin's speech was slurred. After blinking at her with pupils of unequal size, his head suddenly seemed too heavy for his neck, and he lolled against the silk. He must have hit his head on part of the ship as he brought Pascal out of it.

She sucked in a breath. If he'd suffered a concussion, he could drift into unconsciousness. She tucked his hands between the bale and the strings binding it together. But she dared not leave him, lest he begin to slip beneath the surface. Julianne positioned herself behind Benjamin and threaded her arms under his as she too clung tightly to the bale. "It's all right. I've got you." Words she hadn't uttered to him since he was a child and she the only mother he had, soothing him after a nightmare.

If only this were a nightmare from which she could wake as well.

Benjamin turned his head and wheezed. "I was a dead man anyway."

"What? What are you saying? No, we'll ride it out. The worst is over." He wasn't thinking clearly. Julianne could barely think herself.

"Where I'm going now, you cannot follow. Promise me you won't follow. I'll wait for you on the other side."

"I don't—I don't understand," she stuttered, heart rate climbing. Rain and seawater sprayed her face and arms.

"Pascal panicked when we surfaced." Benjamin paused to draw a ragged breath. "I didn't notice he still had his knife in his hand from cutting through rigging below. It was an accident."

Julianne could barely make sense of the words. "An accident?" She cast a sidelong glance at Pascal, drifting on his plank of wood twenty feet away. "Are you injured?" *Or just delirious?*

"His blade. Buried it in my stomach."

No. She saw the foam stain pink on the water. "I will not bury you again, Benjamin." But she would. Of course she would. There would be no recovering from such a wound.

"Forgive me. If not for me, you wouldn't be in this danger."

"Benjamin!" But she was helpless. Julianne knew how to bring babies from the womb, stitch skin back together, use plants to bring healing, dig arrowheads from flesh, concoct cures for fevers—but she could do nothing for the brother growing cold in her arms while the deep pulled at them both from below. He was slipping away from her as surely as if he had already fallen into the sea.

"I forgive," she cried at last, finality weighting her voice. "Now let me go."

Julianne stared at her brother's queue, wet and curling at his neck. "Come, mon frère," she called into his ear, her arms shaking as they framed his sides, her fingers still digging into the bale of silk. "Be strong. Hold on."

The wind sprayed her words back in her face. The coarse fibers of Benjamin's shirt pressed into her cheek as she laid her head against his back. A wave rolled over them, sloshing water into her mouth and nose. She choked on it, then coughed to clear her lungs.

Benjamin didn't choke or cough. Even the shivering had left his frame. Horror gripped Julianne. He was gone.

Shock numbed her, and she embraced it like an old friend that always came to her when she needed it most—at Salpêtrière, at her first wedding, after Simon's death, and baby Benjamin's. And now it was here again, a merciful carving out of her heart, that she may not feel its pain. Vaguely, she registered a persistent clicking and wondered what it could be, until she realized it was her teeth rattling between her jaws.

So it's over. Julianne had found her brother only to lose him. But she would not allow his flesh to feed the sharks. Tears mingled with rain, rinsing the salt from her cheeks. *Lord! I need you now. Please come.* She had no other words but these. Over and again they looped in her mind as she braced Benjamin's body against the bale of silk.

Time grew unreasonable. She felt anchored to the moment of Benjamin's death, while time passed over her like the rolling waves. She could no better discern minutes from hours than she could separate one dark swell from the next. Her thoughts blurred, and she was glad of it, for with clarity could only come pain. Water suspended Julianne between earth and sky, between past and future, life and death, like purgatory.

Then a screaming parted the wind. A bowsprit, broken from the prow of another ship, came hurtling like an arrow launched from Apollo's bow. Blankly, Julianne watched its flight. Wondered, distantly, if it had come to take her life as well.

But it was Pascal who was struck with a sickening thud and knocked into the water.

Was he dead?

Pascal's plank washed toward Julianne, and she caught it. Slowly, something soft uncurled in her middle and warmed through her veins, and she thought that perhaps it might be hope. Hope that the hand of God had struck Pascal Dupree down in perfect justice. Hope that she never need look upon Two Faces again.

Then one of Pascal's arms reached up out of the water, pawing in search of the plank Julianne now held fast. From the deepest, darkest trench of her spirit, white-hot hatred for Pascal Dupree bounded to the surface of her heart like wreckage after a storm. He had killed Benjamin.

But that wasn't all. The full litany of Pascal's wrongs unfurled in Julianne's mind. *Let him die,* said a voice. *Do nothing, and he'll be gone forever. He deserves nothing more than death. Nothing less than a painful one.*

"Help me." Pascal's voice was weak as he thrashed about with one arm. The bowsprit must have incapacitated the other, and he could barely swim with two arms. All she had to do was wait.

So she did. Julianne tightened her grip on the plank she kept from him, and in the corner of her narrowed eye, the lily flexed on her shoulder. The mark of a murderer. It mocked her now. *At last, the brand fits. A murderer after all.*

Pascal splashed with one arm again, then disappeared once more.

Another whisper in Julianne fought to be heard above the rush and roar of hate. *Grace you have received. Grace you must give. Love your enemy. Vengeance belongs to the Lord.* But she did not want to heed those words. Certainly, she felt no love. Still clinging to Benjamin's body, Julianne teetered between judgment and grace.

The list of loved ones she had lost was as long as Etienne's market list. Why was it now in her power to save the one man she despised? Why should he live, when so many others had not survived Louisiana? She licked the salt from her lips and closed her eyes, but she could not stop up her ears against Pascal's desperate splashing.

As his commotion faded, the plank pressing into her palm became a blade, slicing through her grief to the conscience that lay smothered beneath it. One tugged against the other and back again with dizzying speed. *Don't do this thing*, her conscience pleaded.

Who would know? Her anger, combusting.

You. Pascal. And the God who sees all.

I owe Pascal Dupree nothing.

God owes you nothing, and yet He made you His daughter. You are a child of the King; it is His image you bear. King Louis marked you with judgment, but the King of Kings covers you with grace. Whose mark will you now display?

The plank burned in Julianne's hand. Her eyes popped open, and she blinked the water from her lashes.

"Pascal!" she called as he slipped under again. The water bubbled above him.

With a hasty check to confirm Benjamin's hands were strapped securely to the bale, she released her brother's body and swam with the plank of wood toward where Pascal should come up again.

Suddenly she was underwater, Pascal's hand around her

ankle, pulling her deeper. Her white chemise wrapped her like a shroud.

I will not go down with this man. She doubled over, trying to peel his fingers from her leg. That failing, she kicked him in the nose as hard as she could. When his good hand went to his face by instinct, she wrapped her arms around his middle and swam to the surface with all her might.

Chapter Thirty-four

✦ ✦ ✦

Gasping for fresh air, Marc-Paul burst up onto the deck, unable to stay below a minute longer. All the ginger water in the world would not have made tolerable the rolling, cramped quarters reeking with eau-de-vie, sweat, and vomit.

Inhaling deeply of the rain-scrubbed air, he gripped the rail. The rain slowed to a patter, and the winds eased to a mere ghost of what they had been. The sky softened to pale grey silk, sunlight just peeking on the eastern horizon. There was no frigate in sight.

"A bit smashed up, but nothing as can't be repaired. Or replaced, in the case of the bowsprit." Captain Armistead strode with impeccable balance toward Marc-Paul, though the waves, still calming after the hurricane, were twelve feet high. "Worst I've seen in these parts yet. Still, we'll make it back to New Orleans fine, even if we do limp a bit."

Bienville joined them at the rail. "Any sign of *Les Deux Sœurs*?"

"Only that." Armistead pointed at a few barrels and bales, several crates and planks of wood, and at least one broken mast bobbing in the troughs and swells among an untold number of wine bottles. "The fools didn't even reef their sails before the storm. I'd not be surprised if they were all at the bottom of the drink right now, saving us the trouble of jailing and trying them."

Marc-Paul scanned the flotsam. "There may be survivors."

"Not if we leave them to their fate and let nature serve justice this time."

Ignoring Bienville's statement, Marc-Paul crossed the tilting deck to peer over the starboard rail. Uneasiness about *Les Deux Sœurs* had churned in his gut during the last several hours of the storm. Benjamin Chevalier was still alive. Would he dare commandeer a frigate in another attempt to desert to Carolina?

Armistead whooped. "We have a live one!"

Marc-Paul scooped up an untidy coil of rope and joined Armistead at the larboard rail.

"There."

He formed a lasso in the rope and cast it into the waves with a prayer it would reach its target. The man in the water caught the rope and let Marc-Paul reel him in while Armistead hung a rope ladder over the side of the rocking brig.

With a heave, Marc-Paul and Bienville pulled the sodden survivor up and over the rail, where he collapsed like any other fisherman's catch.

Marc-Paul knelt beside Matthieu Hurlot. "How many?"

Rolling to his side, the youth coughed and spit before responding breathlessly. "There were eight to start, but—I think there are four others who survived."

"Four men overboard!" Marc-Paul shouted, and a few other sailors came trotting on deck.

Matthieu shook his head. "Captain Girard, your wife." He closed his eyes.

A charge lurched through Marc-Paul. Had Julianne made her choice and left with her brother? "What about her?"

"When the ship capsized, I think she swam out ahead of me. But I haven't seen her—"

He had heard all he needed to. On his feet again, he stormed to the rail and held on as a wave broke over the bow. He barely noticed the spray salting his lips.

"Two more in the water!" Bienville called, the wind flapping his skirted jacket.

"Men?" Marc-Paul asked.

"Yes, men."

Armistead threw a rope out like fishing line.

Marc-Paul kept looking, straining his eyes to see through the mists that swirled over the waves. "Julianne!" he called into the fog.

"Here!" A man's voice straggled up from below. "Throw me a line!"

Marc-Paul leaned over the rail. Shock jolted him at the sight of Pascal Dupree in the water below. He had no idea he'd returned from Yazoo. He threw the rope to Pascal, who hailed without waving, one arm holding fast to a plank and the other in a sling fashioned from his own jacket.

"Where is Julianne?" Marc-Paul shouted down at him.

Pascal shook his head.

"Tell me!" A fury to rival the night's storm exploded in Marc-Paul.

A wave lifted Pascal toward the rope ladder, and with one hand he clutched it. "She's with her brother now. Fifty yards behind me," he panted. Water streamed from his hair and clothing as he climbed the narrow slats.

"I'm going in!" Marc-Paul shouted to whoever would listen. Ripping off his coat and boots, he vaulted over the rail and into the troubled deep.

⚜ ⚜ ⚜

Aching from fingertips to shoulders, Julianne rose and fell with a rolling swell, keeping Benjamin's body latched against the bale of sodden silk. The sun had risen behind the clouds, a pinhole on the horizon, and the wind had ceased its raging. Only the seas still stirred beneath a blanket of muffling fog.

Julianne shook her head to clear her ears and peered into the heavy mist.

"Julianne! Where are you?"

She sucked in her breath at the impossible sound of Marc-Paul's voice. "I'm here!" Water rippled around her as she turned to look in every direction. "I'm here!"

And then she saw him swimming toward her. Lunging away from Benjamin's body, Julianne met Marc-Paul and threw her arms around his neck, though it meant slipping underwater. For one breathless moment beneath the sea, he clasped her body to his, one hand circling her waist and the other plunging through her floating hair to cradle her head.

Before they sank any further, they released each other to kick back up to the surface and grab onto a broken mast. With one hand, Marc-Paul swiped his hair off his brow. "Julianne! What are you doing out here? Was this your decision, to leave me without a good-bye?" Water dripped from his nose.

"No." Julianne panted for breath. "Pascal and Benjamin took me."

A muscle bunched in his jaw, and his eyes burned with anger as he cursed beneath his breath.

"I would never leave you, mon amour, you must believe that," Julianne said. "You are my home, my family." With the mast under her right arm, she reached for Marc-Paul with her left, and he drew closer to her. "I choose you," she whispered, "with all my heart."

"I thought I lost you twice over." He bowed his head to hers. "Your love. Your life. If anything had happened to you . . ." The sentence broke on the crack in Marc-Paul's voice. Water lapped in the space between them, splashing at their chins.

She shook her head. "I am yours, if you truly still want me."

"I do." His hand came around her waist and pressed the small of her back toward him. She lifted her chin, and his salty lips caressed her mouth with slow, deliberate kisses that warmed her to her toes.

When she pulled away, a moan ebbed from her. "Benjamin . . ." She pointed behind her to his body several yards away, still floating with the bale that held it fast. "Pascal killed him."

Marc-Paul expelled a breath and shook his head. "Ah, Benjamin." Genuine sorrow thickened his voice. "We'll get him aboard and bury him properly."

Julianne could not tear her gaze from her brother's body. The tears that should have come did not, and shame wiggled through her that her eyes would not obey her heart. Long moments passed in silence, until Marc-Paul laid his hand gently on her shivering shoulder, and she remembered the cold and exhaustion that shook her.

At length, she thought to ask, "Did you find Pascal? He dislocated his shoulder. I couldn't set it in the water; I could only stabilize it."

Marc-Paul raised his eyebrows in obvious surprise she had even tried. "He's aboard, and he'll live. But he'll be tried for desertion." And with so many witnesses, he'd be condemned for sure. "Come, mon coeur. It's time to go home."

⚜ ⚜ ⚜

Back on the brig, while Julianne changed into dry clothes and rested in the captain's cabin, Marc-Paul found Pascal Dupree locked in the hold.

"Come to gloat?" Pascal asked, but there was no fight in his voice, no spark in his eyes. He slumped on a barrel in obvious pain, feet splayed against the rocking floor. "Twice I've saved your life. And yet you send me to my death with dry eyes."

A great heaviness settled on Marc-Paul's shoulders as he sat on a wooden crate, regarding the man he'd once considered his closest friend. "Why'd you do it?"

Pascal snorted. "Do what?"

"The crimes that condemn you to die."

Leaning his head back on the wall behind him, Pascal closed his eyes. "Am I to give a reckoning? Are you now my confessor, you who once thought to be a priest?"

"Confess your sins to God, Pascal, and He will forgive you. Be man enough to confess the wrongs you've committed against me, and I'll do my best to do the same."

"What you and I would label *wrong* may be completely different things."

It didn't used to be so. But drink and gambling, greed and lust had ruined what Marc-Paul had once admired in Pascal. He raked his hand through his wet hair. "Let's go with my definition. Start with the day I returned to New Orleans. The missing guns from our warehouse. You didn't use them to pay off an opponent larger and meaner than Le Gris, did you? In fact, if I were a betting man myself, I'd wager there never was such an opponent."

A chuckle rumbled in Pascal's chest. "You'd be right."

"Then where did the guns go?"

Pascal stared blankly through the bars that held him prisoner. "I sent them with Running Deer up to Natchez. They were payment to the British for Choctaw scalps. Running Deer then fashioned the scalps to appear Chickasaw, and Bienville paid me generously for them."

French guns given to a French enemy, paid for by the deaths of French allies, rewarded by the French governor of Louisiana. Marc-Paul's stomach turned at the utter completeness of his crime. "And your British agent in Natchez?"

"Your brother-in-law."

Benjamin. Marc-Paul gripped his knees as the brig rolled gently in the waves. "How, exactly, did you come to this arrangement?"

In a monotone tale, Pascal told of being tasked with Benjamin's execution and the deal the two settled on instead. This, while Marc-Paul was sailing to France to meet with the Regent.

At the end of the story, Marc-Paul could only nod that he had heard. But not that he understood. Benjamin had been so young and had been isolated from his fellow Frenchmen too long. But that did not negate his crime.

Drawing a deep breath, Marc-Paul changed tack. "The cache of food Julianne found by the bayou behind your property," he prompted.

"Mine, of course. But you knew that already."

"To what end?"

Pascal rolled his eyes. "Have you no imagination?" A dramatic sigh blew from his lips. "I used what I wanted and sold the rest to those who could afford my prices."

"Which were astronomical during the famine, no doubt."

"Still a bargain, when the alternative is starvation. It was going smoothly until Bienville sent me up to Yazoo, surrounded by warring Chickasaw. Thanks to your wife, I might add."

He didn't have to remind Marc-Paul of the brutalities suffered by the soldiers at that post. "Was your assignment in Yazoo the reason you decided to desert? Was Benjamin still working for you even then?"

Pascal shifted his weight on the barrel, then winced and curled over his dislocated arm. Moments later, he spoke again. "In theory, he was. Running Deer served as a conduit between us, or one of several. We were both selling information to the British, which they used to support the Chickasaw. But Benjamin grew sloppy and careless with his visits to Julianne. If I didn't find myself at the wrong end of a scalping knife at Yazoo first, it was only a matter of time before Benjamin exposed our activities and got us arrested."

Inhaling deeply of the damp, salty air, Marc-Paul leaned forward. "So it was time to cut your losses and head to Carolina, is that it? And you took as many of our garrison with you as you could persuade."

"I needed crew for our hijacked ship."

Selfish to the end. "Those men—the ones who survived, at least—will be tried and executed alongside you." Standing, he gripped one of the bars between himself and Pascal. "I pray for your soul, Pascal."

"Is this good-bye? Ah well, you'll always have me with you. I know you'll take good care of my daughter."

Marc-Paul said nothing, felt nothing as he sought to make sense of the words.

"Lily can't be yours, you know. You never slept with Willow. I did, while you snored. But you're a much better father to her than I ever would have been."

The brig groaned, and footfalls sounded overhead as Marc-Paul studied Pascal's half-scarred face. Sorrow hovered near his heart that he wasn't really Lily's papa after all. But the guilt of sleeping with Willow dissolved, slowly but completely. God had seen fit to give Lily to him and to Julianne, to love and raise as their own. The bond that made them family was stronger than blood.

"I know how this ends," Pascal said. "I know how I seem to you now. But once we were like brothers." A rare sincerity laced his tone.

Footsteps on the ladder grew louder until Bienville himself stood scowling beside Marc-Paul, his white wig made wild by the salty wind. "My turn, Girard."

Fear poured into Pascal's eyes. He reached through the bars toward Marc-Paul. "I never meant you any harm."

"Yet you kidnapped my wife and daughter and attempted to rape Julianne. Harming them harms me, Pascal." His throat tightened with regret that the man he had once called friend had sunk so low. With Bienville's fiery gaze burning into him, he took Pascal's trembling hand for the last time. "Good-bye, old friend."

⚜ ⚜ ⚜

"Oh no." With the brig in the harbor at her back, Julianne stood on the shores of New Orleans wearing sailor's clothes, Marc-Paul's hand on her shoulder. The hurricane had battered the settlement to pieces. Half-drowned piles of ruined cypress posts, pine planks, and palmetto fronds obliterated the lines that had once been a grid of streets and canals. Residents shielded their eyes from the glaring sun and picked their way over the rubble, searching for something—anything—to salvage.

Tears sprang to Julianne's eyes. In that moment, she felt a kinship with New Orleans that she hadn't before. For didn't she know what it was to be buffeted, broken, and in pieces, an unrecognizable version of one's former self?

Wordlessly, Marc-Paul threaded her hand through the crook of his arm and guided her around the wreckage. She sensed in her husband the same dread that wrapped her heart as she thought of the little girl with the thick black braids and brown eyes. Lily had been born of a fleeting union between Pascal and Willow. But in the ways that mattered most, she belonged to Marc-Paul and Julianne.

"Ah! You've both returned!"

Julianne spun toward the voice.

"Etienne!" Marc-Paul pulled the Canadian into a hug, slapping him on the back. "You weathered the storm, I see!"

"And you as well." Etienne's nose stained pink and tears glistened in his eyes as he kissed Julianne on the cheek. "Wasn't sure when I'd see you again, ma chère. Forgive an old man for letting harm befall you?"

She embraced him. "It wasn't you who harmed me!"

Sniffing, Etienne nodded.

"Is Lily with you? Is she home?" Marc-Paul asked, voice tight.

"No, monsieur. There is no home to speak of, unless you count two walls standing and a scant patch of roof."

Marc-Paul nodded, lips tight.

"Lily." Etienne shook his head, looking past Julianne. "Lily!"

Julianne's breath seized in her chest. Was he mourning her? Or calling her?

"She should be around here somewhere." Etienne's voice rumbled in his chest. "She was playing with Angelique Villeroy, so if you see a shock of red hair, the black braids won't be far." He chuckled, and the sound brought a laugh to Julianne's lips.

Marc-Paul whirled around. "Lily!" he called.

The little girl came running, braids streaming behind her. "Papa! Papa! Madame! You came back!" Vesuvius hustled and panted after her, struggling to keep up. Etienne took the leash from Lily's hand as she passed him.

Tears filled Julianne's eyes as Marc-Paul met Lily on a mound of fallen thatch and swung her up into the air. "Of course we did, ma chère!" Only the slight catch in his voice betrayed his profound relief.

Lily squeezed her arms around his neck, then reached for Julianne, fingers outstretched. "Madame," Lily said, and Marc-Paul lowered her gently to the ground.

Julianne knelt, and the little girl rushed into her arms, nearly knocking her over. "Where did you go, Lily? How did you escape?"

Lily still clung to Julianne's neck as if she would drown without her. "Running Deer showed me a good place to hide. I stayed there all night, just like he told me to. When the storm came, Red Bird found me and took me home to Etienne. It was awful, Madame. Fist Face ran away, but I saved him. Just like you saved me. I missed you and Papa so much. I was afraid you would never come back. Only—" Lily leaned back and searched Julianne's eyes. "Did those bad men come back too? The ones who took me?"

Marc-Paul knelt on one knee and patted the other, an invitation Lily readily accepted. "They're gone, Lily. You don't need to worry about them."

"But will they come back and surprise me? Like you did?" Sitting on Marc-Paul's thigh, Lily twirled his queue around her finger.

Julianne shook her head and wiped the tears from her cheeks. "No. They won't." Her chest ached with the truth of her words. Pascal would soon be hanged, and Benjamin was already gone. Lily smiled and helped Julianne to her feet.

"*Magnifique!*"

Julianne turned to find Adrien de Pauger, the city engineer, walking about the rubble with his arms spread wide. Lifting his beaming face toward the heavens, he said, "Merci!"

"Not the conventional response to a hurricane," Marc-Paul observed quietly.

"Ah, but don't you see?" Etienne volunteered. "A single storm wiped out all the structures he'd been fighting to pull down. Now New Orleans will build again from the ground up, according to his master plan."

The elated engineer strode away, still praising the saints for every piece of debris.

Chuckling, Marc-Paul scratched Vesuvius behind the ears, then rose again. "Well, mon amour?" His hands slid behind Julianne's waist as he drew her close. "Shall we begin again too? Lay a new foundation and rebuild our home? Our family?"

"My family is already here." Julianne winked at Lily, then

fixed her gaze once more on Marc-Paul. "Forgive me for ever making you feel like you weren't giving me what I wanted most. I have what I want. Right here."

He bent his head to hers. "*Je t'aime*, Julianne. I love all that you are, with all that I am."

She looped her arms around his neck and kissed the smile on his face. No longer did she feel cursed by the mark on her shoulder, not with her husband and daughter by her side and God's grace covering them all. "You are more than I deserve."

AUTHOR'S NOTE

In 2014, I discovered a list of names. It was a list of girls from Salpêtrière, aged between twelve and twenty-six years old, sent to Louisiana in January 1720. Why were they in Salpêtrière, Paris's most notorious prison for females? How were they chosen for Louisiana? What did they do once they arrived? These questions and many others took root in my imagination. The character of Julianne began to take shape when I read in a New Orleans archive center about the mass marriage of convicts in Paris in September 1719, right before they were sent to La Rochelle for transport to New Orleans. It was a story that begged to be told!

The forced immigration represented in the novel took place mostly between the years 1717 and 1721. In addition to orphans and convicts—prostitutes, smugglers, criminals, and vagabonds—others came voluntarily, including the German and Swiss farmers who settled the German Coast upriver from New Orleans. Repeated riots in Paris over the forced exile to Louisiana persuaded the monarchy to discontinue its unpopular policy. With a few exceptions, including a shipment of girls to be wed in 1728, immigration of European settlers virtually halted after 1721. The Company of the Indies shipped additional cargoes of African slaves to Louisiana for another decade. (The infamous Code Noir was established to govern the slaves in 1724.) Of the seven thousand Europeans who entered the Lower Mississippi Valley during this time frame, at least half of them either perished or abandoned the colony before 1726.

Though *The Mark of the King* is a work of fiction, the circumstances with which the characters interact are straight from history. Some of the people mentioned or characterized in this novel are historical figures who really lived, including John Law, whose colonizing scheme included marrying and sending convicts to Louisiana; Sieur Jean-Baptiste Le Moyne de Bienville, the Canadian-born governor of the colony; and Adrien de Pauger, the French engineer who came to lay out the streets.

The soldier characters of Marc-Paul Girard, Pascal Dupree, and Benjamin Chevalier were inspired by the terrible conditions the French military endured in Louisiana, especially during the first two decades of the eighteenth century. Barely supported by France, the garrisons would simply not have survived if not for the hospitality of several native nations. Desertion was widespread.

The war between the French and the Chickasaw that took place in this novel is now known as the First French–Chickasaw War. More wars would follow—with the Chickasaw, the Natchez, and even with disillusioned Choctaw—before the French and Indian War broke out between the British and the French and their native allies in 1754.

Other historical events portrayed or referred to in the novel include the famine, the annual gift-giving ceremony in Mobile, the spring flood that dislodged coffins from the levee, the burning of Pensacola, the hurricane in September 1722, the subsequent destruction of the settlement, and Adrien de Pauger's delight

4

that he could begin working in earnest on what is known today as the French Quarter.

My research for this novel included first-person accounts written by several colonists themselves and dozens of volumes by today's historians. For those of you as interested in New Orleans's founding—and her people—as I am, I recommend *Building the Devil's Empire: French Colonial New Orleans* by Shannon Lee Dawdy and *Indians, Settlers, and Slaves in a Frontier Exchange Economy* by Daniel H. Usner, Jr. Those interested in the history of French midwifing might enjoy *The King's Midwife: A History and Mystery of Madame du Coudray* by Nina Rattner Gelbart.

I hope you enjoyed experiencing a lesser-known slice of history in this novel. Even more than that, I hope the idea of grace that eclipses judgment is one that resonates with you. If you remember nothing else from this story, remember this: Even those marked by judgment—be it a physical or emotional scar—can be covered by indelible grace.

DISCUSSION QUESTIONS

1. During Louisiana's early years, France was desperate to send women to the colony. Other than reproduction, what do women contribute to the establishment of a culture?

2. Julianne's brand is on her skin, but many of us are marked by invisible scars from pain or judgment in our pasts. Do you believe those scars are also curses? Why or why not?

3. Think of an event that has marked you in some way. Are you better off now, because of how you've grown? Or is it something you're still striving to overcome?

4. Marc-Paul thought keeping secrets from Julianne was merciful. Do you think his withholding was truly for her best interests, or for his?

5. Are secrets ever justified? If so, under what circumstances?

6. Julianne does not have typical courtship romances. How did Simon show his love for her? How did Marc-Paul?

7. How does our culture define love today? In what ways does that definition fall short?

8. In many ways, the French monarchy did not support the colonists in Louisiana's infancy, but according to Governor Bienville's writings, the colonists could have worked harder to support themselves as well. Think about our own country. In what ways do we rely too much on our government? In what ways could we do more to better our own lives?

9. Marc-Paul loves the law but grows to love grace more. How do you see the two fitting together in your spiritual life? In your family?

10. Francoise advises Julianne to love her enemy not just for his sake but so that her own bitterness will dissipate. What effect do you believe loving your enemy has on you personally?

11. Lily comforts Julianne by telling her, "I see you." What difference does it make for you personally when you feel seen and heard? How do you feel when you feel invisible or voiceless?

12. During the storm, when Pascal is in danger of drowning, Julianne decides that not doing the right thing is the same as doing the wrong thing. Have you felt this way in your own life?

13. Galatians 6:17 reads, "From now on let no one cause trouble for me, for I bear on my body the brand-marks of Jesus." What do you suppose it means to bear the brand-marks of Christ? (NASB)

14. What would it look like for you to have a life marked by grace?

15. At the end of your days, if you could choose one thing your friends and family remember about your life, what would you want it to be? What would you want them to say your life was marked by?

ACKNOWLEDGMENTS

My heartfelt thanks goes to:

The team at Bethany House Publishers, for believing in this story and dedicating their time and talents to bringing it to life, with special thanks to my tireless and brilliant editor, Jessica Barnes.

My agent, Tim Beals of Credo Communications, for his unfailing support and management of my wide-ranging projects.

My incredible husband, Rob, and children, Elsa and Ethan, for sharing me with another book baby; to my parents, Peter and Pixie Falck, and my friend Heather Hruby for help with child care; to my French sister-in-law, Audrey Falck, who spent days translating French documents for my research and answered all my French questions with a willing spirit. Special thanks to both Audrey and my brother, Jason, for planting in my mind the idea that evolved into this book.

My critique partner, Joanne Bischof, for her invaluable help from the brainstorming stage to the edits, and for burning the midnight oil to get it done.

My prayer team, who prayed for every step in the process from the signing of the contract until I wrote the final page.

I am indebted to Bob Thomas, director of Loyola University Center for Environmental Communication in New Orleans, for helping me understand the natural environment in which New Orleans was settled in 1720, and to the incredibly helpful staff at both the State Library of Louisiana in Baton Rouge and the Historic New Orleans Collection—Williams Research Center in New Orleans for bringing treasure troves of information to me. Special thanks to Pastor Tommy and Karen Middleton, for so graciously hosting my family during my research trip.

I owe my thanks to Chief Wesley Harris, for serving as my firearms expert; Jordyn Redwood, for answering my medical-related questions; and Jennifer James, for Paris research help directly from the American Library in Paris.

Most of all, thank you, Lord, for your incredible, indelible grace. May you use this story to bring grace and peace to the hearts of those who read it.

About the Author

Jocelyn Green is an award-winning author of multiple fiction and nonfiction works, including *Faith Deployed: Daily Encouragement for Military Wives* and *The Five Love Languages, Military Edition*, which she co-wrote with Dr. Gary Chapman. Her first novel in the Heroines Behind the Lines series, *Wedded to War*, was a Christy Award finalist and the gold medal winner in historical fiction from the Military Writers Society of America. She and her husband live in Cedar Falls, Iowa, with their two children and two cats. Her goal with every book is to inspire faith and courage in her readers. Visit her at www.jocelyngreen.com.

Sign up for Jocelyn's newsletter!

Keep up to date with Jocelyn's news on book releases, signings, and other events by signing up for her email list at jocelyngreen.com/subscribe

If you enjoyed *The Mark of the King*, you may also like . . .

After a night trapped together in an old stone keep, Lady Adelaide Bell and Lord Trent Hawthorne have no choice but to marry. Dismayed, Adelaide finds herself bound to a man who ignores her, as Trent has no desire to connect with the one who dashed his plans to marry for love. Can they set aside their first impressions before any chance of love is lost?

An Uncommon Courtship by Kristi Ann Hunter
HAWTHORNE HOUSE, kristiannhunter.com

BETHANYHOUSE

More Historical Fiction . . .

Cassidy Ivanoff and her father John have signed on to work at a prestigious new hotel near Mt. McKinley. John's new apprentice, Allan Brennan, finds a friend in Cassidy, but the real reason he's here—to learn the truth about his father's death—is far more dangerous than he knows.

In the Shadow of Denali by Tracie Peterson, Kimberley Woodhouse
THE HEART OF ALASKA #1, traciepeterson.com
kimberleywoodhouse.com

Despite her training as a master violinist, Rebekah Carrington was denied entry into the Nashville Philharmonic by its new young conductor Nathaniel Whitcomb, who bowed to public opinion. Now, with a reluctant muse and a recurring pain in his head, he needs her help to finish his symphony. But how can he win back her trust when he's robbed her of her dream?

A Note Yet Unsung by Tamera Alexander
A BELMONT MANSION NOVEL, tameraalexander.com

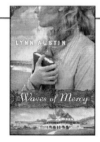

In 1897 Michigan, Dutch immigrant Geesje de Jonge recalls the events of her past while writing a memoir, and twenty-three-year-old Anna Nicholson mourns a broken engagement. Over the course of one summer, the lives of both women will change forever.

Waves of Mercy by Lynn Austin
lynnaustin.org

BETHANYHOUSE

You May Also Enjoy . . .

When her mother suffers a stroke, Deirdre puts her medical career on hold and persuades Dr. Matthew Clayborne to help her treat Mrs. O'Leary at her family's farm. But since the doctor has no intention of leaving his life in Canada, and Deirdre has sworn off marriage altogether, how will they deal with the undeniable spark between them?

Love's Faithful Promise by Susan Anne Mason
COURAGE TO DREAM #3
susanannemason.com

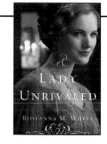

Lady Ella Myerston is determined to put an end to the danger that haunts her brother. While visiting her friend Brook, the owner of the Fire Eyes jewels, Ella gets entangled in an attempt to blackmail the newly reformed Lord Cayton. Will she become the next casualty of the "curse"?

A Lady Unrivaled by Roseanna M. White
LADIES OF THE MANOR
roseannamwhite.com

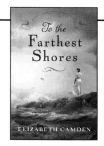

Naval officer Ryan Gallagher broke Jenny Bennett's heart six years ago when he abruptly disappeared. Now he's returned but refuses to discuss what happened. Furious, Jenny has no notion of the impossible situation Ryan is in. With lives still at risk, he can't tell Jenny the truth about his overseas mission—but he can't bear to lose her again either.

To the Farthest Shores by Elizabeth Camden
elizabethcamden.com

◊ BETHANYHOUSE

Made in United States
North Haven, CT
17 April 2022

18331315R00250